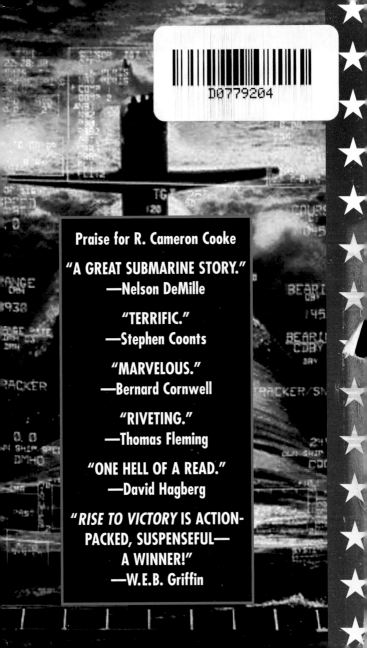

RISE TO VICTORY

R. CAMERON COOKE

J

JOVE BOOKS, NEW YORK

THE BERKLEY PUBLISHING GROUP
Published by the Penguin Group
Penguin Group (USA) Inc.
375 Hudson Street, New York, New York 10014, USA
Penguin Group (Canada), 90 Eglinton Avenue East, Suite 700, Toronto, Ontario M4P 2Y3, Canada
(a division of Pearson Penguin Canada Inc.)
Penguin Books Ltd., 80 Strand, London WC2R 0RL, England
Penguin Group Ireland, 25 St. Stephen's Green, Dublin 2, Ireland (a division of Penguin Books Ltd.)
Penguin Group (Australia), 250 Camberwell Road, Camberwell, Victoria 3124, Australia
(a division of Pearson Australia Group Pty. Ltd.)
Penguin Books India Pvt. Ltd., 11 Community Centre, Panchsheel Park, New Delhi—110 017, India
Penguin Group (NZ), Cnr. Airborne and Rosedale Roads, Albany, Auckland 1310, New Zealand
(a division of Pearson New Zealand Ltd.)
Penguin Books (South Africa) (Pty.) Ltd., 24 Sturdee Avenue, Rosebank, Johannesburg 2196,
South Africa

Penguin Books Ltd., Registered Offices: 80 Strand, London WC2R 0RL, England

This is a work of fiction. Names, characters, places, and incidents either are the product of the author's imagination or are used fictitiously, and any resemblance to actual persons, living or dead, business establishments, events, or locales is entirely coincidental. The publisher does not have any control over and does not assume any responsibility for author or third-party websites or their content.

RISE TO VICTORY

A Jove Book / published by arrangement with the author.

PRINTING HISTORY
Jove mass market edition / February 2006

Copyright © 2006 by R. Cameron Cooke.
Text design by Kristin del Rosario.

ISBN: 0-515-14097-X

JOVE®
Jove Books are published by The Berkley Publishing Group,
a division of Penguin Group (USA) Inc.,
375 Hudson Street, New York, New York 10014.
JOVE is a registered trademark of Penguin Group (USA) Inc.
The "J" design is a trademark belonging to Penguin Group (USA) Inc.

PRINTED IN THE UNITED STATES OF AMERICA

10 9 8 7 6 5 4 3 2 1

Prologue

"**WOULD** you like another cigarette, Ahmad?"

That's what the unsuspecting fatigue-clad youth had said to him only moments before. Now, Ahmad had the youth in a submission hold from behind, one hand covering his mouth, the other thrusting the serrated knife through the perplexed young man's throat with little difficulty. The handle vibrated as the blade sliced through flesh, tendon, arteries, and cartilage, emerging from the other side in a spat of dark blood, painting the side of the tent and the damp jungle floor almost black in the night.

Ahmad had always wondered how it would really feel to cut a man's throat, and now he finally knew as his victim's teeth and fingernails, previously imbedded in his forearm, started to weaken and the blood and breath quickly escaped the doomed body. As the body went limp, he rolled the head back to check the upturned dead eyes just to be sure. As the head came back, one last grotesque gasp of smoky air was expelled from the severed windpipe, the remnants of the cigarette the two had been sharing mere seconds before.

It had been three years since he had last killed a man, but that was with a gun from a few feet away. He had always wondered how it would be with a knife, whether he could bring himself to actually do it. And now it was done, just like he had been trained to do all those years ago.

The dead boy's eyes glimmered in the moonlight and seemed to stare back at him.

Just a foolish boy, Ahmad thought. *Will your mother know you met your end in some jungle on the other side of the world? Did she care when you went off to follow Musa?*

A mere boy, but the youth must have been at least eighteen

years old, and educated, or at least it seemed so from the conversation they were having before his knife had mutilated the boy's throat. Ahmad had seen the boy around the camp a few times. He was typical of all the others, angry and full of hate.

Full of emotion, Ahmad thought. *That's the key. That's what threw him off balance and allowed me to kill him so easily.*

In the moonlight it was hard to see just how much of the boy's blood had run down his arms and legs, but he could feel it. It wasn't the cleanest maneuver and he mentally reprimanded himself for not using better form. He dragged the body through the jungle, skirting the camp's perimeter, until he came to a thick copse of trees adjacent to the supply tent. He wasn't overly concerned about the body being found. He knew that it would be found. When morning came, the camp would awaken and discover both sentries missing, and they would know what had happened.

Musa would know. Musa had been suspicious for the last two weeks at least.

Musa and his men would see the blood on the tent and on the ground the next morning. They would find the boy's body, then rant and rave, praying to God that the infidel Ahmad would burn in flames. After that, they would grab their rifles and grenades and come looking for him.

Ahmad tapped the left breast pocket of his fatigue jacket and felt the square object inside. It was still there. Musa might have suspected him for the last two weeks, indeed had been watching his every move, but not closely enough to prevent him from making this one last disk.

Now to get away with it.

A Kalashnikov rifle hung loosely from the dead boy's limp arm, and Ahmad briefly considered taking it, before he reminded himself that speed and only speed would save him now. Wiping his bloody knife on the boy's pants, he sheathed it, then stood back and stared at the dead boy for one last moment.

The boy was an Arab, just like him. He didn't hate the boy, or Musa either, for that matter. It was all just business.

The first indication that the boy's body had been found

came an hour later as Ahmad ran through the moonlit jungle on the path he had carefully selected over the past few weeks. From one of the few barren hilltops he looked back in the direction he had come. Several miles away across the densely covered valley he saw two, then three flares appear over the spot where he knew the camp to be. The flares hung in the air for what seemed like an eternity, bathing the foliage beneath them in a flickering white phosphorescent light until their small parachutes finally carried them down beneath the living canopy and they disappeared from sight completely. Moments later they were replaced by three more. In the distance, he thought he heard a faint whistle. The camp was mustering.

Damn! he thought. They had found the body sooner than expected. Some late night pisser must have tripped over it.

Undaunted, Ahmad pressed on into the underbrush at a comfortable pace, conserving energy, hopping a log here, ducking a frond there. The path was difficult, but he had deliberately chosen it because it was impassable to vehicles and any pursuers would have to follow him on foot, and he was in much better shape than anyone else in the camp. It was a daunting trek, but he had already run four miles through the obstacle-laden jungle and was making good time. He was still quite fresh, too, and patted himself on the back for having had the foresight to do a discreet carb-loading the night before. Despite his excellent progress so far, he knew the real challenge lay up ahead.

He only hoped Musa did not anticipate what he was going to do, how he was going to escape. If Musa could think straight after finding the boy's mutilated body, he might figure it out. If he did, then the jig would be up. Musa would certainly block his escape route long before he could get there. Musa was smart, and indeed his intellect was one of the reasons for this abrupt departure tonight. Musa had been growing much too suspicious of late. Dangerously suspicious.

Ahmad chugged along through the forest putting mile after mile behind him, never looking back. It was dark, but the path was burned into his memory and he jumped, skipped, and ducked invisible obstacles that he knew to be there.

An hour passed with no sign of his pursuers. He kept running, fighting the urge to rest, knowing that any fanciful notions that Musa had forgotten about him were simply fantasies conjured up by his fatigued mind.

Then he heard it, a thundering in the night. He stopped and caught his breath for a moment, squinting to see the starry sky through the high jungle canopy. A low vibration filled the forest. A heavy staccato pulsation that was getting closer with every second.

Musa had decided to use the Huey to come find him, and it was a move Ahmad had not anticipated.

Musa must be pissed off! Ahmad thought, as his mind scrambled. *He's taking a big chance flying that thing around here!*

The Huey's rotors pounded the night air and filled the forest with their intimidating throb as the helicopter grew closer. The foliage was thick and Ahmad could see no more than the small sliver of sky directly above him. Likewise, one would think the men in the helo would have a tough time spotting him, too, especially at night. But Ahmad knew better. He knew there were at least a dozen sets of infrared headgear in the camp, and the men in the helo would almost certainly be wearing them.

The sound grew progressively more deafening. The Huey was obviously heading in his direction. Could Musa have guessed his escape plan? Could Musa have known about his secret jungle path? Maybe someone had been watching over the past weeks as he had mapped out the trail. Either way, the Huey would be on him in a matter of seconds.

He had to find some mud! Cold mud worked best for hiding from infrared. Ironically, Musa had taught him that. The ground beneath his feet was too firm, no good. He scampered around the jungle floor desperately searching, trying to find a small stream, a gully with some water in it. A fucking puddle would be enough!

But there was no water anywhere. This jungle held hundreds of streams and muddy bogs—in fact, the jungle floor was usually like soft reddish clay—but he'd managed to find the only spot where the soil was solid and dry, and it suddenly occurred to him that he was a rat in a trap. Of course, Musa had known about his "secret" trail through the jungle. Musa knew everything that happened on this island.

The helo thundered overhead and he looked up to see a looming black shape block the shining stars above. The noise was unbearably loud.

He felt naked and helpless under the helo's menace. Grabbing an armful of the loose mulch, he crouched behind the closest trunk and covered up as best he could in the two seconds he permitted himself. Any further movement at this point would be of no use and would only aid the helo in finding him.

The helo's shadow ran back and forth across the forest floor blocking the few beams of moonlight that managed to pierce the dense canopy. The recurring Doppler effect of the rotors indicated that the helo was now circling above his position. He suddenly wished for his Kalashnikov, but of course not having it eliminated the temptation to use it, which would give away his position and almost certainly lead to his death. Instead, he closed his eyes and did not move.

The helo circled relentlessly. It circled what seemed like a hundred times, but he did not move. The deafening noise and the rhythmic vibration seemed to grow louder and louder until he felt it inside his head, rattling his brain, but still he did not move.

The rotors changed pitch now, the Doppler effect was no longer there, just a steady thunderous pulsation that shook the very earth around him. His eyes opened in time to see the helo's shadow cease its movement across the jungle floor. The helo was hovering now. It had found something. It hovered overhead for a moment and then began inching lower, ever lower, until it was practically touching the jungle fronds, most likely to gain a better view of its prey.

Now Ahmad knew they had found him. It was hopeless. He pictured in his mind a fatigue-clad man with infrared goggles leaning out of the open doorway of the helo, aiming the door-mounted M60 heavy machine gun directly at his heat signature, correcting the aim ever so slightly before squeezing the trigger. They *had* to have found him. The helo was not moving and there was no other explanation.

He felt the surging wind on his face. The trees above swayed awkwardly in the unfamiliar downward draft. If he ran now, he might have a chance. Maybe he could run faster than the door gunner could shift his fire. Run toward the noise, that's what Musa had taught him. Run under the helicopter, so that the helo has to reposition itself before it can shoot again. Then run and find a stream somewhere or anything that could better hide him. Maybe, just maybe, he could run fast enough.

He had just made up his mind to do it, when something suddenly moved out of the darkness to his left. He looked in time to see a shadowy figure bolt out of a patch of low brush less then fifteen yards away. It moved like lightning, charging in his direction. Instinctively, he prepared to defend himself, but before his attacker could reach him, the sky exploded above. All hell seemed to rain down from above as the helo's heavy machine gun opened up in an ear-splitting crescendo, ripping apart the jungle's canopy with a torrential downpour of 7.62-millimeter bullets. Forgetting about his attacker, he lay flat on his back and did not move as the foliage, the trees, the mulch, everything was turned to jagged splinters by the heavy machine gun's large missiles. The air around him soon filled with flying dust and atomized pieces of trees that filled his lungs with every breath. Round after round hit the ground with such force that he felt it in his bones, each successive round drawing closer as the gunner high above methodically swept the powerful weapon across the field of fire.

As the rounds impacted the soil near his feet, he closed his eyes and braced for a quick death. Instantly he felt prickly stings on his face, forearms, and ankles as dozens of projectiles struck his body. The impacts were mildly painful, especially the ones in the face, but he knew something was wrong. He wasn't having trouble breathing and he wasn't losing consciousness. The blasts of the gun and the rhythm of the rotors were just as loud in his head as they had been a moment before, so he wasn't fading. But still the impacts continued as sharp stings on his chest and face.

Opening his eyes and expecting to see wounds, he found hundreds of shiny cylindrical pieces of sizzling metal covering his body. They were the spent 7.62-millimeter cartridges from the M60 machine gun, and they continued to rain down on him by the hundred. Clattering and thudding, fresh cartridges hit the fallen ones, hit the ground, hit the branches and the fronds all around him. He looked up between pelting shells and caught brief glimpses of the muzzle flashes fifty feet above. A few yards away on his left the jungle was being systematically destroyed.

The burning cartridges on his face hurt like hell, but still he did not move.

Then, as suddenly as it had begun, the firing ceased.

He did not move as the helo continued hovering. The dust hung low in the air near the jungle floor. Gutted trees and severed branches lay everywhere. A large section of canopy overhead had disappeared and now much more moonlight reached the jungle floor. The light shone down through the dusty air in eerie rays, like a spotlight focused on the mangled piece of jungle. The dust had begun to settle by the time the helo's rotors changed pitch again.

The helo resumed circling.

Ahmad couldn't believe his luck. Had they not seen him, after all?

The helo did eleven more passes, and Ahmad held his breath through each one, as if breathing would give his position away. Then, the sound of the rotors suddenly began to fade. It diminished rapidly in the direction of the camp, fading and fading, until it was no longer perceptible, and the jungle resumed its former tranquility, as if it had all been a dream.

Ahmad slowly rose to his feet, brushing the shells off his chest and legs. They clinked and jingled with those spread on the ground, but the noise did not concern him. There was no one around. There couldn't be. None of the foot patrols could have come this far yet.

Then it suddenly occurred to him what had happened. What it was that had saved him.

He walked over to the demolished area of jungle, only a few yards away. There, under a twisted tangle of branches and leaves lay the remains of what, a few minutes before, had been an adult male orangutan. The unfortunate beast must have been hiding from the helo, too. Only it broke before he did, and when it ran the gunner in the helo assumed he had sighted his target.

Ahmad had never been much of an animal lover, but he came close to kissing what was left of this animal. Now Musa would think he was dead. That was good. On the other hand, Musa would send a foot patrol to collect his body. That was bad.

He had to keep moving. Speed was his only hope. Taking a few sips from the small water bag slung across his chest, he darted into the bush and quickly resumed his original pace.

It took him another hour to make it the four miles to the southern beach. When he finally broke out of the jungle and onto the snowy white sand leading down to the water, the stars had already begun to fade and the eastern sky was showing the first signs of dawn. The jungle behind him was coming alive with the morning calls of a thousand different species of bird.

He removed and buried his boots, socks, and jacket in less than a minute, then looked across the water at the only land in sight, a dark mass rising out of the sea six miles away to the southwest. Dim lights from a local village speckled its coastline, betraying its position to the darkness. A few red and green lights dotted the open ocean east of the distant island. Local fishermen getting an early start, maybe a few merchant ships, or maybe even a patrol craft snooping around after detecting Musa's helo in the air.

He examined the square item he had taken from his jacket pocket just before burying the jacket with his boots and socks. The mini-disk rested inside a clear plastic container.

"I hope this thing stays dry," he said to himself, glancing at the six miles of dark water between the sandy strip of beach on which he now stood and the distant island. "Shit! Now I'm just stalling. Let's get this over with!"

Buttoning the disk into the side pocket of his fatigue pants, he jogged briskly down the sandy slope toward the lapping water below. As the first wave of frigid salt water stung into the half dozen burns across his face, it revived him. His training quickly took over, and within seconds he had reached his cruising stroke.

The weather is clear and the water is calm, he kept thinking to himself. *Just a nice early morning swim is all this is.*

REAR Admiral Quentin Chappell hated it whenever the two men in brown suits showed up, barging into his office like they owned the place. And who wore a suit in Hawaii, anyway? But, of course, they were not from Hawaii. They were from Virginia, and their stay in the islands would be brief. It always was.

"You don't look happy to see me, Admiral," the older of the two said, as he plopped down on one of the chairs opposite Chappell's desk, his younger counterpart doing the same.

"Of course I'm glad to see you," Chappell lied. "You've just caught me at an inopportune time. Perhaps if you'd called first—"

"Ah, yes," interrupted the older one. "But then, that's not the way we operate. After five years in this post, you should know that."

"Of course," Chappell said. Then, assuming a false smile, he added, "*Mister Sinclair.*"

Over the years he'd learned to call the gray-haired man that, but who knew what his real name was. His visits were always unannounced, for that was the nature of his work. Like now, he was always accompanied by some muscular, flawless youth who said nothing and looked like a castaway from some lost colony of androids.

"We need your services again, Admiral," Sinclair continued. "We need one of your fast attacks for a mission."

"Who doesn't?" Chappell mumbled.

"Excuse me?"

"I said who doesn't?" Chappell grunted. "ComSubPac's got every damn boat in the fleet committed right now. We've got boats off Korea, off China. We've got boats in the Gulf. We've even got boats under the ice! This isn't the good old days, you know, when we had more than enough to do the job. Your knowledgeable people back in Washington decided to gut our sub fleet ten years ago, and now we're facing the fucking consequences."

Staring blankly at Chappell over the miniature submarine models adorning his desk, the austere Sinclair appeared unmoved, and Chappell began to wonder if he'd gone too far. His predecessor had warned him never to piss off the men in brown.

Don't ask stupid questions! his predecessor had told him. *When they come by, just make sure they've got the national security advisor's signature, then carry out whatever orders they might have for you. I'm not joking, Quentin, if you get in their way, they'll have you sacked before you get back from your next head call. Those guys have connections. Hell, they'll do it with one damn phone call. How do you think I got this job?*

"Anyway," Chappell said in a more conciliatory tone. "Needless to say, we're stretched a bit thin right now. I doubt ComSubPac could part with a single boat at the moment. At least, not until things quiet down in Korea."

"Are you forgetting what your job is, Admiral?" Sinclair asked as he picked up and examined a model of a German U-boat.

My job? Chappell thought. *What the hell does this fucking civilian from Virginia know about my job?*

"Of course not," Chappell finally said. "But even the Special Ops Deputy to ComSubPac has his limitations."

Sinclair rose from his chair and walked over to observe an elaborate painting of the *USS Nautilus* on a windswept sea as she completed the first nuclear-powered circumnavigation of the globe. The painting commanded the entire western wall of Chappell's office, but it fit in well with the various other submarine trinkets and paintings covering every other square inch of wall space.

"Are you feeling tired, Admiral?" Sinclair said as he stared at the painting. "Worn out? Like you need a rest?"

"Now wait just one damn minute, Sinclair!" Chappell barked, rising from behind his desk, and beating on the gold dolphins and the mass of ribbons adorning his left chest. "I'll be damned if I'm going to stand here and take threats from the likes of *you*, a fucking civilian who doesn't know a fucking ballast tank from a snorkel mast! I've seen too much fucking action in my career to take that from anybody! So, why don't you and your cyborg brute here go fuck yourselves!"

Sinclair turned slowly with his hands behind his back, and Chappell could see the small sliver of a smile on his face. As he collapsed back into his chair, Chappell inwardly cursed his own short temper. What the hell had he just done? His career was over now, for sure. Thirty-five years of slogging it out in the dog-eat-dog world of the submariner, only to be ruined at the end by smarting off to a fucking spook!

Sinclair walked slowly back to Chappell's desk and resumed his seat, glancing once at his counterpart.

"No," he said, expressionlessly. "No, I don't think we'll do that, Admiral. Now, if you're quite through with your pointlessly dramatic displays of bravado, we can get down to the business at hand."

Chappell breathed a sigh of relief, though his pride kept him from showing it. Apparently, Sinclair was going to give him another chance.

"Now," Sinclair intoned, continuing as if the outburst had never happened. "*You* say that you don't have any boats available for this mission, while I and my associate here counted no fewer than five attack submarines moored at the pier during our drive over."

Chappell shook his head. "Those boats are in a refit and training status, right now, and are *not* available for missions. Refit and training may not be important to you people back in Washington, but it's damn well important to us. It's what brings our boys home safely from those missions *you* send them on. All of the other boats are already spoken for, either on deployment, or sitting off the coast of who knows where."

"You have boats coming off deployment, surely."

"Well, yes, of course. There's usually one boat headed home at any given moment, but—"

"Excellent!" Sinclair interrupted. "That's just what we need!"

"Wait a minute, Sinclair. Those boats are coming home for a reason. They're coming home because they've been at sea for six months and the crews need a rest. Do you know what it feels like to spend six months at sea? Do you have the foggiest idea?"

"No. I can't say that I have, Admiral. But I think your boat coming off deployment will suit our purpose, just the same."

"I'm telling you, I won't fucking stand for it, Sinclair!"

"That would be impressive, Admiral, if it were your decision to make. Thankfully, though, it's not. Your submarines exist to serve the National Command Authority in the defense of this country, and the orders I carry with me bear their signatures."

Fuming, Chappell squeezed the arms of his chair and did his best to contain his anger. He hated this damn supercilious civilian who seemed to always draw out his orders like a trusty trump card.

"Well," Sinclair said in a different tone, "now that we've dispensed with the usual pleasantries, Admiral, what boat do you have for us?"

"The *Providence*'s coming off deployment," Chappell said in a voice so low and resigned it was almost a whisper. "She should arrive home any day now."

"Ah, the *Providence*!" Sinclair said, finally with some emotion. "Captain Christopher, isn't it? He'll do nicely, I must say, if his past missions with us are any gauge to measure him by. That man has always come through for us, no matter the danger."

"It *was* Captain Christopher," Chappell corrected him. "*Providence* has a new captain now. Dave Edwards. He's a good man."

"Well, if he's anything like his predecessor, he's sure to measure up."

What the hell do you know about submarine captains? Chappell thought. *What do you know about what it takes to command a submarine on one of your damned missions?*

"This should be a nice easy mission for your new captain. A simple agent extraction," Sinclair said as he held out his hand for the young man to fill it with a red file folder. Without even looking at it, he tossed the file onto the desk in front of Chappell. "It's all right there, Admiral. Everything you need to know about this operation. As usual, your captain is to know as little as possible. We've outlined in blue highlights what you can tell him. This is a tedious precaution, as you well know, but we can't have every sailor in the Pacific in the know, now can we?"

Chappell nodded. He knew the drill. Compartments within compartments within compartments. Classified information was never an easy thing to handle. He hated sending any captain into a mission blind, but he had a special affection for Dave Edwards. Dave had done wonders on the *Providence* during his first months of command. He'd worked hard to turn a demoralized crew into one brimming with pride, something *Providence*'s crew had not experienced for many years, despite what Sinclair might think. Now, Chappell wondered how much this mission would tear down what Edwards had worked hard to build up. The news would not break easily. Any sailor hated to be denied a home port he'd been promised for the last six months.

But, of course, Edwards was a submarine captain. He would overcome this adversity, and accomplish the mission, just as he was expected to do.

As Chappell ran his fingers over the red folder he noticed the classification markings, and the odd name for this "simple" agent extraction mission.

TOP SECRET: OPERATION HYDRA-IOLAUS

Chapter 1

THE digital wristwatch chimed in Lieutenant Scott Lake's ear and woke him from a deep sleep. Reaching under his pillow he silenced the alarm and struggled to find the switch to the small fluorescent lamp hanging above his head. The lamp flickered a few times as if it too had been sleeping and then suddenly shined with its full wattage only eight inches from his face. The brightness stung his eyes and, unable to turn over, he lifted one arm to bury his face in the crook of his elbow.

Lake took a few moments to gather his senses. Like so many previous nights, he had been dreaming about a place far from this one, and the return to reality was never a happy one.

The coffin-like bed felt small and cramped. He was not overweight, but the top was too low for him to turn over onto his side. Some smaller men could do it, but not him. Likewise, the walls on either end of his bed were a few inches too short to be comfortable. Without stretching, he could touch both ends at the same time with the bottoms of his feet and the top of his head. The bed itself was not wide enough for him either, but that was not as much of a problem because, while one side was a solid wall, the other was bordered by a dark blue curtain through which his arm could protrude without obstruction. The rack was indeed small. Small, but in some ways cozy since the rest of the ship was always cold.

The gentle hum of the ventilation system and the dull vibration of the hull were soothing, almost hypnotic in nature, and in the pitch blackness of his stateroom, Lake always managed to get to sleep.

As his eyes became accustomed to the light, Lake remembered what day it was, and a broad smile crossed his face. Normally, waking up to go on watch would be a miserable task for Scott Lake, but today of all days, he was happy, even eager to do it.

Thrusting aside the blue curtain, Lake swung his legs out to emerge from the hole that was his bed into the cold air of the ship. He silently cursed as his bare feet touched the stateroom's cold deck and in the dark he almost tripped over one of the desk chairs. He steadied himself against one of the side lockers, taking care not to rouse the other two officers sleeping in their racks. Not out of any courtesy to the other two men, he just did not feel like the annoyance of a conversation with either one of them.

There was a small knock at the stateroom door and Lake glanced at his watch. It read 0448.

The door cracked open slightly and a sheepish teenage boy of no more than eighteen stuck his head in.

"Mr. Lake?" the boy said, squinting to see in the dark stateroom. "Lieutenant Lake? Your wake-up call, sir."

"You're late," Lake said from the darkness, causing the boy to start and pull back. He obviously did not expect to find Lake up and out of his rack.

"My wake-up call was for 0445. Now go away!"

The boy looked injured by the abrupt reply. He mumbled a weak "Aye, aye, sir" and silently closed the stateroom door.

Lake grinned in the dark. He knew that he had hurt the boy's feelings, but he didn't care. He no longer had to pretend to care for this pathetic crew or his loser fellow officers. After today, he would not care one damn bit about this ship either, and he would never see these idiots ever again. This was his last day.

The deck tilted slightly and Lake felt the ship decelerate. The ship was coming shallower. Soon they would be surfacing and he would need to relieve the watch. He was in no rush. It would only take him fifteen minutes to shower, shave, and don his uniform. An effortless ritual he had performed a thousand times. There would be plenty of time to get a quick breakfast and do his pre-watch tour of the ship.

He sat in the chair and flipped down a panel from the wall until it rested horizontally. It was his desk and, just like everything else on this godforsaken ship, it barely provided enough room to do anything. He could fit his laptop computer and perhaps one drink on the surface at the same time, but that was all. Lake flipped the switch that activated the desk lamp and a calendar appeared in front of his face, hanging from the locker above the desk. The calendar had most of the dates crossed out, like a giant game of tick-tack-toe filled only with Xs and no Os. Each box had a handwritten number in the lower right-hand corner. With each successive day the numbers counted down until they reached today's date, the only date not yet crossed off. The box for today's date had a "1" in the lower right-hand corner.

Lake stared at it for a few minutes, tapping his fingers on the desk. Then, yawning with a long sigh, he reached for the felt tip pen dangling from a nearby string and nonchalantly crossed off the last date, adding a crooked smiley face to it.

Today he ended five years in the navy, three of which had been spent in anguish on this vessel. It had been a long and miserable five years. From the incompetent men placed in seniority above him to the simpleminded enlisted sailors he had to work with, he had grown to hate every aspect of the navy. He longed for the professionalism and efficiency of the business world. Or so he assumed it would be. Never having been on his own in the civilian world, he did not know. But nothing could be worse than this. Since his first day in the navy, he had counted the days until his service commitment would be fulfilled and he could get out. Many times over the last few years, he had cursed his decision to take the navy ROTC scholarship. It had seemed like a good idea when he was a starving engineering student at UCLA. But he quickly came to regret it.

He remembered five years before when he first reported to the Naval Nuclear Power School in Charleston. His first impression had been one of disbelief when he saw an alligator saunter across the parking lot in front of him and disappear into the murky snake-infested swamp surrounding the building on the Cooper River that housed the nuclear engineering classrooms. He could not believe that the navy had selected such a dismal place to train the top one percent of its people.

It had been summer. June to be exact. Right after he graduated from UCLA. The heat and humidity, the biting insects, the incessant buzz of a million locusts all made the place virtually unbearable, and the discomfort was amplified by his brand-new half-polyester khaki uniform, adorned with the bright gold bars of an ensign. Not to mention, he had taken ill. Exhausted from his marathon drive across the country, he had come down with a bad case of strep throat, a very bad case. On his first day in Charleston he could barely muster the energy to drive to the doctor. He went to a civilian doctor because he did not want his illness to jeopardize his chances in the nuclear program. The doctor recommended that he spend the next several weeks in bed to allow the antibiotics time to take effect, but in Lake's mind that was not an option. He was motivated at that time and he wanted to make a good first impression on his instructors and his fellow classmates. He convinced the doctor to give him a steroid shot so that he would have enough strength to attend class on the first day.

But on the first day at school, as he walked across the steamy parking lot feeling both weak and dizzy, he knew it was foolish to try to attend class. The Naval Nuclear Power School was one of the hardest and fastest-paced engineering schools in the country, and doing well there meant long sleepless nights hitting the books. He could not possibly hope to put his body through that kind of regimen in its current condition. So he set up an appointment with his class "counselor," a pointy-nosed lieutenant who had spent his entire career teaching in a classroom. Lake didn't dare mention his illness, but instead pleaded with the lieutenant to allow him to start classes with the next group of officers in the fall, citing personal reasons. It was an innocent enough request, and certainly three or four months of light duty would see him completely recovered. But the deprecating answer he received from the lieutenant-counselor served only as a portent of the many injustices to come in Lake's young naval life.

"You'd like that, wouldn't you, Ensign Lake?" The lieutenant had spat out the words. "Anything to postpone the day you'll have to join the fleet, eh? I've seen this a hundred times. You piece-of-shit ensigns are all alike, looking for any excuse to get out of your commitment. Maybe you'll find another excuse when it's time for the next group to begin, huh? Then you'll have a whole year off, and I'll have to explain to the CO why I held a student back. Now you tell me, why the hell *I* should put my ass on the line for some sorry-ass ensign who probably just wants the time off so he can spend it with his girlfriend?" The lieutenant paused, eying him with open antipathy. "Well?"

Lake had no answer. Obviously, the counselor had already made up his mind. Any further groveling would just give the bastard more pleasure.

"You have two options, Mr. Lake," the counselor continued. "Whichever you choose makes no difference to me. You can dispense with your stupid request chit and get your ass back in class where you belong—or you can drop out of the program."

As Lake left the so-called counselor's office, the lieutenant called after him.

"Oh, Ensign. One more thing."

Lake turned to see an evil sneer on the lieutenant's face.

"If you end up failing your exams and dropping out of the program, don't worry! The Supply Corps's always looking to pick up our table scraps. I'm sure, with enough training, you'd make a fine motor pool supervisor someday."

Lake stood in the hall outside the lieutenant's office for several dejected and speechless minutes. When he finally headed back to class, he could still hear the lieutenant-counselor laughing through the closed door—laughing at *him*. The lieutenant had practically called him a liar to his face. These days, Lake would never let some desk-jockey asshole treat him like that. But back then he was just an ensign, and far too afraid of challenging a senior officer's authority. So, he rejoined his class and resolved to make the lieutenant eat his words.

He spent every night for the next six months with his nose buried in the books, fighting back the chills from the fever that never seemed to go away. Somehow he found the energy to sit through eight hours of lecture each day. He struggled through calculus, physics, thermodynamics, mechanical engineering, electrical engineering, reactor dynamics, chemistry, and radiological controls. For every two tests he passed he failed one. The engineering student who had graduated from UCLA with a 3.88 grade point average had to make do with an average far lower than any he'd ever experienced in his life. Some of his fellow officer-students failed too many tests and were abruptly dropped from the program. They were bound for the surface fleet or the Supply Corps. Lake came close to failing out many times but always managed to keep his head above water. At last, he passed the final comprehensive examination, a grueling eight-hour test, with just four points to spare. His class ranking was nothing to write home about. In fact, he was ranked dead last—but at least he had passed!

He spent the next six months learning how to operate a nuclear power plant by practicing on an old decommissioned ballistic missile submarine sitting in the Cooper River. Through that experience and the four months spent at the Submarine Officers' School in Groton, the label of "last in his class" dogged him at every turn. His confidence shot, he had trouble in almost every course in the curriculum. For the first time in his life, the sigma cum laude UCLA graduate learned how it felt to be in the bottom 10 percent. He resented the jerk-of-a-counselor for that, but he resented the navy even more. An institution that employed such people and gave them such power to make or break an officer's career right from the start did not deserve his allegiance.

Lake had hoped that his attitude would change once he got to his boat. Once he made it to the *real* navy. There he could start with a clean slate. The day he received his orders to the USS *Providence* (SSN 719), a fast attack submarine based out of Pearl Harbor, he actually felt excited about it. He felt optimistic for the first time in a long time. The thirst for adventure he had once known as a midshipman began brewing once again in his blood. Had he known then what awaited him on board the *Providence*, he would have found a way out of the submarine service altogether.

Two months later, he graduated from sub school. The navy gave him six travel days to get to his new ship in Hawaii, but he traversed the distance in less than four days, reporting a whole day early. Orders in hand and brimming with excitement over his new life at sea, the bright-eyed Lake marched across the *Providence*'s gangway for the first time with the lively step of a man with a positive outlook. But all his hopes and dreams of a brighter future soon faded. He met Captain Carl Christopher on that first day. Everything after that was just a blur. A bad dream that was better left forgotten.

Lake felt a chill run down his spine as he sat and stared at the calendar on the wall. Now his navy career was about to end, and he was not sad to see it go. With the pen still in one hand, he reached up and crossed out the smiley face.

"CAPTAIN in control!"

The alert helmsman seemed rather proud of himself as Commander David Edwards entered *Providence*'s control room by the thin door leading from the forward upper level passage. Edwards gave a polite nod to the young sailor, although the obligatory announcement had slowly grown more and more irritating over the last six months. Of course, the teenage helmsman had only done his duty. He was required to announce his captain's presence to the dozen other sailors in the room, just as it was required on all other U.S. Navy warships—but sometimes Edwards wished he could move about unseen. Sometimes he didn't want to be disturbed. Especially during the quiet morning hours like these, his favorite time of day at sea.

Edwards had donned a fresh cotton khaki uniform for entering port, and his black hair still felt wet from his morning shower. It had been a long time since he had worn the khaki shirt and pants, but they still fit perfectly, despite the weeks at sea. Edwards made it his regimen to spend at least an hour a day on the ship's exercise bike or treadmill, and it always paid off. He was resplendent in his uniform and took care to ensure that he always set a good example for his men. The gold dolphins and command star pins near his left breast pocket always sparkled in any light, not to be outdone by the equally polished silver oak leaf pins adorning his collar. He exuded authority and had a natural leadership presence. He was a submarine captain.

As he surveyed the men at the various stations around the room, Edwards thought for a moment about how much he was going to miss the daily routine at sea. The men in the control room went about their morning tasks, preparing the ship for the first surfacing since leaving the Indian Ocean over four weeks ago. The helmsman and planesman nursed their aircraft-like controls on the forward port side of the room. Using only electronic gauges, they gingerly held the ship on course and speed at a depth of one hundred fifty feet, their every move under the watchful eye of the diving officer who sat just behind them. Master Chief Ketterling, the burly African-American chief-of-the-boat and the best diving officer on the ship, spoke in his low deep voice as he directed the two planesmen to keep a wary eye on their depth and angle gauges. To their left, another sailor under Ketterling's eye operated the ballast control panel and kept a good trim by moving water from one tank to another to counterbalance any change in the ship's weight distribution.

In the aft portion of the room, beyond the two side-by-side periscope wells, several quartermasters pored over two chart tables, preparing the day's charts for entering port. Although the ship's gyroscopic computers kept track of the ship's exact position with an error of only a few feet, the quartermasters were still required to maintain the written plots, a tried and true back-up to satellite navigation.

On the starboard wall, a single petty officer appeared lonely as he sat at one of the four tactical computer consoles. The other consoles were empty, only manned during battle stations. Leaning on one arm, the petty officer casually dialed in a solution on a distant sonar contact. Though he appeared bored, he had a firm grasp on the tactical picture. At the drop of a hat he could rattle off the course, range, and speed of half-a-dozen active contacts in *Providence*'s tactical computer registry.

Just forward on the starboard side of the control room, a sliding door led to the sonar room. It was shut as it usually was while at sea, but Edwards could envision his headset-laden sonarmen sitting at their consoles just a few feet beyond. A speaker in the control room's overhead broadcasted the ocean sounds for all to hear, but there was little to hear this morning. *Providence*'s own flow noise gurgled loudly from the speakers as the ship glided through the water, and it would have been the loudest sound in the room had it not been for the officer of the deck's rattle-like typing.

At the podium on the periscope platform the officer of the deck, a slightly balding and pudgy lieutenant commander, whacked something out on his laptop computer keyboard seemingly oblivious to all around him, including his captain. But Edwards knew better.

This was Edwards' favorite time of the day. He loved the silent routine of a submarine in the morning. Each sailor going about his duty, instinctively speaking softly so as not to disturb those sleeping in the lower level bunkrooms. The smell of bacon and toast wafting up through the ventilation system from the galley one deck below. The fluorescent lights dimmed in every passageway. The gentle roll of the deck as the ship passed through eddies in the ocean. Every item stowed in its proper place, ready to take any angle the ship might experience.

He loved it all, especially the fact that this was his ship, his responsibility.

He, *Commander David G. Edwards,* commanded a Los Angeles Class fast attack submarine and all of her one hundred and twenty eight officers and men, and though he had been in command for over six months now, he still had a hard time believing it. After all, command at sea was the high point of a naval officer's career, and few ever achieved it.

Providence was far from being the youngest submarine in the fleet, but Edwards still loved her like she was his own baby. Her three hundred sixty feet of cylindrical nuclear-powered black steel was twenty years old. But periodic refits and modernizations had kept her up to date with the latest submarine technologies from stem to stern. She had state-of-the-art sonar systems and electronic surveillance systems as well as a lethal arsenal of weapons. Her four torpedo tubes amidships could fire torpedoes, cruise missiles, or anti-ship missiles, and the twelve vertical tubes in her bow could fire more cruise missiles. She was virtually self-sufficient at sea, making her own fresh water, oxygen, and power. Her two hundred twenty-five megawatt nuclear reactor could power a small city. Its refueled uranium core could supply enough energy to run *Providence*'s propulsion and electrical systems for fifteen years. Were it not for the needs of her human crew she would seldom need to touch the land.

She was indeed an impressive ship, and Edwards was proud to be her captain. There were newer submarines out there, like the Virginia and Seawolf Classes, but he had always preferred the Los Angeles Class, mostly because he had spent his entire naval career in them. At times, it felt like he had spent his whole life in attack submarines, and sometimes it was hard to remember what life was like before the navy. He had come a long way from his days as an air force brat growing up on Offutt Air Force Base just outside Omaha. As a child he had watched his dad's B-52 take off countless times and disappear into the blue skies over the plains. He came to hate airplanes because they reminded him of his dad going away all the time, and of the countless times his mother had threatened divorce. When he was young, he decided he could never be a pilot like his dad. As he watched his mother turn from alcohol to extramarital relationships looking for the comfort and warmth absent in his father, he decided that when he grew up he would never fly off into the sunset and leave his own family. He would never place his own personal ambitions above his duty to his family.

At least, that's what he set out to do. His father, of course, had other plans for him. His senior year in high school, Colonel Edwards worked hard to secure him an appointment to the

Air Force Academy. Perhaps in his dad's mind it was his way of making up for all those lost years. His dad pulled a lot of weight with the academy's superintendent and the general called many times to impress upon the seventeen-year-old Edwards that he was being handed the opportunity of a lifetime.

But one day, two men in loud red shirts and white pants came to visit Edwards during his school lunch hour. They were football coaches from the University of Nebraska, and they cared little that he was the son of the decorated Colonel Nathan Edwards. They were more interested in his status as an All-Nebraska state linebacker. The choice was clear, and when it came time for him to make his decision he dashed the colonel's hopes by choosing a football scholarship at the University of Nebraska over an appointment to the academy. He had high hopes and lots of potential. As a freshman he started in three games and racked up thirty-two unassisted tackles and one interception. Things were all set for him to start in his sophomore year and he was already entertaining thoughts of a pro career when all of his dreams came to an abrupt end. That summer he tore the ligaments in his left knee playing pick-up basketball with his college roommates. He attempted several tries at rehabilitation but his knee was never the same again. He had lost his cutting ability and, with it, his edge on the field. Too stubborn to quit, he remained on the team, but his moment in the spotlight had passed, and he never played another down in a regular season game. Depressed and bewildered as to what he would do with his life, he buried his head in the books. He chose mechanical engineering as a major and eventually ended up with decent marks. But his father's recruiting efforts never ceased, and as Edwards' meager bank account dwindled away, the colonel's advice started making more and more sense.

Then one day during his senior year, a navy officer wearing a dapper navy blue double-breasted suit came to speak to his engineering class. He told of a life of adventure in submarines and about learning everything there is to know about nuclear power. More importantly, he promised hard cash, and lots of it. Any engineering student accepted into the program would receive a check for four thousand dollars. Edwards could not resist the temptation and signed up that afternoon. He saw it as a way to be successful and independent from his father at the same time. The colonel met the news with mixed emotions, but Edwards felt nothing but pride the day he donned the uniform of an ensign and headed off to nuclear power school. And now sixteen years later, as a thirty-eight-year-old commander, he was at the zenith of his naval career.

He had come a long way to be a submarine commander, he thought, as he glanced casually around the control room. It hadn't been an easy road. There had been many pitfalls along the way. But quiet mornings like these seemed to make it all worth it.

The officer of the deck suddenly ceased his typing and pretended to have just noticed him. Alan Miller was a slightly balding and pudgy lieutenant commander, but he was also the ship's weapons officer, and a very capable one at that. Having been on watch all night, Miller still wore his seagoing uniform, a long-sleeved navy blue jumpsuit-like coverall. All submariners wore the same style uniform at sea, officers and enlisted alike. All officers, commissioned and noncommissioned, wore khaki belts while the enlisted sailors wore blue belts. The only items that identified Miller as a commissioned officer were his gold dolphins and his rank insignia, in contrast to the silver dolphin insignia worn by chief petty officers and enlisted men.

"Good morning, Captain," Miller said with a broad smile and droopy eyes. "We're almost home." He looked tired. He had been on watch since midnight and probably up for the last twenty-four hours.

"Good morning, Weps. How close are we to the surfacing point?"

"We're ahead of schedule, sir. At ten knots we'll be there within the hour." Miller's eyes met Edwards' momentarily, and then shifted nervously to the tactical viewing screen on the forward bulkhead. "We're currently at one hundred and fifty feet. We've come shallow to check for surface contacts. So far, all contacts are well outside twenty thousand yards. Nothing but the usual fishing and merchant traffic out there."

Edwards knew that during the night Miller had probably exceeded the speed called out in his night orders. He would have had to for *Providence* to arrive ahead of schedule. But who could blame him? They all wanted to get home. Six months was too long to be away. The long deployments never really bothered Edwards, but during his extensive naval career he had learned to respect the feelings of those under him who had families waiting back home.

"Good. Maybe we'll have a smooth run on the surface then," Edwards said, deciding not to question the early arrival. Miller had been known to exercise his own initiative on a few too many occasions, but he was a good department head. As the head of the weapons department he had more than demonstrated his abilities to keep his men trained and well supplied during the months on station in the Red Sea. He ran a tight department and left very little for Edwards to manage, which was the way Edwards liked it.

"There is something else, Captain," Miller said.

"What is it?"

"Last night, I gave permission to the engineering officer of the watch to cross connect the seawater cooling systems for maintenance on one of the heat exchangers. Your night orders stated that low level engineering maintenance was authorized, and so I saw no problems in conducting a simple procedure like that one."

Edwards nodded, "Yes, go on."

"A couple hours after I gave authorization I find out that one of the mechanics performing the maintenance operated a valve out of sequence, knocking out the whole auxiliary seawater system. It was only a temporary loss, very brief. The system was back up by the time I found out about it, so I thought to not wake you, sir."

"Who was the watch officer in the engine room?"

Miller paused, "Ensign Yi, sir."

Edwards knew the answer before he had asked. Ensign Yi had been having trouble of late. Of course, he was an ensign. And ensigns were prone to such things. Disasters followed them like a wake. But Yi, a very green junior officer who was still learning the ropes back in the engine room, was having an especially tough time of it. He was an anathema to the ship's engineer, an excitable lieutenant commander named Aubrey Van Peenan, who had a reputation for being especially harsh on the junior officers in his department.

"The engineer has also been informed, sir," Miller added with the slightest indication of a smirk on his face.

Edwards detected it and suddenly felt annoyed.

"In the future you will also inform me when such things happen, Mr. Miller. My night orders are quite clear on that point."

Miller's smirk evaporated. He hesitated for a moment as if he was about to dispute what was written in the night orders, and then obviously chose to exercise better judgment.

"Aye, Captain," he said simply, then strode over to the chart table in the aft corner of the room to confer with the quartermaster.

Department heads were all alike, thought Edwards. They quietly celebrated when one of their rivals had problems, because deep underneath the open display of camaraderie they were all competing with each other. Every department head wanted to command his own boat someday, but with less than ninety submarines on the navy's list and three eligible department heads on every boat, the odds were not in their favor. Only one out of every three would ascend to command. With competition that tight they had to be careful in everything they did. A few bad marks on an officer's record, or even one, could sink all chances of ever reaching that coveted position. A department head had to want it. He had to be willing to make sacrifices. And, he had to be lucky.

Lately, the engineer's luck had been running thin, and Edwards was growing concerned about him. The engineering department had failed a surprise inspection by the Department of Naval Reactors when *Providence* stopped in Diego Garcia in the Indian Ocean, just before starting the journey home. The failure was a potential blow to the engineer's career, and he hadn't taken it very well. The man was naturally high-strung, but his anxiety since that day had been beyond anything Edwards had ever witnessed.

Edwards could understand his reaction, in part. The poor marks on the inspection would go down in his record, and it might prevent him from obtaining command someday. Edwards thought back to his own days as a department head. It was several years ago, but the memories were still fresh in his mind. His own thirst for command had driven him to volunteer for every tough assignment and to run a meticulously flawless department. A department head spent most of his time putting out fires, and sleep was considered a luxury. Whether a drunken sailor needed bailing out of jail in some foreign port, or a critical ship's system needed immediate repairs, running a department on even a good day was pure organized chaos. Being a department head meant being in a constant state of anxiety about the future. It meant wondering every day if your whole life's pursuit would end in failure.

But I never cracked under the pressure, Edwards thought. *I managed to deal with failures.*

It was a truth he couldn't deny. He had taken every challenge the navy had thrown at him and had succeeded at every turn, gaining promotions and honors. He had taken every mission, every tough assignment, and logged tens of thousands of hard miles beneath the sea. It was the story of his career.

During the cold war as a junior officer, he had learned the basics of undersea warfare and in virtually every corner of the world he had played cat and mouse with Soviet submarines of the Red Banner Fleet. But those were the simple days, the days when there was only one enemy. The aftermath of the cold war brought new challenges, tougher challenges, and a new kind of warfare. A warfare in which the enemy was everywhere and nowhere at the same time. Smaller enemies popped up in all parts of the world while Congress was cutting the size of the fleet in half. It was a time of terrorists and petty dictators and their elusive defiance to the world's sole superpower. As a department head and an XO, he learned the ins and outs of this new warfare in which one day he would distribute aid to the citizens of a country and the next he would launch cruise missiles against it. It was crisis management on a global scale, and with fewer ships to cover each new crisis, the deployments got longer and the brief respites at home grew fewer and farther between. While many of his comrades left the service, he stayed with it. Like a college football player vying for the pros, he kept his eyes on one goal, *command*. And he dedicated everything he had to the navy in order to achieve it. Time, emotion, love, hate, all of it belonged to the service.

She had left him during those years too, just after he made XO. Even after five years of marriage, she had left him. It had not been a rosy marriage in any sense, but the divorce wasn't entirely his fault, he kept telling himself. He had to do it. Competition for command was too tight. He kept telling himself that he had no choice. He had to spend that time away from home. Whether he believed it or not, it did little to alleviate the guilt he felt when the memory of that day came to mind. The day he came home from deployment to learn that she had taken their daughter and moved in with her ponytailed kickboxing instructor. That day he had realized that even the cold depths of the ocean could not keep him from becoming his father. Like his father, his dedication to the service had driven a wedge between him and his family and had cost him the love of his wife and the company of his daughter. He felt even more ashamed because deep down inside he was glad to be free of their encumbrance. And now, as a submarine captain, he was at the top of his game, the envy of all other officers who had not achieved that rank. In his mind, command of the *Providence* and all that it meant made all of the loss worthwhile. At least, that's what he thought most of the time.

His past experiences, both personal and professional, were supposed to help him understand how best to lead his own department heads. Knowing full well the stresses a department head can experience, he had been watching his engineer closely and he still did not know what to think of the man's behavior. In the four weeks since the inspection, Van Peenan had become virtually unapproachable. The engineer had transformed into a taskmaster, losing his temper and flying off the handle for the minutest discrepancies. And now, with no signs of improvement, Edwards was especially concerned about the man's mental state and his ability to run the engineering department. This latest problem with Ensign Yi would not make things any easier. Edwards was glad that *Providence* would be putting in to Pearl Harbor for a while. It would give the engineer some time to unwind and get a grip on things.

"We're within ten miles of the surfacing point, Captain." Miller spoke from the chart table, dividers in hand. "Request to take the ship to periscope depth?"

"Proceed."

"Aye, Captain. All stations, Conn, proceeding to periscope depth."

Miller had a small microphone attached to his collar, which allowed his voice to be heard over speakers in the sonar and radio rooms. He waited for acknowledgments from all of the watchstanders in the room before positioning himself behind the port-side periscope.

"Raising number two periscope."

Miller grabbed the periscope hydraulic actuator in the overhead and turned it to the "raise" position. The room abruptly came to complete silence as the foot-wide periscope, looking more like a polished metal telephone pole, began the laborious ascent from its well. It was the signal for every man to cease what he was doing and concentrate on his watch station. For the safety of the ship, only the officer of the deck and the diving officer could speak during a trip to periscope depth. Should an undetected surface ship suddenly appear above the *Providence*, there could be no margin for error. A misunderstood order could mean collision and death for them all.

Edwards moved to the starboard side of the control room to stay out of the way and to observe. As the captain, it was his duty to observe and to train his officers. Although he sometimes longed to have the first look at the outside world, he seldom if ever took the conn for a routine procedure such as a periscope depth excursion. It was one of the many prices of command.

The scope continued to rise until its handles and eyepiece emerged from the well and came to a stop even with Miller's face. Slapping down the handles, Miller put his eyes to the lens and quickly searched the surrounding waters above. He flipped a switch with his left hand, activating a circuit which transmitted the periscope image to a view screen on the starboard side of the control room, just forward of where Edwards was standing.

Edwards watched as the image on the screen appeared fuzzy, then improved rapidly. When the static cleared, he could make out the tiny ripples on the ocean's surface one hundred and fifty feet above the *Providence*. As Miller rotated the scope back and forth, Edwards could see a glimmering disc of refracted light at the top of the screen, indicating that the sun had risen on the world above.

"All ahead one third," ordered Miller. He was proceeding with the trip to periscope depth, obviously satisfied that there were no ships above them.

"All ahead one third, Helm, aye sir," said the helmsman as he dialed in the ordered speed on the engine order telegraph, a small knob on his panel that instantly transmitted the order back to the engine room.

"Diving Officer, make your depth six zero feet."

"Make my depth six zero feet, Dive, aye," Chief Ketterling responded. Resting his arms on the backs of the planesmen's chairs, he spoke a few words to the two men and they gently pulled back on their controls. Slowly the deck tilted upward and the digital depth gauge on the panel in front of them started counting down.

"One hundred forty feet," announced Chief Ketterling. ". . . One hundred thirty . . . one hundred twenty . . ."

All the way up Miller kept his eyes glued to the periscope lens, slowly turning it back and forth across the forward field of view. Likewise, Edwards' eyes never left the view screen. He imagined what *Providence*'s black hull must look like emerging from the dark shadows of the deep, rising to the illuminated water near the surface, her high-protruding periscope reaching to see into the other world, her tall sail coming within a few of feet of breaking through to that world.

The deck rocked slightly as *Providence*'s hull felt the first suction forces from the waves overhead, and Edwards placed one hand on the railing surrounding the periscope stand to steady himself. The surface was getting closer on the view screen. He could make out a few distorted clouds through the watery barrier. Then suddenly, the scope broke through the waves and he could see the blue sky and the flat horizon. Initially, the periscope window received several dousings from the bothersome two- and three-foot waves distorting his view on the screen, but once the *Providence* leveled off at sixty feet the periscope was high enough to prevent any more interruptions.

Miller swung the periscope through several three hundred and sixty degree rotations before calling out, "No close contacts."

The danger was over now and the bond of silence that had stifled all conversation in the room was broken.

"It's a clear day out there, Captain," Miller said, still looking through the eyepiece. "Just a few patchy clouds. No visual contacts. A perfect day for coming home."

Everyone in the control room smiled at the thought. After six months away, they would finally see their loved ones again.

"Very good, Weps," Edwards said. "Let's see what kind of messages we have waiting for us."

"Aye, sir. Chief of the Watch, raise number one BRA-34."

"Raise number one BRA-34, aye, sir," the petty officer sitting to the left of the planesmen at the ballast control panel responded. His panel contained hundreds of buttons and switches that operated everything from pumps and valves to the various masts and antennas. He reached up and flipped a switch and the massive communications antenna started its journey skyward. The sound of the antenna's hydraulic lifting system filled the room and soon the oval-shaped pole appeared on the view screen as it climbed higher than the periscope. The communications antenna towered over the periscope by several feet and its large diameter completely blocked the field of view off the starboard bow.

A voice sounded over the control room speaker. "Conn, Radio, request permission to query the satellite."

"Radio, Conn, query the satellite," Miller replied. "Download all message traffic."

Edwards imagined his radiomen, back in the radio room, frantically lining up the various satellite radio receivers with the appropriate cryptography equipment in preparations to communicate with the satellite several miles above the Earth. The messages traveled from a shore station, which could be several thousand miles away, to the satellite and back down to the *Providence*. General administration, e-mails, news and sports updates, all of the message traffic came in one large data download, and it all happened in the blink of an eye.

"Conn, Radio. We are in receipt of all message traffic. We have received a flash message addressed to us only."

Edwards' ears perked up and Miller briefly took his eyes from the scope. A flash message meant the highest priority. It was not something that a ship received very often, let alone in the last few hours before returning to home port.

"Radio, Captain," Edwards said into one of the control room microphones. "What is the subject of the flash message?"

Several seconds passed as the radiomen accessed and opened the message on their computer. The wait seemed like an eternity and Edwards noticed that the whole room had become silent again. A flash message seldom meant good news.

"Captain, Radio," the radioman's voice finally intoned. "The message directs you to establish a video-teleconference with ComSubPac immediately, sir."

Edwards' eyes met Miller's. The weapons officer's previously happy face now showed bleak consternation, as did all the other faces in the room. The Commander of Submarines Pacific Fleet would not call for an immediate video conference unless it was something serious, and they all knew that their anticipated shore leave had just become an uncertainty.

"Shit!" muttered a sailor standing back by the chart table.

"Let's not panic, everyone," Edwards said with a smile. He had to do something to keep them concentrating on their watch stations. "First, let's find out what ComSubPac wants. Weps, let's get on the surface so that we can have a clear signal for the conference." He paused for a moment then added, "And somebody please wake up Commander Bloomfield."

A few men chuckled at the remark. At least his executive officer was good for something, Edwards thought. If nothing else, the man provided a humorous outlet for situations like these.

Miller's face drew a smile too. He could see right through Edwards' attempt to get the men's minds off the message, but he played along with his captain like a good department head should.

"Aye-aye, Captain," Miller said, then returned his face to the eyepiece. "Diving Officer, prepare to surface!"

SHOWERING and shaving in the tiny accommodations offered on a submarine were cumbersome tasks, and Lake was happy that he had completed them for the last time. Fresh water was a closely guarded commodity on a submarine, thus it was a rule that only one minute's worth of shower water was to be used per man per day. Thirty seconds to lather, thirty seconds to rinse. But Lake smiled at the thought of his shower this morning, which had been long and thorough. It had been a true "Hollywood" shower, as some sailors were known to call it. Who was going to say anything? He was leaving the ship in a few hours, so what could they do to him?

Lake wore his best cotton khaki uniform for entering port. As he conducted his tour of the ship in preparations for assuming the watch, his mind drifted to all of the events that had taken place on this ship in the last three years. The torpedo room, the auxiliary machinery room, the clerk's office, and the berthing spaces. The galley, the crew's mess, then aft through the watertight door that separated the forward compartment from the engine room. As he walked through the three different levels of the engine room, he recalled those difficult days as an ensign and the time he had spent learning every tank, panel, pump, and valve. And he thanked God that he would be saying goodbye to it all today.

Finishing his tour of the engine room, Lake walked back

through the watertight door and into the forward compartment. As he passed through the crew's mess where two dozen or so men of the oncoming watch section ate their breakfasts at small booth tables, he saw the burly figure of Chief Michaelson rise from his seat and approach him. Lake kept walking into the passageway beyond as if he did not notice him. He had a feeling he knew what the torpedo chief wanted and he did not feel like dealing with him right now.

"Mr. Lake." Michaelson had followed him and caught up with him in the passage. "Mr. Lake."

"What is it, Chief?" Lake said with forced irritability. "I'm right in the middle of my pre-watch tour and I'd really like to grab some breakfast before I relieve the watch."

Lake saw that Michaelson's face showed little sympathy, in fact it showed contempt. The man was no taller than Lake, but his broad shoulders and chest gave indication of the years he had spent working with block and tackle in the torpedo rooms of countless ships.

"Mister Lake," Michaelson put the emphasis on the word "Mister," "One of my boys, Fireman Jepson to be exact, told me you snapped at him this morning when he tried to wake you. I would like to know why, sir. It's hard enough to train these boys properly without you officers . . ."

"Oh, Chief, must you bother me with such pettiness this morning? I'm really not in the mood. And to tell you the truth, I really don't care. I'm so short I can hang my feet off a dime and not touch the ground."

Michaelson's face grew beet red with anger. His khaki shirt grew taut in the arms as his large biceps flexed and the small stabilizer muscles twitched and fluttered. "I don't much care how short you are, sir. You are an officer, and until you leave the navy, you are expected to act like one. You may have resigned your commission, but you still have a duty to the tradition of the fleet."

"I don't have a duty to anything or anyone. In a few hours, I'll be on a plane to the mainland and you'll still be here worrying about poor Jepson. Now, if you'll excuse me."

Lake walked on and left Michaelson seething in the passageway. He never really had gotten along with the torpedo chief at any point during his tour on the *Providence*. In Lake's mind, the man was old navy in disguise, trying to pretend that he really cared for his men because that's what got you good marks in today's navy. Just one of the many reasons Lake was leaving the navy forever.

Taking the passageway forward, Lake reached a fork and took the passage on the starboard side that led into the officers' quarters and wardroom. He ducked into the wardroom and found Lieutenant Commander Aubrey Van Peenan sitting at the dining table that took up most of the room. Standing before him, looking rather pale and slight were Ensign Philip Yi and MM3 Dean, an engineering petty officer. Van Peenan had a massive volume of the ship's engineering instruction manual open on the table in front of him and he read the book in silence while stroking the hair behind his ears with the fingers of both hands. His fingers shook as they moved across the short red hair and Lake could see the telltale vein protruding on his forehead, a sure sign that the man was falling into the midst of one of his rages. Yi and the petty officer looked tired and had obviously just come off watch. Both appeared to be the source of Van Peenan's anger and they stood in foreboding silence like convicted criminals awaiting their sentence.

A small bar on one side of the room contained a pitcher of milk and several assorted cereal boxes. Lake slipped by the standing ensign and petty officer, grabbed a box of cereal and poured some milk into a bowl before sitting down at the other end of the table. None of the other three said a word to him or even acknowledged his presence in the room.

One of the engineer's hands suddenly shot from his ear and slammed hard on the open book in front of him, shaking the table enough to spill some of Lake's milk. The sudden noise made the other two men start from their motionless stance.

"Tough shit!" Van Peenan said. "It states right here that auxiliary seawater valve 101 is not to be opened without first venting the auxiliary seawater expansion tank." The engineer's visibly shaking finger pointed to the words as he read them out loud. "There is nothing wrong with this procedure, Petty Officer Dean. The problem is you and your sorry ass excuses. The problem is that you can't seem to follow the procedures as they are written in the fucking manuals. And this isn't the first time you've caused an incident, Dean. You're disqualified as of this moment. And I'm also recommending you for captain's mast for this blatant disobedience of a direct order."

"S-Sir." Yi feebly attempted to intervene. "I don't believe this incident warrants . . ."

"Tough shit, Mister Yi!" Van Peenan recommenced stroking the hair behind his ears. "It most certainly does warrant captain's mast. And you had better keep your damn mouth shut, or you'll be under investigation too!" He shifted his gaze back to Dean. "You, *Petty Officer* Dean, disobeyed a direct fucking order. You're directed to follow fucking procedures as they're written in the fucking manuals and you failed to fucking follow them. How many times do I have to fucking beat it into your head? You're going before captain's mast, as sure as shit! We'll see if a couple months' restriction and half-pay will make you a better sailor. Get out of here, you're dismissed!"

Dean, who was no more than eighteen, seemed too afraid to even respond to the engineer's tirade. He simply turned and left the wardroom with Van Peenan's piercing eyes following him the whole way out.

Lake chuckled a little as he ate his cereal. "Jeez, Eng. Wake up on the wrong side of the bed this morning?"

Van Peenan ignored him and stood to face Yi. The engineer's face was rather boyish, which made it look all the more hideous when it was screwed up and bulging veins during one of his moods.

"Mister Yi, I hold your sorry ass responsible for this incident as well. You were not in control back there this morning, and I don't think you're capable of leading men at all. It was your fucking division that failed the inspection for us back in Diego Garcia and your ass seems to be involved—or not involved, I should say—whenever something goes wrong in my engine room. You are hereby disqualified as an engineering officer of the watch. You will complete the entire qual card all over again and you will not stand watch in my engine room unless I'm right there with you, holding your fucking hand. Is that clear?"

Yi's face visibly languished as he muttered a weak, "Yes, sir." The ensign appeared completely dejected.

Lake even felt a twinge of sympathy for him. He knew how long and hard the engineering officer of the watch qualification was to obtain. It was a six-month task at least. To have to start all over and go back to the beginning would be disheartening, if not utter misery. Not to mention what the embarrassment would do to him in front of his men.

But he had been in Yi's shoes once, Lake thought, three years ago, and no one had come to his aid. Thus any thoughts of speaking up on Yi's account quickly dissolved and Lake chose to think about all the different ways he could pack his luggage for his flight out that evening.

Chapter 2

PROVIDENCE rode on the surface like a giant whale heeled over on one side raising a single giant fin to the sky. She was not made to ride on the surface, but rather for the ocean depths where her long torpedo-like hull could cruise with ease. Unlike the smooth knife-like bow of a sleek destroyer, *Providence*'s rounded bow, when on the surface, wastefully plowed the water before it, leaving a stretching wake behind that could easily belong to a ship ten times her size. Her long cylindrical hull bobbed back and forth in both light and heavy seas and had the effect of turning more than a few stomachs, even those of the more experienced hands. A crewman need not look at the depth gauge to tell the ship was on the surface. The files of pallid sailors waiting in line outside the heads were indication enough.

The seas were light today, but Edwards still had to steady himself several times while he climbed the twenty-foot ladder leading up the narrow tunnel to *Providence*'s open bridge. The dank tunnel traversed the full height of the towering black sail and was filled with the aroma of the petroleum grease used to lubricate the assortment of masts and antennas housed there. Each cold steel ladder rung drew him closer to the open hatch. The first waft of the fresh ocean air revived his skin, banished from the natural elements for so long. Edwards grew closer to the open hatch above, climbing faster, anxious to see the sky above with his own eyes, and not through a periscope lens.

As Edwards made it to the top of the ladder, he was met by Lieutenant Lake, who dutifully stepped aside to allow him to come through the small hatch. The conn had been transferred up to the bridge after surfacing, and Lieutenant Lake was now on watch as the officer of the deck.

"Good morning, Captain," Lake said, smiling, his hair blowing wildly in the wind, his binoculars hanging loosely around his neck.

"Good morning, Mr. Lake. Fine day."

"It is indeed, sir."

Edwards suspected that Lake's ear-to-ear grin had more to do with the fact that this was his last day in the navy than it had to do with the fine weather. He knew that Lake was a sort of outcast in the wardroom. He had an insurmountable wall built up around him, shutting everyone out. Edwards knew the other officers seldom socialized with Lake on or off the ship, and Edwards himself had found the young lieutenant rather hard to become acquainted with, though admittedly he hadn't put much effort into it. Perhaps it was the warning *Providence*'s previous captain had given him concerning Lake. The legendary Captain Carl Christopher had passed judgment on the young man, and maybe because of that—subliminally— Edwards had too.

That was six months ago, the day Edwards took command. Christopher was in a rush to catch a flight that day and took Edwards through a whirlwind review of the ship's records, hardly pausing for any of Edwards' questions. The review included *Providence*'s officer files. Christopher gave the records little attention, simply tossing one on top of the other, summing up the full character of each man in two or three words. When they came to Lake's file, Christopher paused and his composure changed slightly. Even today, Edwards remembered that moment distinctly. It was the only instance throughout the whole haphazard turnover process that Christopher seemed to be genuinely engaged.

"Watch this one like a hawk, Edwards," Christopher had snarled beneath his bushy gray eyebrows, turning the file over several times in his hands. "Lieutenant Lake is trouble with a capital 'T.' He's your most senior lieutenant, but senior *only* in years of service, I assure you. He's a sorry-ass excuse for an officer if ever there was one. The worst I've seen. Immature obstinacy bordering on insubordination. I should've canned his ass years ago, but no matter—he's getting out of the navy in a few months. It's good riddance, too. If I were you, Edwards, I'd isolate him and leave him be until that time comes. No sense in wasting your efforts on a lost cause. He'll only end up corrupting the others."

Christopher had paused for a moment as he gripped Lake's file and stared at it. Edwards remembered seeing a bead of sweat trickle down his temple and had thought it odd that the great submarine legend Christopher could be affected so by this unruly yet insignificant junior officer. Just as quickly the moment passed, and Christopher tossed Lake's file on the desk with the others.

"Anyway, he's not my concern any longer," Christopher finally said, just as brusque and domineering as he had been moments before. "You're *Providence*'s captain now, Edwards, you call it the way you see it. Deal with Lake in your own way. But never forget, I warned you about him!"

Edwards ended up taking Christopher's advice to heart. Who could blame him? After all, Christopher was a submarine superstar. Having rounded out a successful command tour on the *Providence*, Christopher had been selected for promotion to the rank of full captain. For his successful command tour on the *Providence*, the admirals had appointed him as chief of staff to the Commander Submarines Atlantic Fleet, a coveted position and one that earmarked Christopher for eventual flag rank. That was why the turnover ceremony had had to be rushed. Christopher had to leave immediately for Norfolk on the East Coast and his new assignment. Who wouldn't take the advice of such a man, who had accomplished so much and who was rising like a star?

As the departing Christopher had advised, Edwards never did try to breach the wall around Lake. He let Lake have all the space he needed, and left him out of the close-knit cadre of officers he was molding to run the *Providence*. But there were many moments, especially in recent months, when Edwards came to regret that decision. For all his nonchalance and ogre-like behavior, Lake was actually quite an effective watch officer, and Edwards found himself trusting the young lieutenant more and more each day. True, Lake's administrative skills were lacking as was evident by the radio division's constant personnel problems, but on watch it was a different story. When on watch, the young officer seemed to step outside himself for a few hours, absorbed in what he was doing with an alertness and intuition that was second to no other officer on the ship. After witnessing *Providence*'s numerous port entries over the course of the deployment, Edwards found Lake to be his best conning officer. Certainly, he had talent, whether he got along with anyone else or not. And surprisingly, in Edwards' eyes anyway, the disobedient rebel that Christopher had warned about never materialized.

Sometimes, like now, Edwards regretted isolating Lake in the beginning. He was sorry he hadn't spent more time trying to keep him in the navy. But it was too late now.

Edwards shifted around a bit to get comfortable on the small sheltered portion of the bridge, or bridge "pooka" as submariners called it. Like all other spaces on the *Providence*, the bridge was cramped. Only two men could fit in the sheltered portion, which was no more than an open hole in the top of the sail about five feet across. A man standing in that hole could comfortably hang his arms over the bridge coaming and look out at the surrounding sea. If a rogue wave were to crash against the sail, the two men in the hole could duck behind the coaming and thus avoid being swept away. With the seas as light as they were today, Edwards had authorized the flying bridge rigged, which consisted of an iron bar railing around the top of the sail. It allowed for additional personnel to stand on top of the sail itself. The flying bridge also allowed the lookout to stand a few feet higher than the officer of the deck and thus he could see a little farther over the horizon.

Edwards glanced back at the lookout standing alone on the flying bridge with the national ensign flapping behind his head from a flimsy pole and lanyard. The sailor scanned the horizon for any visible ships, his face pressed permanently against his binoculars. Edwards noted that the sailor instinctively stood well over to one side, careful not to stand on the heads of any of the masts or antennas hidden inside *Providence*'s sail. He was no fool. A careless operator down in the control room might accidentally hit a switch and raise a mast, and any man standing on that mast would more than likely find himself catapulted over the side and into the sea. Even worse, the unfortunate sailor might find himself getting sucked into *Providence*'s massive screw.

"There's Oahu, sir," Lake said above the wind.

Edwards brought his binoculars to his face and scanned ahead. Just poking above the horizon were the distant peaks of the lush green mountains on Oahu. Somewhere over the horizon and at the base of those mountains lay Pearl Harbor and home, that almost forgotten place that until now had only lived in his crew's dreams. Sadly, Edwards feared that the pending conference with ComSubPac would dash any hopes of seeing it anytime soon. But he had to be optimistic in front of his men.

"So, you leave us today, Mr. Lake."

"Yes, sir." Lake nodded, still watching the mountains with his own binoculars.

"I don't suppose you're having any second thoughts about getting out?"

"No, sir." Lake came close to chuckling. "No second thoughts, Captain."

"That's good." Edwards considered stopping the conversation there, but something in Lake's response surprised him. He sensed a small amount of anxiety in the young lieutenant's voice.

"So, what are your plans?" Edwards asked with indiscernible hesitancy.

Lake glanced at Edwards like a son reluctant to share his thoughts with his father.

"Get an MBA, sir," he finally answered. "Go to Wharton or Harvard . . . or at least a top ten school. Then I'm going into business. I'm going to do something—whatever it is, it won't be like this."

"Like this?"

"Like the navy, sir. Like submarines."

"And what's wrong with submarines?"

"It's not so much the boats, Captain. It's the people. It's the culture."

"I'm not sure I follow you."

Lake smiled and hesitated. Speaking his mind to his captain obviously made him uncomfortable.

"Go ahead and give it to me straight, Scott," Edwards said in a friendly tone, and then added. "You'll be a civilian in a few hours anyway. What've you got to lose?"

Lake sighed and took the binoculars away from his face.

"I don't like the idea of a system that is made to serve itself, sir. I've been on board now for a little over three years, and things have never changed. Captains come and go, department heads come and go, but nothing ever changes. So, I've come to the conclusion that this is a culture that's been going strong for fifty years and will continue to go on forever. The system serves itself. As individuals, everything we do is designed to make the man above us more eligible for promotion. Promotion, promotion, promotion. It's everything. It's all submarine officers are taught to care about. I learned that on my first day in the navy, when a desk jockey lieutenant didn't want to grant me a medical waiver so his numbers would look good. I learned that from my first day on this ship when Captain Christopher made it clear to me, in no uncertain terms, that he viewed me and all other ensigns as walking disasters with the potential to ruin his career. He started off hating me, so I started off hating him. Captain Christopher embodied everything that is wrong with the submarine culture. Do whatever you have to do to get promoted, that was *his* motto. You know what his first words were to me, sir?"

Edwards said nothing, but made it obvious to Lake that he had his attention.

" '*Fuck you.*' " Lake quoted, perhaps a little too vociferously. "How about that, sir? '*Hello, Captain Christopher. Ensign Lake reporting, sir. I'm looking forward to serving under you, sir.*' And his response was '*Fuck you.*' " Lake scratched his head, shaking it. "Let's see, I think I read somewhere in the naval officers' guide that a captain is supposed to mentor and train his junior officers, but all Captain Christopher ever did was make sure I stayed out of his way. I learned later that he'd looked up my nuke school grade point average before I even reported to the ship. Well, I don't have to tell you, sir, but I wasn't exactly at the top of my class. Captain Christopher made up his mind about me before he even set eyes on me. He identified me as a threat to his career, and made sure I . . ." Lake stopped, as if he suddenly didn't want to talk about it anymore.

Edwards noticed that Lake was firmly gripping the bridge coaming. The smile had long since faded. This was the first time Edwards had ever heard Lake mention the name of *Providence*'s former captain, and he was surprised to learn about the grudge he had been harboring all this time.

The day Edwards relieved Christopher of command was the only time he ever met him. There had not been enough time to get to know the living legend, not with such a short turnover. Over time, as he began to get more familiar with his crew, Edwards found himself also becoming more familiar with the captain who had established such a legendary reputation around the fleet. Edwards began noticing pieces of evidence, mere glimpses really, of the fiendish mind that had been at work here. Seemingly minor incidents here and there, though singularly yielding no clues, when taken together formed an un-ambiguous portrait of his predecessor's methods. Like a men-acing shadow, his essence lingered everywhere. The navy's crew rotation schedule somewhat mitigated this effect, since nearly one third of *Providence*'s crew and most of her officers were replaced with fresh sailors before she left home port six months ago. For this third of the crew, Edwards had somewhat of a clean slate to start with. But for *Providence*'s veterans— and Lake was no exception—he had to contend with the scars left behind by the former captain. And those scars were deep.

"Mr. Lake, you're one of the only officers left on board who served under Captain Christopher, isn't that right?"

"Just the XO, the Eng, and me, sir." Lake nodded. "All the other officers either showed up in his last few months or after you took command, sir."

"He was your captain from the time you were an ensign all the way to lieutenant. That's an important time in a young of-ficer's career."

"Sometimes I can't believe how naïve I was in those days, Captain. I mean, I really believed I was going to do great things in the navy." Lake smiled again. "I thought I might someday command my own ship. Now, all I want to do is find a nice quiet corner of the world as far away as possible from any naval vessel, any naval person—*hell, anything that floats*—and just settle down. No more navy, and no more Captain Christopher."

"You can't be getting out just because of Christopher," Edwards speculated. "After all, he's just one man. You have shipmates that you respect, certainly? What about the other officers and what about the men in your division?"

"Pawns, sir. With all due respect, Captain, they are pawns. The pawns of a system that will take their lives, turn them upside down, separate them from their families, pay them less than poverty wages and spit them out as soon as they're no longer useful. And they all willingly follow this madness as if they can't see it going on around them. It certainly happens on this ship." Lake hesitated for a moment, eyeing Edwards before he added, "Sir, I'll bet you didn't know that three sailors were admitted to the funny farm during Captain Christopher's reign. Did he tell you about that? You see, Captain Christopher determined that these three sailors were troublemakers. Don't ask me how he came to that conclusion, he just did. Knowing him, he had some screwy, half-baked reason. One day, the captain called all of the officers and chiefs into the wardroom and told us to watch these guys, because *he* had determined that these three sailors, out of the entire crew of the *Providence*, were the ones most likely to cause an incident. He wanted us to ride them. Christopher saw them as a threat, so he rode them. He rode them in a way that only Christopher could. He made their every waking minute on this ship an endless mind-numbing hell. He blamed them for everything that went wrong. If the evaporator shit the bed, it was their fault. If a valve leaked, it was their fault. If the freaking captain's head smelled bad, it was their freaking fault. Hell, those guys spent more time at captain's mast than they spent in the rack. One by one, privileges were taken away. First rank, then pay, then liberty. These guys walked on board as second class electronics technicians and by the time they left they barely had enough stripes to scrub the head. He rode them and rode them until they simply went crazy. Every man has his limit, and Christopher knew theirs. They broke, one by one, and got sent off the ship for psychiatric care. They never returned to sea again, and the captain got his wish. I'll bet he never told you about that, sir."

Christopher had certainly not told Edwards anything about the incident, and this was the first he'd heard of it. Perhaps it was the short turnover, Edwards thought, or perhaps Christopher simply had forgotten to mention it. Deep down, he knew different.

"I remember the day after one of them checked off the ship," Lake continued, "this whole damn crew went about their duties, acting like nothing happened. They were probably scared crapless if they said anything, they'd be next. And that's exactly the kind of culture I'm talking about, sir. One of their own gets driven insane by the captain, *one of their own shipmates,* and they don't do a damn thing about it! That poor sailor was here one day, gone the next, and nobody ever complained even once or even sent a freaking grievance to ComSubPac. No one had the balls to do it, and that makes me sick. Not that anyone up at ComSubPac would have listened to a complaint, but it's the principle of the matter. That's what I can't stand. To hell with 'em, sir!"

"How about you, Mr. Lake? Did you file a complaint?"

Lake smiled complacently and looked out at the sea. "What do you think, Captain? I'll bet Christopher warned you about me. I'll bet he told you that I was a slug and a trouble-maker. Well, sir, now you know why."

It was too bad, Edwards suddenly thought, that junior officers only spoke candidly to their captains on their last day aboard.

"Bridge, Radio," The speaker on the portable bridge suitcase squawked. "Captain, a conference has been established with ComSubPac. We are piping the signal to your stateroom."

Edwards nodded to Lake, who then spoke into the microphone, "Radio, Bridge, aye. The captain has the word."

Before starting down the ladder, Edwards took one last look at the distant mountains of Oahu and breathed a long sigh.

"Quite a view isn't it, Mr. Lake? Just think, this may be the last time you'll ever see it. Better cherish it," he said grinning, and then disappeared into the sail.

Lake gazed out at the clouds drifting down to touch the sharp cliffs beyond the blue horizon. A small wave crashed against the sail, washing his face and shirt with a cold salt spray. A dolphin leaped from the wave as if to say "hello" and then fell back into the sea just off *Providence*'s port amidships. All the memories of the past three years came rushing to the forefront of his thoughts.

The conference with ComSubPac probably boded ill for the *Providence*. He had been in boats long enough to know that. But, it did not matter to him. The ship would pull in to reprovision and he would catch the first taxi to the airport and be gone from this place forever.

ADMIRAL Quentin Chappell's static image appeared on the display of the small laptop computer in Edwards' stateroom. The image looked snowy and faded in and out as the ship's communications transceivers and the satellite link synchronized. The video teleconference was a relatively new capability for submarines. Surface ships had had it for years, but with submarines and their limited antenna space it had always been a question of bandwidth. On a good day with a good connection the quality of a conference equaled that of an Internet meeting. Add to that the cryptography modems required for top secret conferences and the image became choppy and the sound erratic. The other person's voice often sounded like it was coming through a fan blade. Still, it was an invaluable means of communicating with ComSubPac. Voice messages lacked the personal interaction. They lacked the feeling and intent that could be expressed in a videoconference.

From the small booth bench seat adorning one side of the room, Edwards waited impatiently for the video conference to begin. He would cast an occasional irritated glance at his executive officer whose bulky body engulfed a small fold-up desk chair in the center of the room and who nervously flipped through the pages of a spiral notepad.

Edwards did not think much of his XO and made very little effort to hide his feelings. What was the point? Lieutenant Commander Warren Bloomfield, overweight in a uniform two sizes too small, always out of breath, always in the background and never in the lead—no matter how many times Edwards had mentored him—never put forth any extra effort to assist in running the ship. The executive officer's duty was to help enforce his captain's policies and to act as an advisor when needed. Bloomfield, on the other hand, spent most of his time in his quarters. He had no ambition, no passion, no command presence, and—to Edwards—no apparent talents. In Edwards' mind, Bloomfield was useless as an officer, and Edwards had little to no respect for the man. He was sure Bloomfield would be perfectly content to spend his time in complete anonymity, and it was obvious to all, including the crew, that he was simply biding time, waiting for the day he would retire. Through some miracle, he'd achieved the rank of lieutenant commander, though Edwards couldn't imagine how.

A rumor floating around the ship suggested that he had given up years ago when his ex-wife supposedly left him for another woman. But Edwards had trouble mustering even a small amount of sympathy for the slug. What bothered Edwards the most was Bloomfield's apparent reluctance to help him understand anything about the ship's history. When Edwards first took command, he had expected Bloomfield to help him get up to speed on *Providence*'s problems, the ship's personnel, any nuances that a new captain might want to know, especially after the quick turnover from Christopher. Instead, Bloomfield had feigned ignorance with statements like "Captain Christopher knew about that, sir, I was not in the loop," or "Check with the engineer, sir, he might be able to help you." It baffled Edwards how the man could have held the position of executive officer for four years and be so evasive about everything. He was one of those few who slipped through the cracks and managed to finagle an XO spot, in spite of his incompetence.

Bloomfield's chubby fingers suddenly removed a pen from his left breast pocket, as if he were preparing to take notes, but Edwards figured it was more likely to be used to calculate his retirement pay.

The speakers crackled and buzzed and the image of the admiral became much clearer now. Admiral Quentin Chappell's face with its immense age lines and crow's feet appeared on the small screen. The admiral's close-cut gray hair was immaculately maintained at the same length, to the point that it looked like a skullcap. His khaki shirt, now only visible down to just below his shoulders, displayed the gold stars on his collar. They represented his rank and the immense responsibility he bore as the special operations deputy to the Commander Submarines Pacific. Chappell's immediate boss, ComSubPac, commanded all forty-two submarines of the Pacific Fleet and all of their supporting units. And Chappell spent most of his time thinking of different ways to use them.

"Hello, Dave. Hello, Warren," the admiral said cordially. The encryption made his voice sound electronic. He could obviously see them now too from a small camera mounted above Edwards' laptop.

"Good morning, Admiral," Edwards replied. "We were quite surprised to get your message this morning, sir."

"Yes, I know. It can't be helped. Listen, you did an excellent job out in the Red Sea, Dave. It being your first deployment with *Providence*, you should be proud of what you've accomplished. You deserve to come home with honors."

"Thank you, Admiral, but my crew certainly deserves the credit." Edwards knew what was coming next. It was inevitable.

"Fine, Dave. Whatever way you want it. Unfortunately, *Providence*'s return home is going to have to wait. We need her immediately. We're sending you to the Moluccas down in Indonesia."

Edwards glanced at Bloomfield. Bloomfield raised his eyebrows high above the rims of his glasses, causing the skin on his forehead to scrunch up, before he scribbled something on his notepad.

"The Moluccas, Admiral?" Edwards said, searching the far recesses of his mind to remember the geography of the waters around Indonesia. "That's quite a distance."

Chappell nodded. "Yes. It can't be helped. This is a most unusual assignment, gentlemen, but it calls for a submarine and I'm afraid you're the lucky bastards."

"Admiral, before you begin, I'd like to remind you, sir, that my crew has been at sea for the past six months. They've been on station in the Red Sea almost that entire time. They're tired and worn out, sir." Edwards noticed the admiral's expression change slightly, and he wondered if he was overstepping his bounds. He personally did not care whether *Providence* pulled in today or next year, but he had to try for the sake of his crew. He hoped Chappell at least recognized that. He decided to continue on another tack. "My men haven't seen their wives and children since we put to sea six months ago, Admiral. They have personal business to take care of, lives to live outside the navy."

Edwards knew his reasoning was falling on deaf ears. He already knew what Chappell's answer would be. Chappell wouldn't have cared if *Providence*'s crew had been at sea for two years straight. The special operations deputy to ComSubPac had more to worry about than the families of a few sailors. The *Providence* and her crew and their families were simply a number on the wall. A resource that was now available to be used somewhere else in the world.

"My men need a rest, Admiral. Besides, *Providence*'s main engines are in serious need of an overhaul. My engineer will be pulling his hair out."

"Damn your engineer, Captain! It can't be helped!" the admiral snapped. Chappell's face started to turn red. He obviously had heard enough. "The overhaul can wait. After your engineer's pathetic performance on his last ORSE, another few months at sea will be good for him. It'll give him time to get his damn department back in order before they fuck around and fail another one."

Out of the corner of his eye, Edwards saw Bloomfield bring a hand to his mouth and cough a few times. Edwards suspected it was to disguise a laugh. He had scolded Bloomfield so many times in the past months that it must be amusing for him to see Edwards receive the same from Chappell. Edwards knew the admiral had already made up his mind. It was pointless to keep arguing.

"I understand, Admiral," Edwards finally said. "I had to try, sir. What's the mission?"

"Good," Chappell said. He waited a few moments with his ear cocked toward the camera, as if he half-expected Edwards to give him another argument. Then in a more conciliatory tone, he added, "Good. The fleet is stretched pretty thin these days, Dave. All the other operational boats are actively employed in the usual hotspots, otherwise I'd . . . Anyway, just tell your engineer that *Providence* will get first priority in dry dock when she gets back from this one."

"Thank you, sir. He'll be glad to hear it."

"Well, then, that's settled. Let's get to your assignment. What do either of you know about the Bunda Islands?"

Edwards exchanged looks with Bloomfield, and Bloomfield shook his head.

"Never heard of them, Admiral."

"It's a small atoll a couple hundred miles west of Halmahera just on the edge of Indonesian territory. It's officially territory of the Republic of Indonesia, annexed back in 1969 along with the western half of New Guinea. I didn't expect you to know where it is. It's not something you would ever know unless you've been there. It's not on any major shipping lanes and it's definitely not strategic. You can download all the details from the secret net, but the atoll consists of three islands. Most of the people live on the namesake, Bunda, and that's where the main harbor is, if you could call it that, a town called Ujungpang. Most of the population reside there, except for a few small villages along the coast. There's also a workable airstrip and some local government offices. That's where you're going, to Ujungpang."

"To do what, sir?"

Chappell paused for a moment, then said, "Humanitarian mission, Captain. You're going there to rescue an American doctor who's about to get himself trapped in a situation he's unaware of. Dr. Gregory Whitehead's a kind of self-financed philanthropist, you might say. He goes to places like Bunda and sets up his own little field hospital and offers medical attention to the kids and old folks and anyone else who wants it. Spends most of his time in the trash dumps of the world."

"And why does he need rescuing, sir?"

"Because a rebel element on the island is threatening to overthrow the local mayor and declare the Bunda Islands as an independent autonomous region. They're going to try to break away from the Indonesian government, and we have reason to believe they're planning to make this move in the next few weeks. I guess they watched the East Timorese do it, and now they think they can get away with it, too. They call themselves *The New PKI*. Don't ask me what it stands for but it's in reference to the old communist party of Indonesia. Of course, the Indonesian government is denying that this group poses any real threat to security on the island and they've guaranteed the safety of Dr. Whitehead, and all that load of crap, but our government's decided to pull him out nonetheless."

"I thought the State Department issued warnings for such situations, Admiral," Bloomfield said with a sudden abnormal interest. "Can't this guy just hop on a flight and get the hell out of there, sir? Why not just send a plane or a helo to whisk him away?" Just as Bloomfield finished speaking the deck took a heavy angle as *Providence* battered her way through a strong cross wave. Bloomfield's blubbery figure lurched to catch his coffee cup as it slid across the desk beside him. His taut shirt lost its tuck in the back and Edwards instantly shifted his eyes to avoid seeing the disgusting sight of his XO's fleshy white backside protruding from his beltline. The cup was saved from a messy spill and Edwards found himself wondering if his executive officer would ever jump to his duties like he jumped to rescue his coffee. The camera's field of view was wide enough for the admiral to witness the whole event but his expression remained unchanged as if nothing had happened. He simply waited for Bloomfield to regain his seat.

"We're not sending aircraft, Commander Bloomfield," Chappell said. "Yesterday, an Indonesian commuter turbo-prop was shot down as it took off from the Ujungpang airstrip. All seventeen people on board that aircraft were killed. Hence the heightened tensions we now enjoy and the urgency of your mission. The Indonesian government has subsequently closed the Ujungpang airstrip and restricted the airspace around Bunda. It's considered hostile airspace now. No flights are going in or out of there until the rebels who shot that plane down are caught or killed. We don't know if they'd fire on a U.S. aircraft. We suspect not, but the NCA's not going to take that chance. The NCA has decided *not* to ask the Indonesian government for assistance because they don't want it to look like the United States is taking sides in this matter. Their conflict is strictly an internal matter for the Indonesian government and the people of Bunda, and we want no part of it. We're also not asking for help from any of our allies for . . . *other* reasons. Other reasons that you don't need to know."

Edwards silently cursed. He hated going into a mission not knowing the whole story. Chappell was holding something back for national security reasons and now he would be left in the dark. Some desk-riding son of a bitch back at the National Security Agency in Washington had probably made the decision that the commander in the field should not know. He thought about arguing the point with Chappell, but held back, knowing it would be futile.

"Assuming it doesn't conflict with the *real* reason we're going, Admiral," Edwards said with forced sarcasm, "why the *Providence*? Why not a destroyer? Why not any number of ships that didn't get back from deployment today?"

Chappell appeared annoyed at Edwards' tone. "We're sending the *Providence* because she's fast and because she's available, Captain! And because she's an attack submarine! It can't be helped, damn it!"

Edwards said nothing, but stood his ground and waited for Chappell to expound on the comment.

"The rebels issued a statement yesterday declaring that no ships or aircraft near the Bunda Atoll would be safe as long as the Indonesian government is in charge there. They've hinted that they have some sort of undersea threat, too. Now, it's quite improbable that the rebels have a submarine. The Indonesian navy doesn't think they have anything, and we don't either. But our own National Command Authority thinks it might be helpful for U.S.-Indonesian relations if we send a fast attack sub for this mission, to act as a sort of . . . *presence*, if you like, a stabilizing presence. It might help the local merchant traffic to sleep better knowing that one of the good guys is around."

"I'm liking this less by the minute, Admiral," Edwards said skeptically.

"Diplomacy is a tricky business, Captain. Indonesia is an important ally in the war on terrorism. On the surface, the NCA doesn't want to take sides in this conflict in order to protect U.S. citizens in the region. Below the surface, they want to show the Indonesian government that we are dedicated to keeping international waters safe and free, regardless of whether or not the region contains a third of the world's oil reserves. If we send one of our own submarines to act as a stabilizing presence, the NCA feels that the Indonesian government will view it as a gesture of goodwill. And that's why *Providence* is going."

Edwards nodded. So the *Providence* would be used as an instrument of diplomacy. He didn't like the sound of that, either, and wished that he felt as certain as Chappell that the so-called "undersea threat" was nothing more than a sham.

"This should be a simple operation," Chappell said. "In and out. The Indonesian government has informed the local magistrate that you're coming. They've even promised to provide you with provisions or anything else you might need. Just go in there, get the good doctor, and get the hell out. And *remember*, stay the hell out of Indonesian internal affairs. Is that clear?"

Edwards did not know what to say. How could things be clear? For some reason, part of the mission was classified and

Chappell wasn't going to share it with him. He knew the character of Chappell from many past dealings. Any attempts to get more out of him would be fruitless. Chappell was quite used to keeping submarine captains in the dark, never revealing where they fit in the grander scheme. He would never budge an inch.

"Has the doctor been informed that he's to be evacuated, sir?" Edwards asked.

"He has, and I know what you're thinking, Dave, but don't worry. You'll have some assistance in convincing him to go. I'm sending a Seahawk out to you with a personal dispatch for the doctor. The package contains instructions for his eyes only. Don't worry, he'll follow his instructions and go with you quietly." Chappell paused for a moment, and then added, "He knows what he has to do, Dave, so don't bother him too much. I don't think he'll cause you any problems. Just get him out of there as quick as you can."

Edwards winced at the thought of entertaining the doctor all the way back to Pearl. Just what he needed, another useless rider to use up air, consume food stores, and fill up tanks. He suddenly winced at the thought of eating every meal with the doctor on the homeward leg of the trip. But there was something else—something in Chappell's tone that sounded a bit rehearsed.

"Is there anything else, Admiral?" Edwards asked openly.

Chappell's lips moved but his voice could not be heard. He had turned his head to the side and was obviously talking with someone not in the camera's field of view. Edwards assumed that it must be the flag lieutenant, or whoever was feeding him the briefing sheets. Chappell paused for a moment and then turned back to face the camera. He cleared his throat several times and said, "There is one more thing, Dave. This is for yours and Warren's information only, you understand?"

"Yes, sir," Edwards said, sitting up on the edge of his seat. Was the admiral about to give him a bone? Some clue as to the real purpose of their mission?

"This is not confirmed, you understand," Chappell said, "but the NCA believes that the rebels are being assisted by a small terrorist group called Al Islamiyyah. This group is believed to be supplying arms and equipment in exchange for safe haven on Bunda, much like Al Qaeda's arrangement with the Taliban in Afghanistan. It's an Islamic extremist group with connections to other groups that are hostile to the U.S."

"Islamic terrorists and communists, Admiral?" Edwards asked. "Isn't that kind of like oil and water?"

"It may just be a marriage of convenience, but we believe the terrorists are there and helping them all the same. Now you can see why the good doctor's in imminent danger. If there is a shift of power over there . . . well, I'm sure you know what the Islamic extremists do when they get their hands on a Westerner."

Who hadn't seen the news in recent years? Several kidnappings and some of the hostages beheaded. A rather grisly prospect for the doctor.

"I'll send you all the latest intelligence and some amplifying information on your next top secret download," Chappell added. "I want you in Ujungpang in six days."

A quick passage, Edwards thought. That was good. At the normal cruising speed, it would take twice that time. The morale of submarine sailors seemed to be linked to the speed of the ship. If the ship was going fast then they knew they would be home that much sooner.

"Any questions, Dave?" the admiral finally asked.

"No, sir." Edwards was lying, of course. He had a thousand questions. But where to begin? On the other hand, the mission did seem straightforward enough. Yes, there were uncertainties, but if all went well, *Providence* would be back home in two weeks.

"We'll stay in touch via normal message traffic and e-mail, Dave. Keep me informed of all developments on your end."

"Aye aye, Admiral. Goodbye, sir."

"Good luck and Godspeed. Chappell, out." The admiral's transmission ceased and the screen turned blue as the monitor lost the signal.

Edwards and Bloomfield sat awkwardly silent for a few moments staring at the monitor, the sound of the sea crashing against *Providence*'s outer hull, drowning out the ticking of the stateroom's clock mounted on the bulkhead.

"Well, fuck you very much, Admiral," Bloomfield finally said, taking a long gulp from his cup as he cradled it in both hands.

"I think that's unnecessary, Warren!" Edwards snapped. He disliked the man more with each word that came from his mouth. "I don't want that kind of attitude coming from my XO, understood?"

Bloomfield looked at him with ambivalence. "Captain, I'm not saying that—"

"You're supposed to be an example to this crew," Edwards interrupted, "I would advise you to just shut up and do your job."

"As you wish, sir," Bloomfield said with an overly dramatic sigh.

"Go make arrangements for the rendezvous with the helo."

Nodding, Bloomfield hefted his big frame out of the metal chair and left the stateroom through the washroom door, his own stateroom lying just beyond another door on the opposite side.

Edwards inwardly cursed his quick temper with Bloomfield. Perhaps he had been at sea too long with him and the prospect of another few weeks had him on edge.

He stood up and walked over to the mirror mounted above the sink in the corner. A dangling picture of a little brown-haired girl of no more than eight years old caught his eye. The sun shined on her hair and her yellow flowery dress. She had a smile that could melt icebergs and she held a sign made of pink construction paper that said "I love you, Daddy." Edwards smiled every time he saw it, but then his thoughts invariably strayed to his ex-wife and how she was probably at this moment poisoning the little girl's mind, turning her into a manhater. Would his own daughter hate him someday? Would she blame him for all the separation?

Next to the picture on the bulkhead was a printed sheet of paper, the ship's plan of the day. It would have to be changed now, Edwards thought. The plan of the day ended at 1400 hours because that's when *Providence* was originally scheduled to dock. Instead, after traveling halfway around the world and back again, the weary *Providence* would remain at sea. He would have to keep the crew together. A hundred thoughts occupied his mind all at once. He thought about the crew's readiness, about the maintenance that would need postponing, about the repairs that would have to be done at sea, about the amount of food and stores on board, about the weapons' status, and about the mission.

He knew Chappell had not told him the whole story. Rescuing single individuals and exercising diplomacy while doing it was not work for a fast attack boat that was designed for spy missions. There was more to this mission than met the eye.

Chapter 3

THE Seahawk helicopter appeared just above the northern horizon first as a small gleam among the low cumulus, then steadily grew larger and more recognizable with each passing minute. Electronics Technician First Class Julio Reynoso held his hand to his face to shade the afternoon sun and caught a glimpse of the black markings on the Seahawk's gray metal skin as it banked briefly then continued on toward the *Providence*. From the bobbing main deck of the hove-to *Providence*, Reynoso thought he could see the mountains of Oahu in the distance. It was hard to tell, and he was always disoriented after weeks under water. Only the officers and a few select enlisted men ever got to look through the periscope or stand on the bridge. He seldom got a glimpse of the world above. Even his time on the open main deck was usually limited to the last hour before the ship moored when he performed his collateral duty as a line-handler. Usually by that time the ship had entered harbor and was already in relatively peaceful waters.

Today, however, he would not be handling lines as he thought he would be.

Providence was out on the open sea, and he was on deck to receive cargo from the approaching helicopter. An underway replenishment, as it was called. The navy had a way of trivializing the most hazardous of procedures.

"Reynoso! Quit skylarking and take this thing." Master Chief Ketterling forcefully shoved a four-foot rod into his hands. The rod had a hook on one end; just the sight of it sent shivers up Reynoso's spine.

Ketterling, Reynoso, and several other sailors stood on the black rubber-coated deck of the *Providence* waiting for the helo to arrive. They all wore Sperry sneakers for traction since the deck of a submarine rolling in the open ocean was not a very safe place. Its cylindrical hull, like a large log, extended only a few feet above the water's surface. Any speed above fifteen knots would immerse the deck completely, washing them off like flies. Although the *Providence* presently had no way on her and the seas were moderately light, they still kept a sharp eye out for any wave that might be large enough to swamp them.

But at this moment, being swept over the side was the least of Reynoso's worries.

He checked the lanyard to his safety harness for the third time, pulling it tight to ensure that it was securely fastened to the runner which in turn was anchored to *Providence*'s towed array housing, a long hump-like shape that ran along the ship's starboard side. If a wave came over the side he would probably get knocked off his feet, but the lanyard would prevent him from being carried away. He noticed two of the junior sailors fumbling with their lanyards. A small wave smacked against the starboard side, spattering them with heavy salty droplets.

"Tepper, Jorgenson! Are you fucking brain dead?" Ketterling shouted at the two sailors, obviously not satisfied with their respect for the sea. "Get those damn lanyards secured, before I beat your ass!"

Reynoso looked up and noticed that the helo was much closer now. He was about to do something very dangerous, something that could kill him, and he instinctively clutched the long grounding rod more tightly in both hands. In stark contrast, Tepper and Jorgenson didn't have a care in the world and he envied them.

He should have kept his big mouth shut. If he had, he wouldn't even be up here. He'd be down below watching a movie, or something. He should have kept his mouth shut, but it seemed that he always ended up inadvertently volunteering for things like this. Maybe he was just too damn gullible.

It had happened innocently enough. He had been in the crew's mess cavorting with his shipmates talking about what they were going to do in Honolulu that night, when Master

Chief Ketterling entered the room and asked if anyone had ever done helo ops before. Like an idiot, he had raised his hand. Like an idiot who wanted to impress his shipmates. Well, he impressed them all right.

Reynoso pulled on the rod to make sure he had enough slack on the heavy-duty cable. One end of the cable attached to the rod, the other end disappeared into the open hatch in *Providence*'s main deck. The cable connected to the ship's electrical ground, somewhere down there. He didn't know exactly where. He left that to the electricians. But he did know that he was about to act as a human switch connecting the thousands of volts of electricity generated by the helo's rotors to that same ship's ground.

He should have kept his big mouth shut!

"Get ready, Master!" a wind-muffled voice yelled from *Providence*'s towering sail, rising out of the deck a hundred feet forward of where they stood.

The voice belonged to the officer of the deck up on the bridge. It was hard to see him in the glare, but he knew that it was Mr. Lake, who also happened to be his division officer. Even with the glare Reynoso could tell that he wasn't very happy at the moment. Reynoso guessed that he hadn't taken the news very well, the news about not pulling in to port. He knew that Lake was eager to leave the navy. For the past six months, Lake had reminded every man in the radio division every time he entered the radio room, announcing how many days he had left and how he couldn't wait to be rid of them and all their troubles.

At this moment, Reynoso wished that *he* were in the small quiet radio room, operating his radio equipment, instead of holding this damn lightning rod. He imagined his division-mates, who were probably at this moment sitting in the radio room, watching him on the close-circuit monitor and laughing it up. It must be funny for them to see their leading petty officer, that asshole who gives them all that boring maintenance to perform each day, shaking in his sneakers.

He looked up at the number two periscope, projecting from the top of the sail standing tall against the bright sky.

The periscope lens was trained in his direction. They would be watching for sure, making wisecracks at his image on the small black and white screen in the radio room. He would have given them the finger, too, if the officer looking through the scope right now wouldn't also see it. Who knows, maybe it was the captain. Then he would be in deep shit. No chance of making chief petty officer after flipping off your captain.

Whoever it was looking, they would have to stop now. Both periscopes began to sink into their wells and, like some kind of silent ballet, the rest of the masts followed in succession until the black sail reverted to its sleek fin-like shape. Reynoso knew that lowering the masts was a precaution against the helo's whirling rotors, and he took a deep breath at the thought of the many different things that could go wrong.

Reynoso could see Lake's head poking above the high bridge coaming. Lake pointed to the approaching helo and said something to the headset-laden sailor on the bridge beside him. Another sailor standing on deck beside Master Chief Ketterling wore a similar headset, allowing the bridge and the deck to talk directly to each other. The circuit was very necessary during helo ops. Any orders shouted from the bridge would get drowned out by the helo's immense noise.

The Seahawk looked like a mosquito, its landing gear hanging beneath it like legs. It approached the *Providence* from the stern at a low altitude. One slow flyby, then it began to circle the submarine in tight close arcs. The whirring rotors kicked up a salty spray, temporarily blinding Reynoso and reminding him to don the goggles currently resting on top of his head. He could see the open side door and two of the helo's helmet-clad crewmen preparing the pallet of cargo for lowering. He could see the pilot's face too, peering through the Plexiglas window. The pilot was focused on him, apparently singling him out as the lucky one with the rod.

Reynoso glanced at the spinning rotors and wondered how much static electricity was in the air today, or even if it mattered. He wasn't as knowledgeable on the concepts of electrostatic discharge as he was on radio wave propagation. Mr. Lake had explained it to him once before. How did it go? The spinning rotors impacted the air molecules around them, stripping the negatively charge electrons from the helo's surface, thus creating a huge potential difference between the helo and the earth's ground. The first thing on the ground to touch the helo would act as the electrical conduit for all of that electrostatic charge to equalize. In other words, if a man touched the helo first, or if he even touched the cargo dangling from the helo, he was in for one hell of a shock. The grounding rod in his hand was well-insulated and would prevent that from happening, theoretically. The rod would route all the current through the stout cable and to the ship's electrical ground, instead of through him. Or did the current flow the other direction? He couldn't remember. He just knew that he wasn't supposed to touch the helo's grounding lanyard for any reason whatsoever.

Still, it gave him chills to think his hands would be inches away from a violent death. One unexpected gust of wind, one stumble on his part, and it could all be over.

The Seahawk signaled, it was ready to lower cargo. The circling ceased and the helo took up a position close off *Providence*'s port quarter. Reynoso saw one helo crewman lean out the side door and make eye contact with him. The crewman spoke into his headset, guiding the pilot closer and closer, until the helo was directly above Reynoso. Then the helo came to a stop and hovered. The helo's crewman cast out a few lengths of the grounding lanyard, and Reynoso quickly identified the small loop at the end of the dangling cable. That was his target.

The man in the helo began to pay out more of the lanyard, and Reynoso watched as the loop slowly descended. Out of the corner of his eyes, he noticed that Jorgenson and Tepper had moved a few paces further away from him, probably thinking that if anything went wrong, the further away from him the better off they'd be. He couldn't blame them. He'd have done the same thing.

He'd have done the same thing if *he* weren't such a chief's kiss-ass, he scolded himself. If he'd only kept his big mouth shut.

As the loop came down, Reynoso held up the rod with both

hands. The trick was for the helo to lower the loop low enough so that he could hook it, at the same time keeping it high enough so that it wouldn't come in contact with his body if a sudden gust of wind came along.

The loop was close enough now. At least he thought it was. His first swing with the extended hook snagged nothing but air. The loop was still several feet away.

He inwardly cursed. He'd never been much of an athlete. He'd be lucky to make one free throw in ten. What the hell was he doing here?

Just then he saw the helo's crewmen exchange glances. Maybe they were thinking the same thing. Maybe they could tell that he'd never done this before. The loop was lower now, much closer. It had to be low enough now!

He took another swing, and missed.

He was starting to panic now. The noise, his inept depth perception, the tossing deck, all seemed to gang up on him and he felt every eye in the helo and on *Providence*'s deck focusing squarely on him. Even the three or four seagulls floating near *Providence*'s bow seemed to be waiting for him before they swooped down to grab their next fish.

I can't do it! he suddenly thought.

He turned his back to the swinging lanyard, and was about to move away when he saw Ketterling's solid bulk in his path. In contrast to Jorgenson and Tepper, Ketterling had moved closer to him. The big black man said nothing, but simply stood with hands on hips, the eyes behind the weathered face meeting squarely with his own. The eyes spoke volumes to Reynoso's conscience, which was always eager to receive encouragement and guidance from his superiors. They said, "I'm here to support you." They said, "You can do it." They also said, "I'll personally beat your ass if you don't hook that damn fucking lanyard right now! And you can forget ever fucking making chief!"

Reynoso turned in his tracks and faced the swinging lanyard, now only a foot above his head. It was close enough that he could easily reach up and grab it. Ketterling was watching him. He *had* to do it!

He brought the rod up even with the loop. He couldn't miss now. He could practically guide it in.

But, just as the rod's hook met with the eye of the loop, *Providence*'s deck took a swell and the hook twisted in his hand. A loud "*Pop!*" resonated and a shower of sparks descended around him as the hook glanced off the loop, almost sending him over the side and into the water.

Reynoso was on his hands and knees now, his heart skipping several beats as he caught his breath and gathered his senses. He was okay as far as he could tell. He hadn't been shocked, just scared half to death. Through his gloved hands he felt the rough texture of the rubberized deck and noticed that he had dropped the grounding rod on the deck beside him.

Behind him, he thought he heard the sailor with the headset shout, "Master Chief, the officer of the deck wants to know what the hell's the problem!"

He wasn't sure why, but at that moment something clicked inside him. Letting down Ketterling was bad enough, but the thought of letting down Lieutenant Lake made him reach for something deep inside himself. Lake was his division officer. Division officers had come and gone in his career. He had never let down any of them before. From his days as a seaman through each successive stripe affixed to his sleeve, he had taken pride in being the one guy in the division that a div-o could count on. Lake wasn't the best div-o he had had by far. He was disorganized, which Reynoso loathed, and the guy was condescending, often ignoring his suggestions. But there was one thing that Lake did long ago, one noble act that Reynoso would never forget, and he simply could not let him down.

Ketterling had moved to pick up the grounding rod, obviously planning to do it himself, but Reynoso snatched it up from him. With the calmness and dexterity of a completely changed man, Reynoso locked his eyes on the swinging loop, allowed three seconds to judge the period of its motion. Then he lunged with the hook in a wide arcing swing. This time the hook landed squarely in the eye of the loop and Reynoso quickly pulled on it once to engage the locking mechanism. Then he raised his hands and backed away, a signal to the helo that the grounding lanyard was securely latched to the ship's ground. The helo and the ship were now at the same electrical potential, and the danger was finally past.

The man in the helo's doorway waved his hand then disappeared inside to prepare his cargo for lowering. Reynoso continued backing away until he was even with the open hatch in the deck where the rest of the men stood, immediately receiving several pats on the back from Ketterling and the other sailors.

"Damn helo pilots!" Ketterling shouted in his ear. "They never can hold that thing steady! Good job!"

Reynoso smiled at Ketterling's kind remarks. Very generous in front of the junior sailors, but they both knew he had panicked. Reynoso knew Ketterling would never say anything about it. The seasoned master chief was above that. In the end he had done it, and that's all that mattered to Master Chief Ketterling.

They both looked up to see the pallet, laden with boxes of food and supplies, swing out from the helo's side door on a small pulley.

"Tepper, Jorgenson!" Ketterling yelled, "Get your asses over here and guide that pallet down!" He winked at Reynoso before following the two junior sailors aft.

Reynoso grinned, happy that Ketterling seemed pleased with his performance. He then cast a searching glance toward the bridge, half-hoping to see Lake's smiling face and maybe a "thumbs up." But Lake wasn't even looking in his direction. He already had a phone to his ear, probably talking to the engineering officer of the watch, telling him to complete all his overboard waste discharges before the ship submerged again.

Reynoso shrugged and returned aft to help the others unload boxes from the pallet and pass them down the hatch to the waiting bucket brigade of sailors below. The supplies were few, yet they were eagerly received by the distressed supply chief in the crew's mess two decks below. Boxes of fresh fruits, fresh vegetables, and milk. Boxes containing Kimwipes and spare parts. All made their way down the long ladder to the second deck and were neatly stacked for the supply chief to take proper inventory of each one. The pallet was soon reduced to its wood frame base, which was fervently hefted and cast over the side by Jorgenson and Tepper at the direction of Ketterling.

Finally, a satchel of mail and dispatches was lowered from the helo and Reynoso, being the only member of radio division present, took custody of it. The man in the helo doorway waved that there was nothing more to lower, and Ketterling skillfully pulled the quick release on the ground rod releasing its hold on the helo's lanyard, severing the electrical link between the Seahawk and the *Providence*. Then, like an eagle newly released from captivity, the helo increased power, nosed down, and banked away to starboard, the forceful draft from its rotors kicking up a splattering sea mist that coated the men on deck in salty spray.

The men on deck watched with silent envy as the Seahawk quickly gained altitude and speed, settling on a direct course back to Oahu.

"Those bastards," Ketterling said. "They're in a damn hurry. Must have a tee time to meet or something."

Reynoso chuckled and was about to make a comment when a stern voice came from the bridge.

"You men quit skylarking and get below, damn it!" Lake shouted from his high perch.

Lake was certainly in a foul mood, and Reynoso wondered what the next few weeks in Radio Division would bring. Lake wouldn't be much help now, though the short-timer lieutenant had been of little help before. Reynoso would have to run things again, like he had always done. In the absence of a radio chief and with a languid division officer, Electronics Technician First Class Julio Reynoso would have to fill the gap once more. Who knows, he thought, maybe someday someone would take notice of all his hard work and approve his promotion to chief petty officer. Then again, maybe not.

"Do what the asshole says, boys," Ketterling muttered under his breath. Lake and the lookouts on the bridge were already disappearing into the sail.

Reynoso and the rest quickly stowed the equipment on deck and one by one dropped down the hatch. Ketterling was the last one down and pulled the hatch shut behind him, shoving the hatch lanyard into Reynoso's hands to hold while he spun the wheel and dogged the hatch tightly shut against its ring.

Reynoso glanced at the satchel of dispatches he had dropped on the deck at the base of the ladder below.

Who knew where *Providence* was going now? He was sure the answer lay in the satchel, nicely sealed in a robust envelope marked all over with "Classified Material: Top Secret."

"The officer of the deck has shifted his watch below decks!" the 1MC speaker announced, echoing throughout the ship. "Rig for dive!"

With the hatch secure, Reynoso followed Ketterling the rest of the way down the ladder and scooped up the satchel. He took the forward passage heading up to the radio room, his thoughts drifting from his near brush with death to his routine duties. He needed to make sure they copied the latest broadcast before the ship went deep.

Wherever *Providence* was headed it didn't matter to him. Deep down, he loved this life. With no attachments ashore, it was all he had. This cruise was nothing more than another chance to excel.

Chapter 4

"SO, let me get this straight," Edwards said sternly. "You hacked into *Le Temeraire*'s computer network and downloaded a virus infecting all of their machines. Is that it?"

"It wasn't exactly a virus, sir. It was just a little program I wrote. It wasn't nothing dangerous, sir."

The accused, a very nervous-looking Fire Control Technician Second Class Shoemaker, stood in his best white jumper uniform at the opposite end of the table, his bleached white "dixie cup" hat pushed low on his brow, his eyes appropriately staring straight ahead. Edwards glanced at Shoemaker, then at Shoemaker's chain of command standing at attention and lining the table's left side, and then to the forty or fifty other faces in the crew's mess staring back at him. He sat alone at the head of one of the long dining tables, the off-watch hands filling the other tables and those without seats crowding the walkways, some only able to poke their heads into the room from the fore and aft passageways for lack of adequate space. Captain's mast usually drew a large crowd. An unpleasant yet intriguing diversion from their daily tasks at sea.

Providence had been cruising southwesterly through the dark ocean depths at full speed for the last two days, maintaining a good twenty-five knot average only to be broken by the periodic trips to communications depth to copy the latest message traffic. The strain of continuous high speed was putting her engines through the paces, but the big twins kept turning and gave no indication of their desperate need of servicing. As an added precaution, Edwards had ordered the main engine lube oil strainers, normally cleaned daily, to be cleaned every watch in an effort to provide them with the cleanest oil possible. The engine room mechanics were not happy about it. It was but one more annoyance in their miserable lives. The dashed hopes of returning to Pearl Harbor had not gone over well with most of the men, but once *Providence* got well on her way and the dream of seeing home port faded from a reality to an uncertainty, from an uncertainty to fantasy, the crew resumed their daily tasks and the seagoing routine, though it seemed most were merely going through the motions. It had taken them a couple of days to get back into the swing of things. That's why Edwards had chosen to wait until now to hold captain's mast.

Now, as he stared across the table at Shoemaker's slight, almost comical, form, he wondered what they all were thinking. The silence in the room seemed amplified tenfold. Even the steady hum of the mess' ventilation fans was absent, silenced whenever captain's mast was in progress. Had he gone too far in holding captain's mast at all? They had been through a lot already. But discipline had to be maintained, especially now.

A worn maroon-jacketed *Uniform Code of Military Justice* lay on the table in front of him, its border haphazardly stamped with *Providence* hull number, SSN 719. Instead of the usual blue leather table cover, a resplendent forest green wool tablecloth covered the table, a mast tradition. The green tablecloth made the table appear much longer to Edwards, and it reminded him of the sailors' euphemism for captain's mast, "playing football with the captain." He loved the thrill of being a captain but he dreaded this part of the job. Maintaining discipline was essential for any ship at sea. It had to be established and enforced or the ship would be lost at some crucial moment when it made the difference between life and death for all hands. Captain's mast was a tradition as old as the navy itself and a very effective, if not oppressive, means to maintain the discipline. Edwards couldn't count the number of Sundays he had spent in similar ceremonies, either as captain or investigating officer, or as one of the accused's superiors. It was a tradition that served as a stark reminder to the crew. A reminder that the country they served, though itself a free republic, demanded their time, their pay, their freedom, and even, at times, their lives, without question.

Edwards' thoughts were interrupted by Bloomfield, who noisily cleared his throat and then used his thumb to push his glasses back up his round, sweaty nose. Red-faced and out of breath, as usual, Bloomfield stood to Edwards' immediate left. He fumbled with a folder for a few minutes, from which he eventually produced a printed sheet of paper. Edwards took the paper and read it. It was the message Commander-in-Chief Pacific, a four-star admiral, had sent informing him of the incident in question. Most captains wanted to avoid getting messages like this one.

"I've got to tell you, Petty Officer Shoemaker, never in my career have I received a message telling me to send an apology to another ship's captain, not to mention to a *French* captain," Edwards said, holding up the sheet of paper that bore the message. "What you did was extremely foolish."

"Yes, sir. I'm sorry, Captain. I'm sorry to have embarrassed you, sir."

"I want the whole story from the top. I need to know exactly what it is I'm apologizing for. Tell me everything." He paused before adding, "Everything, Shoemaker!"

"Yes, sir." Shoemaker shifted a little in his stance, and Edwards could tell he was worried about what was going to happen to him. This was the first time Shoemaker had to be sent to captain's mast in the two years he had been on board. From what Edwards knew of him, he was an overall good sailor who mostly kept to himself, a skillful fire control technician and one of those few chosen ones who manned the weapons console during battle stations. He was known to have an affinity for networks and programming and liked to dabble in different areas of information technology. In fact, he was the only sailor on board who moonlighted as a contract website developer whenever *Providence* was in homeport. The dual talents of Shoemaker had never come in conflict with his navy duties. That is, until now.

"Well, sir," Shoemaker reluctantly started. "When we pulled into Diego Garcia a few weeks back, me and some of the guys went to the Brit Club to have a few beers. Nothing but a few beers at the club, sir, that's all we wanted seeing as how there's nothing else to do on that island. Well, there were some French sailors there too, from the *Le Temeraire*. Being fellow submariners and all, sir, we figured we'd buy them some beers and see how good the French can shoot pool. The evening started out innocently enough. We bought them drinks, they bought us drinks, we must have shot a couple dozen games, but at some point those Frenchmen started to change their manners and started insulting us, Captain."

"They started insulting you?" Edwards knew where this was going. Sailors would be sailors, no matter the nationality.

"I don't know if it was because they had lost nearly every game, Captain, or if it was because they just didn't like the smell of us, but they started to cut us down, bad mouthing the President, talking trash about the whole Iraq thing. We tried to brush it off as best we could, sir, but they just kept the insults coming. They even called the *Providence* an over-designed piece of American shit, begging your pardon, sir. They said we didn't hit jackshit with our missiles, begging you pardon, sir. That we just blew over a few goat herder tents in the desert. Well, you and I both know that's a flat-out lie, Captain. I mean, I fired those missiles myself, sir! We couldn't believe those guys, just cutting us down like we were some merchant seamen or something."

Edwards held up the message and examined it. "It says here that a comment was made about . . . let me see, here it is . . . 'you (expletive) Frenchies shoot pool about as good as you fight.' Did you say that, Shoemaker?"

Shoemaker's eyes shifted high and to the left momentarily.

"Yes, sir, I said that." Shoemaker's shoulders slumped ever so slightly from his rigid attention stance. "But not until after they'd said all those other things, Captain."

Edwards didn't respond. He didn't know why, but Shoemaker's transparent honesty suddenly amused him. Shoemaker didn't have the cunning to lie about the incident, and Edwards had to force himself to keep a straight face in front of the watching crew. He'd have probably said the same thing to the French sailors.

"One of them wanted to fight us," Shoemaker continued,

"and, well, we were all for it. A fight would've happened too, sir, but some British officer came in and broke up the whole thing before it got started . . . uh . . . I mean, thank *God* he broke it up, Captain . . . I mean, we weren't looking for trouble, sir. The British officer ordered us all back to our boats, so we headed back to the ship, like he said. But as you remember, Captain, the *Le Temeraire* was moored just down the pier from us, so we ended up walking with the Frenchies the whole way back, and they never did stop their wise-ass remarks . . . uh . . . begging you pardon, sir. They really were trying to get a rise out of us."

"So after you got back," Edwards said, then paused, holding back a smile, "that's when you sent them a virus, huh?"

"Not a virus, Captain. Like I said, it was just a little program. And I didn't exactly *send* it to them either, sir. I hacked into their network." Shoemaker blinked as he obviously, and suddenly, realized that he was playing at words with the captain, so he added quickly, "I mean, *Le Temeraire* was hooked up to the base network just like we were, sir, so it was easier that way . . . to hack in, I mean. The French are years behind us in security, Captain."

"This message doesn't tell me exactly what it was that you did, Shoemaker. It just states 'petty officer in question loaded an illegal program onto the information systems of a ship belonging to a foreign navy.' Why don't you expound on that for me? What *exactly* was the illegal program?"

Edwards saw Shoemaker glance at a few of the onlookers who were holding back snickers. Edwards figured that most of the crew probably already knew about the program. Probably some of the chiefs and officers did, too. There were some things that happened on a ship the Captain was the last one to know about.

"Well?" he prompted the hesitant Shoemaker.

"It was a simple program, sir, just involving a little j-peg image I created. The program would make the image their default desktop background and their default screensaver. Then if they tried to delete the program it would transfer itself to another directory and reset itself. In other words, sir, they wouldn't be able to get rid of it, not unless they had someone on board who really knew what he was doing. I accessed their network server from our FT division computer and made my way around to each of *Le Temeraire*'s workstations, loading it onto each one."

"What was the image?"

"An American flag, sir," Shoemaker answered simply, immediately followed by a few hastily conjured coughs from somewhere in the back rows of onlookers. He then added, "Mostly, sir."

Edwards held the message up again and read out loud, "'. . . illegal program contained pornographic image . . .'"

Shoemaker's eyes fell to the floor briefly and then returned to attention. He obviously knew that he was caught.

"What was the pornographic image, Petty Officer Shoemaker?" Edwards forced himself to ask with vigor.

"We found this picture, sir, . . . I mean *I* . . . *I* found this picture on the web, sir. It must have been from some strip club somewhere or something like that, but it was a picture of a guy with a . . . well, he was naked, sir, and wearing nothing but a white dixie cup hat. I cut and pasted the picture onto an American flag background, and added some text lines." Shoemaker paused for a moment, then added, "The text read, 'I get off on American sailors.'"

Edwards did his best to keep from laughing. He had met *Le Temeraire*'s pompous captain briefly in the officers' club on Diego Garcia. The mental image of the captain waking up one morning to a naked American sailor on his stateroom's computer screen was almost too much to bear. A few chuckles emanated from the sailors clogging the forward passageway, but Edwards couldn't bring himself to stare them down. He was having enough trouble controlling his own urge to burst out in laughter. But then his conscience got the better of him and quelled any thoughts of levity. Shoemaker's action could have resulted in serious consequences. Suppose the program had interfered in some unforeseen way with *Le Temeraire*'s navigation computers and the big French submarine ended up crashing into an underwater sea mountain at twenty knots. He would have to make Shoemaker an example for the rest to take notice.

"And that's everything, Captain," Shoemaker said innocently. "That's all I did, one hundred percent!"

"Petty Officer Shoemaker, I don't know what to say. One of the reasons we haven't read your charges is because the XO's still trying to count them all. Besides this illegal program and the hacking, you're also guilty of accessing pornographic images on a government computer. Not to mention the damage this incident could do to our relations with the French navy."

"I'm sorry, Captain."

"I don't know if you're sorry enough!" A hush descended on the room as Edwards took on the role of their captain once again. "You've really gone too far, young man. I'm not the only one who has to apologize to the French because of your little joke. The whole chain of command will have to apologize, all the way up to the Secretary of Defense himself. If we hadn't been called away on this mission, the shore patrol would've been waiting for you on the pier with handcuffs and irons ready to whisk you away to the brig. The JAG lawyers are chomping at the bit to get their hands on you. You're literally one step away from making big rocks into little rocks for the rest of your life."

Shoemaker's face took on a deathly pale color as he suddenly realized the weight of the charges against him. Edwards could see a million things going through the twenty-year-old's mind. He felt sorry for him. He could think of at least a dozen crazier and possibly more costly stunts pulled by his own fraternity when he was merely twenty. Boys would be boys. But there was no room for youthful transgressions in today's navy. Everyone had to walk the walk politically, professionally, and personally, or they were rooted out. He didn't write the rules. They were written by people who lived in a white city of marble ten thousand miles away. But he had to live by them, enforce them, and imbue them into a boatload of mostly kids who risked their lives on a daily basis.

"The only way for me to save you now, son, is to throw the

book at you and just hope the JAG is satisfied when we return to home port. I'm not sure they will be, though."

Shoemaker swallowed what he could in a dry mouth.

"Here is your sentence," Edwards said, pausing long enough for Bloomfield to finish fumbling with his pen and the clipboard containing the mast form. "Petty Officer Shoemaker, you are sentenced to two reductions in rate, half pay for three months, forty-five days extra duty, and sixty days restriction to the ship. The sentence is to go into effect immediately."

Shoemaker seemed to gather some inner strength and faced the sentence with his head held high. Edwards could see that the young man did indeed regret his actions, and Edwards didn't want to put him through any further unnecessary misery.

"You're dismissed, *Seaman* Shoemaker," he said.

Shoemaker saluted, turned on his heel, and marched out of the room, Miller and the fire control chief following in file after him.

"Bring in the next case," Bloomfield announced.

Several officers and chiefs filed into the room taking the spots along one side of the table previously occupied by Shoemaker's chain of command. They were Lieutenant Commander Van Peenan, Ensign Yi, and Chief Hans, in that order.

At the far end of the table, Shoemaker was replaced by a younger sailor also in whites, sweating profusely, visibly more uncomfortable than his predecessor. He saluted Edwards, then came to attention. The broad chest and shoulders, in stark contrast to Shoemaker's feeble form, gave away his trade. He worked with his hands for a living and not in front of a computer screen.

"Nuclear Machinist's Mate Third Class Myron Dean, sir," Bloomfield announced before opening the mast report to read the charge. "MM3 Dean is accused of dereliction of duty in that he failed to follow written procedures as directed while standing watch as the engine room lower level mechanic thereby endangering propulsion plant systems and temporarily reducing the maximum speed capable of this vessel." Bloomfield shut the report with an air of nonchalance as if he had just read the day's lunch menu, and then placed it on the table in front of Edwards. "Dereliction of duty while on watch sums it up, Captain. Another dumb wrench-turner. Pretty cut and dry."

Edwards cringed inside. Time and again he wished for his executive officer to keep his comments to himself, especially in front of the crew. He made no eye contact with Bloomfield, embarrassed as he was by the XO's blundering babble. He noticed that Dean kept staring forward, but the red face and the small vein visible on the sailor's neck indicated a twinge of anger at Bloomfield's last words.

"The investigating officer is Lieutenant Coleman, Captain," Bloomfield added.

Coleman stood on the opposite side of the table from the rest of the officers, a sort of geographic representation that the investigating officer did not take sides, but carried out his investigation in an objective and impartial manner.

"Mr. Coleman." Edwards nodded to the young red-haired lieutenant, who was no more than twenty-five years old, but had an expression to suit the worries of a man twice his age.

"Captain," Coleman said, standing at attention. He turned toward Edwards slightly. Edwards knew Coleman to be a very studious young officer who soundly defeated all others in technical knowledge. He viewed every situation with a logical eye and could see to the heart of a problem easier than most of his peers, whether the problem was tactical or technical. However, whatever Coleman was blessed with in intellect he was denied in charm. Regardless, Edwards considered him to be reliable and the perfect candidate for an investigating officer.

"Sir," Coleman continued, "during my investigation I interviewed Commander Van Peenan, Ensign Yi, Chief Hans, the engine room supervisor who was on watch at the time, and several members of the watch section, including Petty Officer Dean himself. I also reviewed the applicable engineering procedures and the engineer's night orders for the evening in question. It's my opinion, sir, that Petty Officer Dean failed to follow procedures as directed in the engineer's night orders. All watchstander testimonies are in agreement with this conclusion."

Edwards glanced through the report in front of him. Of course, he was familiar with the incident. There was no question as to Dean's guilt in the matter. It was the charge that bothered him. Dereliction of duty and the punishment that accompanied it was extremely harsh for a young third-class petty officer who was still learning how to be an efficient and useful nuclear mechanic. Edwards had hoped Van Peenan would have addressed this issue within the confines of the engineering department, and not taken the case to mast. He had hoped his engineer wouldn't force him to act in front of the crew, but it was not to be. He glanced in Van Peenan's direction and was surprised to see the engineer standing at attention with eyes shut and a smile as insidious, and at the same time gleeful, as any he had ever seen. If Edwards had to guess, he would conclude that Van Peenan was enjoying every minute of the proceedings, as if he were fulfilling some sort of personal vendetta.

"However, I would like to add something, sir," Coleman interjected, and before Edwards could turn his attention back to the lieutenant he caught a glimpse of Van Peenan's eyes bolting wide open, surprised to hear any more words from Coleman in this open and shut case.

"Reviewing Dean's watch and drill schedule of the seventy-two hours prior to the event," Coleman continued, "I found that he had no more than four hours of uninterrupted sleep during that time. I also learned that it is currently engineering department policy that every man must spend the six hours after his watch cleaning the engineering spaces, which leaves only six hours of off-watch time for routine maintenance, drills, and sleep before he has to go on watch again. Petty Officer Dean revealed to me that he has not had six hours of straight sleep since the ship left Diego Garcia!"

A nervous laugh suddenly came from Van Peenan. A high-pitched neurotic laugh that penetrated the formality of the ceremony to the amazement of all present, including Edwards.

The laugh was disturbing. It didn't belong. It was so uncharacteristic, so strange, so out of place that Edwards found himself speechlessly gazing at Van Peenan for a long moment before it registered. As his laugh degraded to a chuckle, Van Peenan seemed to realize that all eyes were on him.

"This is really ludicrous, Captain," Van Peenan's high-pitched voice pronounced, his eyes never meeting Edwards but staring awkwardly at the manual on the table. "Mr. Coleman's observations and his opinions have nothing to do with this issue. Dean is guilty, plain and simple. Anyone can see that."

"With respect, sir," Coleman said, "I have included no opinions in my report, but if you want my opinion, Captain, the entire engineering department is to the point of exhaustion. So much so, that I wouldn't trust them to conduct any reactor maintenance *at all,* let alone a simple procedure like the one Dean was performing."

Van Peenan shot a hateful glance across the table at Coleman, but the young lieutenant appeared unmoved by the senior officer's scowl. Coleman was the sonar officer and therefore reported to Miller, the weapons officer, which meant that he was not in Van Peenan's chain of command, and therefore virtually untouchable.

"These men stand watch over a nuclear power plant and carry the trust of Naval Reactors, sir," Coleman persisted. "If they're not allowed sufficient rest, they're being set up for failures like this one."

Edwards started to speak but was abruptly cut off by Van Peenan who shook a long bony finger across the table at Coleman.

"If the men would clean their fucking spaces *while* on watch, they wouldn't have to clean *after* watch!" Van Peenan said with much agitation in his voice. "If the men had fucking cleaned their spaces before the fucking ORSE, if they'd read their fucking manuals, if they'd done their fucking jobs, then they'd be getting sleep every damn day, Mr. Coleman! But that's not your decision, is it? The last time I checked I'm still the fucking engineer on this ship, correct? So keep your damn junior officer opinions to yourself!"

Edwards and every other sailor in the room gasped at Van Peenan's tirade, completely inappropriate, especially during captain's mast. Edwards stared at Van Peenan's long trembling finger, still stretching across the table at Coleman. The engineer's freckled face was full of rage—no, full of *hatred*—for Coleman. Edwards had seen a lot in his fifteen years in the boats. He had seen it before in other men. These were the signs of a man who was breaking down. Edwards had grown increasingly concerned in the weeks since the ORSE failure, but he never envisioned that Van Peenan's emotions were strung so taut.

The crew's mess remained silent. Edwards scrambled to gather his thoughts. The engineer had problems, yes, possibly psychological. The crew had witnessed the whole outburst, yes. But *Providence* still had a mission to perform. And he needed an engineer. There had to be a way to tactfully reprimand Van Peenan and continue with the mast. He could deal with the engineer later, in private. Before Edwards could find the right words, Coleman responded to Van Peenan in a seething tone.

"No, Eng, you're right. That's not my decision. And, yes, you're still the *fucking* engineer."

The whole room burst into laughter, which was silenced in less than two seconds by Edwards' seething glance at the chiefs, who in turn glanced at the sailors, who in turn glanced at each other with still concealed smiles.

The veins were clearly visible now on Van Peenan's bright red temple and he shook with anger.

"Captain, I won't have him talk to me like this . . ." Van Peenan started.

"Enough!" Edwards scolded the room in general. "Lieutenant Coleman, you are dismissed! Leave the room!"

"Aye-aye, sir." Coleman stiffened, then shuffled his way past the sailors blocking the forward passageway.

Van Peenan fostered a smirk as the room quieted down. Edwards saw it and was immediately annoyed.

"And you, Commander Van Peenan, will refrain from speaking unless I ask you to speak. Understood?" He waited for Van Peenan to nod before continuing to the mass of sailors. "That goes for all of you! I don't know what's gotten into you! Captain's mast is no time for levity!"

Edwards could see he had their attention now. Their smiles had faded.

"I know you've been at sea a long time. I know you haven't seen your families in six months. But you're all submariners! You volunteered for this, nobody forced you. You made a commitment to the navy, to your families, to your friends, that you'd be the ones to stand watch for our country under the ocean. It's not an easy job. Nobody ever told you it would be. Sometimes it just plain sucks. Now, I know you're all here for different reasons, but you all have a common duty to your ship and to your shipmates. And I guarantee you that if I find *anyone* slacking in that duty, I won't hesitate to do *my* duty."

They looked like beaten dogs. He could see the longing for home in their faces. Some looked back at him, some stared at the deck, others looked at the overhead. He knew they were reaching the end of their usefulness. They'd spent too much time underwater, but he had to summon every last ounce of personal honor from their souls. It was the only way to get them through the next two weeks.

"Understood?" he said finally with his most confident and fatherly grin.

"Yes, sir!" came the congregational reply. Some of them smiled, others didn't.

He heard Bloomfield clear his throat. The large man pushed his glasses up with his thumb, his eyebrows raised in abject disdain. Edwards wasn't sure if it was directed toward him or the crew, but he suspected the former.

"In the absence of the investigating officer," Edwards said, resuming the businesslike demeanor appropriate for captain's mast, "I'd like to hear what Petty Officer Dean has to say. Tell me, Dean, why didn't you get enough sleep before going on watch that night?"

Dean glanced briefly at Van Peenan with only his eyes, before answering.

"I was up all day, Captain. I was painting the bilge in engine room lower level. I painted all day, and into the evening, right up to when my watch began. But I wasn't the only one. The whole division was painting. Engineer's orders, sir."

"The bilge in engine room lower level?" Edwards said inquisitively. "I was down there just yesterday. Wasn't your division painting that bilge when I walked through there yesterday?"

"We were *repainting* it, sir."

"That bilge couldn't need repainting in just under two weeks, MM3."

"Yes, sir, it did. Or the engineer thought it did, sir. He found a spot of rust. Ordered us to paint it all over again. Fore to aft, sir."

Edwards shot a glance at Van Peenan, but the engineer avoided making eye contact with him. He simply stared forward blinking his eyes in long uneven blinks. He obviously wanted to speak, to refute Dean's testimony, but Edwards would never let him in his current condition.

It was all very clear to Edwards now. Van Peenan was pushing his men too hard. The ORSE failure was making him paranoid and he was taking it out on his men. Repainting a bilge which required painting only once a year was beyond harsh, and he was sure it was just the tip of the iceberg. He had seen it all before on other boats, of course, and unless he put a stop to it there would be more incidents like this one. Still, he had to show to the men that Dean's actions, though not entirely his fault, could not be tolerated.

"What about the division officer and division chief?" Edwards asked, looking down the file of officers past the engineer. "Ensign Yi, Chief Hans, do you have anything to add? Was Dean being pushed too hard? Was he adequately rested in your opinion?"

Ensign Yi stood in silence on Van Peenan's left. Beside him, Chief Hans shrugged in response to the captain's question. Yi said nothing.

"Mr. Yi?" Edwards prompted.

"Yes, Captain," he uttered weakly.

"Are you paying attention, Ensign?" Edwards said impatiently. "Do you have anything to add?"

Yi wanted to blurt it all out. To tell the truth, that the engineer was a tyrant. That Dean was a hard worker and a good sailor. That he needed a break this time. He wanted to say all of these things, but he didn't dare. The hair stood up on the back of his neck as he caught a glimpse of Van Peenan's veiny fist clenched tight at his side. It was a small signal that Van Peenan was waiting for his answer too, and Yi knew there would be hell to pay later if it was not the right one.

"I'm waiting, Mr. Yi!"

"Y-yes, Captain," Yi hesitated after one searching glance at Dean, then added, "I don't have anything to add, sir."

Yi thought he saw a twitch in Dean's face, but it quickly reverted to the same emotionless expression that had been there before, and Yi immediately hated himself. He had had the chance to speak up for this man in his division, this man who'd done nothing but make a small mistake under duress, but he couldn't find the courage within himself. What kind of a division officer was he not to stand up for one of his sailors? What kind of a man?

He immediately wanted to take it all back and do the right thing. He turned to the captain and was about to speak but Edwards, flipping through the courts-martial manual, didn't see him.

"With no more statements to be admitted," Edwards said, "I find MM3 Dean guilty of the charge of dereliction of duty."

Yi flushed deep red. It was done now. His last minute courage had come too late. He noticed an evil grin appear on Van Peenan's face at the reading of the verdict.

"MM3 Dean," the captain continued, "you have been found guilty, and I sentence you to forty-five days restriction in port, reduction in rank, and three months on half pay."

Dean briefly closed his eyes, and the room appeared collectively shocked. The sentence was harsh. Dean had a wife and two children and he hadn't seen them for six months. Under the restriction sentence he was confined to the ship, not allowed to physically leave until *Providence* had been in port for forty-five days. As if that wasn't enough, his family would have to learn how to get by on half a paycheck for the next few months.

Yi wished he could tell Dean he was sorry. A low murmur in the room became a noticeable mumbling. The crew obviously thought the sentence was too much, but Van Peenan seemed ecstatic. Bloomfield was indifferent, thumbing his glasses as he scribbled the judgment and the sentence on the mast report form. As he reached over to gather up the manual on the table, Edwards stopped him.

"I'm not finished, XO."

Bloomfield looked confused, as did everyone else in the room. The verdict had been reached, the sentence pronounced. What else remained?

Edwards locked eyes with Dean and said sternly, "The sentence is suspended until further review of MM3 Dean's performance."

"Suspended . . . What the . . . ?" Van Peenan interjected, suddenly very hostile. "Captain, I object—"

"This isn't a damn courtroom, Commander!" Edwards shouted lividly at Van Peenan. "And you're not a damn lawyer! So stand there and be silent!"

Van Peenan quickly returned to attention, red-faced, with veins bulging from his temples. Yi instinctively moved a few millimeters backward to try to hide as much of himself behind Van Peenan and out of the captain's view. Edwards had a look that could melt a reactor core.

"Do you understand, Dean?" Edwards said, turning his attention back to the rigid sailor. "I'm suspending this sentence, hoping you'll improve your performance and that we'll see no more haphazard procedures performed in the engine room."

Dean exhaled and swayed a little. A few beads of sweat appeared on his brow. He obviously could not believe his luck.

"Yes, sir," he managed to say.

"I'm going to put this ruling aside for six months. If during that time you perform well there will be no mention of this in your record. On the other hand, if you screw up again and I have to see you at mast, this sentence will go into effect faster that you can say 'Seaman Apprentice.' Is that clear?"

"Yes, Captain."

Yi smiled briefly, relieved to see that Dean was spared the harsh punishment. But his smile quickly faded as he sensed the rage next to him boiling inside the engineer. He could see Van Peenan's fist at his side squeezed so tight that the skin was white around the knuckles. At that moment it occurred to him that Dean's life had not gotten any better. In fact, it may have just become terribly worse. Van Peenan would have his revenge. It was only a matter of time. He would make Dean's life miserable until he cracked and did something stupid again. It was unavoidable. Van Peenan would get his way one way or another.

Chapter 5

"HERE'RE the outgoing messages for your review, Mr. Lake," Reynoso said, out of breath, clipboard in hand. After looking all over the ship he had finally caught up with Lake in the torpedo room. Lake was in sweat pants and a tank top, lifting a pair of thirty-five pound dumbbells in a small space wedged between double racks of the shiny twenty-one-foot-long, green-painted Mark 48 ADCAP ship killers.

"Shit, Reynoso, I'm working out here!" Lake snorted. "Can't you see that?"

"I know, sir, but you haven't been up to the radio room in so long, and these have to go out at the next comms period. They're just routine, sir, it shouldn't take more than five minutes to review them."

"Oh, all right." Lake took the clipboard and flipped through the dozen messages at a pace much faster than he could have possibly read them. He snapped his hands for a pen and Reynoso produced one.

"Thanks, Mr. Lake."

Lake said nothing, signed the release and handed the clipboard back to Reynoso. He picked the weights up from the deck again, but before he could complete one repetition, Reynoso pulled a lengthwise folded document out of his back pocket.

"And if you wouldn't mind approving the maintenance schedule for this week, sir. I've already done it up. All you have to do is sign it, sir."

"Shit! What is this? Can't I get a fucking workout without getting interrupted?"

Lake put the weight back down and snatched the schedule from his hands, signing it haphazardly.

"Thank you, sir."

Again Lake picked up the weights.

"Sir, if you wouldn't mind I'd like to also ask about the status of my promotion package . . ."

"*Yes*, the hell I do mind, damn it! Would you fucking leave me alone, Reynoso?"

Reynoso nodded obediently and scurried from the room through the rear door, his clipboard and maintenance schedule tucked under his arm.

Lake completed a few repetitions, then cast a glance toward the door. He didn't know why he was such a jerk to Reynoso. Reynoso was a good guy, just a little too much of an overachiever in his mind. Overachievers and "lifers" annoyed the hell out of him. Still, he had to admit, Reynoso's hard work had kept him from having to do much on this deployment. Reynoso had been running the division, taking care of many tasks that were normally the responsibility of the division officer. Some things had fallen through the cracks, but Reynoso had done his best, or at least the best his experience had afforded. Still, he took care never to make the same mistake twice. He'd probably make a good chief someday.

Lake couldn't bring himself to tell Reynoso that he hadn't even begun working on the eager first-class petty officer's promotion package. After all, he thought he'd be sitting in some café in the Bay Area by now, growing long hair and a goatee, drinking a caramel macchiato, getting caught up on the new bands he'd missed, *not* out on another mission. He'd fully planned to let that job fall to his replacement, whoever the poor sap was who would become the new communications officer. He'd hoped to avoid facing Reynoso with that fact. Now, with the prospect of another two weeks at sea and Reynoso's persistent nature, he wasn't sure how he was going to get around it.

The deck tilted a little. The ship was slowing and coming shallower, probably coming to comms depth to send the messages he had just approved. A small adjustment in his stance and he continued his set without any problem. Just another nuisance he had gotten used to over the years.

Lake continued his workout in the small space he often used at the aft end of the starboard walkway between the long torpedo racks. Out of the corner of his eye, he saw a large figure turn the corner up forward around the center torpedo rack and stroll aft along the starboard walkway toward him. It was Chief Michaelson, the torpedo chief who had confronted him in the passage regarding his treatment of Jepson.

"Mr. Lake, sir," the chief said, gruffly. "Down here again I see."

Lake ignored him and kept lifting.

"Funny, I don't remember you asking me if you could work out in my spaces, sir." Michaelson said, resting one of his muscular arms on a pipe in the overhead. Lake saw the muscles twitch along the obscene tattoo on his biceps.

"I don't have to ask you, Chief, and the torpedo room doesn't *belong* to you. Besides, I've been working out down here for the last six months and you never said anything. What's the problem now?"

"The problem is you, sir. You're in my way. I'm fixing to move weapons around down here, and you're in the way."

"You're going to move weapons? I don't see any of your boys down here. Do you plan to move them by yourself, Chief?"

"Oh, they'll be along directly. But you're in the way, sir. So, I'm going to have to ask you to leave."

Lake carefully placed the weights on the deck and faced Michaelson. He knew the chief was full of it. Michaelson was just getting even for the whole Jepson incident.

"So this is how it's going to be, huh? Let me guess, the next time I try to work out down here, you're going to have to move weapons again."

Michaelson said nothing, brandishing a smug look.

"All right, damn you," Lake said, throwing his sweat towel over his shoulder and gathering his things. "You know, Chief, this doesn't bother me one damn bit. Once I get off this pig, I'm going to work out every day in a huge gym at whatever grad school I end up at. And there'll be hot bimbos with tight young bodies and skin-tight outfits bouncing all around me.

I'm going to have ass in my face every day, and you'll still be
here protecting your little space, and I really won't give a
shit."

"I know you won't, sir."

Lake's eyes met Michaelson's for a brief second. The big
chief's solid stare held nothing but contempt for him. Without
another word, Lake hefted the dumbbells and walked out of
the room through the aft door.

As Lake climbed the ladder to the second level, he inwardly cursed the ornery torpedo chief. He cursed himself
too, mainly because the chief's attitude had struck an unexpected nerve. He didn't know why, but it did. Later, as he fumbled with his clothing in the darkness of his stateroom, he
suddenly began to think about Reynoso and whether or not the
trusty radioman held the same contempt for him that Chief
Michaelson did. If Reynoso did, he would never know it. The
radioman had a naturally cheery demeanor and carried his
emotions much further beneath the surface. Strangely, the
thought disturbed him. After showering, as he climbed into his
rack, the thought was still heavy on his mind. It wasn't until
several hours later, hours spent staring at the rack's low ceiling, that Lake finally fell asleep.

"ATTENTION in the control room, the captain has the conn,
Lieutenant Commander Fremont retains the deck," Edwards
announced as he took the periscope from the thin, sandy-
haired navigation officer, Ian Fremont.

The requisite acknowledgments came from the helmsman,
the diving officer of the watch, and the quartermaster of the
watch, then all went about their business.

"Thank you, Captain," Fremont uttered before moving aft
to stand between the two chart tables. The quartermaster of
the watch hovered over the portside table, gingerly plotting
the latest GPS fix.

Edwards seldom took the conn but was always happy to
whenever one of his watch officers needed to attend to one of
his critical collateral duties. As *Providence*'s navigator, it was

Fremont's responsibility to supervise and verify the latest fix from the Global Positioning System and then approve its entry into the ship's inertial navigation system, a hardened computer that calculated the ship's position based on every minute acceleration experienced by the ship. Entering a bad fix into the navigation computer could have catastrophic results for the ship. Even a position error of a few dozen yards could transform into several miles of error over the course of a high-speed cross-ocean voyage.

"Looks like a good fix, Captain," Fremont said, finally, as he peered over the chart, his head inches away from the quartermaster's. "We got four satellites that time, much better than last night's fix. We're making good time with a twenty-two knot average speed of advance. I hold us just shy of ten degrees and fifty-five North, one hundred forty-nine degrees and twenty-eight East. About four hundred nautical miles southeast of good ol' Guam, Captain. It's a shame *they* didn't have a boat that could do this errand, instead of sending us."

"Yes, a shame," Edwards said, adjusting the magnification knob on the scope. Fremont was right. Guam was much closer and home to a full squadron of submarines, but they were all off on other missions. Deployed to the "usual hotspots," as the admiral had said.

Edwards looked at the world above through the eyepiece. It looked empty and barren. The mild sea stretched out far in all directions with nothing to obstruct his view except the wide trunk of the starboard communications mast, as if *Providence* was the last ship on Earth filled with the last of the human race. A misty cumulus, hit from above with the sun's rays, turned the sky white, forcing Edwards to squint.

"Captain, sir," the chief of the watch called from the ballast control panel in the forward port corner of the control room, a phone hung loosely from his hand. "The galley requests permission to eject trash and the engineering officer of the watch requests permission to blow down both steam generators."

"Very well. Conduct trash disposal and blow down the steam generators." Edwards half hesitated to give the orders, even though both evolutions were previously arranged. They

were extremely noisy procedures, which made any submariner cringe. But it was better to do them now, here in the
open ocean where they didn't need to be quiet.

"Bring me up a few feet, diving officer," Edwards said.
"Make your depth fifty-five feet."

"Fifty-five feet, aye, sir," the diving officer responded, then
whispered a few commands to the two planesmen sitting in
front of him.

As the periscope lens moved a few feet higher in the water,
Edwards strained his eyes for any undetected ships present,
but he saw none. A small flock of sea birds circled a patch of
water far off to the north. Dashes of mist appeared on the surface in various spots as the fowls descended on their swimming prey. A small ecosystem existing out here beyond the
reach or care of man. It was an otherwise empty piece of
ocean.

He felt a small vibration in the deck as the first weighted
can of compacted trash was launched overboard from the galley below. The muffled sound of rushing water followed immediately as a few thousand gallons of high-pressure seawater
flushed the two-foot-long by ten-inch-wide cylindrical can out
of *Providence*'s bottom-directed trash disposal tube, sending
it hurtling into the deep.

"Sonar won't hear the impact for a while, sir," said the
quartermaster, who had moved to the fathometer against the
port bulkhead. "We're sounding three thousand four hundred
and thirty fathoms here."

Edwards nodded, but didn't remove his face from the eyepiece. The quartermaster was right; it would take several minutes for the lonely metal can to make the long descent to the
ocean floor, four miles beneath *Providence*'s keel. He wondered what other relics of past maritime nations it would join
on the dark bottom. The can would perhaps drop next to a pile
of gold doubloons, the remains of some Spanish galleon that
met its fate centuries ago in this barren stretch of ocean.

Just then a dull roar came from back aft, in the engineering
compartment, and Edwards instinctively trained the scope toward the ship's port quarter. A bubbly agitation appeared on

the water's surface at the spot directly above the port side of the engineering compartment. The boiling seawater soon merged with the scope's wake, barely discernible at the mere five knots *Providence* was making.

On cue came the report from the chief of the watch, "The maneuvering room reports they have commenced a bottom blow-down of the port steam generator."

Edwards focused on the surface agitation created by the massive steam and water jet as the port steam generator emptied its contents over the side. How far they had come, he thought, from the days of Spanish galleons, when wooden ships plied on the surface trusting in acres of stretched canvas to get them to and fro. Now they rode in ships of steel, traveling the ocean depths, extracting the binding energy of the atom to get them where they needed to go. Sure, his father's beloved B-52s were impressive, so were the modern stealth bombers, but they weren't masters of their domain. With all of their extended range and capabilities they were still dependent on a land base or another aircraft to keep them fueled and in the air.

Providence, on the other hand, belonged to the sea. She was a self-sufficient life form that *lived* to be at sea, in symbiotic existence with the world around her. The binding energy of matter energized her heartbeat. Steam fed her spinning turbines and motors to propel her as fast as most sea creatures. Electricity was her blood, providing power to her auxiliary equipment, opening valves, running pumps, operating computers. She breathed seawater, using it to cool her systems, then exhaled it back into the sea. She scorned the frailties of her human crew who brought her back to port more for their own needs than for hers. She needed no other ship, no seaport, no place to rest, only an open ocean and a mission.

Like him in so many ways, happy to be at sea away from those who would hold him back, and away from those he loved. Or rather, the one person he loved. The little girl with his chin and his dimples, and her granddad's eyes. He had long since lost touch with his own father. Their relationship amounted to a short phone conversation at Christmas, and then only if he happened to be in port. Now, time would fog over his image in his own daughter's memory. He knew how it would make her feel, how it made him feel when he was a boy. Her playmates' parents would talk in whispers about the poor girl whose father had left her. The father who had never really grown up, off pursuing adventure and promotion.

Of course, that wasn't the real story. Her mother was the real problem, he kept telling himself.

"The maneuvering room reports both steam generator blow-downs are complete, Captain," the chief of the watch said, as he operated a few switches on his panel, pumping water from one tank to another to compensate for the water used in the steam generator blow-downs. "The galley also reports all trash has been ejected. All compartments report ready to go deep, sir."

"I've got the fix entered, Captain," Fremont added. "We're ready to go deep."

"Very well, Nav. Chief of the Watch, lower all mast and antennas."

The hydraulic systems whined as both the communications mast and the periscope descended into the sail. The sound sent a surge of adrenaline through Edwards' body. He ached to get deep again. It seemed that the closer *Providence* was to the surface, the more his thoughts carried him to another place where shame and guilt lurked. When the ship was deep, it was all business, and he could let the duties of a captain fill his mind once again.

"All masts and antennas lowered, Captain," the chief of the watch reported.

"Very well. Dive, make your depth six hundred feet. Helm, all ahead standard."

The orders were acknowledged and *Providence* angled down a few degrees, quickly picking up speed, sinking away from the warm light and into the cold dark depths. The bold red light emitting from the digital depth gauge counted off each foot as *Providence* descended to her cruising depth. Here and there a popping noise was heard as the outside sea pressure rapidly increased against her black steel skin, pressing in on every frame and deck beam along her length. As she passed five hundred feet, the diving officer whispered something to the planesmen and both men pulled back on their control yokes, leveling her off nicely at exactly six hundred feet and not one foot below.

Edwards smiled. They may be homesick, but they were still damn good submariners. After six months at sea, the ship's control parties were all like finely tuned instruments. They could maintain depth within a foot during a hurricane.

"Course two two eight is a good course, Captain," Fremont said from the chart table.

"Very well, Nav. Helm, right five degrees rudder. Steady on course two two eight. All ahead full."

Providence heeled over to starboard ever so slightly as the small rudder angle placed her on the ordered southwesterly course. She then picked up speed. Her algae-ridden hull shook a little as she passed on through twenty-four knots, and then settled down like a wild beast hitting its stride as she steadied at a strong twenty-six knots.

Edwards glanced at the periscope platform's sonar screen, mounted just over his head. The ship's high speed was turning the waterfall display into a solid wash of green lines all around the azimuth. Each line represented *Providence*'s own flow noise. Edwards remembered how much it had bothered him when he was a young, green ensign. A submarine took a certain risk traveling at high speeds. Her own noise limited the sonar's detection capability. Sure, the noise from another ship would show up as a line on the display, but it would be mixed in with hundreds of other sound lines coming from *Providence*'s own hull. It took a keen sonarman to see and hear the difference between the two.

"Conn, Sonar," a voice said over the speaker in the overhead.

"Go ahead, Sonar."

"Sir, could you come into the sonar room please?"

Edwards exchanged glances with Fremont. It was an odd request not normally made by the sonar supervisor, who usually guarded his space like an eagle protecting her nest. They both made their way to the forward starboard side of the control room and opened the sliding door leading into the darkened sonar room.

They were met at the door by the gaunt face of the sonar chief, Chief Ramirez. A headset hung loosely around his neck, its plug dangling free at the end of the spiral-wound cord.

"Captain, Nav, sirs. I think you should see this."

They entered the cramped darkened space lit only by the green and blue displays of the four sonar consoles along the starboard side. It took a few seconds for Edwards' eyes to adjust, as he and Fremont were ushered to stand behind the sonar operator sitting at the forward-most console. Edwards saw that the operator had the data from *Providence*'s hull array called up on his screen. The hull array was an arrangement of hydrophones strategically placed along the ship's length, vastly inferior to *Providence*'s powerful spherical array in the nose, but useful for determining the location and frequency of noise emitted by the ship itself.

"Zoom in on the last five minutes, Jackson." Ramirez directed the operator, wedging himself in beside Jackson to point to something on the screen.

"We've been getting some strange tonals showing up whenever we've been at periscope depth the last couple days, Captain. At first we wrote it off as flow noise, but it's happened the same way three times now, sir, and we think it's something coming from our own ship."

Ramirez pointed to a thin green line appearing on the display.

"You can see here the time history, sir. We detected it for about thirty seconds right as we went deep, then when we got above fifteen knots our own flow noise drowned it out and we lost it. It's my guess, Captain, that whatever it is, it starts somewhere between five and fifteen knots."

"It's speed-related then?" Edwards asked.

"I'd say so, sir. It happens every time we speed up, then we lose it. Hell, it's probably still there, but at this speed we can't hear it."

"Did you get a chance to listen to it?"

"Jackson got it, Captain," Ramirez said, nodding and, at the same time, nudging Jackson. "We were waiting for it this time so we got a recording. Play that back on the speaker for the captain to hear, Jackson."

Jackson moved his cursor around and pressed a few buttons. The speaker above his panel crackled to life with a long, whiny, spine-tingling noise like that of fingernails on a chalkboard.

"That's the masts coming down, sir, right before we went deep."

Edwards knew that, but said nothing. He had heard mast noise thousands of times in his career.

The noise then stopped and was replaced by mostly silence except for a few whooshing sounds that represented *Providence* starting her rapid descent. The silence lasted for minutes, it seemed. Edwards noticed Fremont edging closer to the speaker as if it would help him to hear the noise in question. Then Jackson, who was monitoring the playback, held up one finger, signaling them to listen closely.

Edwards heard nothing at first. But as *Providence*'s static-like flow noise grew louder, a small sound stood out from the rest. It was faint, barely audible, but it was there, nonetheless. A sound much like a distant violin playing accelerando.

"Well, it's definitely not flow noise," Fremont commented.

Edwards nodded. "I agree, Nav. It's a pump or something. Something that's spinning, in any case."

"It's showing up strongest on hydrophones five and seven, sir," Jackson added, pointing to his screen. "That places it somewhere between frames thirty-six and forty-nine. Somewhere in the engine room, Captain."

"I wish I could tell you what it was, Captain," Ramirez said, scratching his head. "But I've never heard a noise quite like that one before."

Edwards hadn't either. As he stared at the small green line he silently wondered if it really mattered how silent *Providence* was. A humanitarian rescue didn't require stealth. Especially when the plan was to pick up the evacuee in a seaport in broad daylight. Still, the green line disturbed the submariner in him.

His ship needed to be ready to fight at all times, ready to carry out any mission. Suddenly, he wondered if *Providence* had been pushed too far this time. He wondered if she had gone too long since her last refit. Through the Persian Gulf, the Red Sea, the Indian Ocean, she had been faithful as a mustang. Was this high-speed run across the Pacific taking its toll on her at last?

"No worries, Chief," Edwards said, smiling and patting Ramirez on the shoulder. "Good job finding this. You too, Jackson. Let's let the engineering folks figure this one out. Nav, pass the word to the engineer to look for this sound short. I want to know what's causing it."

"NO, Van Peenan, no! For the last time, I won't get involved!"

Bloomfield's bulk appeared uncomfortable in his rack as he replaced the bookmark in the novel he was reading and reached over to set it on his stateroom's small fold-down desk. He fixed the olive drab blanket across his body, momentarily revealing the flabby roll of fat around his waistline which was stretching the fibers in his worn white t-shirt to the limit. As was his manner, he shifted his eyes from one bulkhead to the next, avoiding looking directly at Van Peenan who was standing just inside the closed doorway.

"I'm losing control of my department and it's all *his* fault," Van Peenan said, clenching his fists. "*You've* got to do something about it."

"Oh, why?" Bloomfield said as he got settled, then pointed to the locker above his head. "Could you get me those chocolate almonds up there, Van Peenan?"

Van Peenan fought to maintain his composure as he reached into the locker and handed the can of almonds to Bloomfield's thick, reaching fingers. Bloomfield was a pathetic excuse for an officer, in his opinion, a shamelessly slothful oaf, an ass without a shred of ambition or drive. Van Peenan hated him, had always hated him. How he ever made it to XO was beyond him. He must have given the right guy a blowjob back at SubPac, he thought, or maybe his family had political connections. Either way, Bloomfield was a careless shirker who didn't deserve to be above him. He wanted to plant his fist in the bastard's fat gut and kick his ass out of the rack, but he forced himself to stand at attention. It was the only way he could be in the same room with him.

"Captain Christopher never would've undercut the judgment of one of his department heads like this captain does, XO, especially in matters of discipline. Captain Christopher never once reduced one of my recommendations for punishment. He understood that a captain has to back up his officers. He respected his department heads' judgment."

"I suspect his failure to reduce any of your recommendations had more to do with his agreeing to the severity than any special consideration of your opinion, Van Peenan. As you will recall, he often added extra harshness to any of the sentencing recommendations made by the old Nav and the old Weps, much to their dismay I might add."

"He knew how to run a tight ship. Discipline breeds discipline. Captain Christopher understood that."

Bloomfield listlessly popped a few chocolate-covered almonds into his mouth.

"My whole department is laughing at me behind my back!" Van Peenan added.

"Who's laughing?"

"All of them." Van Peenan licked his lips as he spoke. They were insanely dry and he could see he was making no headway with the XO. "Ever since the fucking mast, they think I'm a fucking fool. How am I supposed to run a fucking department when they're fucking laughing at me? We're going to fail our next fucking ORSE, I can feel it. They think I'm soft and it's all Edwards' fault. They think he'll protect them now. Especially that asshole Dean. He's the fucking ringleader. That asshole thinks he can do whatever he wants now, and get away with it."

"Oh, I find that hard to believe," Bloomfield said halfheartedly as he curiously studied a misshapen almond. "What has he done recently, for example?"

Van Peenan looked at Bloomfield scornfully. "I thought that at least *you* would understand, XO, since you've been around long enough to remember when things ran smoothly on this ship! But of course that wasn't any of your doing, was it. It was all Captain Christopher's. I don't know why he ever put up with you, why he never canned your ass. You're about as worthless an XO as you are a fucking fat pig!"

Bloomfield scampered out of his rack and came face-to-face with Van Peenan, his sweat stained T-shirt brushing up against Van Peenan's immaculate blue coverall.

"Who the hell do you think you are, *Engineer*?" Bloomfield spat out the words, finally meeting the other man's eyes, his putrid breath making Van Peenan flinch. "You don't fucking talk to me like that! I'll take this straight to the captain. Don't think that I won't!"

Van Peenan smirked as he looked down his nose at Bloomfield's pudgy red face. He knew Bloomfield would never say a word to the captain. The spineless fool couldn't carry out a threat if he tried. He fought back the urge to slap him across the face. This certainly wasn't the first time he had pushed the boundaries of Bloomfield's impotence. It had happened often under Captain Christopher. Christopher had favored him over the bumbling Bloomfield, and Van Peenan had exploited that preference whenever it served his interest.

The past seemed to register in Bloomfield's memory too, as the venom left his eyes and he plopped down on the chair.

"You want to know why he never got rid of me, Van Peenan?" he said soberly, staring at the bulkhead. "Because I never rocked the boat, I was never a threat to him. You think you're so smart, do you? Well, if you want to make it through your naval career, you'll learn to do what I've done all these years. Remain anonymous."

"That might suit someone like you, XO, a wash-up who can't leave the confines of his stateroom, but not me. I don't want just a career. I want command. I want it, and I'll have it, one way or another. If my department fails the next ORSE I'll be blackballed, and I'm not going to let that fucking happen! Captain Christopher always said I was destined for great things, and I won't have some damned blueshirt named Dean fucking things up for me!"

"I find that attitude surprising, since you yourself were once a 'blueshirt.'"

"I've crawled my way up through the ranks the hard way. Unlike some," Van Peenan drove the point home. "When I was a nineteen-year-old electrician's mate, I did what my engineer told me to do. I showed him the respect he was due, and I expect the same from my own men. You *have* to talk to the captain about removing Dean from the engineering department. As long as he's there, my authority won't be shit."

Bloomfield shook his head and sighed as he crawled back into his rack. "Talk to him yourself, Van Peenan. Hit the light on your way out."

If he hadn't been on a submarine Van Peenan would have slammed the door as he left Bloomfield's stateroom. He stood outside the door a few minutes collecting his thoughts. He could hear the low murmur of conversation coming from the control room at the other end of the long passage. It was night, so the curtains to the control room were drawn, blocking his view, but he could make out Edwards' voice among the others.

Van Peenan knew Edwards would never reconsider his decision to suspend the mast sentence, nor would he consider removing Dean from his department. He was no Christopher. Hell, Edwards had never even been an engineer before. Van Peenan had heard that Edwards spent his department head tour as a navigator. What the hell did a damn navigator know about running an engine room? But still, the fate of his career rested in the ex-navigator's hands.

He had come too far to be denied command someday, Van Peenan thought. The years as an electrician on the Sturgeon Class boats, his selection for the enlisted commissioning program, his stellar grades at the University of South Carolina, his struggle to make rank ahead of his silver-spooned academy and ROTC peers who were all years younger than him. Everything pointed him toward his destiny to command a ship someday. Captain Christopher had further confirmed that destiny by taking him under his wing. Christopher had opened a new world for him, showing him the secrets to success in a sea

command. He showed him how to make it in the dog-eat-dog
world of the submarine officer both professionally and politically, and Van Peenan had been his willing and eager apprentice. Having an ally like Christopher was crucial for any
aspiring officer whose name was in submission to the command board. Christopher could see it done, no problem. He'd
call in a few favors here, promise a few there, then presto, Van
Peenan would get selected for command.

Unfortunately, Van Peenan thought, no flag officer sitting
on the command board could overlook two ORSE failures, no
matter how many favors he owed Christopher.

The ORSE failure was Dean's fault, and he was certain
Dean was presently seeding insubordination within the department. He had heard the snickers, had felt their eyes on his
back as he walked the engine room. Dean was tearing his department apart under his very nose, he was sure of it. And neither Edwards nor Bloomfield would do anything about it, let
alone acknowledge it. The young third-class petty officer was
craftier than they knew.

Something had to be done. Dean had cost him one ORSE.
He would not cost him another.

Chapter 6

ENSIGN Philip Yi stepped into the tunnel leading to the engineering compartment and closed the three-inch-thick steel door behind him, spinning the handle to dog it shut. With only a few hours of sleep in the last few days, Yi struggled to keep his eyes open. He now stood facing aft at the forward end of the "tunnel." The "tunnel" was aptly named since that's exactly what it was, a fifty-foot-long shielded passageway running through the uninhabitable, radiation-filled reactor compartment. It connected the operations compartment with the engineering compartment, allowing passage back and forth between the two. It also marked the beginning of the engineer's domain on the *Providence*. Everything from this point aft belonged to him. As if to emphasize the point, a blast of cold engine room air wafted up the tunnel and chilled Yi's body to the bone. Yi instantly felt apprehensive as if the sadistic engineer might jump out at any moment to accuse him of some blunder.

From his first day on board the *Providence,* Yi was scared to death of Lieutenant Commander Aubrey Van Peenan. But what could he do? Van Peenan was one of the ship's senior officers, the ship's engineer, his department head, and therefore the master of his life.

Van Peenan hated him, and Yi knew it. Yi had backed down to his upbraiding leadership style, if it could be called that, time and again. He'd seen the brutal engineer unjustly treat the men in his division while he stood by and did nothing— just as he did nothing during Dean's mast hearing. His fear of Van Peenan brought out the coward in him, and the thought was almost too much to bear.

As the son of Chinese expatriates, Philip Yi descended

from a line of bravery. His parents were heroes in his mind, heroes who had stood up against their native land's communist oppressors, writing political pamphlets and brochures until the government finally came after them. They narrowly escaped China with their lives, finding the courage to come to America and make a better life for him and his brother. As the first in their family to speak English better than Chinese, Philip had been the object of high expectations from his parents. They had made a sacrifice, and they expected him not to squander it. And Philip did not squander it. He made his parents proud the day he graduated from M.I.T., having funded his entire schooling with scholarships. He became a star in the poor New York slum of his childhood, and at the dry cleaning shop where he'd made money for the family by pressing nearly a million garments before his sixteenth birthday.

Fortune 100 technology companies came looking for him, and made offers anyone would find hard to refuse, but something was missing in young Philip's life, something essential to inner tranquility. Perhaps he had been cursed from birth by the gallantry of his parents. Their heroic struggles in the fatherland had earned them the lifelong respect of the Chinese community in New York. They were valiant crusaders for egalitarianism, and young Philip found himself driven to confirm that he was made of the same mettle. Of all the offers on the table, only one stood out as a means to strike his own blow for liberty's cause. The Department of the Navy needed engineering graduates to serve as officers on their submarines, and they'd sent him a letter asking him to apply.

Through Officers Candidate School, Nuclear Power School, and Submarine Officers School, Yi had no trouble. Navy training was easy and his technical mind earned him straight As in every class. It wasn't until he arrived at his first ship that he came to learn being a good leader meant a great deal more than scoring high on exams. Understanding the word "leadership" became more of a challenge to him than solving third-order differential equations.

He only wanted to do his part, to fit in like the others, to be a good officer for both his superiors and his subordinates—

and his parents. But instead Yi was discovering things about himself, things he tried hard not to think about. How would his parents feel if they saw him spinelessly standing by while Van Peenan shamefully terrorized an innocent sailor under his command? *They* had stood up to armed communist soldiers, but he couldn't even stand up to his own department head.

Now Yi was resolved to set things right.

A sign on the tunnel's bulkhead read "Radiation Area: Personal Dosimetry Required, No Loitering" and reminded Yi that he should not linger there. He instinctively fingered the small radiation dosimeter clipped to his belt and strode briskly toward the tunnel's aft opening. Though shielded, the tunnel still contained a higher than normal amount of radiation and was at this moment bombarding his body with a gamma ray flux.

Yi reached the end of the long tunnel and stepped into the safety of the engine room's middle level, which stretched the width of the hull, filled with a virtual maze of eight-foot-high electrical panels. Yi took one of the many outboard ladders down to the lower level of the engine room, the spaces owned by his own division. He felt his skin exfoliate as he descended. The lower level was always dank and humid from the various cooling systems exchanging heat with the ocean. These were the literal bowels of the ship and contained a crisscrossing jumble of piping, pumps, valves, and tanks. Yi always found it unsettling to see the curvature of the hull at the bottom of the ship and to see the several inches of water pooling in the bilge from various seal leaks throughout the engine room. He still hadn't gotten use to the idea that the crushing ocean was just on the other side of that steel skin.

Walking aft on a catwalk suspended a few feet above the bilge, he passed from one bay to the next. Turbine generator lube-oil bay, where seawater pipes cooled the lubricating oil for the huge turbine generators. Condensate bay, where the steam condensed into water so it could be sent back to the steam generators and turned into steam once again. Propulsion lube oil bay, where more seawater piping cooled the lubricating oil for *Providence*'s massive shaft and gear train.

Main seawater bay, containing the hefty seawater pumps fixed firmly upon their vertical mounts. And finally, auxiliary seawater bay, the lowest habitable point on the ship, where the auxiliary seawater pumps resided.

Yi found Dean standing watch in the auxiliary seawater bay, holding an oversized clipboard while he took log readings on the number one pump. Dean obviously noticed him, but continued what he was doing as if Yi was not there.

"Petty Officer Dean, do you have a minute?" Yi said airily.

Dean nodded, still scribbling in his log sheets.

"I was wondering if we could talk." Yi stumbled over the words. "You see, I know I've wronged you and I wanted to set things straight."

"There's nothing that needs to be said, sir." Dean shrugged. "You did what you had to do. The captain came through for me. That's all there is to it."

"You're a good man, Dean."

"Thanks, sir," Dean said irritably. "I try."

Dean's sarcastic manner hurt deeply. Yi felt like a complete failure, like he was less than a man, pitifully endeavoring to lead a real man.

The uneasy silence remained between them for minutes, accentuated by a sudden down-shift in *Providence*'s speed. The throttleman was closing down on the throttles up in the maneuvering room two decks above, and the reduction in steam flow significantly reduced the ambient noise level in the engine room. Shortly thereafter, the deck angled upward. *Providence* was coming shallow for some reason.

Yi thought it odd since the ship had just been at periscope depth only a few hours before. The next comms interval wasn't for several more hours. With Bunda still thirty-six hours away, the captain's night orders called for high-speed steaming all night. But with all that was on his mind, and Dean staring back at him, he could not afford to give this distraction more than a passing thought.

Finally deciding it was best to leave Dean alone, Yi turned to leave the bay, but a wave of the sailor's hand stopped him.

"Don't worry about it, Mr. Yi," Dean added sympathetically. "The engineer's got it in for me. You might as well steer clear of me."

"It's wrong that he has it in for you," Yi said. "It's very wrong. You're a good sailor. He's never even given you a chance. He's never given *me* a chance, either. We're both new and we both make mistakes like anyone else but he takes *our* mistakes personally, as if we're deliberately trying to screw up. It's almost like he's paranoid."

Dean suddenly looked uneasy and Yi could kick himself for venting his personal problems to a junior enlisted man. The inter-relationships between officers and all the inner turmoil that went with them were supposed to remain just that, *between* officers. They were not to be shared with members of the crew. He didn't know what made him do it. Perhaps he was trying to relate to Dean on some common level. Perhaps it was an attempt to reach out in some way to this sailor he had let down in so many ways.

"Well, anyway," Yi said, awkwardly professional again, "keep up the good work and I'm sure there won't be any more problems."

Dean gave a perplexed nod, then moved toward the number two pump to continue with his logs.

Yi was about to make another gesture at small talk when a high-pitched voice resounded from above. The voice chilled Yi to the marrow.

"What an interesting pairing this is! Ensign Schmuckatelli and Petty Officer Gronk, alone at last, eh?"

Yi turned to see Van Peenan climbing down one of the nearby ladders from the engine room's middle level.

"Good evening, sir," Yi and Dean said almost in unison.

Van Peenan reached the bottom of the ladder and plopped onto the deck, his face twisted into a wicked grin as he regarded them both.

"What the hell is this, a fucking conspiracy? You trying to corrupt Ensign Yi now, Dean?"

"No, sir."

"No, sir . . ." Van Peenan repeated strangely. Then he shot a glare at Yi. "Dean's in enough trouble without your help, Yi, so I suggest you leave him the fuck alone." Then Van Peenan moved quickly to the nearest auxiliary seawater pump and pointed his long finger at its base. "What the hell's all that oil doing there, Dean? Don't you know how to use a fucking Kimwipe?"

"Number three always leaks a little, sir," Dean said, meekly. "I was going to get it cleaned up after I finished taking my logs."

"Tough shit!" Van Peenan thrust out a wrist brandishing his dull diving watch, the sudden movement causing both Yi and Dean to flinch. The black band and face piece stood out on the surly engineer's pale skin. "It's ten minutes after the hour and you haven't finished your fucking logs yet? What the hell are you doing down here, beating off?"

It was Yi's fault, of course. His meager attempt at interaction had prevented Dean from finishing his logs on time. The accused sailor now shot a beseeching glance at Yi, fully expecting him to speak up on his behalf. But Yi was silently retreating into a corner. Dean's eyes searched for help, but as much as he wanted to, Yi did not have the ability to step in. Van Peenan's presence had a numbing effect on him. The hateful engineer's aura squelched any semblance of nerve he could summon. Yi suddenly wished his quivering form could somehow melt into the bulkhead and migrate hundreds of feet through the ship's cold steel all the way back to his stateroom, where his body would reform as a sniveling mess.

A weary smile appeared on Dean's face as he realized he was once again on his own.

"I'm sorry, sir," Dean finally said to Van Peenan. "I'll go faster next time."

"There won't be a next time, Dean," Van Peenan said between gritted teeth. "You have my word on that."

Dean nodded amiably then ducked quickly into the next bay to finish the rest of his logs.

Yi watched him go, feeling guilty but yet relieved to be free of Dean's condemning eyes. Then he realized that he was all alone in the bay with Van Peenan. Expecting the engineer to turn his venom in his direction at any moment, Yi was surprised when Van Peenan stared for what seemed minutes at the flood door through which Dean had exited. The transfixed gaze made Yi uneasy, and even more disturbing was Van Peenan's mouth muttering something inaudible as if he were talking to himself.

The deck leveled off and shook slightly as *Providence*'s hull absorbed a small swell, forcing both officers to grab a nearby stanchion to stay on balance. From the pressure gauge on the nearby panel Yi could see that the ship was now at periscope depth. The swell seemed to snap Van Peenan out of his trance, and he appeared visibly startled to discover Yi holding the stanchion next to him. Almost as if they hadn't seen each other for days.

"What the hell are you doing standing around here?" Van Peenan scowled.

Yi made to speak but stopped when Van Peenan placed one arm around his shoulder.

"Stay away from that asshole Dean, Yi," the engineer said in a bizarrely warm, almost fatherly voice. "He's trouble. Not good for your career. We don't want his kind in our department. Always remember, my boy, the blueshirts will fuck you."

Not knowing how to react, Yi simply nodded and uttered something akin to a concurrence. Van Peenan had always been quite odd, but Yi had never seen him this way before. It made Yi uncomfortable, and he much preferred to receive one of the engineer's verbal lashings.

Just as Yi started thinking of ways to excuse himself, the 1MC speaker on the bulkhead intoned, "All department heads report to the control room!"

Van Peenan held Yi in his gaze for a few seconds longer before his eyes reverted to their former fierceness.

"I'm going to Control to see what the hell they want," Van Peenan said tersely, suddenly his old self again.

Van Peenan headed for the ladder and Yi breathed a sigh of relief. But before the engineer could begin to climb, he turned around and shot a fierce glance at Yi. "By the way, *Mister* Yi, have you found that sound short back here yet? I'll be damned if the captain's going to ask me about it!"

"Uh, no, sir. Not yet."

"Did you check the equipment data logs, like I told you to, shithead? And you better the fuck say you did!"

"Yes, Eng," Yi lied, unable to muster the courage to tell the truth. The truth was he hadn't had time to look through the logs. He'd been busy with maintenance schedules, training plans, qualifications, standing watches, and a dozen other things Van Peenan had tasked him to do.

"Well? Were there any discrepancies? Anything unusual? Anything that might point to what the hell this noise is they keep hearing up there in Sonar? Holy shit, Yi, taking a report from you is like pulling fucking teeth!"

"No, Eng, nothing out of the ordinary."

"There better not be!" Van Peenan eyed him suspiciously. "If I find one fucking gauge reading out of spec during my monthly review, you'll wish you were never born, asshole."

Standing alone next to the big pumps spinning incessantly on their proud mounts, Yi felt a cold comprehension come over him. What if the logs *did* show something was wrong? Van Peenan would almost certainly find it, sooner or later.

Yi had a dozen important things to get done before he could catch a few hours' sleep, but now they all seemed trivial. *He had to check those logs!* The impending doom would hang over his head until he knew for certain they were all in spec.

Chief Hans would have them now. Most likely, the chief had already bound the log bundle in preparation for filing them in the engineer's monthly review file.

Yi reached for the phone near the pump control panel.

"Maneuvering, Auxiliary Seawater Bay," he said evenly. "This is Ensign Yi. Is Chief Hans in the engine room?"

A few moments later a voice came back, "Auxiliary Seawater Bay, Maneuvering. Yes, Chief Hans is in Maneuvering. Do you want to speak to him?"

"*No*—tell him to wait! I'll be right there!"

With a fervent determination, Yi clambered up the ladder to the middle level, past the refrigeration plant, past the massive horizontal cylindrical tube that held *Providence*'s giant spinning shaft, and on upward to the upper level of the engine room. He groped his way forward, past the distilling plant, past the colossal reduction gear, past the domineering main engines, past the school-bus-sized turbine generators, past the sailors on watch whose greetings he obliviously ignored, the whole time bewildered and dazed, focusing only on the worst possible outcome. Somehow it became more and more a certainty in his mind the closer he got to the maneuvering room.

He made his way to the starboard side of the insulated box-like engineering control room and reached the heavy, sliding, metal door. The whiny noise of high-velocity steam pervaded the air in this part of the engine room. Yi did not need to look up to be reminded of the robustly lagged piping that ran through the overhead. The main steam header. The whole reason for this huge metal door and the sealed insulation around the maneuvering room. In the event of a steam line rupture, everyone in the engine room would be killed instantly. The whole compartment would fill with steam in less than a second. The insulation around the maneuvering room would protect the men inside long enough for them to shut down the reactor and remotely shut the main steam isolation valves. Then they would die too. The thought usually bothered Yi, but at this moment he didn't care. He could only think of his lie, and the possible consequences.

Unlatching and sliding open the door, he found the watchstanders inside going about their business. On the far side of the small room the throttleman stood in front of his wheel-like throttle control panel. Next to him, the reactor operator monitored his panel bristling with various displays of temperature and pressure within the reactor system. Closest to the door, the electrical operator yawned as he fiddled with a calculator, his panel displaying a graphical representation of *Providence*'s electrical distribution system. And behind these three sailors sitting at a raised desk, the engineering officer of the watch, Lieutenant (junior grade) Kemper, conversed with Chief Hans who had a thick manila pocket folder tucked under one arm.

"Request to enter Maneuvering?" Yi announced, slightly out of breath.

"Enter." Kemper gestured casually with a hand, then continued his conversation with Hans.

"You know why we're at periscope depth, Mr. Yi?" the sailor sitting at the electrical panel asked, as Yi filed in behind him.

Yi shook his head, only half hearing the question. He didn't care why they were at periscope depth. He was focused on only one purpose.

"Is that the log bundle, Chief?" Yi said, trying to sound casual. "I need to look at that."

Hans uninterestedly handed the log bundle over to Yi and kept talking to Lieutenant Kemper.

Forcing himself to maintain a calm outward appearance, Yi plopped the ream of logs onto the watch officer's desk. There were a lot of them. Every gauge and meter reading on every piece of equipment in the engine room for the past month was contained in these papers. Every temperature, every pressure, every voltage, current, and flowrate was tediously inscribed in the appropriate time-block. Thousands of data points, all marked by the human eye and recorded by the human hand.

Yi cursed this archaic way of maintaining historical data, a relic of the navy's infallible nuclear power program. If he had needed to find a piece of data on any of the equipment in the forward compartment he needed only to access the electronic files from the appropriate computer. The navy's nuclear power methodology, however, was completely different. When it came to nuclear power the navy's philosophy was to never rely on computers for anything, except in the case of certain reactor protection features which needed a computer's quick reaction time in order to save the core from a meltdown.

As Yi began examining the logs, the bored electrical operator attempted to strike up a conversation with anyone that would listen.

"Know what?" the electrical operator said to no one in particular. "I just called Williams up in the crew's mess. He said we're at periscope depth cause there's a boat up there that's in trouble."

Yi was oblivious to everything as he pored over the data,

flipping from one page to the next, searching for an alarm, a trend, anything that might be out of the ordinary. One page after another, Yi's eyes scanned as fast as they could and still maintain comprehension of what they were viewing. Nothing was jumping out at him. There were no alarms, which would have been indicated in red ink. Nothing unusual that he could see at a glance. He allowed himself to breathe a momentary sigh of relief, the thought entering his head that he would not have to answer for his lie after all.

"Williams told me that sonar guys heard gunfire up there," the electrical operator continued to the room in general, this time drawing the attention of the other two operators.

Yi tried to blank out the sailor's meaningless gossip. He didn't care about some mess cook's overly dramatized rumor. But the mention of sonar brought something to his mind that he needed to check. Van Peenan had told him the sonarmen isolated the sound to frames thirty-six through forty-nine. He knew all the equipment in that part of the engine room well enough; the lube oil purifiers, the freshwater pumps, and, of course, the main engines. Just to be certain, he decided to check the logs on that equipment one last time. If he found nothing, then he could walk away with the secure feeling that he was in the clear.

"Williams said there are actually two boats up there." The electrical operator spoke again, doling out each tidbit of information to his fellow watchstanders, each now curious and paying attention as if the operator was the all-powerful keeper of the knowledge.

Yi found the logs for the lube oil purifiers and scrutinized them. He checked every pressure and temperature, read every operator note and found nothing out of the ordinary.

Good, he thought.

He quickly flipped over to the freshwater pump logs and paid them the same amount of scrutiny until he was satisfied that they contained nothing that he had missed.

Good, he thought again.

Finally, he attacked the main engine logs, starting with the starboard main engine. He scanned down each bearing temperature, each stage pressure, each RPM. Everything looked normal. Then he switched over to the port main engine. Pressures were good, so were RPMs. But as he looked at the hundreds of numbers representing the temperature of the engine's forward bearing every hour for the past month, something wasn't right. He saw a slight trend that didn't jibe with the changes in pressure and RPM. The forward bearing temperature had been creeping up for the last month, not at a noticeable rate to the watchstander, who sees only six hours' worth of data at a time, but very identifiable when viewing the data for the whole month.

"Williams told me they think one of those boats up there is a pirate," the electrical operator said, then closed one eye mockingly. "D'ar, ye matey!"

"Let's give it a rest, Royce," said the watch officer, Kemper, who had obviously had enough of his electrical operator's speculation and rumor. "Quit your jawing and mind your panel."

"Aw, Mr. Kemper," Royce said, brandishing a smile. "You're no fun to stand watch with. I wish Mr. Yi was our watch officer tonight. He lets us do whatever we want. Isn't that right, Mr. Yi? . . . Mr. Yi?"

Yi didn't hear him. His face was as white as snow, his eyes glazed over as they stared fiercely and unbelievingly at the data before them. He had found the source of the noise.

And the noose around his neck.

THE starlight glittered on the dark sea, making it difficult for Edwards to distinguish the horizon. Every few minutes the periscope lens took a dousing from the two-foot seas, forcing him to find the horizon all over again.

"They should be visible now, Captain," Lake said from the starboard side of the blackened control room. "Bearing one six six."

Edwards withdrew his face from the eyepiece for a moment and centered the periscope on the bearing. He glanced in Lake's direction but could see little in the darkness, except for two shadowy figures hovering over the forward fire control consoles. Lake and the fire control technician of the watch were tweaking in the solution on the fishing boat *Providence* had been tracking for the last hour.

It had started off as a quiet evening. A normal watch routine of high-speed steaming with Bunda now less than two days away. Edwards had just settled down in his rack for a few hours' sleep when Lake sent the messenger to rouse him, requesting that he come to the conn.

Sonar was picking up gunfire to the south. Small arms fire.

Edwards had regained his senses as he forced himself down the passage to the control room. The gunfire could have meant anything. A bored fisherman taking pot shots at a trailing shark. An Indonesian naval vessel conducting training. Anything really. But the fact that it was midnight on a moonless night raised an instinctive red flag in his mind. The rule at sea was similar to that on land. Nothing good ever happened past midnight.

Providence had slowed to investigate, and it wasn't too long before sonar picked up two distinct contacts in the same direction of the gun noise. One was without a doubt a fishing boat, trolling along on her purring diesels. The other one was smaller and faster, a lighter craft with an outboard motor. Within minutes the two contacts converged, and soon thereafter the speedboat's engine shut down and the fisherman's diesel assumed an idling tone. The bearing held steady and didn't change for fifteen minutes, and Edwards and Lake agreed that the fisherman had come to a stop.

With Lake at the conn, *Providence* had spent the better part of the last hour closing the range to the stopped fisherman. Edwards merely observed as Lake guided her in like the expert conning officer that he was. Despite the bitterness the short-timer lieutenant had exhibited over the past few days— who could blame him after getting extended on board for a few more weeks?—Lake appeared to have put his animosity aside, at least for the moment. He now seemed absorbed in the situation of the moment.

The desire to perform was definitely there, Edwards

thought, beneath the sour exterior. Lake just needed a good challenge. He would have made a fine submarine officer, if only he'd been properly tutored along the way. Such a shame that men like Carl Christopher often drove away some of the navy's best people.

"Our solution holds the fisherman three thousand yards off the port bow, sir," Lake announced.

"Very well." Edwards flipped the toggle switch above his head, activating the periscope's night vision circuit. Unlike an infrared detector that measured infrared radiation *emitted from* an object, the periscope's night vision device amplified starlight *reflecting off* an object. Any reflection appeared fluorescent green in the field of view, and that's exactly what Edwards saw as he leveled the lens on the horizon. A bright green line ran across his field of view, representing where the ocean met the sky. Above it, the stars beamed in the extreme amplification. Below it, the wavelets flickered wildly like a mass of fireflies as they reflected the starlight in all directions. Though he had seen it countless times before, Edwards still needed a moment to adjust to the night vision view, a monochrome world painted only in green hues.

At first, he saw nothing but the sea and the sky. But as he panned the periscope to the left he easily observed the fishing boat about a mile and a half off *Providence*'s port bow. In low-power magnification, it resembled nothing more than a small green dot resting on the ocean's surface. But as Edwards turned the magnification handle to the maximum setting, the shape transformed into the clear image of a coastal fishing boat presenting its starboard beam. He could see every line along her forty-foot hull, from the snub-nosed bow, to the high-profile pilothouse atop the single-level structure running along her length, to the low squatty stern with the towering fishing booms, all bathed in a brilliant emerald hue. She was dead in the water, and obviously did not plan to engage in any fishing activity anytime in the near future. Though she displayed no visible identification lights, her haphazardly stowed booms with their dangling cables swinging to and fro spoke volumes about her state of readiness.

"You were right about the trawler, Mr. Lake. There she is, sitting idle like an innocent child. Angle on the bow is right ninety degrees. Mark this bearing."

As Edwards pressed the red button on the periscope's right handle, the bearing was electronically transmitted to the fire control computer and appeared on Lake's console display.

"Bearing one six three," Lake called.

"Now let's see if we can find the other contact," Edwards said, straining his eyes as he examined the sea surrounding the lonely trawler.

It took several minutes, but he finally found it. As *Providence* passed across the trawler's bow from starboard to port, still a mile distant, a low shape emerged from the trawler's port side. It was a small speedboat, the kind one could ski behind, and Edwards could clearly see that it was moored to the trawler. The starlight reflected off the wet lines that held the two craft together. This image, coupled with the gunfire, could only mean one thing, and Edwards prayed that he was wrong.

As he watched through the periscope, a figure suddenly appeared on the trawler's deck, discernable enough that Edwards could make out a cigarette held in one hand and an automatic rifle casually clutched in the other. The figure watched something intently through a window in the trawler's low structure. Something was happening inside the trawler's living structure, and whatever it was it held this man's attention completely.

Within minutes he was joined on deck by another figure, also with a rifle, and then by another figure that seemed to have difficulty moving. It took Edwards a few seconds to realize that the third figure was bound, and Edwards' heart suddenly hit his throat.

"Mr. Lake," he tried to say calmly. "Start the camera. Make sure we get all of this!"

The image darkened slightly in Edwards' field of view, signifying that Lake had activated the periscope camera. The camera intercepted some of the light the periscope received from the image before it reached the eyepiece, thus reducing the brightness of the image in the periscope eyepiece, but Edwards could still see enough to tell what was going on.

The next events seemed to happen in mere seconds. The two figures with the guns dragged the apparently struggling bound figure to the edge of the trawler's port quarter. They forced the bound figure to stand upright facing out to sea. Then, in the blink of an eye, one raised his rifle to the back of the bound figure's neck, and suddenly the bound figure had less of a head. His body fell forward into the sea, the splash reflecting the starlight in all directions.

Edwards swallowed hard and heard several of the men in the control room murmuring among themselves. They obviously had seen the same thing he had. Anything filmed by the camera appeared on the video screen above Lake's console, clearly visible to anyone in the control room who felt like looking.

Just then the speaker near Edwards' head intoned, "Conn, Sonar. We just picked up gunfire and splash noises on the same bearing as the trawler."

Edwards hesitated a moment to collect his thoughts. Glancing at the sonar waterfall display above his head, he could see the bright green dots on the same bearing as the trawler scroll down the time history. They represented the end of a man's life.

"Sonar, Conn, aye," he said solemnly. "We saw it."

Chapter 7

PROVIDENCE'S darkened control room hid their faces in shadow, but Edwards did not need to see them to feel the skepticism exuding from his three department heads standing before him. Their questions about what he was planning had been pointed and appropriate, given the circumstances. Were he in their shoes, he would have asked the same things. Bloomfield, for his part, had already articulated his dissent and had relieved Lake at the periscope to get a better look at the beleaguered fishing boat.

A submarine was no democracy and Edwards was silently grateful for it, but even though he held absolute authority over the *Providence* and its crew, he felt it important to keep his senior officers in the loop as much as possible.

The control room personnel continued their periscope depth routines while Edwards allowed his three department leaders time to consider his decided plan of action. Miller, the weapons officer, rubbed his bald head. Fremont, the navigator, rubbed his chin. While Van Peenan, the engineer and least talkative of the three, stood uncharacteristically silent, hands behind his back. Edwards could feel his piercing eyes even in the low-level lighting, and thought he must be in another one of his moods.

"Oh," Bloomfield uttered from the periscope stand as he rotated the magnification handle. "What's this now?"

Edwards and the department heads and everyone else in Control glanced up at the video monitor to see what had caught Bloomfield's eye. The fluorescent green fishing boat sat idle as before—it now presented its port beam. Two figures with rifles and a bound figure had emerged once again from the living structure. But there was something different about this bound figure. This one was slightly built and much shorter than the first.

"A woman," Fremont said.

Everyone watched in stunned silence as the armed figures took the woman to the stern, where they had committed their previous murder. She appeared to receive several severe blows with rifle butts as the men made her get onto her knees and face the ocean. Once again, a rifle was raised to the back of the hostage's neck.

"Captain," Fremont said restlessly, "why don't we emergency surface? Maybe we'll scare them away. We've got to do *something*!"

"Easy, Nav." Edwards felt certain the fate of this woman was sealed, no matter what course of action they took. Admittedly, he had to fight back the urge to order an immediate emergency surfacing. Perhaps the sons of bitches would notice *Providence*'s black shape darting out of the sea in a frothy tumult only a mile off their beam and piss their pants. Maybe it would frighten them into inaction, or maybe even flight. But he didn't dare give the order.

Expecting the woman to die the same horrible but quick death as the previous victim, Edwards was surprised when several minutes elapsed and nothing happened. The gun was eventually removed from the woman's neck and the two figures with guns appeared to be arguing, their arms gesticulating wildly. A few minutes later the two dragged the still-alive woman back into the structure. Edwards could only guess what for.

"We can't just let this happen, Captain!" Fremont interjected.

"We don't know what we're facing here, Nav," Edwards said in a calming tone. "Pirates are unpredictable in these waters. They come in all shapes and sizes, some carrying big weapons, some carrying nothing more than knives. These particular pirates have automatic rifles. We can't be sure they're not packing more. We also don't know if there are more hostages. If we make these pirates too nervous, they might kill the whole lot."

"And these are definitely pirates, Captain?" Miller asked skeptically. "What if this is just a drug deal gone bad?"

"In any case, it's not our problem," Bloomfield said peremptorily from the periscope. "I see no reason to endanger our ship, Captain. Let's move on."

"It's our problem because the law of the sea says it's our problem!" Edwards snapped. "*And so do I!*"

His executive officer's apparent lack of feeling for those unfortunate people made him fume inside. Then, as if to perturb him even more, a flagrant sigh came from the direction of the periscope stand. Edwards knew that Bloomfield would never live up to any of his expectations. He'd never be the dependable right-hand man Edwards had once hoped for in an XO.

But he needed to put Bloomfield out of his mind for the moment.

"They're following the standard modus operandi, Weps." Edwards forced himself to keep his voice steady. "I spent some time in these waters when I was a junior officer. I've seen it before. A swift speedboat, unlit, filled with armed bandits, overtakes and boards an isolated and unsuspecting fisherman in the dead of night. They kill the crew, or kidnap them, and make off with whatever cargo their little boat will hold. I know it sounds like some Errol Flynn movie but it happens every day down here. Indonesian waters are notorious for piracy, more so than any other place in the world. Mostly because the geography caters to it. Thousands of uninhabited islands lying across long trade routes. Perfect conditions for the opportunistic pirate to speed out of his hiding place and overtake the victim of his choosing, then speed back to his hole before any authorities can respond.

"The pirate of the twenty-first century may not have a patch over one eye or fly the Jolly Roger, but rest assured he's ten times deadlier than any of his predecessors, and much more tenacious. You all, of course, remember our run-in with the pirate boat in the Straits of Malacca on our way to the Gulf some months back. He ran right up on us in the middle of the night."

"I remember it well, sir," Miller said. "A couple fellas in one of those junks with a long-tillered outboard. They came right up our wake, right out of nowhere. Must've seen our running lights and thought we were a small merchant or something. I would've given anything to see the looks on their faces when they realized they were running up on a surfaced L.A. Class sub."

"Yes, Weps. Lucky for us they weren't suicide bombers with a boatload of explosives."

"Right, sir, like the *Cole*," Miller added quickly. "But whoever they were, they learned better when Chief Michaelson's M-79 dropped a few grenades off their bow. Two or three close rounds and they turned tail and ran as fast as their little boat would carry 'em."

Miller said it with pride, obviously pleased with Chief Michaelson, his torpedo chief who also doubled as the security chief. But Edwards felt another motive in his crafty weapons officer's tone. Always the competitor, Miller never passed up on an opportunity to shine over the other department heads, or to remind Edwards of his past successes.

"So what do we do, sir?" asked Fremont eagerly, perhaps to divert the conversation away from Miller.

"We're finally up on the command link with CinCPac, Captain," Lake interrupted from the back of the room. Hovering over the starboard chart table, his face glowed in the bluish light as he pointed to something displayed on the chart table's tactical screen. "The nearest allied ship's an Aussie destroyer, HMAS *Stuart*, cruising near Timor. She's at least two days away. I've got no information here on her status, sir, but even if her air wing's aboard, her helos couldn't make it this far."

"That's no good," Fremont commented.

"It looks like it's up to us, gentlemen," Edwards said earnestly, intent on gaining their confidence. "We could, of course, contact the Indonesian Navy but I doubt they'd respond in time, if at all. These things happen every day and the Indonesian government scarcely has the resources to deal with each act of piracy. As you can see, gentlemen, we're the only ones who can save those people."

Another sigh came from the periscope stand. Edwards ignored it.

"These crooks obviously think they're all alone out here," Edwards continued. "Otherwise they'd have made off with the cargo by now. We can use that to our advantage. Dealing with an American submarine is probably the last thing on their minds right about now. That being said, I'm ruling out bringing the *Providence* close aboard. Getting close enough to send a boarding party across would be tricky at best. If we overshot them our stern planes would likely punch right through the fisherman's hull and she'd go straight to the bottom. And they've got automatic weapons, then hell, they could have R.P.G.'s too for all we know. Any brash approach is likely to make them panic and start shooting, and the last thing I want is casualties on our side. The hostages stand the best chance if we can sneak aboard and confront the pirates up close. We'll use the dinghy, just like we did during blockade duty in the Gulf."

In the low light, Edwards saw Fremont and Miller exchange uncertain glances, while Van Peenan stood emotionless as before.

"We'll take up position a mile off the fisherman's starboard beam and surface quietly to let off the boarding party. I want two officers and two men, armed heavily. Weps, have Chief Michaelson select two of his best security petty officers, preferably trained in close-quarters combat. Be quick about it. There's no time to lose."

"Aye aye, Captain," Miller said, smiling. "I'll have Chief Michaelson get them up right away. As for the officers, sir, I'd like to volunteer to lead."

Before Edwards could respond, Bloomfield's grumbling came once again from the periscope stand.

"At a minimum, Captain," Bloomfield said snootily, "we should at least seek guidance from SubPac before proceeding any furth—" Bloomfield stopped abruptly. He had been looking through the periscope as he spoke, but now his mouth hung open. An audible gasp escaped his mouth before it uttered, "My God!"

Edwards and everyone in the room gaped at the monitor to see what had so disturbed the XO. The fisherman lay hove to as before, but now another figure had been brought on deck by one of the armed men. Very slim, very small, bound like the others—however, this figure appeared to be nude. The light reflected off the bound figure's bare skin and shone brighter than the others. The small figure was forcibly dragged to the fishing boat's gunwale, where it appeared to vomit over the side into the ocean.

For a moment the retching figure's head moved back in a jerky motion, and then Edwards saw the long, glimmering, wavy hair. His mouth went dry when the realization suddenly hit him.

It was a young girl.

THEY looked like commandos from some World War Two movie, Edwards thought, as he adjusted his position straddling the rounded portside bulwark of the small inflatable dinghy, a paddle clutched in both hands. An occasional wave broke against the side of the small craft, tossing it to and fro like a leaf riding a river's rapids, soaking his left leg up to the knee. The water actually felt good. It wasn't cold, or anything like cold, but it offered some relief from the humid equatorial night.

Next to him, straddling the starboard side, Lieutenant Coleman stared into the darkness ahead, his head and face presenting the misshapen silhouette of a pair of night vision goggles. Like the rest of them, he was bedecked in black ski cap, black pullover sweater, and black pants. Commandos they may have appeared to be, but commandos they were not. The pants belonged to the naval winter uniform and they were lucky to find enough on board to fit all four of them since *Providence*'s travels seldom took her to the colder regions of the Earth.

Edwards allowed a glance behind him at the shoe-polish-blackened faces of the two petty officers, Donizetti and Velasquez, straddling the dinghy's inflated sides. Their young yet experienced, nervous yet eager eyes were fixed on him, waiting for the command to continue rowing. Plastic wrapped weapons rested on the floor of the dinghy next to each sailor's one dry foot. For Donizetti, an M-16 assault rifle. For Velasquez, a shortened, twelve-gauge, pump-action shotgun. Like Edwards and Coleman, each man wore a holstered forty-five caliber pistol affixed to the black web belt around his waist.

They were well armed for close-quarters action, Edwards thought. He only hoped they were armed well enough to do the job.

Looking past Donizetti and Velasquez into the blackness astern of their tiny dinghy, he could see nothing. Somewhere back there, about a mile distant, *Providence* lay hove to on the surface waiting for their signal that the fishing boat had been secured. Then, and only then, would she approach the fishing boat. Those were his orders.

In his mind he could picture Bloomfield and Miller standing on *Providence*'s darkened bridge, binoculars glued to their eyes. Bloomfield would no doubt comment on the futility of the plan, how it might be negatively viewed at SubPac, and how it could wreck their careers—or in Bloomfield's case, his retirement. Bloomfield might even speculate openly about how he planned to make his objection known by an entry in the ship's logbook. Edwards took comfort in the fact that the blathering Bloomfield could never undertake such a bold action by himself. The underachieving executive officer would never run the career risk, would never let his name appear alone on any log entry. Almost certainly, he would try to convince Miller to do it, to make a log entry first. But Edwards felt no anxiety about Miller's response. Miller was behind him 100 percent on this, so much so in fact that Edwards had toyed with the thought of leaving Miller in command of the ship instead of Bloomfield. But as much as it left him ill at ease, the appropriateness of command hierarchy dictated that the XO should assume command whenever the captain is away.

What the hell was *he* doing leading the boarding party,

anyway? Edwards asked himself. A captain's place was on his ship. This was work for his promotion-thirsty lieutenants and lieutenant commanders, not him. He could kick himself for letting his personal emotions cloud his judgment, but the sight of that young girl in the hands of those sons of bitches pulled the image of his own daughter to the forefront of his thoughts. He couldn't help but think about the young girl's parents, about her own father. Surely, she belonged and was loved in some part of the world by parents who would be devastated by her loss. But despite any emotions summoned by the sight of the captured young girl, Edwards knew deep down that he had no choice. He had to go with the boarding party. If anything went wrong, if anyone was hurt or killed, he alone would carry the blame. He would have to explain it to the families back home, deprived of their loved ones, first for a six-month deployment and now for a lifetime.

"The fisherman's about five hundred yards away, Captain," Coleman whispered, still peering into the darkness with the night vision goggles. "We're drifting a little to the west. We need to change course about ten degrees to the left."

"Very well," Edwards responded softly, then turned to the two men behind them. "Let's go. Bear left, quietly."

As they began to row again and the dinghy started to move through the water, Edwards held his paddle firmly over the side, pulling their head further to the left until he got a thumbs up from Coleman that they had turned far enough. Then they all pulled together, quietly but swiftly, heading toward the unseen object up ahead. Edwards strained his eyes to see a light in a window, a candle, a flashlight, anything that might give away the fishing craft's presence. But he could see nothing. The pirates were at least smart enough to extinguish all the lights. They likely were experienced enough to know that any lights would only serve as beacons. A nosy vessel passing within visual range might get curious and come take a look.

A slight change in the wind sent a breeze across Edwards' face, cooling the beads of perspiration gathering on his forehead. Though he was in top shape, the rowing exerted stresses on new muscles he hadn't used since his last stint in the weight room back on the Pearl Harbor sub base. That, coupled with the heat and humidity, made the five-hundred-yard pull quite a workout. Behind him, Donizetti and Velasquez puffed away, also feeling the unusual exertion. Coleman, on the other hand, kept stride easily without missing a stroke, his concentration on the boat ahead seemingly unbreakable. An academy graduate and truly a military machine, Coleman was a little scary to be around sometimes. In a way he was a captain's dream, qualified in everything from ship's diver to small arms marksman. He even went to the army's parachute infantry jump school when he was a midshipman. He could go far, Edwards thought, if only he could develop a personality. But personality or not, Edwards had him in mind for this foray from the moment of its conception. In a situation like this, one clear head under pressure was like a pot of gold.

"We're getting close now, sir," Coleman whispered urgently.

Edwards could make out a low shadow ahead of them now, a black void against the starry sky beyond. During a brief lull in the breeze, the faint clanging of a swinging chain wafted across the water, then diminished when the breeze picked up again. Something that sounded like laughter replaced it. The muffled laughter of two men, then voices. As their dinghy drew nearer to the dark fishing vessel, the voices became more distinguishable. Edwards listened intently for any female voices, but heard none.

Now a mere thirty yards away, with the fifty-foot length of the fisherman's starboard side laid out before them, it appeared much larger. The long booms stretched toward the star-filled sky above her stern and rocked with the ocean swell in an uneven, but periodic, motion, as if they were giant conductor's wands keeping tempo for a great celestial orchestra. The low living structure started about fifteen feet forward of her low stern and ran along the length of the boat, ending with a two-story pilothouse just above her blunt bow. All of the porthole-like windows were dark, save one near a door amidships, where a dull glow emanated, and no one appeared to be on deck. She was obviously a fisherman of the coastal variety. And though she might be considered slightly decrepit in

American waters, she was fairly modern by any standards used in these islands. An archaic surface-search radar sat motionless beside a twiggy radio mast mounted atop the raised pilothouse. It made Edwards wonder if the crew had managed to send a distress call before they were overtaken. Maybe patrol craft were already on the way to the rescue from Jayapura, four hundred miles away.

Perhaps it was the puny size of their dinghy that made the fishing boat seem so menacing. But menacing or not, they did not stop rowing toward it. Stopping would only give them more exposure to any unseen pirate on deck. They made straight for the protection of the fishing boat's high bow. It was high enough that they would be hidden from anyone on deck, barring no one leaned over the side and looked down.

The rubber dinghy glided gently against the slimy hull and Edwards reached out to grab the rusty bow as best he could. He finally found a firm handhold on the high anchor port and instantly felt vibrations from the fisherman's purring generator tickle his fingertips. As the frail dinghy slowly got in synch with the rocking fisherman, the stagnant fumes of burnt diesel choked the four men's lungs, and they strained to fight off the urge to cough. The toxic smell seemed to defy the warm southwesterly breeze as it hung about the idling boat like a low fog.

Coleman peeked around the bow's blunt edge to see the vessel's port side.

"The speedboat's still tied up, sir," he whispered. "No sign of anyone."

Edwards nodded and reached for one of *Providence*'s rope ladders in the bottom of the dinghy. The rolling swells would have made it difficult for most sailors, but Coleman stood straight up with perfect balance. The fisherman's bow was made for plowing through rough seas, not for accommodating boarding parties, and it towered a few feet too high for a six-foot man to reach it. But Edwards had anticipated this and, as planned, Velasquez moved forward on the raft until he was even with Edwards. Coleman then employed both men's shoulders as a makeshift stepladder. With both hands scraping along the fisherman's hull for balance, Coleman gingerly made his way up to a full standing position until he was just able to reach the bow's bottom rail. In seconds he had pulled himself up and over the side, tying off the ends of the ladder for the rest of them to use. Edwards went first up the swinging ladder and got some help from Coleman as he bounded the three-rung railing. Instinctively, he crouched low with his forty-five-caliber pistol at the ready, but not before he tripped over a haphazardly coiled clump of fishing cable and came close to knocking over a bucket full of horrid-smelling fish guts.

Whoever this fishing captain was, Edwards thought to himself, he needed to learn the fine art of stowing for sea. Cables, chains, dirty buckets, and various tools lay strewn about the short deck forward of the pilothouse. Lines of hemp—some coiled, some not—also adorned the deck, made slick after years of contact with fish intestines. The boarding party would need to move with the utmost caution.

Moments later, all four were on deck, hunkering in the small space just forward of the two-story pilothouse, their faces stern, their weapons gleaming. Off to the horizon, Edwards could see the first shades of gray in the eastern sky. Dawn was rapidly approaching. Soon the surfaced *Providence* would be starkly visible to the north. They had to move quickly.

Voices could be heard again coming from within the low structure. They spoke a language not familiar to him, but he assumed it to be one of the hundred different tongues spoken in these islands. The voices were lively. Laughter erupted in uneven bursts, and it didn't take long for him to conclude that they were drunk. He heard what sounded like books being thrown against the wall and concluded that they must be ransacking the boat for any loot they could find. With dawn coming they would certainly be planning to debark soon to seek the cover of a nearby island. Again he heard no trace of a female voice, and he began to fear the worst for the young girl.

"Proceed with Velasquez down the port side," he whispered to Coleman. "Donizetti and I will take starboard. At any sign of resistance, don't hesitate to kill them."

"Aye, aye, sir." Coleman answered quickly and without emotion, then waved for the shotgun-wielding Velasquez to follow him.

Edwards motioned to Donizetti, and the two began moving aft along the starboard side with Edwards in the lead. He could see the open door only a couple dozen feet aft and the porthole beside it where he had seen the dull light. From his perspective, low and flat against the structure's outer bulkhead, there was no way to see inside the door, at least not until he was right on it.

With each step aft he could hear the wild voices growing louder and louder. He thought about peeking into one of the portholes above his head, but then quickly thought against it. If they saw him in the window, the element of surprise would be lost. Their best bet was to go right through the door and take them in the middle of their drunken pilfering. Coleman and Velasquez would cover them from the portholes on the port side if anything went wrong.

Edwards looked back to check on Donizetti behind him. The nineteen-year-old's expression was not as bold as it had been five minutes before. With imminent conflict mere seconds away, the frightened boy was emerging from the stalwart young man. A reassuring nod from Edwards brought a nervous smile from him in return.

Now determined to pounce upon the murderers, Edwards brought his weapon up and held it at arm's length as he began to move toward the open door. He had advanced less than two steps when a loud clanging broke the night air behind him. Practically jumping out of his skin, Edwards swung around to see Donizetti stumbling over a plastic bucket that had been lying on the deck. The young sailor must have been so anxious that he forgot to check his footing. The bucket skidded across the deck, bouncing several times in what seemed to Edwards the loudest noise he had ever heard. He shot a venomous scowl at the startled Donizetti and wanted to curse him up one side and down the other.

Then the voices stopped.

Edwards held his weapon at the ready, aiming it for the

doorway, waiting at any moment for a response from the pirates, hoping Coleman and Velasquez on the port side would have the good sense to do the same.

"Ali!" a voice said from inside the structure.

Several seconds of silence followed before the voice was heard again, this time sounding more urgent.

"Ali!"

Footfalls could be heard inside and Edwards soon realized that someone was coming out. In his crouched stance, he held the weapon with both hands, his aim steady on the door.

Then a man strolled out of the door with a rifle held loosely in one hand, a burning cigarette in the other. He was much shorter than Edwards had expected, forcing him to adjust his aim accordingly. The periscope's magnification had played the usual tricks on his mind with regard to distance and size. He had forgotten to expect the men of these islands to be shorter than most Westerners.

The man stood in the doorway pulling hard on the cigarette. He hadn't noticed them yet, and Edwards assumed his night vision had not yet fully adjusted after being in the low cabin light. Edwards, however, could make out almost every feature of the inebriated pirate's face. In fact, he was close enough to smell the alcohol exuding from his skin. The man was brown-skinned, like the Javanese of this region, and hard-faced. Though bare-footed, he wore a dirty, loose-fitting, button-down shirt, and a pair of equally filthy loose trousers rolled up to the knee. His rifle had an oversized banana-style magazine and looked similar to an AK-47 assault rifle, but Edwards couldn't be sure since there were so many variations on the market these days.

"Apa kabar, Ali!" the figure cried in a slurring voice as he held his arms high above his head, appearing to stretch.

The man then glanced over his shoulder and Edwards could see the realization sink in as their eyes met.

"Ali!" the man cried suddenly as he struggled to bring his rifle up.

But his drunken reflexes were too late. Edwards' forty-five and Donizetti's M-16, held steady on the man from the m ment he had emerged from the cabin, erupted in a staccato of reports and muzzle flashes that shattered the tranquil dawn. Edwards instantly lost his night vision to the blinding muzzle flashes and the man disappeared entirely from view. He had little time to think about measure of force and emptied the weapon's entire magazine in the direction of the armed man. Donizetti did the same, apparently recovered now from his momentary lapse. The young sailor fired his weapon without remorse, the muzzle not ten inches from Edwards' left ear. Spent cartridges ejected en masse out the right side of his gun, ricocheting off the bulkhead and clattering onto the deck.

With Edwards' eight round magazine and Donizetti's thirty rounds expended almost simultaneously, the dawn became silent once again, the rich aroma of gunpowder filling the air. The former cold steel of Edwards' forty-five now felt warm in his hands, and indeed the barrel was hot to the touch. Wafting trails of smoke escaped from the muzzles of both guns, and between them Edwards and Donizetti saw the bloody mess of a man lying prostrate on the deck. The force of the bullets had moved him several feet further aft from where he had originally stood, and dark oozing spots covered the white bulkhead, portholes, and deck everywhere.

Inside the doorway, rapid footfalls thumped from fore to aft. The dead pirate's accomplice was obviously scrambling for the port side door in an effort to reach his speedboat and escape. The sound of the port side door creaking open, then slamming shut, followed instantly by the blast of Velasquez's shotgun and then a heavy splash indicated that the pirate's attempt to escape had not succeeded.

"Clear?" Edwards shouted, hanging just outside the door.

A few seconds later came Coleman's voice. "Clear!"

Both parties entered the structure from opposite sides. One of them found a light on the wall and pulled its short chain switch. The room, which contained a galley and a small booth table, was a complete mess. Opened lockers, papers, food, liquor, and clothing littered the room everywhere. Bottles— some empty, some broken—rolled loosely across the deck. Strangely, a cooking pot sat undisturbed on the small stove.

"Those assholes must have taken the poor bastards when they were about to sit down to dinner," Velasquez said.

Coleman held up a hand, silencing him, and pointed toward the passage leading to the forward staterooms. A muffled sound could be heard coming from the first stateroom on the left, its door still shut. As Edwards and the boarding party exchanged glances, it became evident that the sound was that of a young girl crying.

Edwards thrust open the stateroom's door to be greeted by a deplorable sight. A double bed occupied most of the room. On it, two outstretched and naked females lay side-by-side, both bound with duct tape at the wrists and ankles. They looked Malay, probably Indonesian too, but it was impossible to tell. One was quite young, obviously the girl he had seen through the periscope. She was young but certainly a young woman and no girl, and Edwards rebuked himself silently for jumping to conclusions. She stared at him through teary eyes, her body shaking involuntarily, her long black hair falling in disheveled clumps across her flawless face and breasts. The other woman appeared to be in her forties, though Edwards found it hard to tell from the many bruises and dried blood discoloring her face. She had obviously taken the worst of the pirate's beatings and appeared to be unconscious. No doubt they had both suffered a terrible night of rape and torture.

Edwards quickly covered them both with a nearby blanket, then Velasquez tossed him a pocketknife which he used to cut their bands. As he removed the last tape from the young woman's trembling wrists, she turned her head away and stared distantly at the bulkhead. Tears rolled off her face and fell onto the bed sheet beside her.

Her look of utter despondency, of complete mental breakdown, left him speechless and half-wishing he had emergency-surfaced the ship as Fremont had suggested. He felt somehow responsible for what had happened to these poor women, and suddenly he could no longer be in the same room with them. He couldn't breathe the dank smelly air anymore. He had to get out.

Leaving Velasquez to attend to their wounds, Edwards

stepped out into the passage and was immediately met by Lieutenant Coleman.

"We've cleared the rest of the staterooms, Captain, and the hold. There's no one else aboard. The diesel appears to be in good shape, no serious damage."

"Good." Edwards nodded with forced bearing.

"I also found some papers, sir. She's the *Mendar,* out of Ujungpang. From what I can make of the logs she's been at sea for a week. But there's something strange, Captain." Coleman looked puzzled.

Edwards looked at him inquisitively.

"The cold stores are empty, Captain. No fish on board. I'd think a week in these waters would pull in more than this boat can carry."

"Maybe they're just out here for a cruise." Edwards regarded him warmly. "It's perfectly legal, Lieutenant, and none of our business. Besides, I'm not about to start questioning those women right now. They've been through enough. Let them be, for now."

Coleman nodded heavily and stared fixedly past him at the door to the stateroom.

"See what you can do for them," Edwards added. "Remember, no questions. Let them know they're safe now. I'm going to signal *Providence* to come alongside."

"Aye, aye, Captain."

Grabbing a flashlight, Edwards went out on deck through the starboard door. The eastern sky was glowing now, and he could see Donizetti up forward hauling on the dinghy's line, dragging it aft where it would be more accessible.

Just then, a shot rang out and he saw Donizetti's left shoulder shudder from an impact, atomized blood filling the air beside him. Donizetti fell to the deck with a groan, dropping the dinghy's line and clutching his dripping shoulder with the opposite hand.

Edwards looked up to see a figure with a gun standing on top of the high pilothouse.

Of course, he thought with terrifying realization. This third pirate must have been keeping watch for the others. *Ali.* He must have fallen asleep while on watch and then woke up after the shooting started.

Edwards brought his weapon up quickly and took aim at the figure above. The man appeared to notice him at the same moment and likewise swung his weapon in Edwards' direction. With his weapon in front of his face Edwards suddenly realized that the slide mechanism on his pistol was still locked in the rear position. In all the excitement, he had forgotten to load another magazine! He was a submarine captain amateurishly playing commando, and now he would pay the price!

The man on top of the pilothouse leveled his carbine-style rifle at Edwards, bringing it to his shoulder in one motion. The gun was in perfect alignment with Edwards' head, and Edwards expected it to be over at any moment. The pirate would certainly put a round between his eyes.

Just then a flurry of blood filled the air near the pirate's head as it jerked violently to the side. The rifle dropped from his lifeless hands and clattered to the deck two stories below, joined soon after by the limp body of its owner, landing only a few feet away from the wounded Donezetti.

Edwards breathed a sigh of relief, but then immediately began to wonder where the bullet that saved his life had come from. It could not have come from Donezetti, and Coleman and Velasquez were still inside the superstructure. It had come from somewhere else, and Edwards suddenly got the notion to look over the rail at the morning sea.

A rush of adrenaline flowed through his veins as he saw *Providence*'s black magnificence surging through the seas less than a hundred yards away, the dark waves of the early dawn parting before her towering sail like the Red Sea. She came on with a destroyer's dash, making a good twenty knots, leaving an extended sky-blue wake behind her.

On the bridge atop the sail, Edwards could make out Miller's and Bloomfield's windblown faces, Miller waving one hand wildly and brandishing a grin from ear to ear. Just behind Miller, standing on *Providence*'s raised flying bridge, a matching grin appeared on the face of Chief Michaelson, his big tattooed arms clutching a scoped M-16 rifle across his broad chest.

Edwards sighed heavily, taking a few seconds to recover from his near brush with death, and then waved back. He couldn't help but feel a surge of pride at seeing his beautiful ship in all her glory. It was a view he seldom got to see, but a view he would cherish for the rest of his life. Even the sight of Bloomfield's sulky round face could not destroy this moment.

Providence was his ship, and he was her proud captain.

Chapter 8

"BRIDGE, Helm. Steady on course two nine one."

The bridge railing's sun-soaked steel felt warm under Lake's fingertips as *Providence* gently settled on the next leg of the circuitous track that would safely convey her through the reef maze surrounding the Bunda Islands. His cotton khaki uniform was soaked from the humidity in the mere one degree of northern latitude. Lake cursed the heat as he felt drops of perspiration trickling down his arm, making the railing slippery. Above him, an endless sky of small fluffy clouds wafted low over the sea, providing brief but consolatory moments as each took turns blocking the hazy sun from *Providence*'s small patch of ocean.

Lying across *Providence*'s bows and just a few miles to the west, three sharp islands rose out of the turquoise sea, their green canopied hills and mountains spotted with distinct shadows from the same low-flying cumulus. Lake wondered how anyone could live in this humid weather, but obviously many did since he could discern several villages lining the shores of the two southernmost islands.

"That big one in the center, that is Bunda Island," said a cheery, ball-cap wearing Moluccan man standing beside him on *Providence*'s bridge. "Ujungpang is there."

Lake returned an emotionless smile only out of courtesy.

The small happy man, who looked like he had just come from a beach party in his T-shirt, shorts, and sandals, was Bunda's idea of a harbor pilot. He seemed thrilled to be standing on the bridge of a United States submarine, guiding her through the shallows as his smoky harbor craft followed closely in *Providence*'s wake. English was obviously a second or third language to him, but he spoke it reasonably well.

Probably because his trade demanded it. Lake surmised a great number of English-speaking merchants came this way to fill their holds with Bunda's precious minerals.

"The one to the south is Teluk," the pilot said, pointing in the direction of the southernmost island. "Much fishing there."

Lake took a few moments from his conning duties to scan the islands with his binoculars, mostly as a gesture to placate his annoying companion. Each of the three islands were elongated with jagged mountain ridges running along their lengths like the spines of great ocean beasts hiding their heads in the sea. Great crevasses and valleys ran from the tops of the ridges down to the shorelines creating hundreds of tiny coves and inlets, mostly hidden from the sea by great outcroppings of volcanic rock where—unlike the rest of the rich land—no living thing grew. The high-ridged Bunda in the center, together with her lower-altitude sisters, came close to forming a semicircle bounded on the open side by the sharp reefs through which *Providence* now transited. During a particularly long and painful watch with Fremont—his department head—Lake learned that these islands were formed thousands of years ago by a massive volcanic eruption rivaling Krakatoa. Even in his callous mood Lake had to agree that they were breathtakingly beautiful. It was hard for him to imagine such a place was on the edge of unrest.

"Bridge, Navigator," the bridge speaker intoned. Fremont's voice sounded slightly nervous. "We're sounding eight fathoms here, Officer of the Deck, and getting shallower. Please inform the pilot that our last fix places us forty yards to the right of the channel. Recommend we come left to course two eight nine."

"Navigator, Bridge, aye," Lake acknowledged and glanced at the pilot.

"*Tidak.* Not yet, Officer of Deck," the pilot said, then smiled. "This is good course. Wreck under water in channel up ahead. Officer of Deck needs to stay right. Five kilometers until next turn."

"Tell the Nav to keep passing us soundings, Mr. Lake,"

Edwards chimed from the flying bridge behind them, a pair of binoculars held to his face, his short hair blowing wildly in the warm breeze. "We'll do what the pilot recommends. He knows these waters better than we do."

This brought a grin from the pilot who looked tickled to death that Edwards had sided with him over his own navigator. "*Terima kasih*. Thank you, Captain, sir."

Lake spoke into the small microphone to relay the order to the control room, inwardly chuckling. He could picture Fremont down in the control room feverishly hovering over both chart tables at once, surrounded on all sides by his flustered quartermasters, some plotting, others looking through the periscopes marking bearings and ranges to different landmarks, others manning the radar and fathometer, still others holding clipboards to take logs on every bearing and range called. Frantically, almost certain of a collision with an unmarked reef at any moment, the navigator would be checking every fix three or four times, trusting no one. Fremont had come close to a heart attack when the confident but outwardly unimpressive pilot arrived on board to guide *Providence* through the treacherous approach. Fremont's career had certainly flashed before his eyes.

With that in mind Lake was suddenly pleased to be on the bridge during the port entry. Things may have been frantic down in the control room, but the world above was peaceful. *Providence* glided through the gentle surf at a slow five knots, leaving a long wake behind her to mark her many turns. At this slow speed, the water rolled off her bow, never reaching the base of the sail. Her rubber-skinned deck remained dry and bare except for a small group of seagulls congregating far aft near her waterline and shouting challenges at their counterparts circling overhead. The only sounds were those of the put-putting harbor craft and the squawking birds.

"What's that northern island?" Lake asked the pilot in an attempt to make conversation. "I don't see any villages over there."

"Oh, no," the little man replied. "That's Wijaya. No one lives there."

"Why not?"

"It is a refuge. Some animals live there, but no people. Some orangutans have been moved there from Borneo."

Lake examined the low foothills before the ridge as if he could see one of the apes from this distance. All was covered in a thick jungle running right down to the gleaming white strip of sand at the water's edge. An undisturbed paradise on the edge of a nation comprised of a thousand such islands. Studying the breathtaking islands before him and the heartfelt smile of his harbor pilot companion, Lake wondered if the central government in Jakarta—almost two thousand miles away—even cared about such a remote place.

Certainly they had showed little concern for the fishing boat *Providence* rescued the day before. Lake had sent the message himself—or rather ordered Reynoso to send the message—notifying the Indonesian navy, or *Tentara Nasional,* about the incident and requesting arrangements to pick up the surviving female passengers. *Providence* then waited for six hours with no response. Lake had a tough time believing it. After all, a bullet had taken a healthy nick out of Donizetti's left shoulder. And even though the wound was superficial, it was a big sacrifice to make in order to rescue a bunch of people who didn't pay U.S. taxes. They should have sent a thank you at least. But nothing had come from the Indonesian authorities.

Of course, SubPac was notified too and their response came back promptly via a flash message. It was not a "thank you" and Lake thought he detected an instance of irritation when he delivered the message to the captain. *"Proceed with the assigned mission without further delay."* A tactful way of telling Edwards to get on with *Providence*'s mission before he got himself in deep shit with the admiral.

Reluctantly, the captain had ordered the fisherman cast adrift, and brought the two women aboard *Providence* for transport to Ujungpang. Lake had been there to meet the women as they came down the ladder through *Providence*'s forward hatch, the suffering of the past twenty-four hours very visible on their bruised faces. The scars had to be deep and in-eradicable, not withstanding that every male crewmember was now dead. Lake learned later that there had been three men in the fisherman's crew, all related to the two women and all executed in the same fashion.

Such a damn shame, he thought.

The only bright moment came when he informed Bloomfield that the captain wanted the executive officer stateroom vacated to accommodate the female guests. Lake wished he could have taken a picture of Bloomfield's face at that moment, all aghast. Sonar probably heard Bloomfield's blubbery jaw hitting the floor. Lake had enjoyed it more than anything else he had done in the last few months. As a lowly lieutenant, he seldom got the chance to rain on Bloomfield's lazy pleasure cruise.

In the last week Edwards had been shaping up to be his kind of captain. Well, sort of, if that was at all possible. And for the first time in his naval career, Lake actually felt sympathy for a superior officer. Two innocent people were alive today because the captain cared more about doing the right thing than protecting his career. That kind of reasoning had been foreign to Captain Carl Christopher. Of course, SubPac would reprimand Edwards for it. The ass-covering Christophers of the world always seemed to fall into their admirals' good graces while men like Edwards suffered for doing what was right. It was a methodology Lake was eager to separate himself from forever, and soon.

Providence continued the transit through the reef passage under the expert eye of the pilot. The shallow reef barrier came within a few fathoms of her keel in several places, but the pilot guided her through safely and without incident. As they drew closer to Bunda, approaching from slightly south of the island, Lake could make out Ujungpang Bay, which opened to the southeast, hidden from view earlier by a large outcropping of land. The town of Ujungpang, nestled along the shoreline of the placid bay, was now clearly visible. Its houses and buildings lined the waterfront, advancing inland until they disap-

peared into the dense forest at the base of the mountain ridge
beyond. The prominent land outcropping—now off *Providence*'s starboard beam—rose sharply several hundred feet,
presenting a natural land shield for the small seaport against
any westerly weather patterns. The crumbling remains of a
colonial-era fort adorned its crest with several dingy long iron
cannons still protruding from their vine-covered embrasures.

Under the old fort's lee, dozens of bamboo rafts and
prahus plied the calm waters of the bay, traversing back and
forth between Ujungpang and the scattered fishing villages
along the coast of Teluk Island, ten miles to the south. The
people riding in the closer rafts waved at the men on *Providence*'s deck and several of *Providence*'s sailors waved back.
From his high perch on the bridge, Lake could see Master
Chief Ketterling walking briskly fore and aft along *Providence*'s sun-dried deck getting the dozen or so life-vest-clad
sailors in position to receive lines. Many of the Malay women
in the nearby boats pointed and giggled at the mostly pale
American sailors lined up in formation in the hot sun.

"Everyone seems happy to see us." Lake commented to the
pilot.

"Ya. Everyone has heard what *Providence* did for the *Mendar* women. They are grateful for that."

"That's nice to know. Tell me, what's that up there?" Lake
pointed to the fort high above them.

"That is Fortress Arnhem, sir. It is an old Dutch fort. They
built it long ago when they ruled here."

The spice trade of the colonial era Dutch East India Company had reached far across Southeast Asia even to remote islands like this one. Lake could picture the fort in its better
days, guarding the precious resources on this far extension of
the Dutch Empire, its watchmen on the high stone walls looking out for any sail that might indicate an English line of battle. These islands, remote as they were, could claim their fair
share of the history of Western civilization.

Providence made her way past the promontory with the
Dutch fort and turned northwest, allowing a better view of the

inner bay. Lake could see that it curved back further to the east now. The promontory was no more than a quarter mile wide where it lined the bay's eastern edge, and now he could see fishing vessels tied to a dozen small piers jutting out from a section of shore that resembled a fish market. Buildings sat on the shore end of each pier obviously to receive fish cargoes and then process them for shipment. The five miles of open bay between the fisheries and *Providence*'s bridge did little to dissipate the stench hanging in the air.

"I see the Indonesian navy beat us here," Edwards said from his perch.

Lake scanned to the right of the fishing piers and saw a much longer pier extending out into the bay. Two gray warships flying the red over white flag of the Indonesian navy sat idly one behind the other, their port sides moored to the pier.

"Can you make them out, Mr. Lake?" Edwards quizzed.

Lake gave an inaudible sigh. He had abandoned ship recognition charts the day after he got his dolphins.

"Uh, looks like two escort type warships, Captain."

"Nice try. The furthest one looks like a guided missile frigate of the Fatahillah Class. You can tell by the Bofors forty-millimeter gun mounted on the stern. You can't see her bow from here, but she's got a 120-millimeter turret gun mounted up there, along with a 375-millimeter twin-barreled mortar. She's a 'G' frigate because she carries Exocet anti-ship missiles amidships. You should know that."

"Yes, sir." Lake nodded, feigning interest. He planned to flush every last naval fact from his memory within a month.

"The other one's a corvette," Edwards continued, completely absorbed. "Kind of looks like a Russian 'Grisha.' She's got a good-sized turret on her stern, probably a twin-barreled Soviet fifty-seven millimeter rapid-fire gun. I'm going to say she belongs to the Patimura Class." He glanced down at the pilot. "Am I right?"

"Ya, Captain!" the pilot replied excitedly, seemingly overjoyed at Edwards' interest. "*Malahayati* and *Nuku*. Both are fine ships!"

Edwards gave a sly smile then looked at Lake again.

"Is that all, Lieutenant? You guessed a couple escort ships. Is that all you see over there? I'm surprised at you."

Lake brought the binoculars back to his eyes and scanned the distant pier once again. On the right side lay the frigate and the corvette just as Edwards had described them, their decks and pier speckled here and there with blue-clad sailors going about in-port routine. He examined the ships closely. Their low superstructures and whirling radar and communications masts seemed like any other he'd seen in various parts of the world. As he examined the dozen or so pennants flapping from the frigate's flagstaff, he finally came across something noteworthy.

"A pennant with two stars," he announced triumphantly. "The frigate has a flag officer on board, Captain."

"While that's interesting, Mr. Lake, it's not quite what I was looking for."

Lake noticed that Edwards didn't remove the binoculars from his face but was staring intently at something. Something near the pier.

Looking once again, Lake focused not on the ships this time but on the pier in general. Then he saw it, and immediately felt like an idiot. On the left side of the long pier, opposite the warships, a low grayish black shape hugged close to the water. A smoothly faired low structure protruded from its middle anointed with an array of masts and poles that just barely reached the height of the pier. He had mistaken it for a strange-looking fender, but of course he shouldn't have.

"A submarine," he said unnecessarily.

Through the binoculars, Lake could see the nylon lines connecting the submarine's cleats with those on the pier. The submarine's deck was so far below the pier that the lines appeared to be at right angles. She was moored with her starboard side next to the pier and her bow pointing toward the land, allowing Lake a clear view of her stern. Obviously she was a diesel-electric boat of some sort. The twin black tips of her X-style rudder just poked above the surface a few yards astern of the exposed portion of her rounded hull. The wing-like shapes of her raised bow planes were also clearly visible just forward of her short sleek sail. She looked like a midget next to her surface cohorts, and she would look that way next to *Providence*, too. She could be no more than one-third the length of a Los Angeles Class boat.

"Not just a submarine, Mr. Lake, a submarine of the future. Unless I'm mistaken that's a Type 214, the latest German model."

A confirming nod came from the pilot. "The *Hatta,* sir. She is also a good ship. An excellent captain, too."

"That's a fine boat you're looking at, Mr. Lake," Edwards said excitedly, as if he wanted Lake to share in his thrill. "Not many officers get to see one this close. Consider yourself lucky."

Fuckin' A, Lake thought sarcastically. "She's not a nuke, Captain," he said glibly.

The binoculars came away from Edwards' face in an instant, his eyes regarding Lake in such a pitiable manner that Lake actually felt below par for a brief moment.

"Maybe not, Lieutenant, but if you ever did littoral operations, you'd want her on your side. She's got the latest in air independent propulsion systems. When she's using it, she's as quiet as a hole in the ocean. I bet she can stay submerged for a couple weeks without recharging."

Littoral operations? Lake wondered. Ah yes, the navy's term for shallow water ops. Or, more appropriately, operations close in to the shore. The air independent propulsion system he knew little about, except that if you stuck hydrogen and oxygen in one end, you got water, heat, and electricity out the other. Nowhere near the power output of *Providence*'s nuclear reactor, but probably enough to push the smaller sub along at a good pace.

"I wasn't aware that Indonesia had bought any new subs," Edwards commented. "But of course our intel is usually a day late and a dollar short."

As *Providence* neared the protracted pier, the ships came

alive with activity. Indonesian sailors lined the pier and deck in an unorganized deluge of blue short-sleeved uniforms, all scrambling to see the United States submarine.

"Sir," the pilot said meekly. "If the *Providence* will please take the position aft of the *Hatta*. There is enough space there. One hundred fifty meters of pier space for the *Providence*."

"Very good," Edwards said confidently. "Mr. Lake, we've got no tugs to assist us this time. You're on your own. Take the ship in, please."

"Aye, aye, Captain." Lake clutched the bridge coaming with both hands, his knuckles white from the strength of his grip.

No pressure, Lake thought, as he sized up the distances to the other submarine's stern and the crowded pier. *I just have to parallel park a three-hundred-foot submarine with the entire fucking Indonesian navy watching me.*

Of course, he'd docked the ship dozens of times, but seldom without a tug. Submarines lose their steerage at low speeds, making them extremely difficult to maneuver. Under normal conditions, a tugboat would tie up near the bow to help push the head around whenever it got too far right or left. Without a tug the bow could swing freely at low speeds, sometimes right into the pier, or worse, into a nearby ship. Without a tug, the officer of the deck needed to use the nearly forgotten art of delicate ship-driving.

The pier was now only a couple hundred yards away, and Lake could clearly see the slimy fenders bobbing at the spot where *Providence* was to moor.

"Helm, Bridge." Lake spoke into the bridge box. "All stop. Maneuvering, Bridge, lower the outboard."

The order was acknowledged by the helm, followed a few moments later by the maneuvering room's report that the outboard had been lowered.

Lake pictured the secondary propulsion motor—or outboard, as it was called—emerging from its faired housing on *Providence*'s underbelly. The small electric motor, strategically positioned near the ship's stern, was essential for mooring when no tug was available. Its propeller was small when compared to *Providence*'s giant screw and therefore gave a minimal amount of thrust, but it could be rotated and trained in any direction yielding that small moment of rotation at the critical moment when it was needed.

Lake checked the speed indicator on the bridge box. *Providence* had slowed to four knots. She was a mere hundred yards from the pier, slightly to the left and approaching at a thirty-degree angle.

Now came the tricky part. As *Providence*'s way came off her, she would rapidly lose the ability to steer. While she still had enough speed, Lake needed to point her bow at the *Hatta*'s stern and keep it there, at the same time he needed to allow for currents and drift. On the way in he had noticed most of the rafters rowing on the west side of their vessels, and he suspected there was a slight westerly current in the bay.

"Bridge, Navigator. According to GPS we're being set to the west at zero point five knots."

"Nav, Bridge, aye." Lake smiled at the affirmation of his presumption. He had the information. Now he needed to point *Providence*'s head appropriately. "Helm, Bridge. Right ten degrees rudder."

As the helmsman acknowledged, Lake looked aft to see *Providence*'s exposed rudder angle to starboard. The rudder created a small disturbance on the surface and its drag slowed the ship even more. He knew this would be the last chance to guide *Providence* before she lost steerage completely.

As the bow swung slowly to the right, pointing first at the shore, then at the *Hatta*'s bow, then at her sail, then at her aft deck, Lake had his eyes glued to the ship's heading indicator mounted on the bridge in front of him. The bow came over slowly, slowly, until she nearly pointed at the *Hatta*'s exposed twin rudders. The distance had closed now to fifty yards.

"Helm, Bridge. Rudder amidships!"

"Rudder amidships, Helm, aye," the answer came back immediately.

Instinctively Lake glanced aft to ensure that the rudder had returned smartly to the amidships position. The deck tugged at his feet ever so slightly, the hull feeling the sudden loss of the rudder's drag. *Providence* had slowed to two and a half knots. She was too slow now to respond to any rudder angle. Even with the rudder amidships, her head still swung minutely to the right but Lake was happy with it.

He glanced up at Edwards, but the captain was staring off at one of the lush hillsides behind the town, seemingly unconcerned. Lake guessed that it was just a show. A show specifically meant to display trust in Lake's conning abilities. Behind those eyes, Lake was certain all of the captain's senses were focused on the docking evolution.

It was a waiting game now. How long should he wait before ordering an astern bell?

As *Providence*'s nose inched closer and closer to the pier now only twenty yards away, Lake caught a glimpse of a face down on the deck among the waiting line-handlers. It was Reynoso.

Of course it was Reynoso, he thought. Every freaking opportunity to volunteer, the brown-noser put his overly eager ass forward. He probably volunteered to handle lines again.

Lake thought he saw Reynoso look up at the bridge for a brief moment. He figured the petty officer was probably trying to lay a guilt trip on him. After all, Lake had been avoiding him like an alpha particle for the last few days, skirting the issue of the promotion package, which Lake had every intention of leaving to his successor. It wasn't that Reynoso didn't deserve it. He certainly did, if anyone in the radio division did. But Lake found it hard to give a damn so close to the end of his tour.

As *Providence* edged closer, almost at a stop, the men on deck positioned themselves to toss their lines to the waiting men on the pier. As she came under the lee of the pier, Lake decided it was finally time.

"Helm, Bridge. All back one third! Train the outboard to starboard ninety degrees and start the outboard!"

Churning bubbles appeared just ahead of *Providence*'s rudder as the astern throttles were opened for the first time since surfacing. The giant screw reversed direction and quickly brought the ship to a stop, her bow nearly touching the pier with her stern still well out. *Providence*'s length and the pier now formed a thirty-degree angle—the apex being where ship's bow met the pier. Lines simultaneously flew across the space of water and were caught dutifully by Indonesian sailors on the pier.

When Lake was certain that *Providence* had come to a complete stop, he ordered, "Helm, Bridge. All stop."

The shaft stopped turning, and now it was up to the churning outboard motor to thrust *Providence*'s stern from its current flared position to its moored position up against the pier's fenders, which it did with the gentleness of a nursing mother. The sailors quickly looped the nylon lines around the cleats on both *Providence*'s deck and the pier and tied them off, the bitter ends neatly coiled on the black deck beside each cleat.

With her beam secure against the pier and her lines doubled up and fastened tightly, *Providence* was a beast in captivity once more and Lake waited until he received the requisite nod from Edwards.

"Well done, Mr. Lake. Secure the main engines and secure the maneuvering watch."

"Aye, aye, Captain."

Lake relayed the orders over the bridge microphone. Edwards followed the pilot down the bridge hatch, patting Lake on the shoulder as he went. Then the lookout followed them, leaving Lake on the bridge all alone.

The afternoon sun had lowered in the western sky, leaving the pier and most of the bay in the refreshing shadow of Bunda's high mountain ridge. The relief on Lake's sunburned face felt good as he leaned on the bridge coaming's cooling black steel and watched the bustle of activity on the pier. Water lines were being installed forward, while aft a group of men hoisted a small gangway across the deck to allow access on and off the ship. Some of *Providence*'s sailors conversed with Indonesian sailors on the pier, exchanging cigarettes and who knew what else. He never got over how quickly a ship went from a "sea mode" to an "in-port mode."

A 1MC announcement intoned over the bridge speaker as if to second his thoughts. It was Miller's voice. "Secure the maneuvering watch! Station the normal in-port watch, section three! Lieutenant Commander Miller is the ship's duty officer! All divisions bring all maintenance work orders to the control room for approval!"

A moment before, *Providence*'s bridge had been the center of the universe, where all the decisions were made, where the safety of the ship depended on the orders he gave. Now, it was nothing more than a high perch on a useless tower. All his authority as the officer of the deck went away the instant the in-port watch took over, and Commander Miller was now in charge as the duty officer. How quickly had he reverted from the star of the show to a mere short-timer lieutenant again.

He heard a clattering and had to stand aside as a sailor in camouflage fatigues emerged from the bridge hatch, an M-16 rifle slung muzzle-down across his back.

"What the hell are you doing, Chase?" Lake chided.

"Duty officer's orders, sir," the slightly overweight and red-faced Chase replied. "We're setting hostile port conditions. I'm the sentry up here."

"Well you're not going to fool anyone in that outfit. They'll just shoot at the tree growing out of our sail." Lake laughed heartily at his little joke, but Chase did not seem amused. He'd probably heard it once too often.

Glancing down at the brow, Lake saw two more of *Providence*'s sailors dressed just like Chase taking up sentry positions on the pier. At first, Lake thought it absurd in such a pristine place, but then he noticed the Indonesian ships across the pier also had armed sentries at their brows. As if to further stress the point, something that sounded like distant gunfire—automatic weapons fire—came from the forested hills beyond the town. Miles away, a flock of birds took to the air, rising out of the thick trees. Moments later, the gunfire diminished until it could be heard no more, and Lake shuddered at how eerily quiet it had become all of a sudden.

The ships rode at their mountain-shaded moorings, rising and falling from the gentle swell in the bay. The town beyond was alive, its streets and alleys active with people going about their daily tasks, but somehow everything seemed hushed and inhibited. Something hung in the air of the place, and Lake could feel it. As if the calm before a great storm. Something is looming over this place, he thought.

Lake found himself studying the Type 214 submarine—the *Hatta*—moored just a dozen yards ahead of *Providence*'s bow. *Providence* dwarfed her and from this stern view he could see just how skinny the little submarine's beam really was, no more than half *Providence*'s width. Her crew couldn't number more than thirty or forty people. But still, he had to admit that she had a smart look about her. The teardrop-shaped hull, newly painted and free of blemish, had a smooth rounded cut that appeared to be more hydrodynamic than *Providence*'s. While *Providence*'s sail rose sharply at right angles to tower above her main deck, the *Hatta*'s shorter sail met her deck in a curved hyperbolic arc conforming nicely both fore and aft to the sleek taper of the hull.

If she were a car, Lake thought, she'd be a Corvette.

As Lake further examined the exposed tips of the *Hatta*'s strangely angled twin rudder, he noticed a solitary figure standing on her stern. The figure was facing him, wearing the blue-on-blue, short-sleeved uniform of the Indonesian navy. Lake thought he could make out officer epaulettes too. Standing all alone with hands clasped behind his back, the man seemed to move only to adjust a curvy pipe smoldering from his lips. Distance and the shadow of a ball cap hid the man's features from Lake, but he appeared to be staring directly at him. The man—coupled with the strange feel of the place; add to that the distant gunfire—it all made Lake uneasy.

"I wonder who that is," Lake said uncharacteristically.

"I don't know, sir." Chase looked surprised that the sour Lake would make conversation with him. "But he looks like he's interested in our ship, doesn't he? You want me to take him, sir?" the eighteen-year-old joked immaturely as he clutched the rifle in a mock-ready stance.

"Nah." Lake grinned. "Better not. When I get off this pig, I don't want to spend the rest of my life in the Federal pen."

As Lake headed down the bridge hatch, he cast one last glance at the *Hatta*. The man was still there, the smoke from his pipe swirling above his head, his stare unbroken.

*   *   *

"SECURE the main engines, Maneuvering, aye," the electrical plant operator, Electrician's Mate Second Class Peters, said into the sound-powered phone set hanging around his neck. He swung around in his chair to face Van Peenan standing next to the watch officer's desk. The other operators in the maneuvering room obediently attended to their own panels, not wishing to provoke the wrath of the engineer.

"Well, Peters?" snapped Van Peenan. "I'm waiting, damn it!"

"We have the word, sir. Didn't you hear me acknowledge the order?"

"How many times do I have to keep fucking saying this, gentlemen? Verbatim repeat backs! I want verbatim repeat backs." Van Peenan scowled from one operator to the next, each avoiding his gaze, including the watch officer, Ensign Yi, who was sitting at the desk. "You fucking pieces of shit cost me the ORSE because you weren't following standard engineering practices! Now, when you get a fucking order from the officer of the deck, you fucking repeat it back word for word to the engineering officer of the watch, then *he* gets permission from me! Is that fucking clear?"

"Yes, Eng," Peters said impassively. He then turned to Yi and, in an emotionless voice, said, "Engineering Officer of the Watch, sir, from the officer of the deck, secure the main engines, sir."

"Secure the main engines, aye," Yi said promptly, then turned to Van Peenan. "Engineer, sir, request permission to secure the main engines and to place the engine room in an in-port steaming line-up."

"That's fucking better," Van Peenan said, more restrained. He would teach these assholes how to do their jobs correctly if it was the last thing he did. "Very well, Engineering Officer of the Watch. Secure the main engines and place the engine room in an in-port steaming line-up."

"Secure the main engines and place the engine room in an in-port steaming line-up, aye, sir," Yi acknowledged.

Van Peenan eyed Yi pathetically as the young ensign picked up the desk microphone and feebly relayed the order over the engine room loud speaker.

"*With some balls*, please, Mr. Yi! I don't want any of your watchstanders out there to miss an order because of your damned mealy-mouthed bedside voice."

"Aye, aye, sir," Yi responded weakly.

Though he was mere inches from Yi's right ear, the ensign avoided eye contact with him, instead looking straight ahead at the panels in front of the row of operators. Van Peenan shook his head in disgust. Not only was his department plagued with a group of loser sailors, he had the weakest bunch of lame-brained junior officers ever to sail a ship. And Yi led the pack.

The room was silent as Van Peenan looked for the next blaring deficiency. None of the men in the room dared speak unless it was to give a required report. Peters spoke into his phone set as he received the order acknowledgments from the engine room's various watch stations. On a small board beside his panel, he checked off each station with a grease pencil as they reported in.

". . . Engine Room Lower Level, Maneuvering, aye . . . Engine Room Upper Level, Maneuvering, aye . . . Engine Room Supervisor, Maneuvering, aye . . . Auxiliary Electrician Aft, Maneuvering, aye." He checked off the last one, and turned to Yi. "Engineering Officer of the Watch, all stations acknowledge the order to secure the main engines and place the engine room in an in-port steaming line-up."

Van Peenan looked at his watch.

"Fuck!" he said, then wrenched the microphone from Yi's hands. "Give me that thing!"

"This is the engineer!" his voice echoed from the speakers outside the sealed room. "It took two whole minutes for the engine room to acknowledge that last order. That's unsat, gentlemen! I want it done in thirty seconds next time, or we'll be running drills all the way back to Pearl!"

Shoving the microphone back at Yi, Van Peenan boiled inside.

It was a damn conspiracy, for sure. They were *trying* to

fuck up, he just knew it. They knew they had him by the balls, and they were starting to squeeze. Things had changed after the captain's mast. They no longer feared him. And what the hell did they care if they failed the next ORSE? It made no difference to them. Only he would get fired over it. They'd take their failing grade and continue on, business as usual—but with a *new engineer.* That would probably make them all very happy. He hated every last lazy one of them.

Just then Peters' phone whooped again.

"Maneuvering," Peters answered, while Van Peenan watched. Silent seconds followed as the person on the other end spoke. Peters listened, shooting a momentary glance at Van Peenan, then quickly turning away. Cupping his hand around the mouthpiece, he muttered something into it that sounded like, "This isn't a good time right now."

"What did you say?" Van Peenan demanded. "This isn't a good time for what?"

Peters turned in his chair, then hesitated.

"Tell me, Peters, damn you! This isn't a good time for what?"

"It's the port side main steam root valve watch, sir. He's calling to ask for a head break. Says he's got to go really bad."

"Asking for a head break while we're in the middle of changing engine room line-ups? Tell him, tough shit! He can fucking hold it!"

Peters nodded, then relayed the answer to the main steam root valve watchstander.

As Van Peenan fumed over the lack of professionalism, the room returned to its former thick silence. He imagined what would happen if someone called Maneuvering for a head break while the ORSE inspectors were on board.

Then a thought suddenly entered his head.

"*Who* is the port side root valve watch, Peters?" he asked pointedly.

Peters turned again in his chair, his expression filled with trepidation.

"It's Petty Officer Dean, sir."

Instantly, Van Peenan felt the blood rush to his head, the

telltale vein protruding on his temple. He gripped the side of Yi's steel chair until it visibly shook with him. The room suddenly felt smaller, stuffy, confined. A thousand thoughts occupied his stressed mind all at once. Thoughts of career, of promotion, of all his struggles to get where he was, and thoughts of conspiracy.

He looked at each of the men in the room. They watched their panels, seeming to pay him no mind. But he knew better. He still had the wherewithal to realize he was losing it in front of these men, and that they were carefully monitoring his every move out of the corners of their eyes, recording every moment to retell their shipmates over the evening meal.

"I'll be in my stateroom," he managed to say to Yi.

The latch to the room's sliding door felt cold in his hand as he muscled it open and stepped outside into the hot air of the engine room. It was always hot when the ship was steaming pierside, and at this moment he was thankful for it. Warm bay water didn't have near the cooling capacity of the cold ocean depths. And the warm air felt good for some reason as his forehead broke out in a sweat. The white noise of steam rushing through the pipes overhead was strangely soothing to his troubled mind.

Heading aft he walked along the bank of circuit breaker panels lining the port side and froze suddenly when he noticed a sailor hovering over the ladder well just ahead. The sailor wore a phone headset and had his back to him.

It was Dean.

A valve hung from the overhead above him, its hydraulic controller only an arm's reach away. In this part of the engine room, the main steam header ran along the overhead toward the main engines. Whenever the steam plant was operating in port, a mechanic was always stationed at the root valve. In the unlikely event that the main engine throttles suddenly came open, the mechanic would shut the root valve, thereby stopping steam to the engines, hopefully before the ship went barreling into any nearby ships. Although the valve controller was easily within the mechanic's reach, it was sometimes difficult to operate because it hung directly over the port-side ladder well, the only vertical ladder anywhere on the ship to traverse all three of *Providence*'s levels in one sheer thirty foot drop. It was a boring watch to stand, and Dean with his full bladder hovered over this very ladder staring down into the open well as he fidgeted from side to side on the very brink of the steep drop.

Van Peenan suddenly had an evil thought as he watched the young sailor he believed to be responsible for the conspiracy. Checking fore and aft and certain that no one was nearby, Van Peenan advanced toward the unsuspecting Dean, the source of all his misery.

Moments later, he found himself directly behind Dean, waiting for the right moment when his fidgeting left him off balance. Then it came. And he pushed Dean forward with both hands, at the same time kicking his feet out from under him.

Dean gasped as he lurched toward the open well, his hands desperately reaching for a handhold, but in vain. He fell sideways through the opening, striking his head on the edge as he passed through, then disappearing from Van Peenan's sight. The coiled phone cord on the deck unraveled in a rush as Dean's falling body pulled the slack down with him. Van Peenan entertained a gleeful thought that he might be hanged, but that hope faded when he heard the two distinct thuds of Dean's body hitting the middle level opening's edge, followed a second later by it hitting the lower level deck thirty feet below.

Hmph! Van Peenan thought coldly as he ran his fingers along the loose phone cord. So there *was* enough slack after all.

The sound of rushing feet came from the lower level. The lower level watch had discovered Dean's body.

"Man down in engine room lower level!" the sailor far below shouted.

As much as Van Peenan desired to look down the ladder well at Dean's broken body, he didn't dare. Instead he carefully skirted the well's edge so as not to be seen by anyone looking up, then made his way rapidly but calmly to the forward compartment and his stateroom. Once there, he calmly closed the door behind him, sat at the small desk and waited for the certain call from Maneuvering, his mind clearer than it had been in months.

Within seconds, the phone on the bulkhead whooped as expected.

It was Ensign Yi. There had been a terrible accident.

"Don't worry, Mr. Yi," he said consolingly, a wicked smile on his lips. "I'll be right there."

Chapter 9

"AND the room we are dining in, Kaptan, once housed the Portuguese governor's library. Like the rest of the mansion that you saw before dinner, it is a relic of Bunda's best-forgotten past, when European powers exploited our islands for their rich resources."

Edwards regarded with courteous interest Bunda's portly mayor who sat at the head of the long ornate table. Next to him, Fremont looked on with unabashed enthusiasm, feeding on every detail. The finely dressed mayor, or *Walikota* as Edwards learned to call him, was gray-headed and appeared to be in his sixties. He had a pleasant countenance that was offset by wild darting eyes that perhaps indicated a trace of an inferiority complex. Earlier that evening and all throughout the tour of the old government buildings, the mayor seemed to show the same fixation for the colonial era, as if it had occurred days ago, not decades.

"I find this place fascinating, sir," Fremont chimed in. "Could I ask if that was a colonial cemetery we passed on the way to the government buildings this evening, just after we were met by that delightful Gamelan orchestra?"

"Feel free to go there tomorrow, Commander, if you wish," the mayor said, smiling. "I think you might find it interesting. You will find the headstones of mariners from every part of the world. Arab, Chinese, Dutch, Portuguese, English—they are all there. The dates give a glimpse into our turbulent past."

"Thank you, sir. I'd enjoy that very much," Fremont said gleefully, but drew a stern face once he caught Edwards' masked scowl. "Uh . . . but, I'm afraid I have duties on board ship tomorrow, sir. I appreciate the kind offer, though."

Before bringing Fremont along for the mayor's dinner, Edwards knew he would have to restrain him—the ship's most ardent history buff. He was infatuated with anything and everything to do with history, and had placed his desire to view ancient ruins or battlefields above his own safety during more than one port call. But he was an easy choice over the only other senior officers available this evening—Bloomfield and Van Peenan. As easily sidetracked as Fremont tended to get, he at least would not embarrass Edwards in front of the local mayor and his guests.

Edwards glanced around at the many conversing guests sitting at the mayor's table that evening. The dinner was a routine event that doubled as a meeting between the leaders from the various villages, government officials, and the military. Representatives of international N.G.O.'s were there too, including the United Nations Human Rights Commission. Everyone seemed to be discussing the growing crisis in the islands. They all conversed in English for the sake of their American guests, and Edwards found himself a bit humbled by the generosity of all those present. Perhaps it was for the sake of the U.N. people too, but either way it made him feel inadequate knowing only one language.

"Although I myself am from Ternate, only two hundred kilometers to the southwest of here," the mayor continued, "I sometimes feel like a colonial governor. All of this talk of rebellion, a battalion of marine commandos roaming my streets, and the naval rendezvous my little district seems to have become, it is a wonder the people don't side with the rebels in the jungle." The mayor gestured to the four blue naval uniforms and one marine uniform sitting along the opposite side of the table from the two white-clad American naval officers.

"Have no fear, Walikota Umar," the Indonesian two-star admiral, or *Laksda*, said, sitting directly across the table from Edwards. "The Tentara Nasional is here only to keep the peace. The marines are combing the forest to root out these insurgents as we speak. Once we have found them, we will blast them out of the countryside. Those we don't kill, we'll take back to Jakarta for questioning, and then the military will leave you to go about your lives in peace."

The mayor grinned briefly, then quickly assumed a straight face when he perceived the watchful eye of the United Nations envoy at the other end of the table. The suave middle-aged Frenchmen from the U.N. sat with his arms folded on the table and spoke quietly with one of the N.G.O. reps sitting next to him. By all appearances he was absorbed in the conversation and had not even heard the admiral's brash comment. But all experienced diplomats—no matter how absorbed they might appear—always kept an ear turned toward every other conversation in the room.

"But really, Laksda Syarif," the mayor continued, addressing the Indonesian admiral, "these are nothing more than rumors. Nothing more than boys in the hills. That is what my social secretary assures me. They could hardly have the capability to cause a widespread revolt in these islands." The mayor turned and raised his glass to the slightly built man with slicked back hair sitting to his left. "Is that not correct, Imam?"

The refined-looking secretary sipped from a wineglass, and then gave a slight nod to his mayor, a small smile appearing on his lips. Imam had been sitting silently throughout the whole evening, only responding when directly spoken to. Edwards had been inside the Indonesian culture for only six hours, but he already knew this man could not be trusted. Deviousness lurked behind those eyes, and more than once Edwards caught the man casting a glance in his direction before quickly looking away.

"Jakarta does not share your secretary's assessment, Walikota Umar," Rear Admiral Syarif said sternly. "Perhaps you are not aware of what's transpiring on your own islands. Boys in the hills do not shoot down passenger planes full of civilians. The separatist movement is gaining momentum here. We have seen an increase in the boldness of terror attacks in Aceh and Sulawesi too. Something is happening, and you would do well to restore *Pancasila* before the governor in Ternate moves to replace you."

"Pancasila, ah yes." Umar gave a nervous laugh, then glanced at Edwards. "But, we are being rude talking politics while we have guests here. Forgive us, Kaptan. We have not even asked about your unfortunate sailor. He is resting comfortably at the hospital, I trust?"

"Yes, most comfortably," Edwards replied. "You were very generous to offer care for him."

The news of Dean's fall had come as a shock just as Edwards donned his crisp half-polyester short-sleeved summer white uniform to leave for the dinner. Remarkably the young man had survived the fall, albeit with a concussion, two broken ribs, and a broken collarbone. The contusions on his head and body told the story. His head hit the lip of the upper ladder well, then—fortunate for him—his shoulder took the brunt of the impact on the lip of the middle level opening. It must have been a serious jolt, but it slowed his plummeting body just enough to prevent any internal injuries. Dean hit his head again when he finally reached the lower level deck, and now lay unconscious at the local hospital, if it could be called that. Edwards, along with *Providence*'s corpsman, had seen Dean to his room before coming to dinner. He couldn't remember the last time he had seen such filth. The hospital was a single-story, open-windowed, fly-infested structure that looked more like a shelter than a hospital. In America the building would be condemned and bulldozed on the spot. But as bad as it was, at least it had a larger bed for Dean to stretch out on in the place of his confined rack on board the *Providence*.

"He started to come around as I left," Edwards added. "He's just mumbling, but my corpsman says it's a good sign that his head's okay. Again, thank you for your most kind help."

"It is the least we could do for such a gallant *kaptan* and crew. Indeed, it is *we* who are indebted to you for saving the women on the *Mendar*. Our own navy obviously had better things to do." Umar shot a snide glance at the admiral.

"Hrmph!" Admiral Syarif muttered as he mouthed a bite of food.

"Anything you would like while you are here," Umar continued, "please feel welcome. Your sailors, of course, can peruse our shops and beaches if they would like. They need only use their identification cards as passports. I'm sure they will find this a most excellent place to relax from a long cruise at sea. I would advise against travel in the country, but the streets of our town have been free of violence thus far. In fact, we once had a vibrant tourist economy here before this most recent unrest began. We were fortunate to be spared the religious conflicts that have plagued the other Moluccas. Here, *Obed* and *Acang*, or should I say Christian and Muslim, live in peace together, sharing in this fruit basket of God's great blessings."

"Spared religious conflict, yes," the admiral snorted. "But free from the separatist vermin, I think not!"

"But surely, Laksda Syarif, you must be happy to have Kaptan Edwards here with his submarine, to add to your naval force, no? His presence will certainly put to rest these rumors of a rebel submarine prowling these waters. Hopefully, it will provide a sense of security to the merchant shipping that has abandoned our port in recent days."

Edwards cleared his throat, suddenly uncomfortable at the mayor's implication.

"With all respect, Walikota Umar," Edwards said politely. "We are here for one reason, and one reason alone, and that is to evacuate Dr. Whitehead as soon as possible. The United States has no intention of getting involved in any internal matters."

"Really, Captain?" a deep slurry voice interjected from the other end of the table. "I find that difficult to believe knowing firsthand your government's manner of conducting business."

Edwards looked down the table into the suspicious blue eyes of the United Nations envoy, Jean-Pierre Descartes. He had been introduced to the Frenchman earlier that evening. It had been an extremely curt introduction, with Descartes paying him the minimal obligatory courtesy required of his position. The rest of the evening Descartes had ignored him, not speaking one word to him—that is, until now.

"Isn't it curious that the United States government should send a nuclear submarine to evacuate a simple doctor from this forgotten corner of the world?" Descartes spat the words out of his curly, protracted lips, his tone conspicuous in its utter disgust for the country Edwards bore allegiance to. "Interesting that I was never informed of your coming, either."

Suddenly all conversation at the table drew silent and all watched Edwards' face for a response.

"A nuclear-*powered* submarine, Monsieur Descartes," Edwards corrected simply. "And I apologize if our presence here is alarming to you. ComSubPac is not in the habit of informing the U.N. on submarine movements."

"Nor is your government in the habit of keeping the U.N. informed about *anything*, Captain. I fear we're seeing the same cowboy diplomacy at work once again, gentlemen. Here you see the U.S. sending in armed forces to sabotage the U.N.'s efforts to resolve the conflict peaceably. What, has your government found weapons of mass destruction here too, Captain? Are there Al Queda hiding in the hills of these islands?"

Several of the N.G.O. representatives chuckled and slapped their hands on the table, obviously sharing the envoy's sentiments. The Indonesian officers laughed, too—all but one. A lieutenant commander, or *mayor* in Indonesian ranks, sat calmly with his arms crossed, his face placid, his dark eyes meeting Edwards' across the smoky space. Edwards could see that the Indonesian officer's eyes held no amusement, but rather sympathy for him. The man appeared to understand the awkward position he was in.

As a military man, Edwards would be completely out of place responding to the envoy's chiding comments. And though Edwards wanted to answer the smug Frenchman with several very colorful words, his discipline kept him from turning the dinner into an international incident. Anything he might say would simply give the French more ammunition at the U.N. General Assembly, as they tried to persuade the rest of the world to imbibe their bedrock policies of indecision and inaction while the unfortunate peoples of the world suffered at the hands of dictators and murderers.

Eventually, conversation resumed among the various parties, and when dinner concluded the guests moved to the parlor where those who weren't already smoking lit up cigarettes, turning the whole room into a foggy cloud within minutes. Edwards shared some words with Mayor Umar about arrangements to retrieve Dr. Whitehead from his mountain camp the following day, then he was abruptly cut out of Umar's presence by Descartes and his entourage, who obviously desired to speak to the mayor without him.

Edwards suddenly found himself standing alone. The room was alive with discussion, though he took part in none of it. Leaning against the far wall, Fremont's arms gesticulated wildly as he absorbed himself in a regional history talk with some of the local village chiefs. Edwards never felt comfortable in social functions. He could never make conversation as easily as Fremont, unless the conversation centered on nuclear physics and submarine systems. He believed himself a complete bore.

The smoky air was thick and Edwards wondered if it would expunge the oily stench that inundated his uniform from the months at sea. It had been ten years since the regulation prohibiting unrestricted smoking was enacted on U.S. warships, and in that time Edwards' eyes had grown accustomed to a smoke-free environment. Now, with the acrid air filling the parlor all around him, he could feel just how accustomed they had grown. His eyes began to feel dry and scratchy and he sought fresh air on the mansion's balcony, which extended beyond the parlor's open French doors.

The night air was humid but pleasantly warm. Thin mosquito netting hung from the roof and fell over the balcony's outer railing, keeping most of the million biting insects away. From the balcony's edge he could see the nearby government buildings, dimly lit here and there in a yellowish glow by the scanty streetlights. Beyond the government complex to the south, he could just make out the single lightpost that marked the hospital where Dean now lay. And beyond that sprawled the small town of Ujungpang. The dimly lit town was quiet this evening. It had a population of no more than seven or eight thousand, and it suddenly reminded Edwards of one of those sleepy urban farming communities he had visited so often in

Nebraska. Beside it, the bay glistened with the lights of fishing craft, but the most predominant lights came from the large loading cranes parked on the merchant pier, where *Providence* and the other warships now lay moored. He could just make out the silhouettes of the Indonesian ships, but his own ship was hidden by the pier. He doubted he could have seen it from this distance anyway since its low black hull was designed to blend in with the water. Beyond the town to the west lay a vast black expanse that he knew to be the tropical forest and foothills leading up to the mountain ridge.

Somewhere, several miles away, in a jungle village beyond the ridge, Dr. Whitehead would be preparing for his departure. Tomorrow Edwards would send a shore party to fetch him. The thought of sending some of his men across that dense jungle made him uneasy, but he had no choice. Originally, he hadn't planned to send anyone ashore, but when Umar's people finally contacted Whitehead by radio late that afternoon, the doctor had insisted on a military escort across the rebel-seeded countryside.

That's just what I need, Edwards thought, *a demanding rider. He's not even aboard my ship yet and that son of a bitch is already placing demands on me.*

But the day's turn of events hadn't been all bad. By a stroke of luck, the doctor happened to have a daughter in Ujungpang working for one of the N.G.O.'s at the hospital. She had come to the government offices shortly after *Providence*'s arrival and had offered transportation to and from her father's camp. Frankly, Edwards was surprised to see her since his orders stated nothing about her. This was the first he had heard of Whitehead's daughter. Nevertheless, he was grateful for her help and had offered to evacuate her too, before she curtly informed him in so many words that she had renounced her U.S. citizenship and was now a Canadian citizen. She was determined to stay, and he did not make the offer a second time.

At least the doctor was willing to leave, Edwards thought, thankfully. Normally, medical people of his caliber, those who put the natural desire for profit aside and exercised their

professional skills among those who could never hope to pay
for them, would turn away any offer for evacuation, instead
choosing to suffer the same fate awaiting their patients. It was,
at least, one less thing he had to grapple with at the moment.

The sound of distant gunfire floated across the forest on the
heavy night air. Perhaps Admiral Syarif's marines had found
some rebels, or perhaps they had found some innocent farmers they would later claim to be rebels.

"Will my smoking here disturb you, Captain?"

Edwards was half-startled by the sudden voice behind him,
and he turned to see the Indonesian officer who had not
laughed at Descartes' joke standing on the balcony. He was a
full eight inches shorter than Edwards, but his confident demeanor gave him a virtual stature several inches higher. His
dark black hair, accentuated by a high hairline, framed a very
round and pleasant face, and the slight smile on his lips was
not betrayed by the sparkling Asian eyes that creased at their
edges as the smile grew wider. His blue naval uniform was
loosely casual but immaculate, and the gold leaf embroidered
on his shoulder boards twinkled in the light emanating from
the parlor behind him. In one hand he carried a curved
wooden pipe and in the other a lit match, which he held away
from the pipe while awaiting Edwards' reply.

"No," Edwards said, smiling politely. "I don't mind at all.
I'm just admiring the view from up here."

The man nodded, then lit the pipe and puffed out several
sweet-smelling clouds of smoke. He joined Edwards by the
rail and stared distantly into the night.

"I do so detest the chimerical diatribes of bureaucrats," he
said. "Especially those which are filled with promises but lack
any real substance. The air is much cleaner out here. Even for
smoking."

Edwards nodded, not knowing quite what to say, but the officer seemed to sense the awkwardness and extended a hand.

"I do not think we were ever introduced, Captain. My
name is Peto Triono. I command the KRI *Hatta*, moored just
ahead of your ship."

"An excellent looking submarine, sir," Edwards said, shaking the extended hand.

"Thank you." Triono eyed Edwards sparingly. "Actually— we have met before, Captain. Once, several years ago."

Edwards gave a puzzled look. He could see some familiarity but honestly couldn't place the face with the moment. He couldn't imagine when he would have met an Indonesian naval officer.

"It was during the Pacific Rim exercises in Pearl Harbor in 1998. I was an aid to our Admiral Agung, who went there as an observer. You were working on the SubPac staff at the time and gave many excellent briefings each morning for all of the visiting flag officers from other countries."

Of course, Edwards thought. He remembered now, though he was embarrassed that he hadn't recalled Triono's name.

"Very nice to see you again, Lieutenant Commander, or should I say *Mayor* . . ."

"Please, Captain. Call me Peto. I would not trouble you to learn our naval ranking system. I will call you 'Captain,' because I couldn't think of using a more familiar term with one I hold in such respect."

"I certainly don't deserve any . . ."

"Yes, you do, Captain," Peto interrupted. "The others in there may not show much appreciation for what you did for the *Mendar*, but *I* am from this island. I knew the family aboard the *Mendar* well. I have a special appreciation for the risk you took in helping them. What you have done for them will not be forgotten."

"Anyone else would have done the same. We just happened to be there at the right time."

"You and I both know that is not true, Captain. We both command ships, and we both know the potential costs of what you did. Such actions are far more often career-ending moves than stepping stones to promotion. Most American captains, I think, would have sailed away. But you, you helped them because you are an honorable man." Peto glanced back into the parlor and added distantly, "Unlike Admiral Syarif, who could not even dispatch the corvette to assist you. Be assured, the people here are grateful for what *you* have done."

Edwards felt ill at ease with Peto's praise, especially since he still felt guilty for not responding fast enough to save the male members of the *Mendar*'s crew.

Again, the distant sound of gunfire interrupted his thoughts.

"The jungle is lively this evening," Edwards commented. "Your marines must be busy out there. It's giving me second thoughts about sending my men across the island tomorrow to get Dr. Whitehead."

"You are wise, Captain. There is much discontent in these islands, shared by both commoners and merchants alike. Walikota Umar underestimates the size of this insurrection. The governor in Ternate appointed him Walikota of this district. He is not from here and does not have the pulse of these people. Umar was right about the religious tranquility, but he is wrong on the motive. Christians and Muslims have always lived in harmony here only because they could agree on the greater evil that plagues them both, the central government in Jakarta. It is rumored that the central government incited the religious violence in the southern Moluccas to keep the people there distracted away from any separatist movements. Military troops were sent in to restore order, giving the population a sense of dependency on the central government for security. If Jakarta is attempting the same thing here with our ships and marines, it is making a grievous mistake. People here will view our presence as an act of oppression. I know. I have been listening to the dissidents on this island since I was a child." Peto shrugged. "But I am a mere junior officer, and my words carry no weight with Walikota Umar. He will not listen to me. Nor will Admiral Syarif. They do not care what motivates the rebels here, only how to eradicate them."

"What motivates them?" Edwards asked. "The rebels, I mean. What do they want?"

"What did the thirteen colonies in North America want two hundred years ago, Captain? Freedom from a distant government that takes their tax money and resources, providing little in the way of infrastructure, security, or representation in return. The *Mendar* incident is a perfect example. Admiral Syarif received your message requesting assistance, but did he send any help? He cares more about crushing this revolt than he does about protecting our fishermen from piracy. And I'm afraid he is a mirror image of the sentiments in Jakarta. The central government wants the rich resources of these islands, but none of the social responsibilities. It's almost like another colonial power."

"And yet you're an officer in the Tentara Nasional," Edwards commented, quizzically.

"I said I was *from* here, Captain, not that I was born here." Peto eyed Edwards briefly. A momentary shade of sadness fell across his face, as if his mind had strayed to some dark memory. He looked like he was about to say something, but then hesitated, smiling gently. "Would you *know my stops*? Or *sound me from my lowest note to the top of my compass*?"

Edwards thought it odd to hear an Indonesian naval officer quoting Shakespeare. But if he had learned anything in the last few hours, it was that he was a stranger in a strange land. A thought suddenly crossed his mind that he might have offended Peto with his direct question. He remembered something about obtuse conversation being the code of conduct in Southeast Asia. But before he could voice any kind of apology, Peto spoke again.

"Where are you from, Captain? What state?"

"Nebraska," Edwards answered evenly.

"Ah, the Great Plains!" Peto said excitedly. "An endless mass of land covered with corn and livestock!"

"You've seen it then?"

"Yes, yes. I have seen it once. I went to university in America and once rode on a bus that crossed Nebraska on one of your great highways. I never thought it would end. How old are you, Captain?"

Edwards paused for a moment thinking the question oddly out of place, but eventually answered. "Thirty-eight."

Peto nodded, then looked off into the dark night. "I am

forty-two years old, Captain. When you were a baby in the rich American Midwest, I was a little boy living a meager existence with my family in a small village in eastern Java. We were poor, but happy. Or at least I was happy, in my own little world. I know now that my parents were not. Children have a way of making the most out of the beauty in the world around them. Of course, it's the real world that decides our fate as children, and the real world was in chaos during those years, growing ever more polarized by the magnetic pull of the two great superpowers. Our young republic was feeling the temptation of communism and our then President Sukarno had begun to court the nation's blossoming communist party. Little did I know at the time—and of course I was too young to know—but my father and most of our village were members of the communist party. The idea of communism must have been appealing to those poor villagers who looked on it as a means to share some of the country's wealthy resources. I remember very little about those years, but I do remember that my father seemed to be happier with each passing day. I'm sure he must have been excited for the party's future.

"Then in 1965, a group of militants attempted a coup, murdering several high-ranking army generals, and shortly thereafter everything in my little world changed. The communist party was blamed for the coup and the ensuing backlash was directed at all those who were members. The population rose up against the communists in a blood bath that lasted several months. Entire villages were purged—indeed massacred—including mine. All was in the name of defending the republic from the evil communist scourge, but many long-standing scores were being settled at the same time." Peto glanced at Edwards briefly, then continued distantly, "One night that year, perhaps while you, Captain, were being tucked in by your mother in your warm nursery in Nebraska, I awoke in my single-room bamboo house to see my parents being dragged out the door and led away. I was placed on a truck with the rest of the children, where we watched our village burn to the ground through our young teary eyes. Then we were driven far away, never to see our parents again. Years later I learned that they were murdered that night and buried in a mass grave a few kilometers away.

"I was actually luckier than most of the children. Many of them died young deaths on the streets, but I had an uncle who was a naval officer who found me and took me in as his own. But even he and his family were under scrutiny, since it was rumored that the navy had a part in the attempted coup. When the Suharto regime started the policy of transmigration in the early seventies, we moved to Bunda and settled here. And this is where I spent the rest of the days of my youth."

"I'm so sorry," Edwards said. He could see the emotion in Peto's eyes, and he felt guilty at having brought such painful memories to the surface. "I didn't mean to pry . . ."

Peto waved a hand. "It isn't all sad, Captain. I *did* end up joining the navy, of course, and earning a commission. I eventually went to engineering school in the United States, and now I command the newest submarine in the Tentara Nasional. All are things I never would have done growing up in that dirty village as the son of a poor communist. In my adult years I have come to learn that my father was a simpleton. A small-minded, misguided fool."

Edwards fought back the urge to talk about his own father's absence during his childhood, the Vietnam years when his father was deployed overseas. Misery loved company, but his did not compare with Peto's.

Just then a young Indonesian sub-lieutenant emerged from the parlor, seeking Peto's attention. Peto excused himself and the two conversed in Bahasa Indonesian near the doorway. Obviously the young man was one of Peto's officers and he reminded Edwards of his own Ensign Yi. The two were probably conversing about some critical repair issue aboard the *Hatta*, and the thought made Edwards dread seeing his own ship's repair list when he returned later that evening.

After a few minutes, Peto dismissed the young officer and returned to the railing.

"Forgive me, Captain," he said, "but I must return to my ship at once. The *Hatta* may be new, but like any ship she is prone to equipment failures at inopportune times."

"Of course."

Peto made a move to leave, then turned again to face Edwards. "I have enjoyed our conversation, Captain. And I hope I have not left you with the wrong impression of me. It would trouble me deeply if you sailed away tomorrow thinking of me as a disgruntled son."

"That's not my impression in the least," Edwards said, almost apologetically.

"All the same, it would ease my conscience if you could come to my ship for lunch tomorrow. The road over the mountains to the north shore is rocky and steep. It will take your men at least three hours to get to Dr. Whitehead's camp. They won't get back until late in the afternoon. There should be plenty of time for lunch and a tour of my ship before they return. That is, if you are interested, Captain?"

Edwards thought of the million things he had to do on *Providence* before they departed, but his interest was piqued. Not many U.S. navy officers, if any, had been on board a Type 214 submarine. It was the chance of a lifetime, and the submariner in him knew he could not refuse. Besides, it would make the long hot day go by faster.

"Name the time," he said with a grin, "and I'll be there."

AUBREY Van Peenan sat naked in the dim lighting at the foot of the tousled single bed and drank down another glass of the acrid liquor before dragging hard on a cigarette. The owner had called it whiskey, but it tasted like it came from a donkey's ass. The small square room's thick air reeked of residual alcohol, smoke, urine, semen, and other unidentifiable aromas from the countless inhabitants preceding him. Its scanty furniture was filthy beyond belief and he assumed he didn't want to see how it looked during the daytime, probably the only time the room ever had adequate lighting.

"Quit your sniveling, you bitch!" Van Peenan snapped at the small form huddled up under the sheets at the opposite end of the bed.

A few muffled sobs were the only response.

The last few hours were like a blur to him and the whiskey had helped little to take the edge off his troubled mind. Neither the whiskey nor the rough sex he had forced on the unwilling naked prostitute now crying on the bed would make his troubles go away. Dean was still alive. And worse, the third-class petty officer could come to at any moment, and remember. Surely the concussion would cause some memory loss, but would he remember that he was pushed? That was the question that weighed heavily on Van Peenan's mind.

The thought had come over him while Dean was being transferred to the hospital ashore. With horror he had realized that if Dean woke up and remembered the push, it would only take a short investigation to determine that he was the culprit. In desperation, he knew that he had to get ashore and do something. It was easy enough to get permission from Bloomfield to run ashore, under the guise that he was checking in on Dean. But once ashore he didn't go anywhere near the hospital, for fear that he might try to strangle Dean's unconscious body with his bare hands. So, instead he followed the string of Indonesian sailors leading to Ujungpang's tiny red-light district where now he sat in a whorehouse drinking himself to oblivion.

The woman he was given was no more than eighteen or nineteen, and he used her body every way he could during the first part of the night. But the thought of Dean mentally blocked every sensation in his body. When the exhausted woman finally tried to leave, he got angry and beat her until she submitted to another several hours of sexual slavery. But, he never stopped thinking about Dean.

He couldn't wipe Dean from his brain. Not with all the dirty whiskey, not with sex from any cheap whore. Dean would certainly remember, and Van Peenan's hard-won, illustrious career would be over. He'd be court-martialed, convicted, then sent to Fort Leavenworth to spend the next twenty years to life. What was once an honorable service record, listing many distinguished accomplishments and the prospect of command in his future, would be replaced with a prisoner record.

Outside the door, Van Peenan heard several voices belonging to noisy drunk Indonesian sailors mingling with laughing female voices as their owners rustled down the hall to another room. Then a knock came at the door to his room and the bar's owner tipped his head in.

"Bapak?" he called. "Is everything to your liking?"

The man's eyes got wide when he noticed the woman sobbing on the bed, and he ran over to her.

"Oh my God, Bapak!" he cried, holding the woman up and examining her puffy and bruised face with probing hands. "What have you done? I gave you this girl because she is one of our best, and now you have lowered her value. Please leave my place at once, Bapak."

As the owner ushered the woman out of the room, shaking his head in disgust, Van Peenan reached out and grabbed his arm. The man turned with a scowl, but his countenance instantly changed when he noticed Van Peenan's hand held a wad of U.S. cash in large bills.

"I'll make it up to you," Van Peenan said. "Here's five hundred dollars."

The owner pushed the girl out into the hall without another thought and snatched up the cash with a gleeful grin.

"There's more where that came from if you can do something else for me."

The man stared at the money for several moments, as if he were already spending every penny.

"Of course, Bapak," he said in a much more conciliatory tone. "Can I get you another girl? More whiskey? Or maybe you would like some heroin? Or weed perhaps?"

"No, none of that shit." Van Peenan withdrew another wad of cash from his pants draped across the foot of the bed. "Here's another five hundred. I'll bring you four thousand more from my ship if you can do what I ask."

"What is it, Bapak?" the man said, eyeing the money.

"There's a sailor in the hospital here. An American sailor. I don't want him to ever leave the hospital."

The owner appeared confused for a moment, then his face drew tight as Van Peenan's meaning sank in.

"I do not do such things, Bapak," he said, shaking his head.

"Look, you son of a bitch, I've got eyes in my head. I know business is tight around here. These navy sailors don't get paid jackshit. A place like this needs tourists and merchant seaman with their fat wallets, or it falls flat on its face. And you probably haven't had a merchant ship stop by here in weeks. Shit, you're probably taking a loss right now."

Van Peenan could see that his words were hitting the right nerves as the owner's eyes stared more and more longingly at the wad of bills in his hand. Four thousand dollars would probably support his operation for several months. In Southeast Asia, the American dollar still had a high value, unlike its standing in Western Europe.

"I'm offering you a quick profit," he continued. "To make up for the bad weeks you've had, and the bad ones that are sure to come. Four thousand dollars can go a long fucking way. Hell, with that money you could even move your little operation somewhere else more lucrative."

Clutching the cash already in his hand, the owner appeared to undergo a moral dilemma. Obviously he was already caught up in dealing drugs, and probably other things, too. Killing would just be another vice to add to the list. Van Peenan's alcohol-saturated mind hoped that his money would be enough.

"Look," Van Peenan finally offered, "if you don't want to do it, find somebody who will and split the money with him. I'll even raise it to five thousand dollars."

The man's eyes grew wide and locked on Van Peenan in an untrusting stare.

"Believe me, you'll have it! Would I give you all this money up front if I were lying to you? Just get the job done, and I'll fetch the rest from my ship. But you can bet on one thing. If you don't do it, me and my money will sail away tomorrow and you'll be left running this fucking pig-hole whorehouse for the rest of your life!"

The man slowly reached out and pulled the money from Van Peenan's hand. With slightly trembling hands he carefully smoothed out each bill lengthwise. One at a time, he

Chapter 10

"SON of a bitch!" Chief Michaelson exclaimed from the open back seat of the jolting jeep as it caught air on a pothole in the winding mountain road.

"This road too bumpy for you, Chief?" the young woman in the driver's seat called back playfully, her short brown hair blowing in every direction. The sunglasses hid the amusement in her eyes.

"No, ma'am," Michaelson said, deep and manly, as he grabbed a firm hold on the jeep's roll bar, obviously determined never to utter another sound about the wild ride she was taking them on. His other hand clutched the stock of an M-16 rifle draped across his lap, the butt end poking into the skinny thigh of Reynoso, who was crammed in the back seat next to him. Reynoso sat silently, his eyelids sagging from the long morning drive. Between his long, spindly legs his hands clutched a silvery suitcase containing the ship's portable radio equipment.

From the front passenger seat, Lake glanced back at the brawny torpedo chief and the scrawny radioman. He received a scowl from Michaelson, who was obviously less than thrilled to be under his command for the day. The feeling was mutual, and Lake gave him a cynical smile before turning back to the road before them, instantly facing into a cloud of dust kicked up by the police vehicle on the rocky road up ahead. Lake had to remove his sunglasses between jostles to wipe the dust from his eyes.

"You're turning pinker than a baboon's ass!" the woman said smiling, a mischievous look in her eye.

Lake wished she would keep her eyes on the road, but she seemed to know this narrow highway like the back of her hand. He leaned out and glanced at his face in the sideview mirror. White circles appeared around his eyes surrounded by sunburned flesh. He had forgotten to put on sunscreen before leaving the ship that morning, and his skin was suffering from prolonged periods away from the sun, submerged for months in artificial light in the dark recesses of the ocean.

"There's some sunscreen in the glove compartment!" she shouted as the jeep hit a rock and bounced a foot in the air.

Lake nodded and rustled around the glove compartment until he found it. He squeezed out a glob and applied it to his arms and face. The creamy lotion felt warm after sitting in the glove compartment all morning, but he felt instant relief. Holding it up to offer the same to Michaelson and Reynoso, he received a scowl from Michaelson, and Reynoso was dozing. Without a second offer he returned the tube to the glove compartment.

"Do you always drive this fast, Miss Whitehead?" he said, suddenly uncomfortable with the smirk she was sporting.

"Please, Lieutenant, call me Teresa. Miss Whitehead was my mother. And, no, I usually take this road faster, but that Japanese piece of shit up there is holding me back."

Lake glanced at the Bunda police force's mud-coated Japanese SUV leading their advance up the mountain road, then back at the smiling young woman. She was roughly his age, late twenties or early thirties probably, brown hair, blue eyes. Her face was fatless and what was obviously once flawless white skin was now tan and bore the slight glimpse of wrinkles when she smiled. She wore a tight-fitting white tank top that came down no further than her slim waist, and olive-drab cargo shorts cut just high enough to show the firm and shapely legs, tanned by the sun and disappearing into shin-high hiking boots, from which a pair of thick cotton socks peeked and accentuated her well-defined calves.

Lake had to force himself to look away from her. Normally he wouldn't be interested in her type, the rough and tumble tree-hugger, liberal, granola type. Not to mention she had a mouth on her worse than most sailors. But in six months he hadn't been this close to a woman and her mere presence was driving his senses wild with desire.

He had to admit, seeing her pull up at the pier with the Bunda police this morning was a pleasant surprise. When Edwards informed him the night before that he would be leading the shore party, his first instinct was that of irritation. Sure the place was beautiful, but he was going to have to drive the ship out of harbor late this afternoon, and then go on watch again at midnight when *Providence* was submerged. He always preferred to get a few hours' sleep before a long watch as officer of the deck. The watches were long enough when you were wide awake, but they seemed like an eternity when you were dead tired. Besides, he was a short-timer. Why would Edwards waste this opportunity on him and not on Coleman or one of the other junior officers who still might make a career out of the navy?

Either way, he had put aside his misgivings when he saw Miss Whitehead, or rather Teresa, would be their driver. She offset the glowering presence of Michaelson, who had volunteered to handle security for the trip before discovering that Lake was to lead. They had hardly said two words to each other the entire morning, and Lake wondered if Teresa could sense the tension between them.

Probably, he thought. She probably found it humorous, too. Her demeanor, though polite in her own way, had been one of almost insulting condescension since the moment they met her, and Lake felt certain that she regarded them as several notches below her level, as nothing more than silly little boys who still dressed up to play cowboys and Indians.

Then, of course, there was the ever-forthright Reynoso, who had volunteered to serve as radioman on the trip. Reynoso was the best radioman on board, and Lake was thankful for that. But he would really rather have one of the more junior radiomen on this trip. He didn't feel like dodging Reynoso's promotion package issue, which was bound to come up at some point during the long day.

The morning drive had been largely uneventful. Once they

had passed the Indonesian marines' checkpoint just outside Ujungpang, Lake half-expected to see guerillas with assault rifles emerge from the jungle on all sides. But it didn't happen. In fact, they had seen no one on the road at all. Even the small mountain villages they passed through an hour back had appeared deserted, and it gave Lake an uneasy feeling. He almost wished the guerillas would appear out of the forest. At least then he would know whether his fears were justified. The two-man police escort up ahead, while well-intentioned, provided him with little comfort. The dense forest on both sides of the road looked as if it had eyes, and only when they reached the mountain road and started to climb above the dense foliage did Lake start to breathe easier.

The mountain road ran a winding course along Bunda's eastern side, dodging in and out of the deep valleys created by the sharp crests jutting off the central mountain ridge. As the two-vehicle convoy made the dusty journey along the jagged mountain range between thick patches of forest and bends in the road, Lake caught glimpses of the vast turquoise ocean running to the horizon as far as his eyes could see. Living on a submarine afforded very few moments to view the ocean from a high altitude, and he found himself enthralled by the pristine view. Whenever the road wrapped around the outer edge of one of the long ridges descending from Bunda's spine, he could see the small island to the north that he had seen earlier while piloting through the reefs. If Bunda was for the most part undeveloped, then the northern island, Wijaya, appeared completely undisturbed by man. No roads, no villages, no traces of civilization anywhere to be seen. No wonder it was being used as a wildlife refuge, he thought.

Behind them now, several miles away and almost hidden by the promontory with the old Dutch fort, Ujungpang and its harbor speckled the coastline with reddish brown roofs, and from this height Lake could easily discern the treacherous reefs appearing as distinct white lines beneath the water's surface. The white lines snaked all around the harbor's entrance and around most of Bunda's coastline.

He noticed Teresa was watching him as he studied the surroundings.

"The island appears peaceful, almost deserted," he said in an attempt to make conversation.

"It is," she answered, "up here on the north side anyway. The rebel group is concentrated around Ujungpang. We passed through their units about an hour ago."

"Units? I didn't see anything. You make it sound like they're an army."

"They were there, Lieutenant. Sure as shit, watching us from the jungle. And yes, they are an army of sorts. An army of pissed-off fishermen, miners, and farmers, all with a grievance against the Indonesian government, all wanting autonomy and freedom."

Lake stared into the sloping forest on both sides of the road as if they were still flanked by unseen, armed men.

"Don't worry," she said, smiling. "We're safe up here. Their grievance isn't with us, anyway. They're only interested in the Tentara Nasional forces. And I don't blame them, either. I've only been on Bunda for a little over a month now, but I've been here long enough to see what the military has done to these people. Murders, rapes, torture, vandalism, you name it. Rumor has it, they've been trying to spark a religious war on these islands for years."

"So you've spoken with them? You've actually discussed this with the rebel group?"

She glanced at him, slightly annoyed. "It's kind of hard not to, Lieutenant, seeing as how they're everywhere. They're in every village, even in Ujungpang. Hell, some of them are my dad's friggin' patients. This is an island-wide movement, and I don't think Jakarta quite understands that. They're going to need a whole lot more than a couple hundred marines to stop them."

"That doesn't seem to concern you? I mean, the Indonesian government is kind of your protection here, isn't it? If *Providence* hadn't arrived to evacuate you—"

"You're *not* here to evacuate *me*, Lieutenant!" she interrupted. "I'm not going anywhere! You're here for my father because he's an American citizen and he's agreed to go. My father's a good man. He couldn't bear the thought of a U.S. serviceman getting hurt trying to save him. That's the only reason he's going with you. I, on the other hand, am a Canadian citizen. I denounced my U.S. citizenship long ago, and I'm staying right here."

Lake had wondered why his orders mentioned nothing about Dr. Whitehead's daughter. The Canadian government must not be too concerned about Teresa Whitehead's safety. After the few hours he'd spent with her, Lake couldn't say that he blamed them.

"When the United States ignored the rest of the world's opinion," she continued, "and started bombing people in the name of fighting terrorism—terrorism that they and their fucked up foreign policies created—I decided I didn't want to be a part of it anymore. I couldn't stand the thought of my tax money buying bombs that people like you would later drop on innocent civilians.

"My father's made a life out of helping people in some of the world's most isolated places. He helps those who can't pay him back. It's our extension of humanity toward these people that is our protection, Lieutenant. But, I'd hardly expect you to understand that. The world is one big family of peoples of all colors and religions. We have to understand each other in order to have peace. We can't just label someone an enemy because they look different, or because they pray to God in a different way, or even to a different god. My father understands that. It's a shame the U.S. government does not. Dropping bombs on defenseless people will only make more hate. Embracing people with open arms and learning how you can help them will endear them to you. My father and I have proven that. Our safe passage through the rebel lines is the proof. These people see us as helpers, not hurters. And they've accepted us into their community, regardless of the color of our skin or religion. And we've accepted them in return."

Lake hadn't heard so much liberal-speak since he left the

Bay area. Normally he'd find it refreshing after long periods with the staunchly conservative officers on the *Providence*, but after all he'd experienced in the last few years it struck him as strangely narrow-minded. He knew he'd been in the navy too long because he suddenly felt offended by her assertion that "people like him" would intentionally drop bombs on innocent civilians.

"The world is not black and white, Lieutenant," she continued. "It's shades of gray—"

"Excuse me?" Lake heard himself say. She was treating him like an uneducated fool and he had had enough. "If I'm not mistaken, Miss Whitehead, these same rebels you're talking about shot a plane down and killed a bunch of people a couple weeks ago. Tell me where's the gray in that."

Teresa looked across at him, obviously surprised at his interruption, especially since he had hardly spoken all morning. For an instant Lake thought he had gone too far in expressing his opinion to a civilian. The rigid code of conduct for any American military man was to treat all civilians with courtesy and respect, never giving a voice to any personal opinions or political views. If the captain ever found out, he'd be certain to get a reprimand for it. But then he thought, *What the hell. I'm a short-timer. The worst he can do to me is extend my tour of duty, and he's already done that!*

"A terrorist's a terrorist, Miss Whitehead, no matter what way you slice it. Why should we try to understand the guy that squeezed the trigger to shoot down that plane? Why should we try to understand the guy who put a roof over his head? Why should we try to understand anyone who would lend him assistance? Whatever's happened to that guy in his life, nothing justifies setting out to kill innocent people." Lake checked his volume, suddenly realizing that Michaelson in the back seat was probably listening to every word. "And by the way, contrary to popular belief, *people like me* don't just go around targeting innocent civilians. I know, because I've fired the missiles. Several times, in fact. Every time the intended target was military or else it was some terrorist camp. Sure, some civilians were probably killed too. That's the way the terrorist operates. He places himself around as many women and children as he can. But that's the fucking breaks! Does it keep me up at night sometimes knowing I probably killed some innocent people? You bet your ass, it does! But then I have to wonder what kind of man would let his family serve as a human shield for those killers. And that helps some. It helps me to know that there's nothing on God's green earth I could have done about it, and that some people are alive today because that terrorist wasn't able to blow them up."

Teresa did not respond immediately, and they drove on in silence for another mile before any words passed between them.

"Did you ever wonder why you were ordered to come here, Lieutenant? Ever wonder why the United States government gives a shit about some medical doctor taking care of patients in the jungle? After all, my father never asked to be evacuated."

"I would assume because he's an American citizen."

"Oh, bullshit!" she said, as the jeep took another pothole. "Rumors are alive about a terrorist cell operating from these islands. The terrorist Musa Muhammad and his group, Al Islamiyyah. Now can you put two and two together? The U.S. government just wants its citizens out of the way. Then it can let the Indonesian military do whatever it needs to do to put down this revolt, nabbing Muhammad and his group in the bargain. It's an act being played out on different stages all around the world. The United States turns a blind eye to the atrocities of the local authorities and in return they get their terrorists. Once *Providence* leaves port, the Indonesian marines will go on the offensive. But it won't be in the jungle where the rebels are. It'll be on the streets of Ujungpang. They'll make the people suffer to bring the rebels out of hiding."

"Any atrocities would certainly be reported by the U.N. or any of the N.G.O.'s in town," Lake offered.

"Oh, please! The U.N. will file a report. They'll talk a lot and have lots of meetings, but in the end they'll do nothing! They'll probably respond by pulling their team out. That's the way the fucking U.N. responds to a crisis situation. Look how long it took them to help out East Timor, for God's sakes! Besides, most people in the U.S. won't believe any report coming out of the U.N. That's why I'm staying, Lieutenant. I've seen firsthand the effects of the 'war on terror.' I've seen how it's destroyed the lives of innocent people in Afghanistan, Iraq, Yemen, Palestine, just to name a few. When my father wrote me that he might have to leave Bunda soon because of a military build-up here, I knew that I had to come. Of course, Father didn't want me to, but I quit my job with the Peace Corps and came here as soon as I could. And now I work at the hospital in Ujungpang. That's where I've been for the last month, and that's where I intend to stay until this whole thing is over. Only this time, I'm going to record everything I see. I'm going to log every beating, every rape, every torture, every murder and then share it with the world. I'm going to expose the 'war on terror' for all that it truly is!"

Lake stared out at the blue ocean so that he wouldn't have to look at her. He regretted his attempt at conversation and, of course, perished any thought of ever scoring with his dogmatic driver. It was just a sailor's fantasy, and probably a good thing too. Even her liberal mouth couldn't stop him from wanting to look at the shadow created by her breasts in the tight tank top.

He scolded himself. She probably only looked hot because he'd been at sea for so long. After a couple of months on land, he'd wonder what the hell he was thinking.

IT took another hour and forty minutes of jolting and jostling on the poorly maintained dirt road before they reached the camp, the jeep rolling in close behind the police vehicle late in the morning. She didn't say another word to him for the balance of the trip, and he was partially glad for it. He didn't care about her crusade to expose the U.S. government. He just wanted to get the doctor, get back to the *Providence* and head on home, watching movies in the wardroom the whole voyage back.

The camp was located in one of the few open green meadows Lake had seen on the long trip across the island. A long flat meadow nestled under the lee of a great jutting cliff projecting from Bunda's central ridge. A small drive turned off the mountain highway and disappeared into the meadow's tall grass, obviously seldom trampled by the tires of motor vehicles. The mountain highway kept running North, but Lake figured that it could not go much further. They had come back down in altitude, but before descending from the high road he had noticed Bunda's northern coast only a few miles away, along with a few fishing villages.

Both vehicles came to a stop in front of a cluster of makeshift tents and bamboo lean-tos at the far side of the meadow. The camp appeared to be deserted, with no vehicles parked outside. Of course, thought Lake, few of the locals would have vehicles, but still, the camp appeared to have once had a reasonable capacity. The only sign of inhabitance was a white flag attached to a small pole that also served as a stanchion for a large white canvas tent. The flag fluttered briskly in the coastal wind. When the jeep's engine finally shut off, Lake could hear the wind in the trees, and the jungle surrounding the meadow alive with a thousand birds.

Honk-honk! Honk-honk!

Teresa leaned on the jeep's horn, almost causing the half-dozing Reynoso to jump out of his seat and into Michaelson's lap.

"Sorry, Chief," Reynoso said to Michaelson, who ignored the radio petty officer as he scanned the jungle surrounding the meadow.

The two camouflaged policemen had emerged cautiously from their vehicle carrying their rifles at the ready, and Michaelson did the same with his M-16, looking as if he would shoot the first thing that moved from the thick trees.

"Would you put that thing away, Chief?" Lake said irritably. "We don't need to provoke anyone. We're just here to get the doctor and be on our way."

Then Lake hopped out of the jeep and landed with both feet in a soggy patch of mud. He had worn the cotton khaki uniform, by order of the captain since Edwards felt that the blue underway jumpsuit might be mistaken by the rebels for an Indonesian navy uniform. Whether they had convinced the rebels or not, his khaki pants were now splattered with Bunda's iron-rich red mud. The kind that stained permanently. The kind they colored T-shirts with in Hawaii. His misery was further compounded by the cool sensation he felt seeping along the soles of his feet. He'd worn low-top blue Sperry sneakers, the ones normally worn by *Providence*'s deck personnel for traction when handling lines. It was the closest thing he could find to a work shoe, and now he wished he'd brought his shipyard work boots on the deployment with him. They would have held up much better in this mud. But, space on a submarine was at a premium, and he probably couldn't have fit that extra case of Mountain Dew in his locker six months ago if he'd brought the bulky boots along.

As he scraped his shoes off on the bumper, he noticed that Michaelson had chosen not to obey him but rather to continue watching the trees like a hawk. A brief laugh came from Teresa who briskly walked toward the white tent, shaking her head, apparently amused by the silly military men.

Sighing heavily, Lake hurried to catch up with her, leaving Michaelson, Reynoso, and the two policemen with the vehicles.

Before Teresa reached the tent the mosquito netting that covered the entrance flew back and Lake saw the tanned bald top of a man's head emerge as he ducked out of the low opening. The man was Anglo and middle-aged and he instantly greeted Teresa with outstretched arms and a big grin, his white teeth outlined by a close-cut gray beard.

"Resa! It's so good to see you!"

Dr. Whitehead was far from what Lake had expected. His lean legs and arms, clearly visible in his loose flowery shirt and denim shorts, had the long muscles of a marathon runner. His skin was dark from many years living near the equator, and though his beard was gray his features were as young as any twenty-year-old.

"Oh, Papa." She smiled, hugging him and placing one arm tightly around his waist. "I wanted to spend some time with you before you go away." Her gaze fell to Lake who was waiting patiently a few paces away. "And besides, these guys need all the help they can get."

"How do you do, Doctor? I'm Lieutenant Scott Lake. I'm the communications officer on the USS *Providence*."

"Oh, yes, they told me," Whitehead said, his eyes never meeting Lake's but instead gazing beyond him at the men by the vehicles, as if he were examining them. His voice sounded distracted, almost as if he were in a trance. "They told me on the radio this morning that you had left Ujungpang. But the radio went dead soon after. I started to worry."

"I'm sorry, sir? Did you say you're having trouble with your radio?"

Whitehead paused for a moment, still staring at the other men, before turning his eyes directly at Lake. "Well, we don't want to keep your captain waiting, Lieutenant," he said in a suddenly energized voice. "We'd better get moving. Would you mind helping me with my bags? They're just inside here. Teresa, please help Mr. Lake's companions to the cooler by the tent over there. I've still got some sodas left from the last shipment, and I'm sure the road's made them thirsty."

Lake felt like he was in the wrong conversation, but chalking it up to "like father, like daughter," he followed Whitehead into the tent. Inside he found that he had just stepped into Dr. Whitehead's field hospital. Six cots lined one side of the tent, while a few tables and lockers lined the other. The two cots near the entrance were the only ones occupied. Dark-skinned men were lying on top of the sheets, cigarettes smoldering between their lips, their dark eyes locked on him from the moment he entered the room. Lake thought it strange that sick men would smoke in bed, let alone inside a hospital tent. Their piercing eyes carried more than just sickness behind them. These men were nervous about something. He didn't need a degree in psychology to tell that.

But before he could ponder any longer, Whitehead had his arm.

"These boys are from the fishing village down the road, Lieutenant," he said strangely. "Showed up just this morning.

Imagine the luck, they get the flu on the same day that I'm getting evacuated."

The men on the cots did not say anything. They did not smile either. They simply stared back at Lake, hands resting behind their heads, their faces blank.

"This way, Lieutenant."

Whitehead led him through a flap hanging at the far end of the tent that led into another small room. The room had a small table, a desk, and a cot—obviously Whitehead's working and living space. It appeared that most of the equipment had been packed up, except for a small CD player on the desk intoning a twangy country music song. As Whitehead drew the flap shut, he grasped Lake's arm firmly and held a finger to his mouth. With the other hand he reached over and turned the volume on the CD player up a few notches. Lake was startled by his actions, but even more so by the fierce look in Whitehead's eyes.

"Don't talk!" he whispered sternly. "Listen to me! Those men out there are not fishermen. I've never seen them before today. I've checked them out. They're not sick. There's nothing wrong with them."

Lake stupidly glanced over his shoulder, as if he could see the men through the flap. He wasn't sure he understood why the doctor was so alarmed. Then he noticed Whitehead gritting his teeth.

"Don't tell me," he said, a minute sigh passing from his lips. "You're not an *operator*. You really are the *Providence*'s communications officer, aren't you?"

Lake nodded, shrugging his shoulders.

"And you think you're here to evacuate me before this revolt breaks out." Whitehead whispered it more as a statement than a question. "Fuck! I wish those fuckers up at Langley could get their shit straight!"

Whitehead stared at the floor for several seconds as if he were deep in thought, as if he were trying to put the pieces of a huge jigsaw puzzle together in seconds.

"All right," he finally said in a determined tone, "that's okay.

Somebody back in Virginia obviously thought it'd be cute if you didn't know. Well, I've just decided that you have a need to know, so listen up. I don't have time to explain everything. I'm an operative in a highly sensitive operation and your ship is here to extract me and my associate. Understand? I know this is a lot to swallow, Lieutenant, but I know you wouldn't be wearing those bars on your collar if you weren't a big boy."

Lake didn't know what to say. Was this guy out of his mind? Had he been in the jungle alone too long? Of course, if what he said were true, it really wouldn't surprise Lake. It certainly wouldn't be the first mission *Providence* had been sent on with the bare minimum of information.

"You have a package for me, correct?" Whitehead said softly.

Lake nodded. "An envelope. I left it in the jeep."

"Good," he said quickly, shouldering one duffel bag while he shoved another into Lake's hands. "Let's go. We can discuss the details later. After you, Lieutenant."

Lake thought he saw a gun in Whitehead's hand pass underneath the duffel bag, but he couldn't be sure. With a million questions running through his mind, Lake didn't know what to make of Whitehead. Hefting the duffel bag over his shoulder, he walked through the flap that the doctor held open for him, concluding that it would be better to discuss the whole thing on the long drive back to Ujungpang.

They passed into the next room where the two men had been, but now the beds were empty and there was no trace of them anywhere.

"Shit!" Whitehead exclaimed, then brushed past Lake and out of the tent.

Lake followed and caught up with him just as he reached Teresa and the men standing by the vehicles.

"Did you see where they went?" Whitehead said excitedly.

"They ran that way, sir," Michaelson pointed to the dense jungle on the meadow's north border, his eyes hidden by the shade of his blue ball cap. "They seemed to be in quite a hurry."

"It's as I feared then," Whitehead said before glancing at

the two policemen. "Those men were insurgents, you might want to follow them."

The policemen looked at each other, first puzzled, then somewhat fearful. They obviously did not expect to encounter rebels this far to the north, and they appeared to have no desire to chase the two men into the jungle. Halfheartedly one finally motioned to the other, and the two walked carefully toward the northern edge of the clearing with rifles close to their chests, scanning the jungle before them, pausing periodically.

Once they were out of earshot, Whitehead turned to Lake. "Do you have my package, Lieutenant?"

"What is it, Father?" Teresa asked in a puzzled tone as Lake rustled under the passenger side seat to retrieve the large envelope. "What is it? Who were those men?"

"Not now, Teresa. I'll explain everything later."

Whitehead tore open the envelope and emptied its contents onto the passenger seat, while Lake, Teresa, and the rest watched. The envelope contained two passports and a wrapped stack of U.S. currency in large bills, along with a short letter on government letterhead stamped and signed by a name that Lake recognized as one of the President's national security advisors.

As the whole group gaped in awe, Whitehead snatched up the passports and money and placed them into the side pocket of his cargo shorts. The letter he folded neatly, then buttoned it into his shirt's left breast pocket.

"What the hell's going on, Dad?" Teresa exclaimed with an expression of terrified confusion.

Whitehead shot her an intense look that quickly transformed into a tender expression. By her question and her demeanor, Lake knew that Teresa had no idea about her father's true occupation. Everything she had told him on the morning drive, she truly believed. Innocently and proudly she believed her father to be the selfless peace-making philanthropist who bought into her "love reaps love" ideology. Although she had been quite the bitch to him earlier, Lake felt sorry for her now.

Whitehead walked over and took Teresa's hands in his. "Resa," he said gently, ignoring the three U.S. sailors rudely gaping, "your dad isn't everything you hoped he is. It pains me to tell you this, but I'm not the man you've idolized all these years. All this time I've been on Bunda, I've been working for the U.S. government. I'm a federal agent and these men are here to evacuate me." He patted his pocket that contained the passports. "And you too. That's why I didn't want you to come to Bunda. I knew I'd be ordered to leave soon and then I'd have to worry about your safety too. But now that we have a passport for you and this letter to Mr. Lake's captain, we'll get you out too. I won't leave you here."

Teresa's gaze held a myriad of emotions and Lake could only wonder what was going through her mind. She stared into her father's eyes with a brave outward strength that soon dissolved into a quivering lip and watery eyes. Without a word she turned from her father and walked away, stopping only when she had gone thirty or forty paces across the grassy meadow. With her back to them, the tropical wind whipping her short hair, Lake saw one hand touch her hip while the other appeared to wipe away tears.

Whitehead appeared to spend little time lamenting the pain his deception had caused his daughter.

"We must leave now," he said to Lake desperately. "This island's about to erupt into civil war. It's going to happen today. The rebels are massing near Ujungpang, preparing to make their move against the town. They've been gathering for weeks now, taking every able-bodied man into their army, including the ones that used to work for me in this camp. And they're *really* well armed. Shit, I knew the attack was imminent, just not *this* imminent. I misjudged their readiness level when I requested extraction. Otherwise I'd have insisted a SEAL team come here instead of you."

"Excuse me, sir," Lake said, "but how do you know the rebels are going to move on the town today?"

Whitehead smiled condescendingly. "They're jamming communications, Lieutenant. The first step in any offensive operation. That's why I lost radio contact with Ujungpang this morning. Go ahead and try, but you won't be able to reach your ship."

"Reynoso," Lake said with immediacy, "Get on the horn and try to contact *Providence*. Now!"

"Aye, aye, sir." Reynoso nodded, hefting his communications suitcase onto the lip of the jeep's cargo locker.

A sudden chill came over Lake as he realized how quickly this simple jaunt across the beautiful island could turn into a total disaster. If they got caught behind rebel lines, who knew what would happen to them. And now this doctor was telling him they were part of a top secret operation. *He was too short for this!*

"She is strong," Whitehead said to Lake, looking across the clearing at his daughter. "I know she can handle this. It may take some time to win her trust again. She's grown up believing that her father is a selfless peace-loving man. I'm afraid my cover persona has served as the beacon in her life, so I guess I'm to blame for her coming to Bunda, trying to follow in her dad's footsteps. She's much like her mother was. I only hope she's as forgiving."

Lake felt uncomfortable hearing about the Whiteheads' family problems. After all, he'd only just met them, and he couldn't say that he cared much about their twisted relationship. His main concern now was getting back to the ship safely.

"Your daughter seemed to think the rebels would leave us alone," Lake offered.

"She's right. The rebels probably will, but Al Islamiyyah sure as shit won't."

"Al Islamiyyah? The terrorist group?"

"If we had time for explanations, Lieutenant, believe me I would give them. Let's just say that if we don't get the hell out of here, we're going to have a bunch of pissed off Islamic militants on our ass. Those two 'sick' men weren't just passing the time of day. And they weren't local fishermen either, like they claimed to be. They were Filipino, and around here that can only mean one thing. They belong to Al Islamiyyah, and they were sent to kill me. I'm sure they'd have tried to, too, if you hadn't shown up when you did. Now they've probably gone to tell their boss. And I doubt Musa Muhammad will spare any resource in stopping us from reaching your ship."

"So why the big act then? Why didn't they just walk up and shoot you?"

"Because I'm not the catch of the day. The associate I spoke of, the 'field' side of our operation, is their main target. They were obviously stalling to see if I would give away his location. He's the one they really want. And he's the one we *have* to get off this island, no matter what else happens."

"My orders say nothing about anyone other than you, sir."

"Too bad, Lieutenant," Whitehead said stiffly. "I don't give a shit what your orders say. They're bogus anyway. My associate's been hiding in the jungle for eight days. He knows you're here and he's meeting us on the road back to Ujungpang. Whether you like it or not, you're taking him. If it makes you feel any better, I've got a passport right here that says he's an American citizen."

It didn't make Lake feel any better; neither did the blaring static coming from Reynoso's communications equipment.

"He's right, sir," Reynoso said, wearing a thin wiry headset. "I can't raise the *Providence,* or anybody else either. The entire H.F. spectrum's being jammed."

"Shit! Try calling them on the satellite phone. Maybe they've got it turned on, but I doubt it."

Lake did his best to keep a straight face. The situation was getting progressively worse and he had to keep a clear head. Someone on *Providence* would need to line up one of the Extra High Frequency antennas in order to receive a call from the satellite phone. It was an odd configuration and one not normally maintained, since the vital E.H.F. antennas were needed for other things like routine message traffic, email, and web access. *Providence* wouldn't change the configuration until they realized the H.F. spectrum was being jammed. And with Reynoso ashore, who knew how long it would take the junior radiomen to figure it out.

The two policemen were on their way back now, after a less than enthusiastic search of the clearing's northern edge. They had avoided entering the jungle in pursuit of the two Filipino men, probably out of fear of ambush. Their fear was evident on their faces as they crept backward toward the vehicles, their rifles and their eyes never straying from their surroundings.

With no means to seek guidance from the ship, Lake felt the loneliness of command. He had to make a decision and the steadfast contemptuous face worn by Michaelson did little to help his confidence level. Regardless of the rift between him and Michaelson, Lake suddenly found himself feeling very thankful that the big chief and his M-16 were a part of his shore party.

Chapter 11

ENSIGN Philip Yi made his way cautiously through the streets of Ujungpang, looking over his shoulder at regular intervals. The town made him uneasy and he remembered his father once telling him that Chinese were frequently persecuted in the Indonesian Republic, often being viewed as wealthy exploiters of the Indonesian economy. Some believed the Chinese were responsible for the Asian economic crisis, while others just held to ancient grudges, the reasons for which having been long since distorted or forgotten. The Chinese citizenry was simply another place for the poor of Indonesia to lay the blame for their hardships. Pointing a finger at someone else was always easier than pointing it at yourself. How like himself over the past twenty-four hours, in his mind attempting to blame Dean's accident on circumstance, when deep inside him he knew the truth.

Van Peenan had acted far too smug, far too insensitive when the report of Dean's fall reached him—even for him. Yi tried to convince himself that Van Peenan couldn't have pushed Dean down that ladder well. He *had* to convince himself of that. He had to beat all other thoughts out of his brain. After all, what else could he do? Report his suspicion to the captain? Then what? There had been no witnesses. Certainly the captain wouldn't take the hunch of a lowly ensign seriously. And what if Van Peenan found out that he had gone to the captain?

The thought sent a shudder through him even on this humid day. Once again, his course of action was all too clear, and once again he hated himself for it. Silence and cowardice.

Yi walked through a small intersection where two roads met, feeling out of place in his cotton khaki officer uniform.

Trickling streams of muddy water ran down the gutters on each side of the street that led back to the waterfront, reminding him that he was alone, and far from the ship. He felt like all eyes were on him, though the streets seemed oddly devoid of activity. There were no vehicles, no scooters, only a few men on bicycles pedaling here and there. Some shops were open but most appeared to be closed. A handful of civilians, mostly men, loitered here and there, conversing quietly, smoking or just staring. Most of the ambient sounds came not from the town but from the surrounding jungle, alive with chirping creatures and insects. The sound was loud and intense compared with the town's calm, and it seemed to forebode some kind of storm. Yi felt the hair rise on the back of his neck, and he would have marched right back to the ship at that moment if it weren't for the fatigue-clad Indonesian marines standing guard on every corner in the small town, assault rifles and walkie-talkies in hand. Their presence provided him with some sense of security, though not much.

Yi held up a hand to offer his eyes more shade than that afforded by his navy blue ball cap. He could see the hospital down the road, separated from the town by a quarter-mile-long nutmeg plantation. Not far from the hospital, the white buildings comprising the government complex contrasted sharply with the deep green jungle behind them. Beyond the hospital, Yi could see the dirt road Lake's shore party had taken earlier that morning when they left to retrieve Dr. Whitehead. The jungle enveloped the road on both sides, swallowing it whole beyond the first visible turn. There it vanished from view completely, reappearing above the trees miles away as it ascended a bare stretch of slope on Bunda's great mountain range. The jungle and the road looked menacing and Yi did not envy Lake the task. Glancing at his watch, Yi assumed Lake's party had reached the doctor's camp by now. Perhaps they were already on their way back.

The sooner the better, Yi thought. This place made him uneasy.

As he walked up the street leading to the hospital on the low hill, he saw a few dark faces watching him from the open windows of the low buildings on either side. They obviously had no compunction about staring, and their piercing eyes sent a chill through his body. Yi wasn't sure what scared him more, the staring faces or the prospect of running into Van Peenan. Apparently Van Peenan had gone ashore the night before to visit Dean, but had not yet returned. Bloomfield uttered a few words under his breath about Yi looking for Van Peenan. Just to make sure he was okay.

"I don't know where's he's gone to, Ensign," a heavily perspiring Bloomfield had said beneath the hatch ladder as Yi prepared to leave the ship, "but if you see him you tell him he'd better get back here before noon or he'll have to answer to me." The out of breath XO had paused before adding, "Actually, tell him he'll have to answer to the captain."

Yi suddenly had a nice thought.

The engineer was missing ashore. Maybe he'd been arrested, or maybe he'd had an *accident* of his own. Better yet, maybe he'd been kidnapped by the local rebels, never to be seen or heard from again. Yi could only hope. The thought brought a smile to his face, which quickly faded when he once again noticed the faces in the windows staring back at him.

Forget the engineer, he thought. If he wasn't careful *he* could get kidnapped by these people, or worse.

Yi eventually made it to the front steps of the bleak and dingy white, single-story hospital. The building appeared to be a relic of the colonial period, and could probably trace its longevity through three centuries of typhoons to its solid brick construction. A few vehicles were haphazardly parked outside, probably belonging to the local N.G.O. personnel who comprised most of the hospital's staff. Once he passed through the creaky double screen doors, he could see that one wing of the hospital was comprised of an open ward filled with two dozen cots lined in neat rows, each protected by loosely draped mosquito nets. Several of the cots were occupied and nurses of many different nationalities, mostly European, moved about tending to the patients. The hospital's other wing was divided into several rooms, some of them patient rooms, and Yi was quickly met by a smiling nurse who escorted him to one of these, where he found the shirtless Dean lying in bed, staring thoughtfully through an open window that looked out on the dense jungle only a dozen yards behind the hospital.

The room was small but sufficient, and Yi quickly concluded that Dean must have received special treatment to be spared the open ward's congregational suffering. Or perhaps it was the practice of the hospital staff to separate local patients and foreigners. As Yi well knew from the meager days of his youth, even humanitarian organizations with all their noble deeds and selfless generosity could play preferences and dole out their own form of discrimination.

As Yi knocked on the open door and entered, Dean turned his face to reveal a thick piece of gauze covering the right side of his head. He also had a bandaged shoulder and bandaged ribs, and several other bruises left unattended to heal on their own. A thin film of perspiration glistened on his face, and Yi suddenly realized how awfully humid it was inside the building.

"They should give you a fan in here, Petty Officer Dean," Yi said in a cheery manner.

"Hello, sir," Dean slurred, smiling to show a fat lip and two upper right teeth missing.

Yi grimaced at the sight, then instantly resumed a casual expression, hoping Dean had not noticed. Up close, Dean's bruises were much more apparent and even the smallest of movements appeared to cause him a great deal of pain. Remarkably, there had been no internal bleeding—a miracle, considering the short blood supply the hospital probably had to work with.

"I just thought I'd stop by and see how you were doing, Dean. I'm sorry about what happened."

"S'okay, sir. Not your fault. I don't know what happened."

Yi moved to pat him on the shoulder then drew back, cursing his own stupidity. Dean seemed to find it humorous and gave a weak laugh.

"Not that shoulder, sir. That one hurts like hell. It feels like it's twice its own size. I can feel it throbbing with every beat of my heart. My head, too."

"I promise I won't touch you," Yi said, attempting in the only way he knew to be humorous. He paused before asking the question that had been boring a hole through his brain and tried his best to make it sound like it wasn't the only reason he had come to visit.

"Do you remember the fall at all?"

Dean glanced at him painfully before answering.

"I can't even remember what I had for breakfast that day, sir. My head hurts just thinking about it. It's the strangest thing, but all I can remember is waking up with my face on the cold steel deck. I think I was in the lower level. Harris was shaking me, yelling at me to wake up, and I just remember wanting to tell him to stop fucking shaking me, but I couldn't. I couldn't even move. Oh yeah, I also remember my pants feeling wet. I guess I must have pissed my pants, too. At least that's what the corpsman told me when he stopped by this morning. After that, I don't remember a fucking thing. I woke up here, feeling like shit."

"I don't think you'd be lying there if I'd stood up to the Eng and let you go to the head." Yi tried to make it sound convincing. "I seem to keep letting you down whenever you need your division officer."

"Hell no, sir," Dean shook his head as much as he could without inducing too much pain. "Don't worry about that shit. You've got to live with the Eng up in officer country twenty-four hours a day, sir. You've got to eat with him, sleep with him. Hell, you've even got to shower with him. I don't have to be with him near as much as you do. It's one of the nice things about being enlisted, sir. We only have to see the Eng during watch or during training." He paused and then added, "Or whenever he hauls our butt in front of a captain's mast. And the captain's a good guy, so that's not so bad either. Believe me, sir, my life's better than yours. But there is one thing you can do for me."

"You name it."

"Could you call that nurse, sir? I've got to piss like a race horse and I'm not going to put my dick anywhere near this bottle they gave me."

Dean held up a bottle and Yi could see why he was so reluctant. The bottle was a dingy color that probably used to be white but now was stained from the residue of various fluids it once contained. Yi felt like he could get a disease just by looking at it.

"There's a head down the hall, sir. I used that this morning. But I need some help getting there."

Yi nodded and ducked outside to find the nearest nurse. He found a hospital orderly, a not-unattractive local young woman who produced a rickety wheelchair and brought it to Dean's room. With the young woman's assistance, Yi gingerly helped Dean's tender body into the chair. Then Yi made a move to push the chair, but Dean stopped him.

"If you don't mind, sir," he said with a wink only Yi could see. "I'd like her to take me. Something about taking a piss in front of your own division officer."

"No problem," Yi grinned. "I'll be here when you get back."

Once the attractive orderly had rolled Dean out of the room, Yi partially shut the door and sat on the bed staring out the window at the green jungle and spotty gray clouds while he waited for Dean to return. The clouds were getting darker and thicker, and he remembered Fremont saying something at breakfast that morning about rain being in the forecast. The leftovers of a larger storm far north, up near the Philippine Islands, were headed in Bunda's direction. As if to confirm this, the forest trees swayed heavily in the stiff breeze, their massive boughs stretching out in all directions, some leaning to almost touch the window's edge.

Yi actually felt somewhat at peace. What Dean had said relieved somewhat the guilt that hung over him. To know that Dean understood, that Dean even sympathized with him for what *he* had to go through on a daily basis did wonders for his soul. Whatever berating, whatever harassment Van Peenan doled out in the future, Yi would do whatever he needed to in order to survive, and Dean would understand. That thought comforted Yi as he stared out at the swaying jungle, enjoying a brief moment of solace.

Just then, a face suddenly appeared in the window blocking his view of the jungle. The face was followed shortly by another. The men belonging to these two faces were locals of brown complexion, black hair, and dark eyes. The wretched countenance of these interlopers startled Yi far more than their sudden appearance did. From their gaunt faces, disheveled T-shirts, and cracked lips, Yi judged them to be on hard times. Probably victims of Bunda's rebel conflict. Most likely out of work fishermen or service workers from Ujungpang's dead tourist industry.

They obviously had no compunctions about poking their heads into other people's windows and, though it seemed strange, Yi soon dismissed it as a mere cultural difference. After exchanging stares with the two strange men for several seconds, one of them finally smiled and motioned for Yi to come over to the window.

"Hello, mista," he said in broken English. "Do you have any money?"

Yi had learned somewhere in general military training never to brandish a wallet, and never to give money to local beggars—that is, unless you wanted to get mugged. The man continued to smile, but Yi did not respond. Instead, he thought it best to notify one of the nurses out in the hallway. They could deal with the two men as they saw fit.

As he casually made for the doorway, Yi heard a rustling behind him. He had only turned his back on the window for two and a half seconds. Twisting around again, he was shocked to see that both men had leaped over the windowsill and were now standing in the room with him. A stark horror took hold of Yi when he noticed that each man clutched a long slim knife in his right hand. The knives were similar to those he'd seen fishermen use to carve up fish.

Yi hesitated, too startled to say anything, to even yell for help. He made a mad dash for the door, but it was too late.

In a flash, they were on him. One of them must have dived

for his legs because he felt his feet fly out from under him just before his body crashed into a tall metal table. The toppling table and his forward momentum carried him against the door with a *Wham!,* slamming it shut.

Now face down on the floor, Yi felt both men fall firmly on top of him, one of them instantly placing a grimy, sweaty hand over his nose and mouth. The weight of both men knocked the wind out of him, and before he could recover, sharp, stinging sensations began traveling all up and down his back and shoulders. Multiple stings. Some hurt worse than others. It took him a few seconds to realize he was being stabbed. Struggling, jerking, biting the foul-tasting hand over his mouth, Yi tried desperately to turn over, but nothing worked. They had him down, they were stabbing him, and he was getting weaker by the moment.

Then the stabs suddenly stopped, and he felt the hand over his mouth pull his head back so hard that he thought his neck would break. But it did not break. Instead he felt a final stinging blow to the side of his neck, and suddenly he could not breathe.

A moment later, it was all over. The hand released its grip and the weight of the two men came off his back. As his hearing faded he thought he heard footfalls. Then all was silent, and the room was spinning. He was weak and could barely lift his head. After a few vain attempts to look up, he let his face rest on the cold tile floor. A warm wet sensation crept over his numbing lips. He was face down in a pool of his own blood.

As the pool expanded, time took on a different meaning. It seemed an eternity before he felt several hands turn him over. Through foggy eyes, he saw desperate faces frantically working on him. They appeared to shout at one another but he could hear nothing. He even saw Dean's face too, pale and troubled, his lips moving as he were speaking, but Yi heard only silence.

Then something strange happened. A small isolated signal reached Yi's blood-deprived brain. It was Dean's voice. It was the only thing he could hear. The only thing his brain could process. But it was enough to comfort him.

"Hold on, sir . . ." Dean's voice said worriedly. "Hold on . . . Hold on . . ."

Slowly, the voice faded into the void rapidly filling his mind—and then all went black.

"I'VE already shown you the electric propulsion motor that drives the shaft, Captain," Peto remarked over his shoulder as he led Edwards through the *Hatta*'s small engine room, a mere garage compared with the size of *Providence*'s. "I've shown you the hydraulic plant, the carbon dioxide scrubbers, the oxygen-hydrogen generator, and, of course, you can't miss the diesel generator. I would show you the banks that hold our hydrogen, oxygen, and nitrogen, but they are located in the ballast tanks, and, of course, are not visible from here."

Edwards nodded. It seemed that his tour of *Hatta*'s engine room had only just begun. And it had. There really wasn't that much to look at, at least in comparison to *Providence*'s massive engine room, which held so many dozens more systems to support her nuclear power plant. *Hatta*'s engine room was so small, in fact, that Edwards judged the entire room could fit inside *Providence*'s reactor compartment. Small as it was, he had to admit the *Hatta* was an impressive little ship. Everywhere around him the spaces gleamed with the telltale indicators of a crew that took prideful care in their work and in their vessel. Not a single Kimwipe or oily puddle could be found anywhere on the deck, and Edwards noticed no loose items lying about, practically a miracle for a ship in port. Despite the various maintenance that accompanied any in-port period on any ship, Peto had managed to keep his ship stowed for sea and Edwards found himself feeling slightly humbled. Of course, Peto had a much smaller ship to manage, the *Hatta*'s crew numbering only twenty-five compared to *Providence*'s one hundred twenty.

Edwards had met most of *Hatta*'s crew at lunch in the wardroom. One by one they dropped in to give Peto some report or another, Peto proudly introducing each one. They seemed a sharp bunch, but then each man would have to be to get selected for such service. Their uniforms were flawless, their manner professional and courteous. Sailors often say that a ship has a soul, carried with her from keel-laying to decommissioning. It's also said that the faces and demeanor of a ship's crew can reveal the color of that soul to any visitor. In Edwards' judgment, the *Hatta* was a happy ship with a good soul. Her crew appeared content, even honored, to serve under her captain, for whom they carried a deep respect easily discernible to Edwards' seasoned eyes.

"And this, as you say in America, Captain, is where the rubber meets the road," Peto said, as he pointed to a rectangular metallic casing about the size of a small school bus with gas and water piping protruding from one end. Edwards knew what it was before Peto told him. "This is our Air Independent Propulsion system. With it we can cruise close to eight knots for seventeen days without recharging. Perfect for operations close in shore, and of course perfect for detecting pirate activity, smugglers . . . even a rebel submarine. We can cruise off an island or a strait for almost three weeks without detection."

Edwards scanned the glistening metal box with interest, though little could be gained from this vantage point. Most of the nuts and bolts of the system resided within the plain metal housing. Apart from a few gauges and valves, there was nothing to see on the outside. Of course, he didn't need to see inside to know what the housing contained. SubPac's policy of continuous improvement training for senior officers had kept him up to speed on all the latest developments in submarine technology. A few years back he had attended a conference in which A.I.P., or Air Independent Propulsion, was one of the main topics. Of course, his engineering mind had absorbed the knowledge like a sponge, and he remembered the concepts quite clearly.

"I've read about them," Edwards commented. "But I've never seen one up close."

Peto eyed him skeptically, then shrugged. "It's no nuclear reactor, Captain, but it serves its purpose. It's relatively simple, actually, functioning essentially like a battery. An electric current is produced from a potential difference created across an anode-cathode arrangement, the positively-charged hydro-

gen ions acting as the plus side while the negatively-charged
oxygen ions form the minus side. Electrons are removed from
the hydrogen gas at the anode and recombine with oxygen gas
at the cathode, producing current to drive an electrical load.
The hydrogen ions then migrate across a gas permeable membrane to combine with the oxygen at the cathode. Water and
heat are the only byproducts. It's a clean system."

"Are you using a polymer membrane as the electrolyte?"

"Ah!" Peto grinned. "So you *do* know something about our
fuel cells, Captain. Very good. Yes, the electrolyte is a polymer. As you obviously know, there are many advantages to a
polymer over a liquid."

Peto moved forward to continue the tour and Edwards inwardly cursed his own pretentiousness. The surest way to silence any presenter was to let on that you knew something
about the subject. If only he'd kept his damn mouth shut,
maybe he'd have actually learned something. Something he
didn't already know about A.I.P. Many unfriendly nations
around the world used different forms of A.I.P., and it would
be nice to know some crucial tidbits firsthand.

Much to Edwards' dismay, Peto said no more about the
A.I.P. system and continued on with the tour, leading him
through the forward hatch and into the next compartment.
There he showed Edwards the space-age control room with
its dozen different stations for ship, navigation, sonar, and
weapons controls. The big dual-paneled consoles lined the
bulkhead in a semi-circle surrounding the periscope stand
in the center. The room was smaller but much more automated
than *Providence*'s own control room, and Edwards deduced that
during battle stations Peto managed and coordinated the various stations like the London Philharmonic.

The tour then continued forward, bypassing the officers'
quarters, and leading one deck below into the torpedo room.
The room stretched the entire breadth of *Hatta*'s hull but it still
seemed tight with the racks of weapons occupying practically
every square foot. The room's forward end gleamed with eight
polished brass breech doors for *Hatta*'s eight torpedo tubes.

The tubes were situated in two horizontal rows of four pointing directly forward, unlike *Providence*'s four tubes which were separated and angled slightly outward. Much like *Providence*'s torpedo room, the smell of axle grease filled the air from the trucks and pinions of the automatic loading system.

Edwards leaned against one of the long weapons while Peto pointed out a few things. It took him a few moments before realizing he was leaning on the canister for a Harpoon missile.

Peto appeared amused at his surprise.

"We have eight torpedo tubes, Captain. Four can fire missiles as well as torpedoes. We're outfitted with a few Harpoons like the one you're leaning on, bought from your government years ago. But, of course, you yourself know all submariners prefer to use the torpedo. These are our real advantage in an underwater fight."

Peto pointed to one of the long reload torpedoes securely fastened to its rack. Edwards immediately recognized it as a German-made, five-hundred-thirty-three-millimeter AEG SUT torpedo, with "swimout" capability. A swimout torpedo could be fired without a launch transient, thus giving a submarine complete stealth from the moment the target was detected to the moment the weapon exploded beneath its keel.

Peto seemed to pause for a moment, his eyes focusing on Edwards as if he wanted him to fully absorb the meaning of the swimout capability. Edwards tried his best to appear unruffled. Swimout weapons required specially designed torpedo tubes, and *Providence*'s tubes did not have this capability. Her tubes blasted the big weapons out using the age-old water ram method, creating a sound transient that could be heard for miles. *Providence* lost her stealth the moment she fired. That meant that *Providence* would be at a distinct disadvantage in a one-on-one engagement with a Type 214. This was good to know if his career ever pitted him against a Type 214, either in simulation or in real life.

"As you can see, Captain, if we were to come across this phantom rebel submarine, we could more than handle her by ourselves." He said it almost jokingly. "In fact—and please take no offense by this, Captain—the *Hatta* is more suited to the task than even your own fine ship."

Perhaps it was simply a proud captain boasting about his ship, but it had sounded almost like a challenge, and it made Edwards uncomfortable. He was surprised to hear it coming from this officer who had been nothing short of polite since the moment he met him. Either way, he felt it best to avoid the pointless argument over who had the better submarine.

"Rightfully so," Edwards said, shrugging his shoulders. "Especially since that's not *Providence*'s mission here."

"Of course." Peto smiled only with his eyes, the lines once again becoming visible at the edges.

With the tour complete, Peto led Edwards up to his small stateroom. The room was much like his own, spartan and businesslike, with only a few personal touches to indicate that an actual person, and not a robot, inhabited the place. A laptop computer sat open on a small flip-down desk and Peto grabbed up a remote mouse to show Edwards a slide show of his wife and three children. Apparently, they lived on a small farm just inland from the harbor and Peto proudly pointed out a small painting of the farm hanging from the room's starboard wall. The painting showed a cozy single-story white house in an open field on a sunny day, the jungle's vivid colors and Bunda's mountainous spine dominating the background.

"My wife painted this," he said. "She wants me to have a small piece of home with me wherever I go. Sometimes during hard days, I look on this painting and dream of the day I'll finally settle down and become just a simple farmer. I know it is a strange feeling for a sailor to have, especially now that I finally have a command. Do you ever miss Nebraska, Captain?"

"Not really," Edwards said, his mind straying to his daughter after seeing the photos of Peto's family.

"If I had been born in Nebraska," Peto said distantly, "I am certain I would miss it. In fact, if I were born in such a place, I probably never would have left it."

"Why's that?"

"I remember that Nebraska was full of farms and rural

towns, all far from Washington, all far from your government's seat of power, yet I felt just as surrounded by the cradle of freedom and justice there as I did anywhere else in your country. Everyone in every town I visited all across your vast country seemed to have a common bond of entitlement, like they were part of the whole no matter how remote their geographic location. Everyone was represented, everyone a part of the system, everyone respecting the opinions and beliefs of others. And there was an underlying intent of goodwill throughout."

"I think a whole lot of people would disagree with you on that," Edwards said bleakly.

"I'm a proud idealist, Captain, and an optimist. I ignore such people. Even an unfinished house provides more shelter than an open field. I believe that people are capable of so many things if they concentrate on successes and have the courage to hold on to their dreams. Your nation's founding fathers are a perfect example. Despite the perils they faced, look where your great country is today. And now, despite the harsh criticism from so many other countries, people from all parts of the world still flood your immigration system with requests for entry." Peto stared at the painting on the wall. "If my own country were such a place . . ."

A moment of awkward silence filled the air, and Edwards found himself glancing at the books lining the half-filled shelf above Peto's desk. Following suit with the rest of the ship, a single metal bar neatly secured them against any unexpected rough sea. He could not decipher the Indonesian titles of most of the volumes, but Edwards was surprised to see *The Complete Works of William Shakespeare* along the spine of a well-worn book.

"Do you read Shakespeare, Captain?" Peto said, noticing his interest.

"Not since college." Edwards shook his head.

"I took an interest when I went to school in America and have been 'hooked,' as you say, ever since. I make sure I'm in Jakarta every year for the Shakespeare festival there. His writing speaks to my soul, or should I say to the soul of any ideal-

ist. He understood man's inner motivations. Why we do what
we do, why we feel what we feel. Whether they are European,
African, American, Arab, or Asian, men are the same around
the world. The reasons for what they do are the same." Peto
paused for a moment, still staring at the painting of the quiet
farm house. Then he said softly, " '*Now would I give a thousand furlongs of sea for an acre of barren ground. The wills
above be done, but I would fain die a dry death.*' " Do you
know it, Captain?"

"No, I'm sorry to say, I don't."

"It's from *The Tempest,*" he said, never taking his eyes
from the painting. "My life has been a tempest of sorts."

Peto appeared deep in thought, a thousand miles away,
very sad, and Edwards suddenly felt very out of place.

"Maybe a *deep* death is more suitable for a submariner,"
Edwards said cheerily in an attempt to break the mood.

Peto turned to him and smiled heavily.

"Right you are, Captain. The *only* way for a submariner to
die, no?"

Just then a muffled *thump* filled the stateroom. It was followed shortly by another. Then another. Each one sending
small vibrations through *Hatta*'s hull and deckplating. Edwards felt them in his feet, and he instantly identified them as
explosions outside the hull. Peto's expression revealed that he
had deduced the same.

Moments later one of *Hatta*'s officers poked his head into
the room, appearing distressed. He reported something to
Peto and the two exchanged excited words, leaving Edwards
to only watch in eager anticipation of the translation. Peto
spoke what sounded like heated orders to the young officer
and the officer quickly disappeared out the door.

"Captain, we have a most desperate situation," Peto said,
as he reached for his hat on the desk. "The rebels are lobbing
mortars into the town. They appear to be engaging the
marines at the jungle's perimeter."

Edwards immediately thought of Lake and the shore party,
suddenly wishing he had not let them go. They would be on the
road heading back by now. He needed to raise them on the radio

and warn them to stay away from the town. He had to move fast before it was too late, before they ran headlong into a firefight.

"I've got to get back to my ship, Peto," Edwards said, heading for the door.

"Captain, wait! That's not all." Peto clutched his arm. "The mortar rounds are rapidly approaching the waterfront. The ships may be in danger, so the admiral has ordered the flotilla to get underway. I'm sure you know what an eighty-one-millimeter mortar round can do to a ship's hull, especially a submarine's. And mortar rounds don't know the difference between Indonesian and American vessels, Captain."

"I've got one man in the hospital and three others off in the jungle somewhere, Peto! I'll be damned if I'm going to just leave them here! You do what you have to, but *Providence*'s staying till all her people are aboard."

"Captain, wait! I implore you to listen to me! Of course, you're not under Admiral Syarif's command and are not obligated to follow his orders in any way. You can stay if you so choose, but please consider my advice. It makes no sense to put your ship at risk when you don't have to. The rebels would never target the hospital, and your men in the jungle will be safe. Your ship, however, will not be. Imagine if a stray shot were to hit your hull and compromise *Providence*'s watertight integrity. Your navy will have to send a ship to tow you back to Pearl Harbor. How long would that delay your mission? God forbid if any of your crew are hurt or killed! Please trust me and take your ship out of danger. Give the marines time to get the situation under control. It shouldn't take very long. Then you can come back and pick up your men and be on your way."

Edwards knew Peto was right. It was one of those tough moments when a commander had to make a decision to protect the ship over a few members of its crew. As much as his instinctive side wanted to stay and wait for his men, his logical side told him that it would accomplish nothing, and unnecessarily put the ship at risk. Lake would certainly hear the gunfire as he approached on the mountain road. And he'd be smart enough to stay away from Ujungpang until the battle subsided.

"Damn it!" Edwards exclaimed, punching the Formica wall. "All right, Peto, you win."

"Good!" Peto seemed satisfied. "Now, listen to me. Once we get clear of the pier, the ships will form up in column to transit to the open sea. *Malahayati* will take the van position followed by *Nuhu* and then my ship. *Providence* can bring up the rear. Stick close to my stern, mirror my maneuvers *exactly*, and you will make it safely through the reefs."

Edwards could already hear the bustle in the passage outside as the *Hatta*'s crew hurriedly prepared her for sea.

"We'll keep in touch on the bridge-to-bridge radio," Peto added as he grabbed a set of binoculars from a nearby locker. "Now, you better go. Good luck, Captain!"

Edwards wished Peto the same before rushing out the door and toward the ladder. Brushing past a few Indonesian sailors, he scrambled up the ladder and emerged topside on *Hatta*'s forward deck. The pier and ships were frantic with activity. Blue clad sailors ran everywhere, coiling hoses, disconnecting power cables, singling lines, transferring what supplies they could from the pier to the ships.

In stark contrast to this frenzy, Edwards turned around to see *Providence* riding at her moorings as if it were a lazy Sunday afternoon. On her deck, a few sailors curiously watched the Indonesia sailors while some others pointed at the columns of smoke rising from the town. Only the rifle-wielding sentries on the pier showed any sign of heightened alert, holding the weapons at the ready instead of the usual slung-over-the-shoulder position. They appeared to have no idea the danger they were in.

Damn! Edwards thought. Were his men that complacent? Had they been at sea so long that they now stood waiting placidly for the next mortar round to fall?

As Edwards made his way across *Hatta*'s brow, the first close mortar round hit. There was no warning, no screaming whistling sound like in the movies, just a sudden explosion that ripped the air apart. Like the majority of the running sailors, Edwards instinctively flattened on the pier's warm concrete and felt the pressure wave hit his ears like two open hands. Moments later, coupled with the screams and cries of the injured, he heard chunks of metal and wood landing on the pier all round him. He looked up to see debris scattered everywhere. Among the debris, the injured clutched bleeding splinter wounds. The round had landed on a supply shack on the land side of the pier, and the building had disintegrated, its wooden sides and metal roof instantly transformed into a thousand high-speed missiles. A column of black smoke now marked the shack's former location.

After checking his body, Edwards breathed a sigh of relief that he was not injured. The blast had been far enough away to protect him from the lethal projectiles.

He glanced over at the two surface ships, *Malahayati* and *Nuhu*. Dirty brown hues appeared just above their low stacks as their diesel engines roared to life. Dozens of sailors ran to their stations for leaving harbor. On the flagship and larger of the two, the *Malahayati*, Edwards could see several officers observing the mass of seamen from the high open bridge above the windowed pilothouse. Admiral Syarif's gray hair and frame stood out among the others as he gesticulated wildly, shouting orders at his confused officers.

With all her sailors either aboard or lying injured on the pier, *Malahayati* cast off her lines and began backing into the harbor. As his ship gained momentum, Syarif's eyes scanned the pier and noticed Edwards staring back at him. Cupping his hands he shouted, "You had best get your ship underway, Kaptan Edwards. If you know what's good for you!"

Edwards took one last look at the dozen or so wounded men lying all around. He wondered who would care for them. Then he saw a single squad of marine medics emerge from their cover at the far end of the pier. They rushed over to the nearest bleeding sailor and gathered round the prostrate man to carry him to safety.

Then the next mortar round hit.

One moment the marine medics were there, huddled over the wounded sailor. The next, they disappeared into a blood red cloud of dust, smoke, and flesh.

Edwards had dropped again at the moment of impact, and

was far enough from the blast to escape injury, but he had to fight back a churning stomach when he returned to his feet and had to step over several severed fingers and charred bone fragments to continue on to *Providence*'s brow. He had to think of his own ship first. There was nothing he could do. The wounded Indonesian sailors would have to fend for themselves. Though he surmised whoever was spotting for the rebel mortar would continue to mercilessly direct shells down on them.

By now, *Providence*'s loiterers had sought safety below-decks, and Edwards was met at the brow only by his two nervous sentries and an agitated Miller.

"Holy shit, Captain, that was close!" Miller shouted. "We've got to get out of here! I took the liberty of ordering the main engines warmed up, sir. The XO agreed. They're almost ready to go."

Edwards could picture the flustered Bloomfield, probably watching him this very minute through the periscope, eager to get underway and to get his ass away from danger. At least Bloomfield's instinct for self-preservation had worked advantageously in this instance. The main engine warm-up would have taken precious time. Time that they didn't have at the rate the mortar shells were closing.

"I heartily agree, Weps," Edwards forced himself to say calmly in front of the two terrified sailors. "Have the maneuvering watch stationed immediately. We're leaving port."

Chapter 12

"BAPAK! Wake up, Bapak!"

Van Peenan's head spun as the brothel owner shook him—not gently—from his lumpy cot. His head hurt tremendously, the results of last night's whiskey—and whatever else he had managed to drink. As the owner threw open the flimsy curtains, Van Peenan winced, expecting piercing sunlight, but was surprised to see a gray-clouded sky instead.

How long had he been out? It must be noon by now.

He cursed his own stupidity for drowning in the bottle. His all-night absence from the ship would definitely raise some eyebrows. No doubt Edwards was livid by now. He would have to come up with an excuse that would suit.

Perspiring as he lay naked in the sweat-stained sheets, the breeze blowing through the window felt suddenly refreshing against his aching body. The night had been a crazy one. One of those long periods of unconsciousness that followed any heavy night of drinking. He thought he could remember stirring several times, hearing explosions all around him, but he assumed they were just alcohol-induced dreams.

"What time is it?" he muttered.

"Oh, Bapak, it is time for you to get up. You drank very much last night, and I am afraid you must get up now."

There was a different tone in the owner's voice, much different from the greedy runt that eagerly took his cash the night before. Then Van Peenan noticed the two fatigue-clad men standing in the doorway. They were not marines, or at least their uniforms didn't match those of the Indonesian marines he'd seen. Their camouflage uniforms appeared orange, not green, from the rich island soil, haphazardly thrown together, very unsoldierly. The two men glared at him sternly with assault rifles held waist high. Then he suddenly realized they were not Pacific Islanders, but Arabs.

"Who the fuck are you?" he muttered through his cotton mouth.

One of the men moved swiftly to give Van Peenan his answer, a rifle butt across the jaw. The blow knocked him off the bed and sent him rolling in a wad of sheets across the dirty floor.

When Van Peenan collected his senses, instantly sobered by the shock of the blow, he realized that he could hear explosions outside, more distant than those he remembered in his dream. The short staccato of small arms fire accompanied it. It had not been a dream, after all. Something was happening in Ujungpang, and from the looks of things, he was now caught up in it.

The pain in his jaw, accompanied by the throbbing sensation in his rapidly swelling lower lip, soon brought him to his senses. Hovering over him, the two Arab men shouted at him in English and Arabic. They wanted him to get up. One muddy boot after another kicked him in the ribs. He made a quick surge for the window in an attempt to get away but was again struck down by the man swinging the rifle. The blow hit the back of his head this time, and soon after his face hit the hard floor. The last blow was harder than the first and he began to feel as if he might lose consciousness.

Rolling over, he opened his eyes to see the squirrelly owner's face staring down at him, a smirk on the man's thin lips.

"I am sorry, Bapak, but today is independence day in Ujungpang, and you are on the wrong side of the lines."

"What are you talking about?" Van Peenan managed to say through his swollen mouth. At first he thought the owner had betrayed him to the local authorities, but then he slowly began to realize what was happening. The rebels must have launched an attack, or an offensive of some kind, while he slept. They must have captured the town, or at least his part of it. The distant gunfire indicated that the battle was not yet over. How he could have been so drunk to sleep through it, he did not know. He was caught in the middle of a local civil war. That explained a lot of things. Of course, it still didn't explain why these Arabs were beating the shit out of him.

"I gave you good money, didn't I?" Van Peenan struggled to say. "That has to be worth something."

"Oh, yes, Bapak, and I appreciate it very much. And you will be pleased to know that my men have killed the American sailor in the hospital." He paused briefly. "But, you see, there is a problem, Bapak. Your ship has left port. They have left you here and you still owe me money. Five thousand—that was our deal. I have searched your clothes and have found only fifty of your dollars. You still owe me four thousand nine hundred fifty American dollars."

Holy shit! Van Peenan thought. Dean *was* dead! Though his head hurt like hell, Van Peenan suddenly felt a wave of relief come over him. He was off the hook. Now Dean would never talk to anyone. But the moment of twisted joy didn't last long, as he again realized his present dilemma. *Providence* had left port without him. They would have no clue where to start looking for him, if they'd even made an attempt to find him before leaving. And now he would probably never live to reap the benefits of Dean's demise.

"I'll get you the money!" Van Peenan said desperately. "My ship's bound to come back for me once the fighting's over. You have my word that you'll get every penny!"

"Perhaps, Bapak. But I have an even better idea. You have, of course, just recently become acquainted with my two associates here. They belong to an organization known as Al Islamiyyah. They were accompanying the rebel army and have made it known throughout the town that their leader will pay ten thousand dollars for every captured American delivered to them. So, please do not feel bad. You will more than compensate me for the loss."

Van Peenan's skin went ice cold in the humid heat of the room. He'd read enough headlines to know the fate that awaited hostages of terrorist groups. They'd probably use him as a negotiating chip for a little while, maybe even gain the freedom of some of their brothers in Guantánamo. He'd probably be tortured too, but in the end he'd be killed like all the rest. His head severed and displayed for the world to see, all in the name of Allah.

He glanced up briefly at one of the Arabs hovering over him and was met by a solid fist. The hard blow smashed his nose, instantly coating his mouth and chest with a stream of red blood.

"Enough!" the other Arab shouted in English. "You will be paid for him soon enough. Now, Musa wants to see this infidel!"

As the two men dragged him naked and kicking out of the room, the owner following close behind, Van Peenan found himself shouting, even as he spat up blood.

"You little shit! You little fucking piece of shit! I want my money back, you asshole!"

"I do not think you will be needing it anymore, Bapak," the owner said with a smile.

The Arabs dragged him out to the brothel's main parlor, the same place he had spent many hours the previous night drinking. But now no scantily dressed women adorned the place. In fact, there were no women to be seen anywhere. On the room's opposite side stood a few other men in various states of undress facing the far wall, obviously Indonesian sailors and marines, other patrons of the brothel yanked out of bed in a similar fashion. A half-dozen heavily armed Arab and Filipino men held them at gunpoint. Van Peenan was shoved into line with the rest and the whole procession proceeded outside in single file with the gunmen watching them closely.

Half-expecting a town marred with the scars of battle, Van Peenan surprisingly saw throngs of smiling people crowding the streets. Joyous civilians intermixed with fatigue-clad rebel soldiers, all cheering in jubilation. Everywhere, happy people laughed, hugged and threw flowers, acting as if they had just been liberated, and apparently they had. Van Peenan ventured to guess that most of the town's citizenry supported the rebel cause. Some laughed when they saw his pale naked body being led barefoot along with the rest of the prisoners. Beyond that they paid little attention to the column of prisoners, aside from some of the young boys who felt the need to hurl a few stones in their direction. Van Peenan shouted several curses at them and soon found himself their target of choice. Several stones struck his right buttock and leg, leaving painful red welts. He soon passed out of range, however, when the Arab gunmen turned the column down another street and headed south.

The gunfire he'd heard before seemed to be far behind him now. Sneaking a glance over his shoulder, he saw thick black smoke rising from one of the white government buildings on the hill to the north of town. That's where the fighting must be, perhaps the remnant of the Indonesian marines making their last stand.

As he followed the column up the street, he noticed several bodies lying here and there, all of them Indonesian marines. The bodies lay mangled and mutilated, a gruesome testament to whatever form of modern weaponry had killed them. He also noticed several bloody spots on the road where he suspected rebel corpses had once lain but now were removed for burial. Obviously, the rebels had shown little quarter in their push to take the town. Several fierce-looking squads of Malay men met them on the road, hurrying north, paying little attention to the column of prisoners. These were not farmers and fishermen with guns, but well-trained and well-armed soldiers. Van Peenan estimated at least a hundred in this one group, double-timing toward the fighting, exchanging no words with the Arab and Filipino escorts. Van Peenan got the impression that the terrorists and the rebel soldiers, though allies, seldom intermingled.

The column halted at a large warehouse near the edge of town, which appeared to double as a temporary supply depot for the rebel troops. Men wearing green fatigues were everywhere, some standing guard, some running shells to a couple of visible mortar emplacements further on down the road, some resting with their squads, some giving orders. Several men loaded boxes onto a parked caravan of civilian trucks, probably to re-supply the rebels fighting on the north side of town. Van Peenan then noticed a strange-looking heavy vehicle parked by a grove of palm trees. It had an awkward looking turret on top and he suddenly realized that it was a mobile anti-aircraft missile battery.

How long could a couple hundred Indonesian marines stand up against such a well-armed insurgency, he wondered. Obviously not for long, if the town had already fallen.

The escorts forcefully led the prisoners into the stark warehouse through a shipping and receiving bay, then made them stand facing a bare wall, all except Van Peenan. Two Arabs grabbed him out of the line and pushed him toward a solitary table in the center of the big open loading bay. Sipping a drink alone at the table sat a very slim Arab man who appeared to be in his mid-forties. A stubby black beard cradled his face and intense eyes, while his black curly hair just brushed the top of his fatigue shirt collar.

This had to be the "Musa" his captors had referred to, Van Peenan thought. The emblazoned eyes carried with them a whole history of religious zealotry, a fanaticism that focused on little else, and Van Peenan got the feeling that whatever Musa wanted, he eventually got. Here was a man of power and action. A man whose intensity obviously rivaled that of his own.

"Here he is," the brothel owner said proudly. He had been keeping close to the heels of the column the entire way, probably to make sure he got his money. "Did I not tell you I had an American in one of my rooms? And here he is, just like I promised. An American naval officer, no less. Now, about my payment . . ."

The small man stopped talking as Musa rose from his chair, his face stern as he flicked a cigarette across the room. As he approached, Van Peenan could tell from Musa's confident demeanor that he was the leader and that everyone else in the room was subservient. The two Arab guards held Van Peenan's arms tighter as their leader came closer, forcing him to stand with his arms stretched taut between them as Musa's eyes locked onto his blood-dried face. Without a word, he planted a fist firmly in Van Peenan's gut, doubling him over. The guards instantly pulled him back upright as he coughed out several mouthfuls of blood and saliva.

"That is a lesson," Musa said, strangely calm after the violence of the blow. "I would advise you not to play games with me. Tell me who you are."

Van Peenan, still retching from the punch to his stomach, gave no immediate reply. Apparently impatient and unsatisfied, Musa launched his knee swiftly into Van Peenan's bare genitals. This time, the men were not able to hold onto him, and he fell to the floor, assuming the fetal position, his groin screaming with pain.

When they finally got him on his feet again, he caught a glimpse over Musa's shoulder at the brothel owner. His face brandished a big grin. He was apparently enjoying every moment. Van Peenan's whole lower body ached, but he tried to fight away the pain by concentrating on how much he wanted to kill the little son of a bitch.

"Once again, infidel," Musa spoke. "Who are you?"

"Lieutenant Commander Aubrey Van Peenan," he wheezed through throbbing lips. "Engineer on the USS *Providence*."

"Why is your ship in these islands?" Musa snapped.

"We're here to evacuate an American citizen." Van Peenan saw no point in lying about it. Especially not when his life hung in the balance.

The lightning fast punch to his gut, however, indicated his answer did not satisfy Musa. The wind left his lungs in a rush and it felt like one of his ribs had cracked under the force of the blow. After they returned him to his feet he had trouble breathing. Each breath seemed more painful than the last.

"I am going to give you one chance, infidel. After that, I will send you to the devil."

Van Peenan had no clue what he was talking about. What the hell did he want from him? Then he wondered if the terrorist leader was simply delusional, paranoid that the *Providence* had come to capture or kill him. Hell, didn't the son of a bitch know they sent SEALs to do that shit, not submarines? Either way, Van Peenan figured he had better think of something fast, or else he was a dead man.

"They don't tell me everything," he offered lamely. "I'm just the engineer. My job is to make the reactor work. If *Providence*'s here for some other reason, they didn't tell me. Don't hit me anymore."

His request obviously denied, Musa clopped him on the left ear and came close to shattering his eardrum from the sudden change in pressure.

"You are here to retrieve a spy, infidel!" Musa's face was red with anger. "And you are going to tell me where he is!"

Van Peenan's dizzy mind tried to make sense of what he was hearing, but he knew nothing about a spy. The *Providence* was there to get Dr. Whitehead. That was all he knew. Then a thought crossed his mind. Maybe Whitehead was the spy! Maybe the terrorist leader simply wanted to get his hands on Whitehead!

"We're here to pick up a Dr. Gregory Whitehead!" he said quickly. "He's your spy! He's got to be it!"

Musa grabbed Van Peenan's bloody face in both hands and held it before his own, forcing Van Peenan to look into his eyes. The intense stare almost made Van Peenan look away as he saw veins protruding from the black hairline above the terrorist leader's temples.

"What about the *other* one?" Musa asked quietly, but firmly. "Whitehead's partner! The other one you were sent to evacuate. Where is he? Tell me and I will let you live."

"Shit, I don't fucking know. I swear, I don't fucking know about any other. You've got to believe me!"

Musa regarded him solemnly. "You are either very brave, American, or you are a fool. Either way, you will die a painful death."

"Wait, wait!" Van Peenan struggled to think straight, but he'd been hit so many times and his head still throbbed from the earlier rifle blows. "I've got something you want! C'mon, you don't want to kill me. Do you want money? I can get you money!"

"The devil's money is useless to me, infidel."

"All right, how about knowledge? I'm a fucking nuclear engineer. You guys are always trying to get your hands on nukes, right? Well, I've got reams of nuclear tech manuals in my head. Shit, I could build you a fucking nuke from the ground up. I could be your own personal nuclear arms expert!"

"You act as though I do not already have these things, American. You have nothing that I want. If you don't know the location of Whitehead's partner, you are useless to me."

Van Peenan tried to speak again but ended up with a rifle butt in the small of his back, toppling him to the floor.

Musa said a few words in Arabic to his men, then headed for the door. Apparently he was going to leave Van Peenan's execution to his henchmen. But before he could leave, one man guarding the other prisoners against the wall asked, "What about these other men from the whorehouse?"

Musa paused. He appeared annoyed for a moment, then walked over to the man, snatching the AK-47 from his hands. In the blink of an eye he brought it to his waist and leveled it at the prisoners facing the far wall. Then the gun erupted in a rapid succession of flash, smoke, and ejecting shells. The Indonesian sailors and marines fell forward as the stream of bullets sprayed across their lower backs from left to right. It took only one complete magazine to put every man down, leaving two dozen holes and a runny spattering of blood on the wall beyond.

The room suddenly became very silent, although Musa's men appeared completely unfazed by the cold-blooded murders. The terrorist leader shot a glance back at Van Peenan, then suddenly shifted his gaze to the fidgeting brothel owner who was silently inching toward the door. Musa shouted something in Arabic and two of his men quickly grabbed hold of the little man, who instantly looked terrified. Musa tossed the AK-47 back to the guard and removed the MP5 automatic machine gun from its position slung across his back. As the two men held the brothel owner firmly between them, his eyes grew twice their size as Musa clicked off the safety and leveled the gun at his legs.

He fired a short staccato burst into the man's knees, which instantly spewed cartilage and bone fragments as they buckled beneath him. Musa's men released the brothel owner and let him fall to the ground, shrieking in pain, his legs oddly limp and twisted beside him. But Musa was not done and moved closer, now aiming the gun at his torso. The little man tried to scoot himself away, smearing blood across the concrete floor.

"A house of prostitution is not permitted under Allah," Musa said simply, as if passing sentence on the wretched little man.

The brothel owner brought his hands up, but they did little to stop the dozen rounds that Musa emptied into his chest, the MP5 expending the rounds in a *burrrp!* lasting no more than two seconds. The man died instantly, his chest a bloody mess. His body remained in the seated position until Musa kicked it over with a muddy boot.

At least that asshole got his! Van Peenan thought as he tried to roll into a better position to breathe. His ribs felt like they were piercing his lungs with every breath.

Musa glanced at him, naked and beaten on the floor. He said something in Arabic to the two men hovering over Van Peenan. Then he and the rest of his men exited the building, leaving Van Peenan alone with his two guards. From his position lying flat on the floor, Van Peenan wondered why he had not been killed with the rest, and for a moment he tendered the thought that he had been spared.

"They died quickly," the more vicious-looking of the two guards said, glaring down at him. "But you will die an infidel's death! You will pray for their fate before cold death overtakes your lips."

Without a moment's delay, the beating commenced. They kicked him repeatedly, took turns punching him while the other held him, kicked him in the groin, took off their web belts and flogged him across the back. It seemed to go on and on until he lost all sense of time and pain. He lost count as to how many times they'd hit him, his mind overloaded by the pain and bordering on a state of shock. Oddly, he began to think about how good this little entry would look on his officer record if he were to somehow survive it. The navy board could not deny promotion to an officer who had withstood capture and torture by terrorists, no matter how many failed ORSE inspections might tarnish his record. Just let the command board try to turn down his appointment, now. He'd have twenty admirals in front of the board the next day appealing on his behalf. Now with Dean out of the way, he could bring the hammer down on the department and make certain they didn't fail another inspection.

He was golden. That is, if he survived.

Any hopes of surviving seemed to fade when the two men finally tired of hitting him and drew out their long knives. Through swollen eyes, he saw that the knives had serrated edges. Now the real torture would begin.

"You will die without your manhood, infidel," said one of them, flipping his knife several times with one hand, while the other one spread Van Peenan's legs apart. He didn't have the energy to resist. Any move he tried to make hurt instantly, and his arms felt like they weighed a hundred pounds each. The two men seemed to chuckle with delight at the prospect of castrating him. He could not prevent it and simply closed his eyes to wait for the inevitable.

Suddenly, an explosion louder than any he had heard before shook the very foundations of the building. It must have been close outside, and he began to think that the weapons dump had exploded, but then came another distinct explosion, this one even louder. And now he ruled out the weapons dump. It sounded more like artillery rounds hitting close by. His torturers appeared startled and exchanged puzzled looks. They left him on the floor and went over to the door to see what was happening.

They never made it to the door. Just before they reached it, the door, the men, the whole side of the building disappeared in a massive explosion that blasted Van Peenan clear to the other side of the room in a sooty cloud of debris. His body came to rest amid a pile of timbers and sheet metal that had once been the far wall. The dust particles filling the air instantly inundated his mouth and eyes.

More explosions followed, all outside the warehouse among the concentrated rebel troop positions. He could hear men screaming outside, buildings burning, vehicles speeding away. He needed to seek shelter. Using his last ounce of strength, he dragged himself to a spot between two nearby crates. There he lay his face down on the debris-covered floor with the intent to pass out. He managed to roll onto his side to take some of the pressure off his ribs and felt something poking him from behind, something lodged between his lower back and the crate. Almost too weak to move, he thought about leaving it there, but it caused too much pain in his back. He felt around behind him and eventually pulled the odd-shaped, slippery, and unexpectedly heavy object out, lamely tossing it to the floor beside him.

"You got yours too, you asshole," he managed to mutter as a semblance of a smile appeared on his bruised face.

With Van Peenan's last conscious glimpse, he stared into the bulging eyes of the man who was to castrate him, the severed head with its contorted dirty face and tousled hair lying bloody on the floor beside him.

"CAPTAIN," Miller said from the periscope stand, never removing his face from the eyepiece. "I'll be damned, sir, but I think that frigate's shooting at the town now!"

Edwards stood with arms crossed, leaning against the periscope stand railing as he studied the view screen. In magnified view, it showed the two Indonesian warships steaming in a column formation, Admiral Syarif's frigate *Malahayati* in the lead a few hundred yards ahead of the smaller corvette *Nuku*, both bows laced in a white froth and making close to twenty knots. The ships appeared to be touching Bunda's shoreline—Bunda's steep, cloud-shrouded mountains filled the field of view behind them—but Edwards knew it was merely an optical illusion. The periscope magnification coupled with its low height of eye, just four feet above the water's surface, could play games with a person's depth perception. In reality the ships stood several miles off shore and well outside Bunda's reef barrier, through which the small procession of ships had passed under sporadic mortar fire only a few hours before.

The *Hatta* was nowhere to be seen. *Providence* had closely followed her through the treacherous passage, suffering no hits although several mortar rounds came unsettlingly close. Once they had made it beyond the barrier both submarines parted company, *Providence* heading south and the *Hatta* north to prevent any chance of an underwater collision when both eventually submerged.

At Admiral Syarif's advice, Edwards had taken the *Providence* even farther away from the island to give the Indonesian warships plenty of maneuvering space as the frigate's one-hundred-twenty-millimeter and forty-millimeter turret guns began pounding the rebel positions ashore. The bombardment had been going on for the better part of an hour, the high-angled gun barrels puffing out white smoke with each round fired, the smoke leaving a pall several feet above the water's surface marking the frigate's path and masking the corvette behind her. The corvette's guns were silent as she followed in the wake of her consort, the island well out of range of her less powerful guns.

Over the last few hours the situation on Bunda had turned from confusion to chaos. The fight ashore had not gone well for the marines. Electromagnetic interference paralyzed *Providence*'s HF communications, probably due to jamming, but the radiomen gleaned enough information from the chatter on the other frequencies to learn that the battle had taken an unexpected turn. The Indonesian marines, convinced that they faced an inferior opponent, a mere handful of guerillas, had pressed the offensive and ventured far into the jungle to root out the mortar emplacements. Instead they ran headlong into a trap. A rebel army several hundred strong quickly turned the hunter into the hunted. The marine offensive formations assumed hastily prepared defensive positions, which withstood very little punishment before breaking, the marines fleeing for the hoped safety of the town. The town, however, was no safe haven for the beleaguered marines. An uprising had all but ensued; citizens everywhere emerged from their homes and shops armed with newly furnished assault rifles and cut down the terrified marines piecemeal. Before long, the whole town was in rebel hands, the government complex being the last to fall. *Providence*'s radiomen reported hearing a last desperate plea to Jakarta for help, calling for air support, more troops, anything, before all went silent. As if to confirm the report, a thick column of black smoke appeared above the promontory, beyond which lay Ujungpang and the government buildings, completely obscured from *Providence*'s view by the point of land.

Now with the defeat complete, the Indonesian admiral had apparently decided to punish the town of Ujungpang for its betrayal. Up until now the frigate's shells had been focusing on the rebel positions in the jungle, but now she lobbed her shells over the high promontory to come down in the midst of the treasonous civilian population. On the view screen Edwards could see more smoke rising beyond the point of land as the naval shells started fires among the various buildings.

"He can't just open fire on those civilians like that!" Fremont said. He and the quartermaster watched the screen from the chart tables. "Those are innocent people! And our guys are still there!"

"Innocent people harboring a rebel army, Nav," Edwards replied. "I'm afraid as long as rebel troops occupy the town Admiral Syarif can do whatever he deems necessary to fight them. And he's got some face to save here. The rebels defeated his marines ashore while he and his flotilla escaped. To any casual observer in Jakarta it'll look like he deserted them."

Edwards tried not to show the concern he inwardly felt for *Providence*'s men ashore, none of whom had been heard from. There was no word on Lake and his shore party. No word on Dean in the hospital, nor word on Ensign Yi who had gone to visit him. No word on Van Peenan either, who had gone ashore the previous evening and strangely never returned to the ship.

He feared for their safety. All of them, as if they were his own children, and in some ways he felt responsible for being so stupid. Peto had warned him about the dangerous crisis brewing on the island. He should have figured out another way to retrieve Dr. Whitehead other than sending a poorly armed shore party to the other side of the island. He also should have made it clear to his officers that the "no liberty" policy applied to them as much as it did to *Providence*'s crewmen. Now, with Ujungpang under rebel control, and with no idea how his men would be treated at the hands of the rebels, Edwards felt impotent. He could do nothing but watch the events unfold and wait for the outcome.

"Did those situation reports go out to ComSubPac, Nav?" Edwards asked across the room.

"Yes, sir. We transmitted over an hour ago. Still don't have anything back yet."

Shit! Edwards thought. Certainly Admiral Chappell would be watching for *Providence*'s messages. Certainly he would see the note about the missing crewmembers and respond promptly with some kind of guidance. Or maybe the messages caught him in the middle of a round of golf. But Edwards knew that not to be true. Maybe for some other admirals, but not for Chappell. Chappell lived in the darkened SubPac situation room, very seldom enjoying Oahu's warm sun. He lived for the navy and for his sacred special operations projects. Twice divorced, the man had all but given up on devotion to the opposite sex for the one nearer his heart. Most considered him a total fanatic.

Edwards quickly banished the thought, suddenly realizing that he could well be describing himself.

"Strange that the Indonesian air force hasn't shown up yet, Captain," Miller commented. "Those marines could've used some air support. Might've held out a little longer anyway." He paused for a moment, rotating his wrist to increase the scope magnification. "Holy shit! That was a big one!"

Edwards glanced back at the screen to see a large fireball rising in the distance above the promontory. The flames rose several hundred feet into the air before evaporating into a black cloud of smoke. The explosion was too large to have been created by one of *Malahayati*'s rounds, and he concluded it must have been a secondary. One of the hundreds of projectiles being launched over the point of land must have found its mark. A fuel tank, a rebel ammunition depot, or something else highly explosive. Edwards glanced over at the sonar display to see a bright green dot appear on the same westerly bearing as Ujungpang. The explosion had at least been loud enough to send a pressure wave all the way through the water to *Providence*'s hydrophones more than a dozen miles away.

Looking at the green dot on the time history display, Edwards wondered how many people had died at that moment. Probably more civilians had died than rebels. Unless Syarif was still in contact with some surviving marine spotters, which he doubted, the naval bombardment was totally random and indiscriminate. How could Syarif commit such an atrocity?

"Conn, Sonar," the speaker intoned. "I have a new contact bearing three four zero. Designate contact as subsurface. Contact has a high bearing rate."

Edwards glanced at the bearing on the azimuth sonar display and saw a faint green line appear at the northwest position. The line curved sharply from right to left, or northwesterly to southwesterly, and appeared devoid of any rough edges, which would have indicated a civilian craft. It was definitely military and definitely submerged, but it couldn't be the *Hatta*. *Providence*'s sonar would not be able to detect her while she drove on her A.I.P. propulsion system. For a moment, Edwards thought they might have detected the phantom rebel submarine, but then he suddenly realized exactly what he was looking at. The green line was too fine, too smooth to be a ship, or a submarine for that matter. A cold tingly feeling shot down his spine just as the sonar chief's voice echoed his suspicions.

"Conn, Sonar, torpedo in the water bearing three zero five!"

The control room instantly took on a different feel. The helmsman sat on the edge of his seat, fingers twitching, anticipating an order for high speed. The chief of the watch covered the ballast control panel ready to sound the alarm or to flood or blow buoyant weight as needed; more importantly his hand hovered over the countermeasures launch panel to his left. In the aft portion of the room Fremont and the quartermaster plotted the torpedo bearing and began calculating the best evasion course. They all worked anxiously but efficiently, their training very evident. All waited for Edwards to give the order for evasion.

But Edwards didn't plan on evading, not just yet. As he observed the thin green line trace across the sonar screen he noticed that the torpedo's bearing rate—the rate at which it traveled across the azimuth—continued to remain high. If *Providence* had been its target the bearing rate would have fallen off to almost nothing shortly after sonar detected it. The torpedo would have steadied on a collision course with *Providence* coming at her from one steady bearing. The high bearing rate meant one of two things; either it was a poorly aimed weapon, or it was fired at another target. As the thin green line on the sonar display rapidly converged with the larger green line representing the *Malahayati* it removed any doubt from his mind.

"The torpedo doesn't appear to be closing us, Captain." The fire control technician, from one of the fire control consoles, stated the obvious. His computer had been converting the bearings passed from the sonar computers for the last minute. "I've got a solution on the torpedo now. Bearing two eight five, range eight thousand yards, course two two five, speed thirty knots."

"It's headed for the surface ships!" Fremont reported unnecessarily.

"Radio, Conn. Raise *Malahayati* on the bridge-to-bridge circuit," Edwards ordered into the control room's open microphone. He quickly moved to relieve Miller on the periscope stand, and the anxious weapons officer hurried over to one of the fire control consoles to verify the solution for himself.

"Chief of the Watch, man battle stations."

"Aye, aye, Captain." The chief reached above his panel, pulled the general alarm lever, and started the fourteen-bell gong resounding throughout the ship. Within seconds, feet pattered on the decks below. Moments later, the control room became the most crowded room on the ship as junior officers and fire control technicians squeezed into the empty consoles on the starboard side, all donning headsets to quietly communicate and thus keep the din at a manageable level. As the weapons officer, Miller took up position behind them, roaming from station to station making sure they tracked contacts as a team. A bad target solution entered into the system could take crucial minutes to remedy, thus all operators had to obtain his permission before entering a new solution into the system.

Extra quartermasters filed in behind Fremont, who directed them to the electronic plot. There they would maintain the tactical picture throughout the course of the action. A seaman appeared at Edwards' left to act as his periscope assistant, waiting for the order to raise or lower the scope. Another sailor sat next to the chief of the watch and donned a headset. Another sat behind the chief, waiting for any errand that might need running.

Edwards could imagine the other preparations going on all over the ship. Extra engineering watches manned in the aft compartment. The torpedomen scurrying around the torpedo room, preparing their lethal weapons for loading. The mechanics in the auxiliary machinery room three decks down, waiting beside their sleeping diesel generator in case it was needed for any reason. The corpsman transforming the wardroom into a sickbay. The twenty odd sailors that comprised the damage control teams filling the crew's mess, firefighting equipment and breathing apparatus strewn out on every table. Remarkably, the whole transformation took less than eight minutes.

One by one, the stations reported in to the chief of the watch over the phone system.

"All compartments report battle stations manned, Captain."

"Very well, Chief of the Watch," Edwards said calmly. *Providence* was not the torpedo's intended target, but going to battle stations was still an advisable move. He centered the periscope reticle on *Malahayati*'s main mast. Obviously still unaware of the approaching torpedo, the frigate continued to steam parallel to the coast on a northerly heading, her guns blazing away at the town. Likewise, the corvette followed obediently in her flagship's wake showing no signs of evasive maneuver.

"Conn, Sonar," once again the sonar chief's agitated voice intoned on the speaker. "Positive ID on the torpedo. Unit is a five-hundred-thirty-three-millimeter AEG SUT wire-guided weapon, thirty-five knots max speed, fifteen nautical mile tactical range. Torpedo is currently running in passive cruise mode."

"Sonar, Conn, aye."

"Captain, we need to clear datum!" Bloomfield's voice said fervently.

Edwards removed his face from the eyepiece to see his executive officer standing before him looking like a thing from the crypt. His hair was matted and disheveled, his eyes droopy. His belt hung open and loose in its loops, his T-shirted belly protruding through the jumpsuit zipper he had forgotten to fasten.

"XO . . . nice of you to join us. A little late reporting to your battle station, I see."

Luckily most of the men in the room were busy at their panels and didn't hear the exchange. Even if they did, Edwards was sick of this sorry excuse for an officer. Bloomfield regarded him with an open mouth. He had obviously just woken from a long nap. Shaking his jowls a few times, he pointed to the sonar display.

"Captain, there's a torpedo in the water!"

"I know that, XO. Unlike you, I've been in the control room since we left port. I see you took the first chance you could to hit the rack. Why doesn't that surprise me?"

Miller took a step away from the weapons consoles to speak lowly.

"Captain, I hate to side with the XO here. That torpedo

may not be headed our direction, but we still haven't detected the sub that fired it. For all we know, the next one might have our name on it. Wouldn't it be wise, sir, to go deep and stand away from the area?"

"The *Hatta* fired that torpedo, Weps. Of that, I'm certain. And *no*, we're not going deep until we've warned the surface ships."

Both men looked at him incredulously.

"Now, Weps, please resume your station," Edwards said, then faced Bloomfield with a look of disgust. "XO, you'll go below and take over in the crew's mess as the damage control coordinator."

"What?" Bloomfield seemed flabbergasted. "But my place is here as your approach officer, sir!"

"*Your* place is where I say it is, damn it!" Edwards snapped. "I've already got two officers stuck on that island because of your piss-poor judgment, and I certainly don't need any of your tactical advice up here. Now go below!"

As the slighted portly XO bounded down the passage on his way to the crew's mess, Edwards saw a few smirks appear on some of the junior sailors' faces. Perhaps he'd been wrong to treat Bloomfield so harshly in front of them. After all, he too was at fault for sending Lake and his men into the hostile countryside. If Bloomfield was guilty of poor judgment by letting Yi and Van Peenan go ashore, so was he. Either way, he felt relieved to have his bothersome executive officer gainfully employed elsewhere, especially in the present situation.

He was certain the *Hatta* had turned against her surface consorts. The type of torpedo, the lack of a launch transient, the direction from which the torpedo originated, all pointed to the *Hatta* being the shooter. Now, death closed fast on the Indonesian flagship. If she didn't maneuver soon, it would be too late.

"That torpedo's less than a thousand yards from the *Malahayati*, Captain," Fremont reported. "It's closing fast!"

"Conn, Sonar. Torpedo has commenced active homing."

The torpedo was now in its final stages. Edwards stared at the frigate, looking for a sign. Surely, by now, they must have detected the active sonar transmissions coming from the torpedo.

"Radio, what's the status of that comms circuit?" he shouted into the speaker.

"Conn, Radio. Unable to establish the circuit, Captain. Jamming is interfering with the bridge-to-bridge circuit. I can't raise them, sir!"

Seconds later the issue was moot. Edwards saw the frigate perform a sharp turn to port, heeling over heavily as she placed the incoming torpedo behind her. She had detected it now and was running for her life. A churning ocean appeared by her stern as she brought on flank speed, surpassing thirty knots, her stack blowing out a mass of dirty brown diesel exhaust. But the torpedo had also shifted to its top speed, a few knots more than the frigate's. The torpedo's active sonar had already locked onto the frigate's hanging keel, its guidance mechanism steering straight for it. A few yards at a time, the torpedo ate away at the distance to her prey. The outcome had been determined. It was a simple matter of distance and time. The *Malahayati* had detected the torpedo too late and now she could not get away. Her fate was sealed. Edwards thought he saw a few men leaping from the frigate's main deck, splashing into the water beside. Some on board obviously knew what awaited them.

It seemed like hours but it took only minutes. The torpedo closed the distance, and as Edwards watched in the periscope, everyone else in the control room looked up at the view screen to see the inevitable happen. In the blink of an eye the ocean turned white underneath the *Malahayati*'s hull, then the hull erupted in a towering geyser shooting straight up through her mainmast lifting the ship's guts along with it several hundred feet into the air. The frigate buckled like a tin shed in a high wind, then bowed inward, her hull breaking into fore and aft sections as the column of water returned to the earth, raining steel girders, electrical cabling, wooden crates, and bodies, all marked by splashes all around her. It was a perfect hit, the torpedo detonating directly beneath the frigate, the ensuing gas bubble expanding as it rose. The bubble had exposed the rigid keel to an enormous tensile stress for a mere fraction of a second, but long enough to snap it like a piece of balsa wood, breaking the frigate completely in two. Both sections now quickly filled with water, the forward section pointing its sharp bow to the sky while the aft section exposed the still spinning twin screws.

"Sonar, Conn. Torpedo has detonated, bearing two six five."

The report was absurdly unnecessary, but the routine of discipline never stopped on a submarine. So many men must have died in the explosion. Edwards rested his forehead against the eyepiece for a brief moment, certain that few, if any, of *Malahayati*'s crew had survived. If the admiral had been on the bridge, as most likely he was, his body was now raining in atomized pieces over the gray clouded sea.

From the moment Peto introduced himself at the mayor's house, Edwards had suspected him. Or more accurately, he suspected the *Hatta* was indeed the phantom rebel sub. Now, it appeared that Peto and his state-of-the-art submarine had been a part of the rebel movement from the beginning. A critical part of a master plan. It made perfect sense. For Peto's rough childhood, he could certainly blame the government in Jakarta. For the death of his parents he could blame the military establishment. For the oppression of his local community he could blame the appointed *walikota*. But for the suppression of his dreams, he could only blame himself. And though he had only just met Peto yesterday, Edwards felt he knew him well enough to understand his motives. Peto did not strike him as the kind to let others define his own boundaries. He dreamed of a better world for his people. Despite all its merciless violence, the carnage Edwards had just witnessed was merely an action in the pursuit of those dreams. The desperate action of an idealist in pursuit of freedom.

As the smoke cleared away from the frigate's destruction, the corvette *Nuku* became visible again, showing *Providence* her stern as she headed west at top speed. Obviously anticipating that *Hatta*'s next torpedo would be meant for her, she was making a mad dash for the shallow reef boundary. The sharp reef walls, while treacherous to any vessel, could deceive a torpedo by yielding false sonar returns. It was a good idea, Edwards thought, and the only option left now to *Nuku*'s captain. With luck, any incoming torpedo's onboard computer would confuse the *Nuku*'s signal with the mass of returns bouncing off the jagged coral. The torpedo would eventually pick out a big chunk of coral and explode harmlessly on the rocks—the *Nuku* would escape.

But all hope of *Nuku*'s escape dissolved when Edwards again heard the sonar chief's voice over the speaker.

"Conn, Sonar. Launch transient, bearing three four zero."

Edwards swung the scope around to the northwesterly bearing and saw exactly what he expected to see. In the middle of the empty expanse of sea, a tongue of flame shot up from the water and into the sky, leaving a pall of white smoke to mark the launch point. The object propelled itself high into the air, then arced down again until it steadied on a wave-hugging altitude only a few feet above the water's surface. The fifteen-foot flying projectile, obviously a Harpoon anti-ship missile, quickly transformed to a mere blur as its flaming booster extinguished and the internal turbojet engine took over. The missile turned one time, made a minor course correction, then headed straight for the hapless corvette at six hundred miles per hour.

Edwards swung the scope to the left to view the *Nuku*. With impact only seconds away, she shot glittering chaff into the air above her and the twin gun turret on her bow spat out a deluge of thirty-millimeter projectiles at the rate of ten per second. But the corvette's inferior radar and tracking computer could not correct fast enough to intercept the high-speed missile. Instead, the ensuing torrent of shells kicked up the ocean surface in a stretching curtain of water that lagged well behind the missile but clearly marked its path as it raced to its target. Moments later, the Harpoon slammed into *Nuku*'s superstructure on the starboard side, penetrated the metal skin, and exploded. As Edwards watched, the structure and main mast disappeared in a massive fireball that bubbled into a fiery oxygen-deprived inferno in the sky. Like a demonic beast from hell, the churning fireball groped for the oxygen above the ship, then suddenly found itself isolated from its fuel source below. Seconds later it extinguished into a black cloud of dense, ashen smoke, leaving nothing below but the charred and burning remnants of a once living ship. Now, a flat hulk with no semblance of man-made shape or form sat low on the horizon, small fires scattered along its length. It was all that remained of the corvette *Nuku*.

Every man in the control room watched the devastation with disbelief, and it took several reprimands from the chief of the watch before they turned their attention back to their stations. In the space of a few minutes, the *Hatta* had turned Admiral Syarif's flotilla into an oily patch of burning flotsam. It was a perfect example of the immense power one small submarine could unleash when it had the advantage. A striking example that left even *Providence*'s veteran submariners in awe.

"Captain," Miller called anxiously from the weapons consoles, "we've entered a makeshift solution on the *Hatta* based on the last bearing from that launch transient. Bearing three four zero, range ten thousand yards. Recommend warming up the weapons in tubes one and three, and opening outer doors, sir."

Edwards glanced at the burning corvette one last time before motioning for the periscope to be lowered. From this range the *Hatta* posed no threat to the *Providence*. Even if she had hostile intentions toward the *Providence*, which he doubted, her AEG SUT torpedoes could only manage thirty-six knots maximum in the right environmental conditions. *Providence* could easily outrun them at flank speed. There was no point in challenging her.

"We're going deep," he said evenly. "Chief of the Watch, lower all masts and antennas. Helm, all ahead standard. Dive, make your depth six hundred feet. Nav, give me a good course to deep water."

As the deck tilted downward and *Providence* picked up speed, Miller moved closer to him and leaned on the railing.

"Shouldn't we consider the *Hatta* as hostile now, Captain?" he said in a low voice. "I mean, they attacked our allies, didn't they? I think we should take them, sir, before they try to take us out, too."

"Go read your Rules of Engagement Manual again, Weps. A hostile act against another nation doesn't give us carte blanche to engage. Not unless we've got special rules of engagement handed down from SubPac for this specific situation, which we don't. No, we're going to stand off and contact SubPac for guidance. The situation's out of our hands now."

Miller appeared less than satisfied as he moved back over to the starboard side of the room. Perhaps when he attained command someday he would understand the different authorities a captain answered to. A captain always had to consider the international ramifications of his actions. Not only did he answer to ComSubPac, but also to the National Command Authority. A mere submarine captain had no place declaring sides in another country's civil war.

"Course one one two's a good course, Captain," Fremont called from the chart tables.

"Helm, right standard rudder. Steady on course one one two." Edwards caught another glance from Miller out of the corner of his eye. Someday he would learn. "Stand down from battle stations and station the section tracking party. If the *Hatta* so much as sneezes, I want to know about it."

LIEUTENANT Scott Lake couldn't believe what he'd just witnessed.

From the high mountain road overlooking the island's eastern shore, he had looked out at the gray-clouded sea and watched both Indonesian warships meet their fate, both exploding sequentially from what he assumed was a weapons attack. The distance and the poor lighting hid the details, but it appeared that both ships had been completely destroyed. Burning flotsam now remained where the two ships had been cruising only minutes before. As he pondered the meaning of this small Indonesian naval disaster, he noticed smoke to the south, and lots of it, rising above the ridges hiding the distant Ujungpang.

Whitehead's predictions seemed to be coming true.

"Can you get anyone on that thing yet?" he turned around to ask Reynoso riding in the back seat.

Reynoso shook his head. "These mountains are interfering with the signal, sir. I'm only getting one bar. As soon as I try to place a call I get dropped."

The grimacing radioman held the satellite telephone before his face, its bulky foot-long antenna extending out ahead of him. Earlier, after the electromagnetic interference prevented all use of the HF radio, Lake had ordered Reynoso to try to contact the *Providence* on the satellite phone. The satellite phone operated on a much higher frequency and was thus less susceptible to jamming. However, it required an unobstructed line of sight to communicate with the satellites overhead. Not an easy task on this winding road which led through some of Bunda's deepest gorges and crevasses.

"I thought you said that thing was a satellite phone," Teresa commented from the driver's seat. "A lot of good it does you. Your taxpayers' money at work once again."

Why the hell should you care how much it cost? Lake thought to himself. *You're a fucking Canadian!*

Reynoso provided a more civil response, "Actually, ma'am, this phone uses multiple satellites to convey its signal to the network's earth gateway. It uses L.E.O. satellites. That's why we're having a hard time placing a call."

"You lost me already," she said cynically. "What the hell's L.E.O.? Or wait, don't tell me! I've got an idea. Maybe I'll ask my fucking dad. I'm sure he fucking knows! He seems to suddenly know everything. It seems I'm the only one around here that's been kept in the dark."

Reynoso looked slightly confused by her rambling, but chose to answer anyway. "L.E.O. stands for Low Earth Orbit, ma'am. Ideally, we'd use satellites in a geosynchronous orbit around the Earth, but a satellite has to be pretty far away to be in that kind of orbit. Even a light wave takes a couple seconds to travel that distance. The resulting time delay would render the phones useless for normal conversation. That's why we use Low Earth Orbit satellites, so that we can minimize the time delay. But the problem is, low orbit satellites can't remain over the same spot on the earth. They've got to have some speed on them, or else they'll fall out of orbit and burn up in the atmosphere. Because of that, the satellites perform, what we call, a 'handoff.' When the satellite that has the call travels over the horizon, it automatically hands off the call to another satellite just coming into range. On top of that, you have to deal with the crypto synching, and . . ."

"All right, already!" she said, as the jeep took a bump. "I get the picture, you can't call your ship. I'm sorry I asked."

Lake had noticed a curious—although completely understandable—change in Teresa's demeanor since she had learned of her father's true occupation. After a few emotional moments at Dr. Whitehead's camp before they left, she had quickly assumed a posture of loathsome indifference. That is, an attitude of indifference that did not acknowledge her father in any way, shape, or form. All attempts at consolation by Whitehead were shunned and Teresa made it clear that her father would not be riding in *her* jeep back to Ujungpang. Perhaps the doctor knew better, but he had chosen not to argue with his daughter. Instead he had thrown his gear into the police SUV, prompting the rest of them to get a move on before his unseen Islamic militants appeared out of the surrounding forest. About a half-mile up the road from the camp, along a shady patch of thick trees, their little two-vehicle convoy was flagged down by a man standing near the side of the road. The man was an Arab, dressed in green shorts and a tan T-shirt, both in ribbons. His face carried scars in several places, some of them recent, some resembling burn wounds. Whitehead had jumped out of the SUV with a wide grin and vigorously shaken the Arab man's hand, then, soon after, introduced him to the group as "Ahmad." Lake concluded that this dirty, jungle-reeking individual was the "associate" that Whitehead had earlier mentioned. Obviously, the strange man prompted questions from the two Ujungpang policemen, but they were quickly silenced when Whitehead produced the Arab man's passport in one hand, and a wad of cash in the other.

While the doctor insisted that he and Ahmad ride in separate vehicles for redundancy's sake, Teresa insisted that her father not ride with her for malice's sake. Thus, the expressionless Ahmad took his place in the jeep's back seat next to Reynoso and said very little, while Chief Michaelson moved to the SUV's empty back seat next to Whitehead. Without further delay, the little convoy had resumed its long drive on the mountain road to Ujungpang.

Little conversation took place in the jeep on the drive back, Reynoso trying to get the phone to work, Teresa still smarting from her father's true identity, and Ahmad—the man had said hardly two words in as many hours. He simply stared out at the brief glimpses of ocean or at the jungle on either side, whether in a daze or just relaxing, Lake could not tell. From the little Lake had been able to glean, Ahmad had been living in the jungle for several days now. The grime on his clothes and legs confirmed this. He appeared to be only a few years older than Lake, his matted black hair still showing no signs of gray, his skin for the most part free of the creases brought on by age, and, despite his stay in the jungle, he appeared to be in excellent condition. The cut-off fatigue pants he wore clearly displayed the lean muscles pulsating on his thighs and calves, not diminished by an equally impressive upper body. Above all else, his gray eyes stood out from their deep cavities, exuding an intensity Lake had never seen before. Casual and quiet as Ahmad's demeanor might have been, Lake caught those gray eyes several times scanning the jungle on both sides of the road like a searchlight.

The little convoy reached an open stretch on the mountain road, an extension of land bounded on one side by a steep jungle-covered slope, and on the other by a sharp rocky cliff. The sheer drop to the left side of the road ended where the ocean crashed against the rocks several hundred feet below. The combination of the vertical drop, the narrow road, and Teresa's driving made Lake extremely nervous. What made him even more nervous was the serious lack of cover on this part of the highway. The mile-long stretch afforded no hiding place for the vehicles. It was an excellent spot for an ambush, should any rebels be hiding in the dense woods rising sharply to their right. Conversely, the high altitude allowed an excellent view of Ujungpang, still several miles away to the south. He remembered passing this spot earlier in the day, and how breathtaking the view had been from this high vantage point looking over the vast ocean. In contrast to the morning, a cloudy expanse now hung over the dark sea. Rain squalls dotted the horizon here and there as solid gray sheets reaching down to touch the water's surface, some close, some far away. He got a chill as the stiff wind hit his face and flapped his ball cap around. The wind carried with it the heavy smell of rain.

"Lots of smoke over there, Mr. Lake," Reynoso said, pointing toward Ujungpang.

Lake looked ahead to see smoke rising in several places around the distant town, now visible beyond the next ridge. The buildings were tiny from this distance, but a few appeared to burn ferociously, the lapping flames clearly visible. A point of land still hid most of the harbor from view, including the merchant pier where he hoped the *Providence* still waited for them.

"From the looks of things," Lake commented to Teresa while pointing at the distant town, "I'd say we could be driving straight into trouble."

"I couldn't tell you, Lieutenant. You'll have to ask my father," Teresa said sternly. Glancing in the rearview mirror, she added, "Or maybe you could ask Ahmad back there. I'm sure he knows what the fuck's going on."

Ahmad stared off at the ocean, seemingly oblivious to the conversation. Lake didn't press the issue with him. Every shot Teresa placed across his bow seemed to clam him up even more.

Lake cursed his bad luck. He had no idea who the hell this *Ahmad* was, or what the hell Ahmad and Whitehead were up to. He really had no choice but to believe them. Just get them to Ujungpang, he kept telling himself, then all the responsibility would be off his shoulders. Hopefully, *Providence* would still be there, then he could turn them over to the captain. Let *him* decide whether or not they're on the up and up.

"Wait!" An instantly energized Ahmad suddenly spoke and

reached forward, placing a dirty hand on Teresa's shoulder. "Stop the vehicle!"

"Get your hand off me!" Teresa said, stopping the jeep in the middle of the road. "Just who the hell do you think you are?"

Ahmad didn't answer, didn't even seem to hear her protest. He was sitting up straight on the edge of his seat, his head whirling from side to side, his eyes scanning all around.

"Shhh!" he finally said. "Do you hear it?"

"Hear what?" Teresa retorted.

Ahmad's fierce eyes indicated that he was serious, and they convinced Lake to turn an ear toward the jungle to see if he could detect whatever it was that held Ahmad's complete attention. At first Lake heard nothing. Then, his wind-blown ears detected a distinct repetitive sound, emerging from the ambient jungle noise. It rapidly grew louder, and louder, until the wind itself seemed to pulsate with it.

"A helo," Lake said calmly. "Maybe they're coming to pick us up?"

"Everyone out!" Ahmad shouted, obviously not sharing in Lake's optimism. "Get out of the jeep!"

While Lake exchanged quizzical glances with Teresa and Reynoso, Ahmad leaped out of the jeep and darted for the cover of the sloping jungle to the right of the road.

Suddenly, like a huge hornet, the helicopter emerged from the valley up ahead, rising up to hover over the road. It was directly in their path and only a few hundred yards away, its rotors beating the air to a menacing pulsation that shook the jeep's thin metal skin. The SUV carrying Whitehead, Michaelson, and the two policemen, had driven on a bit further, but it came to a sudden stop too when the dark green Huey made its sudden appearance.

Whether the helicopter had been waiting in ambush or simply patrolling the mountain road, Lake could not tell. Whatever its purpose, it instantly spotted the exposed vehicles on the bare cliff, and like an angry beast dipped its head to move toward them, closing the distance at an alarming rate. With no room to turn around, the SUV's wheels spun in reverse, kicking up dust and rocks as it swerved along the narrow road. Obviously, the policemen sensed they were in danger, and Lake guessed that this helicopter was not a friendly one.

The SUV had no hope of escape. Within seconds the helo reached a position just above it. The police driver, in a frenzy to get away, steered erratically and eventually lost control of the vehicle. Still in reverse, the jeep took a screeching turn toward the cliff's edge then swerved sharply away, plowing into the steep embankment on the right side of the road. The force from the impact smashed the vehicle's rear bumper, collapsing it into the rear wheelbase, rendering the vehicle completely immobile. With its prey now disabled, the Huey swooped away from the road to hover just off the cliff's face, directly opposite the wrecked SUV.

Lake watched in disbelief as a man appeared in the helo's open side door hefting a rocket propelled grenade launcher. Lake glanced at the SUV. No one had emerged yet. Whitehead and the others must still be dazed from the crash. Lake desperately cried out to warn them, but the sound of the whirling rotors drowned out his voice entirely.

The left rear door of the SUV suddenly popped open and Chief Michaelson threw himself out onto the ground. He appeared to be in pain, but managed to quickly roll into a small gully between the embankment and the road. No one else emerged. Half a second later, the man standing in the Huey's door fired his weapon. A short blast of smoke appeared out the helo's opposite side as the solid rocket propellant shot the grenade from its short tube. The piercing round went straight through the SUV's front windshield and exploded inside the passenger compartment, blasting the windows out in all directions and instantly igniting the gas tank. Within seconds, the metal shell turned into a blazing pyre. As the flames quickly expanded, they ignited the flammable oil and gas spilled onto the road until the road itself appeared to be on fire. Through the flames, Lake saw three shadowy forms still sitting in their seats all ablaze and undistinguishable.

No one could have survived the grenade blast, or the fire.

"Father!" Teresa screamed. *"Oh my God, Father!"*

She clutched her hair and face in her hands as she watched the holocaust in disbelief, tears streaking beneath her sunglasses. The impact of seeing her father burn before her eyes had paralyzed her, and Lake had difficulty removing her from the driver's seat.

The helo was still there, and now they were the target. He had to get her to safety, and fast. Motioning for Reynoso to grab the radio equipment, Lake slapped Teresa across the face and eventually managed to tear her away from her fixated stare. The Huey had already started moving down the road toward them. It would be on them in seconds.

"We have to go!" he shouted, then grabbed her hand and yanked her from the jeep. Ahmad was nowhere to be seen, so Lake dashed for the closest patch of jungle, with Teresa and Reynoso following close on his heals, Reynoso lugging the silver communications suitcase. They reached the dense woods just as an RPG round screeched through the air behind them, penetrated the hood of the thin-skinned jeep, and blew it apart. Lake could hear pieces of metal whipping by their heads, slicing through the thick green fronds and thudding into the mineral-rich dirt. Once under cover of the dense foliage, the ground angled up drastically and they found themselves crawling on their hands and knees to get farther away from the road.

The Huey began circling above them. Moments later, they learned that it also had a mounted heavy machine gun. The gun opened up in an endless staccato blast, drowning out everything, including the sound of the rotors. The lethal missiles began spraying the jungle in all directions, and the three flattened as multiple rounds impacted the dirt several yards to their left. Too close for comfort, but still not near enough to have been specifically aimed. It led Lake to believe the gunner had lost sight of them and was now shooting randomly in hopes of hitting something. He found himself thanking God for the thick canopy above them. The ground in this area was thick with it, the green belt running up the long slope until it almost reached the crest of Bunda's central mountain ridge. Too steep for cultivation, it had been left virtually undisturbed since the ancient volcanic activity centuries ago. Lake found himself pondering for a brief moment that he now knew how grateful North Vietnamese soldiers must have felt, thirty years ago, for the thick foliage of their own country.

The machine gun continued shooting long bursts into the trees while Lake, Teresa, and Reynoso inched farther and farther away, climbing some, then moving farther to the right in an effort to place as much forest as possible between them and the road. Crawling through the thick reddish dirt on their hands and knees, it soon covered their faces and clothes. Lake and Reynoso found themselves pressing to keep up with Teresa, whose body seemed more attuned to this kind of physical exertion. Her years in the Peace Corps using her legs to get her where she needed to go were paying off. In contrast, the six months the two sailors had spent at sea were quickly becoming apparent.

The Huey moved from one place to the next, hovering over different spots in an effort to find them, coming close many times, many times forcing the three to dodge the unaimed machine gun bullets. After a few more close calls, Lake began to think it was only a matter of time before the Huey got lucky and found them. Then, the machine gun abruptly stopped firing. As suddenly as it had appeared, the Huey increased power and broke away, the rotor sound quickly fading away to the north. Lake began to wonder what had diverted their assailants, then soon found his answer as a roaring squall rolled across the jungle. Within moments the deluge began pouring on their position. The water came down in sheets, clangorously impacting the large green fronds above until Lake had trouble hearing himself think. Within moments, the fertile dirt turned into muddy rivulets streaming down the mountainside in ever-increasing ferocity, forcing the three to take shelter in some thick tree roots to avoid being swept away.

The Huey's crew, whoever they were, obviously had decided not to contend with the squall, and had broken off the hunt.

"We're safe," Lake shouted to the others over the beating

rain. "For the moment, anyway. I'm sure they'll come back once this storm lifts."

A quarter hour turned to thirty minutes. Then thirty minutes turned into an hour, but the squall showed no sign of abating. The downpour lost some of its original intensity, but it still came down in buckets. The low gray clouds, tossed south by a tropical storm a thousand miles to the north, traveled slowly across Bunda's mountain chain, so slow that they seemed to hover there. But the sky was scarcely visible from their current position. The three sat a few feet downhill from a towering clove tree that must have been over a hundred years old. Two twisted jutting roots formed a large "V" and a natural shelter from the streams of water coming down the hillside. Though soaking wet and miserable, Lake welcomed the storm's protection. As he rested his head against a partially exposed root, he saw Teresa sitting against the opposite root sobbing relentlessly, her arms crossed on her drawn up knees, her face buried.

He could not blame her for letting it out. She'd been through a lot today. Much more than the rest of them had. In a rather abrupt way, she'd learned the truth about her father only to see him killed before her eyes a few hours later. Who wouldn't let loose after something like that?

Reynoso made a face at Lake as if he should console her, but Lake waved him off. Such pain and confusion were better conquered in silent contemplation. Or at least, that's what Lake assumed from his limited experience in the matter.

"Lieutenant," a voice said behind him as he felt a hand clap onto his shoulder. Lake nearly jumped out of his skin, turning to find that the hand belonged to a rain-soaked and muddy Ahmad.

"Where the hell have you been?" Lake asked heatedly once he'd recovered from the shock. "You sure as hell didn't waste any time high-tailing it to safety!"

Water streamed from the long black strands of hair hanging down past the Arab's eyebrows as his stern face regarded Lake for several long seconds. Then he shrugged, and said dryly, "I told you to get out of the jeep. You chose to wait."

Lake fought back the urge to punch him in the face. Given the circumstance he decided against it. If Ahmad was an agent, he was probably trained in close combat and could probably kill him with a coconut or any of a dozen other odd weapons nearby.

"We must go," Ahmad said simply. "They will return to look for us on foot. I've found a more concealed spot five hundred yards uphill. I've already taken your comrade there."

"Our comrade . . ." Lake stuttered. "Uh . . . Michaelson! Is he okay?"

"His leg is broken, but he will live. Come, we must hurry."

Lake suddenly felt relieved that he'd refrained from hitting Ahmad. Anyone who could drag the two-hundred-and-thirty-pound Michaelson uphill five hundred yards in the mud had to be a virtual fitness machine—an ironman.

Obviously not one to waste much time with conversation, Ahmad motioned once for them to follow and began climbing up the muddy slope, never once looking back.

"Let's go," Lake said to Reynoso, then suddenly noticed that the skinny radioman was empty-handed. The silver communications suitcase was no where in sight. "Where the hell's the box, Reynoso?"

Reynoso looked like a drowned rat as he responded meekly, "I dropped it, sir. Back there. The hill was too steep, and that helo was shooting at us. I couldn't crawl and carry it at the same time and still keep up, sir. I'm sorry."

"Shit, Reynoso, why didn't you say something? Holy shit, now we're fucked! Of all the stupidest . . . I hope you realize, Einstein, that that suitcase was our only way to contact the fucking ship!" Lake immediately saw his words hurting Reynoso like daggers. He instantly wished he could withdraw them, but the damage was done. His anger had gotten the better of him. All he wanted to do was to get back to the ship and get home and out of the navy, but the whole situation was getting worse by the minute. Now losing the comms suitcase was the coup de grâce.

Reynoso smarted from the verbal lashing, his eyes looking

everywhere but at Lake. His face sagged visibly before he said, "I can go get it, sir. I'm pretty sure I know where it is."

Lake glanced up the hill. Ahmad had already climbed a good distance and would soon be out of sight. They would have to climb quickly to keep up with him. Going after the suitcase would be too risky.

"No," Lake said to Reynoso with forced calm. "It's okay. Just get going up the hill. We can't lose sight of that guy, or we'll never find him again."

Nodding appreciatively, Reynoso started up the hill behind Ahmad. Lake walked over and gently touched Teresa's arm, indicating that they had to get moving. Without a word, and with the inner fortitude of one who had seen anguish in a dozen different places around the globe, she stood up, wiped away the tears, and headed up the mountain behind Reynoso.

Chapter 13

ONE hundred miles east of the Bunda islands in the dark depths of the gray-shrouded ocean, the black-hulled *Providence* cruised slowly on a northerly course at a depth of four hundred feet. Night had fallen over the cloudy sea, rendering the submarine's deep environment pitch black. But her great rounded nose with its spherical hydrophone array listened to any and all noises surrounding her. A thousand different noises at a thousand different frequencies occupied nearly every point on the compass, and gave her drowsy sonarmen much to listen to on their late night watch. Clicking schools of fish, rumbling volcanoes, lumbering whale song, and a dozen other odd sounds made up this great concert of the sea. To this orchestra, *Providence* contributed very little. For that was how her rubber-coated hull and technologically-quieted pumps and turbines were designed. But if one keen and particularly bored sonar operator decided to scan his own ship's noises, he might discover a small pulsating rhythm emanating from far aft, somewhere in the engine room on the starboard side. He might not recognize the sound at first and thus might resort to the computer's historical data files to see if he could cross-reference and properly identify it. No files existed relating to this particular noise, but if such a file did exist the young sailor might find its title to read: *"Treadmill, Submarine Commander, Pissed Off."*

On the treadmill, situated in the engine room's upper level, just outboard of the starboard main engine, a dripping Edwards gritted his teeth as he punched the up arrow to increase the jogging speed. As he rapidly increased his stride, he carefully positioned himself on the belt so as not to hit his head on the low hanging pipes and valves. Discovering that his gray

T-shirt was saturated with sweat, Edwards couldn't remember the last time he'd pushed himself this hard. He'd been running for the better part of an hour but had no trouble handling the added speed. As a couple of mechanics walked by toting tools to do maintenance on some piece of equipment further aft, he imagined that his pumping legs must appear a mere blur to them.

Though intense, the workout felt good. It felt good to let off some steam. It had been over twenty-four hours since he had witnessed the destruction of the Indonesian ships, and the situation had not improved. He still had no clear direction from SubPac and *Providence*'s six crewmen were still abandoned ashore.

The deck suddenly leaned slightly to port, and he felt gravity pulling him to one side of the treadmill belt. Compensating accordingly, he glanced at his watch to confirm that *Providence* was executing one of her long, wide turns to return to the southerly leg of the racetrack course she had repeated for the last three watches. With his ship still close enough to monitor activity around Bunda, Edwards had ordered *Providence*'s towed sonar array extended for long-range monitoring. The dangling array at the end of its mile-long tether streamed far behind the big churning screw, far from any noises created by the submarine. With its powerful beam-directed sensing nodes, the array could easily pick up any sea activity in and around the Bunda Islands, even at this distance, though he doubted it could detect the *Hatta*.

"Captain, 2JV, sir," he heard the engine room speaker intone, just barely audible above the din of the main engine steam piping.

He pressed the pause button on the treadmill's sweat-splashed control panel, then picked up the small towel he'd slung over a nearby pipe hanger. The towel felt scratchy on his face, its fibers hard from six months of washing without fabric softener. As he allowed his heart to settle down to a normal rate, he stepped off the treadmill and found the nearest 2JV phone.

"Captain," he said, placing the phone to his ear and depressing the button to talk.

"Captain, Engineering Officer of the Watch, sir," Lieutenant (j.g.) Kemper's nervous voice responded immediately. Lieutenant (j.g.)'s always got nervous when they spoke to their captain. Especially when their captain was in a bad mood. "I'm sorry to bother you, but the control room called for you, sir. The navigator said to tell you we've received a message from ComSubPac, and did you want him to bring it aft?"

Finally, instructions! Edwards thought.

"No, Mr. Kemper. Tell the Nav I'll come forward."

"Aye, aye, sir," Kemper's voice said before the phone went dead.

Edwards hung up the phone, tossed the towel over his shoulder and started the long walk forward, anticipating what the message might contain. Hopefully, ComSubPac had *some* orders for him. Hours had passed with no clear direction from the admiral.

Going deep after the Indonesian warships' destruction, he'd taken *Providence* to her present position a safe distance from Bunda's coastline, then popped up to comms depth. *Providence* had spent most of the previous midwatch at periscope depth, attempting to reach both ComSubPac and the shore party. But the messages to SubPac requesting guidance appeared to fall on deaf ears, the only reply simply stated that *Providence* should "*hold position and wait for tasking.*" Attempts at communication with Lake's shore party had proved even more frustrating, though much of the electromagnetic interference had diminished. Edwards had been in the radio room hovering over the operators' shoulders as they called on each successive frequency, only to hear static in return. In light of the potential hazards in the area and not wishing to keep *Providence* shallow, Edwards had ordered the officer of the deck to stream the floating wire antenna and take the ship deep. The antenna, floating on the surface several hundred feet above the submerged submarine, could adequately receive any messages from ComSubPac, although at a much reduced baud rate. Now finally, almost eighteen hours later, SubPac had responded.

As Edwards passed the turbine generator sets going forward, he noticed Lieutenant Coleman up ahead, PDA in hand, conversing with one of the engineering chiefs. Coleman caught sight of him and hurried aft to greet him.

"Good evening, Captain." Unlike Kemper, the diligent young Coleman never had any compunctions about approaching his captain, no mattered what his captain's disposition.

"Anything to report, *Acting Engineer*?" Edwards asked with a forced smile. With Van Peenan absent, he'd made Coleman the acting engineer. It would seem an odd choice, since he needed all his sonar resources to listen for the *Hatta*, but in reality the division officer was more of an administrative role and had little to do with the operational side of the ship's sonar suite. *Providence* had an excellent sonar chief in Chief Ramirez, and that was what mattered most. The engineering department, however, could not run without a department head. Too many day-to-day items required the engineer's permission and sometimes intervention. Next to Lake, Coleman was *Providence*'s most senior lieutenant and had recently finished all the qualifications required to be a ship's engineer.

"No problems, Captain," Coleman said in his customary professional tone. "We're seeing a slight decrease in condenser vacuum due to the warm water around here. It's not a problem, but with all the volcanic activity in these islands, it's possible we could drive over a hydrothermal vent and catch a hot up-flow. That might trip a condenser if we're not careful. I'd like to get your approval to shift main seawater pumps to fast speed, sir. Just as a precaution."

"Very well. Put it in the night orders and I'll sign it."

"Aye, aye, sir," Coleman said, before hurrying back to converse with the waiting chief.

For a moment, Edwards wished Coleman were not the ship's *acting* engineer, but the *actual* one. Van Peenan never would have given such a clear and concise request. Had the same request come from Van Peenan, it would have been frustratingly obtuse and laced with ass-covering statements. But still—Edwards corrected his train of thought—it did no good to wish things were different. He had to work with the crew he was given. And now he had to focus on getting his missing crewmen back.

Taking the ladder down to the engine room's middle level, Edwards headed for the long shielded tunnel to the forward compartment. Foot traffic in the passageways was light due to the late hour. He passed through the darkened crew's mess where two dozen hands were watching an action movie on a wide flat-screen monitor. Some faces smiled, thoroughly absorbed in the film. Some appeared distant and gloomy. Several of these hands glanced in his direction as he skirted along the outboard passage. Most likely, they were wondering what the future held. With the present circumstances it seemed *Providence*'s return to Pearl would be delayed once again. More bad news for the anxious families back home.

Darting up the ladder just forward of the mess, he reached the control room where he found Fremont standing at the watch officer's podium, thumbing through several printed messages.

"Anything good?" Edwards asked as cheerily as he could, still in his gym shorts and sweaty T-shirt

"I'm afraid not, Captain." Fremont looked confused, even distressed. "We still have no orders from SubPac, but we've been copied on a rash of area alerts and intel reports going out to all of Seventh Fleet. It's strange, sir."

"What's strange?"

"They cite Indonesian waters as a hot zone, Captain, warning all ships to use due caution when transiting. Of course that's not news to us, but according to this intel report, an armed insurrection has broken out all across eastern Indonesia. Borneo, Sulawesi, Irian Jaya, the northern Moluccas—all have declared independence from the government in Jakarta. All on the same day." Fremont paused and held up one message to read from it. "Let's see here, it looks like they're calling themselves *The Republic of Eastern Indonesia*. And they've already sought recognition from the U.N. too, according to this report. This also says that Indonesian forces are currently on the defensive everywhere, but that the situation is likely to change quickly. *High probability that air strikes are forthcoming against rebel positions. All ships are to remain at least one hundred nautical miles away from the listed provinces. Interference in this internal Indonesian matter is strictly prohibited.*"

Edwards clenched his hands into fists. Indonesian air strikes forthcoming while his people were still ashore in the danger zone. Why the hell wasn't ComSubPac doing anything about it?

"Funny that they don't mention Bunda in particular," Fremont said, turning the message over and back several times, "other than to say the northern Moluccas. But I guess that includes the Bunda Islands. It seems a shame, Captain, that such a lovely place should be in such turmoil. I keep thinking about our hosts the other night. How many of them were rebels, and how many were loyalists? And what's going to happen to them?"

Edwards did not care much what happened to them. They were now a very small piece of a much larger puzzle. The government in Jakarta would consider Bunda's revolt miniscule compared with those on the larger islands. That was the most likely explanation for the lack of air cover for Admiral Syarif's marines. With revolts raging across the country, Jakarta probably decided to employ its air force against the bigger threats in Borneo and Sulawesi. The threats near to the border of their archrival, Malaysia. Combat on these bigger islands no doubt involved thousands of rebel troops fighting against the beleaguered Indonesian garrisons. Saving those garrisons would be the Indonesian military's top priority. Bunda's tiny revolt could remain on the back burner until the larger rebellions had been crushed.

"We'd better worry about our own people first, Nav," Edwards finally answered. "Whatever happened to our hosts, I'm more concerned about getting our people back, and safely." He glanced at the tactical display on the electronic chart table. "Any contacts out there?"

"Only fishing craft, Captain. A whole bunch of 'em. They sortied out of Ujungpang a few hours ago. Apparently Bunda's fishermen go fishing whether there's a civil war on or not. We're monitoring probably two or three dozen different diesel engines out there, in and around these islands."

Edwards glanced up at the sonar display showing the spattering of green lines.

"Have Sonar watch them closely, Nav. Try to identify each one individually. Remember, one of those fishermen could be the *Hatta* recharging her batteries."

"Aye, aye, Captain," Fremont said in a tone indicating the thought had never occurred to him.

"And take the ship up to comms depth again. I'm anxious that we've gotten no tasking from ComSubPac. Shit, I can't believe they've put us off this long. Check and see if we're missing something on the satellite broadcast, or even on email. If you get anything, forward it to my inbox ASAP. I'll review it after I've taken a shower. And you have permission to go deep again after copying message traffic."

"Aye, aye, sir."

Edwards passed through the control room's forward door into the passage beyond and took the first door on the left to enter his stateroom. After a few moments cooling off, he jumped in the small box-like shower. The warm water felt good against his skin after the long run. He felt the toxins leaving his body, and even allotted himself a few more seconds than regulations allowed, hoping the hot water would clear his head so that he could concentrate on what had to be done. The deck tilted slightly and he had to brace himself against one of the shower's cold metal walls to keep from sliding. Fremont was taking the ship to comms depth as ordered. If there were any messages waiting for them, he would know soon.

With his shower complete, Edwards toweled off and sat naked at the desk chair in his darkened stateroom, his laptop screen illuminating his face in a bluish glow. As he watched his email account download a myriad of messages, most of them spam, he scanned through the various subject lines, half-expecting to find a personal email from Admiral Chappell. Sometimes, the admiral chose to communicate via direct email instead of formal message traffic. It was faster, and—more importantly—it crossed fewer eyes. But this time, nothing appeared from Chappell.

Edwards' frown quickly turned into a smile when he noticed a new email from his daughter. The subject was "*Happy Birthday, Daddy.*"

Was it his birthday? he wondered, glancing at the calendar. *Holy shit, it was.*

His little girl had remembered it, even when he had not. The email contained only a few sentences, a typical nine-year-old's writing, but a pleasure to read all the same. He was shocked that his ex-wife had let her send it. Or maybe she didn't even know about it. Kids today were pretty savvy with the computers and the Internet. Maybe his little girl hadn't been brainwashed to hate him just yet.

Giving it one last affectionate look, he closed his daughter's email. Hers was the last one, and he was about to log off when another message suddenly appeared, moving the mass of messages down one notch. *Providence* was still at comms depth, so it must have been sent only moments before. One quick check of the time-date stamp confirmed this. The email had not come from a government source and he didn't recognize the sender's name, at least not at first. It took him a few moments to place the last name, "*Triono.*"

Then it suddenly dawned on him. The message was from Peto.

But how did Peto get his email address? Of course, they had exchanged business cards at dinner that night. Edwards could scarcely believe it. He could scarcely believe Peto would risk a transmission from his ship knowing that the Indonesian navy was looking for him. Reluctantly, Edwards clicked on the email.

My friend, Captain Edwards:

I apologize for the scene you no doubt witnessed two days ago. Please understand there was no other alternative. I am writing to you because it is of the utmost importance that we meet. I am currently in Ujungpang and would like you to join me here tomorrow morning. I have reason to believe your ship is still in the area.

I must inform you with much regret and sympathy that Ensign Philip Yi is dead, God rest his soul. I am deeply saddened by his loss and assure you that the soldiers of the new Republic of Eastern Indonesia played no part in his killing. Your sailor, Petty Officer Dean, is safe and in my protection. You may take him, and Ensign Yi's remains, with you after our meeting tomorrow.

I understand that I cannot easily win your trust again. I would not ask you to enter the harbor with my simple guarantee of your safety. Therefore, the harbor pilot will be waiting at the channel entrance at 0830 to bring you personally while your ship remains at a safe distance away.

Please agree to this meeting. The Republic of Eastern Indonesia wishes no harm to American personnel, and I cannot stress how important this meeting is to both our interests. The survival of your shore party in the mountains depends on it.

Very respectfully, your friend,
Peto

Edwards stared at the message, reading it over and over again in disbelief. His worst fears had become a reality. Ensign Yi—the young guy who didn't have a clue, the guy the other officers made fun of, the guy who tried his best to do his job and learn as fast as he could—was dead! How could it be? What had gone wrong?

He held his head in his hands as sadness, rage, and anxiety joined the hundred other mixed emotions churning inside him. Few captains were made of stone. He certainly wasn't, and no matter how long he'd served in the navy, losses like this never got easier to deal with. He found some solace in mulling over the requisite duties to the fallen sailor. Yi's personal affects would have to be gathered. He'd have to make sure Yi's life insurance beneficiary information was all in order. Last but not least, he'd have to write a letter to Yi's parents. The dreaded duty of all captains.

It took him a few minutes to recover his senses and start thinking clearly again. Peto's letter did have a bright side. Dean was still alive. Lake and his shore party were still alive, too. Though, he gathered, they were trapped somewhere in

Bunda's mountains. He needed to stay focused. *Providence* still had crewmen alive out there, and they needed rescuing.

Peto's request for them to meet was completely absurd, though Edwards found it unusually tempting. To take his ship within missile range of Bunda invited disaster. Not to mention surfacing in broad daylight so that he could go ashore while his ship sat off the coast, a perfect target. ComSubPac would never understand such a move, and he'd probably get court-martialed for it. But with no guidance from above, he had to do *something*.

And why would Peto lie to him, anyway? he wondered. If the whole thing were a trap, Peto certainly would have avoided telling him about Yi. And surely any action taken against the *Providence* would only hurt the new "*Republic's*" case before the U.N.

Edwards knew that he had already made his decision. If for no other reason, saving Dean alone would justify what he was about to do. Justify it in his own mind, anyway.

He reached for the phone on the bulkhead next to his desk.

"Officer of the Deck, this is the captain. Plot a course for Ujungpang. I want to be outside the reefs before 0800."

"HE'S coming back, sir," Michaelson's voice whispered from the blackness.

Lake pulled at his T-shirt a little to allow some air between the soaked cotton and his skin. The rain had finally stopped, but the temperature had also risen and now a steamy mist hung in the air, preventing anything from drying.

Lake could not see Michaelson from his present position, but he knew the muscular chief lay atop the large rock outcropping that had served as their rain shelter for most of the day. Michaelson had insisted on pulling guard duty, despite the pain in his leg. After their narrow escape from the helo the day before, Teresa had applied a skillfully prepared splint made of branches and cut strips of khaki cloth, obviously not the first time she had done so in her career. She had recommended elevation and rest to Michaelson, but the hobbled torpedo chief could not stay down. He desperately wanted to get at the enemy, to fight them, whoever they were. Presumably they were Islamic terrorists, as Whitehead had said. There really was no way to be sure. Ahmad, the only available source of information on the subject, had met Lake's probing questions with near arrogant silence. But, regardless of their identity, the "terrorists"—if indeed that's who they were—had occupied the jungle beside the road for most of the day. From the shore party's position five hundred yards up the jungle-covered slope, they could hear vehicles speeding by at irregular intervals, some heading north, some south. Sometimes they heard distant voices, too, both Arabic and Indonesian. Oddly enough, at no time during the long overcast day did the terrorists attempt to come up the hill looking for them.

Lake spent most of the day turning down Michaelson's recommendations about how best to retrieve the comms suitcase from the militant-infested area, all involving squad-like tactics that the poorly armed shore party was neither equipped nor trained to handle. Ahmad, on the other hand, insisted on a more stealthy approach and, before Lake could even voice an approval, he prompted directions out of the uncertain Reynoso, then disappeared into the jungle.

That had been just after nightfall, several hours ago. The rest of them had spent that time anxiously awaiting his return.

A small rustle in the black night soon proved that Michaelson's lookout skills were still honed. Soon after, Ahmad's form appeared out of the jungle, empty-handed.

"Well?" Lake asked eagerly.

"I couldn't find it," Ahmad said, wiping the sweat from his brow. "I followed his directions, but it wasn't there."

"It's got to be there," Reynoso interjected, suddenly at Lake's side. "Sir, let me go. I can find it."

"Forget it. You'd get lost before you went a hundred yards." Lake said dismissively.

"Your lieutenant's right," Ahmad added to Reynoso. "The ones who pursue us are everywhere down there."

"And just who the hell are they?" Teresa's voice spoke from the darkness where she sat leaning against the rock. "I think it's about time you started leveling with the rest of us, Ahmad. I especially have a right to know."

Ahmad did not reply.

Lake hesitated to press him for an answer, but Teresa was right. Her father was killed for a reason, and she should at least know who had killed him and why. Lake wanted to know, too, especially since it now appeared they all might follow Whitehead's fate. If he was going to get killed in his last week in the navy, he sure as hell wanted to know why. Besides, as the only officer present he had to assume some kind of authority, as much as it went against his grain.

"Tell us what you can, Ahmad," Lake said with a forced commanding tone. "As officer in charge here, I need to know what we're facing."

An audible *hrmph!* came from Michaelson's direction, obviously an attempt to undermine the foundation Lake was attempting to lay. But Lake ignored Michaelson altogether, having faced his share of obstinate chief petty officers in his career.

Ahmad stood in silence, clearly not wanting to divulge anything.

"Let me put it this way," Lake said, more sternly. "Either you tell us what this is all about or I'm going to give up trying to find that damn suitcase and then your ass won't get extracted. I'll give Chief Michaelson here permission to charge the fucking light brigade and we'll all go down in a blaze of glory. Is that what you want?"

"They are Al Islamiyyah," Ahmad said quietly.

"Great!" Lake said cynically. "I understand that. They're not rebels, they're Al Islamiyyah, led by the infamous terrorist Musa Muhammad umpty-scratch, and so forth and so on. Now tell me something I don't know. Why the hell are they after us? Why did they kill Dr. Whitehead? Or more importantly, why are they after you?"

Ahmad hesitated, then sighed heavily. He appeared to consider for a moment, plainly formulating in his mind the risk versus the gain of divulging information. Then Lake thought he saw the shadow of Ahmad's head nod in an apparent capitulation gesture. Maybe he had come to the realization that Lake was his only ticket off the island.

"There is an island north of here, you no doubt know, called Wijaya," he said quietly. "There are no villages there. It's virtually deserted, the terrain being much too harsh to cultivate. Five years ago, a small wildlife protection group petitioned the Indonesian government for permission to relocate some orangutans from Borneo to Wijaya, under the rationalization that the climates were similar and it would be an excellent way to grow and preserve a small number of the near-extinct beasts. Already under pressure from the world community for its poor wildlife protection record, the Indonesian government was very forthcoming in granting the request. Within months, a pier was constructed on Wijaya's north side, the apes were moved, and the wildlife protection group set up a small camp from which they could monitor the small population. With their request, the group managed to obtain exclusive rights to the island, forbidding any ships or aircraft from approaching without permission for fear of disrupting the apes' fragile ecosystem."

Lake raised his eyebrows. He didn't know where this was going, but he hoped Ahmad would soon get to the punchline.

"From time to time," Ahmad continued, "ships would put in at the little pier, to resupply the small group of scientists and veterinarians. At first, the people of Bunda, long at odds with the government in Jakarta, resented this imposition on what they considered to be *their* property. The idea of the federal government handing their land over to foreigners offended them. But it wasn't long before the people of Bunda came to understand how beneficial the arrangement might be. Or, should I say, the rebels came to understand it.

"You see, it wasn't long before they learned that this innocent wildlife protection group camped out on Wijaya wasn't anything of the kind. It was a front, a cover, for an international terrorist organization called Al Islamiyyah, run by the notorious terrorist Musa Muhammad. The rebels contacted

Musa and made a deal with him. They wouldn't expose his operation to the Indonesian government, as long as he agreed to sell them arms." Ahmad paused before adding, "I was one of them, a member of Al Islamiyyah, and a close associate of Musa Muhammad. I've been with them from the beginning. For the last five years, I've lived with them and learned their ways. I've helped them to transform Wijaya into the major distribution center it's become."

"But you're working for U.S. intelligence, right?"

Ahmad did not answer.

"I mean," Lake said, before he paused and rephrased his question to one that Ahmad could answer, "if you've been here all this time, and our government knows about this camp, why hasn't it been destroyed?"

"To understand that, Lieutenant, you must first understand what Al Islamiyyah is. Islamic terrorism is a multi-headed beast. Chop off one head and another grows in its place. Al Islamiyyah is the *neck* of that beast. They serve as a distribution facility for Islamic terrorist organizations all over the world, accumulating arms and supplies on Wijaya from any country that will sell them. From there, they're shipped wherever they're needed. Afghanistan, the Philippines, Yemen, Iraq, even Europe and the United States, or anywhere militants find themselves facing the 'infidels.' Wijaya is a perfect place for such an operation. Isolated, covered with dense jungle, and well beyond the Western powers' reach. Terrorist groups from all over the world use it for training. I've met with Abu Sayyaf, Hezbollah, Islamic Jihad, M.I.L.F., Al Qaeda—the list goes on. The many heads of the beast eventually find their way here, to their source, their lifeblood. Not surprisingly, the Wijaya camp has become a watershed of information concerning these organizations. Cell locations, planned operations, leaders' hideouts, even their telephone numbers. I've collected it all, literally gigabytes of priceless data."

Ahmad hesitated for a second and glanced at Teresa. "Our operation ran smoothly for years. I'd make frequent trips to Bunda under the guise of shoring up relations with the rebel units, and while here, I'd make a drop-off in the jungle.

Whitehead would come along later and pick it up, then transmit it back to our superiors. It worked perfectly. Of course, Musa was always suspicious of the doctor's presence on Bunda, but he didn't dare take action for fear of attracting the West's attention to his quiet little corner of the world. On the other hand, Musa never suspected me for a minute. At least, not until recently."

"So what happened?"

"A feeling. A hunch, call it. Musa began acting strangely. He was watching my every move. I was certain he had others spying on me. When he restricted my movement off the island, I knew my days were numbered. I'd been with him long enough to know how he operates. He was only keeping me alive to try to find out if I had any conspirators. My superiors decided to pull me out. That's why you're here. Besides, we knew this rebellion was imminent. You see, the Indonesian government never learned about the terrorists living on Wijaya, but when the rebels did, the word soon spread through the back channels. Across Indonesia, one separatist group after another came to Musa wanting to set up arms deals. It wasn't long before Al Islamiyyah was supplying every separatist movement in Southeast Asia. Over the years, Musa's made billions, and rebel groups throughout Indonesia have built impressive arsenals. And they've been planning carefully for the day they would use them. A couple weeks ago, we saw indications that that day had come. The rebels were ready to make their move.

"The hope was to extract me before things started popping. You see, Musa's got a special relationship with the rebels here, and while they don't agree with him ideologically, they know he's crucial to their success on the battlefield. Now that they control these islands, he won't have any trouble enlisting their help to look for us."

As Lake digested all that he had just heard, he tried to put the pieces together. Ahmad was the real deal, the front line in the war on terrorism. Ahmad had given him a lot to swallow in such a short time, and Lake had no choice but to believe every word.

"So why keep up the cover?" Lake asked. "Why not have a special ops team bring you out covertly?"

"I don't know." Ahmad shrugged. "It wasn't my decision. I can only guess that international politics had more to do with it than common sense. If the Indonesian government discovered United States forces carrying out covert operations within its borders it would certainly damage diplomatic relations between the two countries. On the other hand, sending your ship in broad daylight to casually retrieve the charitable doctor doesn't sound so bad."

"I can't believe this," Teresa said suddenly, holding her head in her hands. "My father was a total fraud! He was nothing more than a mindless minion for a bunch of greedy oil men in Washington. Didn't he have any freaking shame?"

Ahmad showed little empathy for the sniffling daughter of his late partner. Instead Lake felt Ahmad's firm hand grasp his arm and draw him close.

"All right, Mr. Lake," he whispered low enough so that the others couldn't hear. His voice was stern, almost wicked. "I've told you what you wanted to know. Now know this. I intend to accomplish my mission with or without you. I'm not fool enough to have given my superiors everything they wanted to know in my last data dump. I know how easily a field agent can be written off by a bunch of dogs in Washington running for re-election. I've saved the most crucial information in my head. The missing pieces of the puzzle that can wrap up a dozen terrorist groups in a matter of weeks and save thousands of lives, *and* get some people re-elected. Washington needs me to survive, and I'll stop at nothing to make it off this island, do you understand? Don't underestimate my dedication to this cause. Three years ago I went so far as to kill an American to keep from blowing my cover, and I'll do it again without hesitation, just as sure as I'm standing here. I didn't spend the last half-decade of my life living like a fucking Quaker to see it all fall to pieces now. So you keep that bitch out of my way, you hear? Or I'll send her to join her father."

Lake was taken aback by this sudden ruthlessness from the same man who had displayed such little emotion before. The flippant and casual threat to murder Teresa if she got in his way left Lake rigid. He couldn't see Ahmad's eyes in the dark, but he felt them piercing through him. Then a thought suddenly crossed his mind. In a flash he realized he was face-to-face with America's answer to the threat of terrorism. Ahmad was it, and though he looked Arabic, his accent revealed that he had grown up in the U.S. He probably had family ties in the Middle East and thus would have been an excellent choice to infiltrate a terrorist organization. Islamic fundamentalist organizations were not the only ones recruiting soldiers on America's college campuses. The Central Intelligence Agency's counter-terrorism division must have seen much promise in this fanatical piece of work. In Ahmad, they had the right mix of self-preservation, mission focus, and amorality. Perhaps amorality was the key attribute for such an agent. Terrorists themselves were inherently evil. Evil enough to intentionally kill civilians in order to advance a cause. In order to strike back at such evil and defeat it, you had to be just as evil. In fact, you had to be *more* evil. Ahmad and a few agents like him, cold, unfeeling and single-minded, were the solution.

The group sat in awkward silence for a few minutes before Reynoso suddenly appeared at Lake's shoulder.

"Mr. Lake, I know I can find that suitcase, sir. Just let me try."

"Damn it, Reynoso, why are you always volunteering for shit like this?" Lake said, suddenly annoyed. "Haven't you learned by now? There're terrorists down there, my boy, with guns!"

"I'll go with him," Michaelson intoned from the rock, obviously disagreeing with Lake's reluctance.

"What are you going to do, Chief, limp your way down the hill? They'll hear you coming a mile away."

"I will go with him," Ahmad said out of the blue, his voice once again emotionless. "Mr. Reynoso can show me where it is, and I will watch for our assailants while he retrieves it."

After staring thoughtfully at Reynoso's shadow, Lake decided it was their only choice. Getting rescued depended entirely on communication with the outside world. *They needed*

Chapter 14

"MY friend, I am so happy you could come." Peto smiled warmly as he swiftly crossed the drawing room to meet Edwards.

He appeared somewhat pale and anxious, his hands oddly trembling as he extended one in friendship. This was not the Peto Edwards had lunched with only two days ago. Before him stood a man clearly on the brink. A man who had just forfeited a great deal and now faced a bleak future answering for his actions.

Discovering Peto in the mayor's mansion somewhat surprised Edwards. A half hour earlier, while riding as a passenger in the pilot's harbor craft, Edwards had looked for the *Hatta* in Ujungpang harbor but was surprised to discover that she had not returned to port. As he stepped off the craft and onto the pier he began to suspect a trap, so much so that he came close to activating the tiny distress transmitter taped to the inner band of his navy blue ball cap, a precautionary measure suggested by Fremont at the last minute. It could hardly save him, but it would warn *Providence,* now riding at comms depth just beyond the reefs, of any treachery ashore. Should he activate it, *Providence* was under orders to clear the area and notify ComSubPac.

And he had come close to doing that very thing, only relenting when the pilot reassured him that all was well and that Peto awaited him at the mayor's house. The ebullient pilot appeared forthcoming enough. He seemed to have no reservations about telling Edwards everything he wanted to know, even explaining how Peto had arrived in Ujungpang by truck the previous evening. Apparently, the *Hatta* had pulled into one of Bunda's isolated coves earlier that evening, fearing federal air strikes on the town and the harbor. Edwards wasn't exactly sure why he believed the smiling pilot. The happy little man seemed completely at ease, and cared little as Edwards checked in with *Providence* on his hand-held walkie-talkie every quarter-hour—the back-up plan against treachery.

As he stepped off the tugboat and onto the pier, Edwards was shocked at the transformation Ujungpang had undergone in his absence. There was widespread celebration on the streets and on the waterfront. Amid charred and burned-out buildings whose fires had only died in the recent rains, a colorfully adorned throng of people wearing traditional dress danced and sang. Here and there a gamelan musician smiled widely at the passersby, while banging out a celebratory rhythm on his drums. Rebel fighters, only distinguishable by their green fatigues, laughed and smiled with the crowd, not a single unslung rifle visible in their ranks. If Peto feared forthcoming air strikes, the people of Ujungpang seemed ignorant of the threat altogether.

The hapless joy of the doomed, Edwards thought. If only they knew the tenuous position they were in. If only they knew the almost certain fate that awaited them.

As he was ushered into a waiting jeep to convey him to the government complex, Edwards found himself regarding the happy citizens of Ujungpang with pity. He thought back to the messages he read just before leaving the *Providence*. The messages were from ComSubPac. More situation reports, more updates on the crisis in Indonesia. The messages foretold a bitter end to the widespread revolution of which Bunda was only a small part. Rebel positions in the other provinces had broken on all fronts. The battle had turned against them. In the major hotspots of Sulawesi, Aceh, and Irian Jaya, fresh Indonesian troops backed by heavy air support were driving rebel forces from the captured towns, making little distinction between hostile and civilian. The short-lived rebellion had quickly turned into a massacre, and a means for Jakarta to eliminate some longtime foes. The Indonesian government hardly needed to look for excuses. There were reports citing mass executions of government officials in many of the rebel-held areas. The rebellion had done irreparable damage, ensuring the continued oppression of the people it had hoped to liberate.

As the jeep pulled into Ujungpang's bullet-ridden government complex, Edwards discovered that Bunda was no exception to these reports. A two-hundred-year-old brick wall stretched along the compound's east side, and against the wall lay a crooked line of two dozen or more twisted corpses. Bullet holes marked each torso and matched the bloody pattern painted on the wall behind them. As he passed by the wall on the way to the mayor's house, Edwards caught a glimpse of Walikota Umar's body lying in the middle of the fly-infested row, the wounds on his body still damp like all the others. Obviously, the executions had happened within the last few hours. The unfortunate mayor had been joined in death with most of his staff, along with a few Indonesian marines and policemen. It was a bloody beginning for the new Republic of Eastern Indonesia. Now as Edwards shook Peto's cold hand in the dead mayor's drawing room, the stress quite visible on Peto's face, he believed it would be a bloody ending as well.

"Thank you for coming, Captain," Peto said almost apologetically. "Can we offer you a drink?"

"No," Edwards said firmly, expressing with one word that his business was not social in nature. "I'm here for my crewmen. Where are they?"

"Perhaps you can tell us, Captain?" a voice came from the opposite side of the room, behind the big desk belonging to the late mayor.

The cat-like eyes of Umar's social secretary, Imam, peered over a tall stack of files, his pencil-thin form hidden by the big desk as he sat in his former superior's chair. It came as no surprise to Edwards that Imam was part of the revolt too. The man simply looked deceitful, and Edwards immediately sensed a hierarchical relationship between Peto and Imam, with Imam on top. But to see Imam now in a position of power, indeed in a position that could order his instant death, suddenly made Edwards nervous. Peto's polite demeanor, on the other hand, offered little comfort. He could trust neither of them, and he began to feel small drops of perspiration forming under his short hair.

"Please, Walikota Imam," Peto said pleadingly. "The captain has shown goodwill in coming here. And we have promised to deliver his crewmen. If we expect him to listen, we must first make good on our promise."

Imam's invisible lips smiled slightly, then he nodded. Peto wasted no time in striding to a side door where he disappeared momentarily, reemerging moments later with the limping Dean in tow. The young sailor's face was at first distraught, but then broke into a huge grin when he noticed Edwards.

"How are you, Dean?"

"I'm fine, sir," Dean said, grimacing as he gingerly moved toward his captain. "I'm still pretty beat up, sir, but I'm getting more movement every day."

"Have they harmed you in any way?" Edwards directed the question at Dean, but glanced accusingly into Peto's face.

"Oh no, sir, not at all. They've been good to me, Captain. These two gentlemen have been very good to me. I've been confined to this house for the last two days, but all in all, I've been treated pretty well. I've eaten a hell of a lot better than I did over at that hospital. Did you hear about Mr. Yi, sir?"

Edwards nodded, still looking into Peto's eyes.

"Mr. Yi's body is being delivered to the harbor craft as we speak, Captain," Peto offered somberly under the intense stare. "It will be waiting for you there when you are ready to return to your ship. His body has been prepared for transport, honorably." He paused before adding, "His death was most regrettable and unexpected. You must believe me, that it had nothing to do with the revolt. Some of our well-known town thugs attacked him, apparently to get his money. I assure you they have been dealt with."

From Peto's stern expression, Edwards could only assume that the two men had been executed, perhaps against the same wall where Umar had met his fate.

"Is that what happened?" Edwards asked Dean.

"Pretty much, sir. I don't think these guys had anything to

do with it. Ever since this whole thing started they've bent over backward to protect me. After the battle ended they transferred me over here. I guess so I'd be better protected."

"Okay, here's Dean," Edwards said impatiently. "Now what about the rest of my men?"

"We have had reports of another American officer sighted on the other side of town shortly after the battle started," Peto answered. "I am afraid he was captured by Al Islamiyyah fighters. Our troops in that area did not follow their orders, and we have been unable to locate him. It is possible he was killed in the naval bombardment. The area took several direct hits from the *Malahayati* before I could destroy her."

After all Edwards had witnessed that day, Peto's casual mention of the frigate's sinking shocked Edwards the most. His tone contained no remorse for killing the sailors on those two ships. Sailors he had once called comrades.

"As for your shore party," Peto continued, pausing briefly for an approving look from Imam, "this issue we must urgently discuss, alone."

Edwards caught the implication and patted Dean on the shoulder.

"Dean, why don't you wait for me outside. I won't be long."

Dean nodded, limping expeditiously, the best he could, out the door. When the door shut behind him, Imam rose from his seat and walked slowly to the window looking out on the low gray clouds shrouding Bunda's green central mountain range.

"Your men are out there, Captain," he said, crossing his hands behind his back. "As you know, Al Islamiyyah is after them. It is only a matter of time before they are captured or killed."

The news took Edwards aback, though he struggled not to show it. Of course, he knew about Al Islamiyyah. CinCPac's daily intelligence reports contained several references to the terrorist organization's activity in Eastern Indonesia, but he had no idea they were in the Bunda Islands. The group's presence here was a shock, and now to hear that they were pursuing his own men somewhere in the mountains left him with a sudden sense of despair. It was an unexpected factor in the equation that made the outcome that much more uncertain. The prospect for Lake and his men seemed dismal at best. Hopeless, when added to the fact that *Providence* had not heard from them in the past thirty-six hours.

"Is that a threat?" Edwards asked after collecting his thoughts.

"Call it what you will," Imam said evenly, then shrugged, "but your men will certainly be killed unless you cooperate with us. We are their only hope now."

"The United States doesn't negotiate with terrorists, Imam. You're smart enough to know that. If you've taken control of this island like you say you have and you're allowing Al Islamiyyah forces to operate here, then you're guilty of harboring terrorists, and you can expect the United States to respond accordingly. We don't distinguish between terrorists and their landlords." Edwards paused, keeping his best poker face. "And then there's the U.N. How do you expect them to view this whole thing? Murdering American sailors who were on a peaceful mission. That won't go over very well in the Security Council. Fat chance they'll ever recognize your little government as legitimate. You're operating on shoestrings here."

"Please do not insult my intelligence, Captain!" Imam snapped vigorously. "And do not lecture me about ethics! How many times did your own leaders look the other way during the Suharto regime because it suited their purpose? How many Suhartos around the world remain in power because the United States put them there during the Cold War? The citizens of those unfortunate countries are the true casualties, Captain, written off by your government, no? You and I both know your ship was never sent here on any mission of peace. Let us be honest with each other. Al Islamiyyah is after your men because you came here to extract an agent who had infiltrated their organization. As you well know, that agent is presently with your shore party and is the only reason your men are being pursued!"

"I don't know what the hell you're talking about," Edwards said honestly, irritated by Imam's implication. He also thought it best to withhold the fact that he had been out of communication with Lake and his men.

"Do not take me for a fool!" Imam said vehemently, his voice suddenly intimidating for a man of his slight build. "Nothing happens in these islands I do not know of! You had best mind who you are talking to, Captain!"

"Imam, please!" Peto said in an appeasing tone, obviously in an effort to bring Imam back to center. Apparently, Imam took the hint, pausing for a moment to harness his anger. When his face finally resumed its natural color, he continued in a subdued voice.

"It is interesting that you should mention the United Nations, Captain. You are quite right. They would never recognize a rebel movement with ties to terrorism. And that brings us to our point of business with you, the reason we asked you to meet with us."

Edwards did not know what direction the rebel mayor was trying to steer him, but he got the strange feeling that Imam had just assumed the role of a salesman, and he, the customer, was about to receive an offer.

"You obviously desire to get your men back," Imam said, his lips once again pressed in the squirmy smile. "We share your desire to save them. And while we hold considerable sway over Al Islamiyyah and their leader, Musa Muhammad, we are at odds with their fundamentalist notions. We do not subscribe to their aspirations, nor do we subscribe to their methods. An independent Islamic state is not the goal of our movement. Having a free state with a representative government is. We do not thirst for the blood of your people, or the blood of Christians, or even the blood of our enemies in Jakarta. It is the taste of freedom that we thirst for. In pursuit of that end we have gone to great lengths, have made great sacrifices, and will continue to make any sacrifice necessary to achieve it."

He paused, staring Edwards in the eyes. "Even entering into less than desirable alliances such as ours with Al Islamiyyah. Yes, it is easy to condemn us for that, Captain, but before condemning a fair man would consider our position and the few options that we had. The United States touts democracy in front of the world, but nations such as yours scoffed at our little movement when we appealed to them for help. We appealed through covert channels and they shunned us, afraid of offending their friends in Jakarta whom they needed for their war on terror. They left us with few choices, essentially pushed us into our alliance with Al Islamiyyah, our only means of obtaining supplies and weapons to support our movement. Our alliance with the terrorists is indeed an alliance with the devil, but has been necessary. And now that the need for that alliance has come to an end, we wish to join the world community in condemning the terrorists who are pursuing your men and who have committed so many unspeakable acts around the world. We wish to join the world effort to bring them to justice and to take our place at the table of civilized nations. We want to do this—deeply desire to do this—but before we can, we require a small extension of trust from you, Captain."

"I'm listening," Edwards said guardedly. As much as he had grown to despise Imam, he was willing to play along if it meant saving his men.

"Whether you will admit it or not, Captain, you came here on a mission, a great mission in the noble war on terrorism. Just for a moment, I am going to ask you to put aside your allegiance to that mission and consider a greater, an even nobler, calling. Peto has told me how highly he thinks of you. He has vouched for your character and tells me that you are a man we can trust. If that is so, you must sincerely consider what I am about to request of you."

Peto eyed Edwards thoughtfully and nodded, apparently in agreement with his superior.

"What mission could be greater than defeating terrorism, you might ask?" Imam continued, in a somewhat dramatic tone, as if he were Henry the Fifth on the morning of Agincourt. "I will tell you. It is defeating the *source* of terrorism. It is depriving the fundamentalist leaders of their endless supply of Jihadis pulled from the ranks of the downtrodden and deprived. These are the young men who file in behind the Musa

Muhammads of the world, readily accepting the excuse that America is to blame for the tribulations in their lives. Your government is right, Captain. Democracy is the key! It is the one system that can enfranchise those who have lived under tyranny for so long. It is the only system that can hold leaders accountable for their actions."

He paused for a moment as his look grew increasingly grave. "Peto and I have heard the news from our brothers in Sulawesi and Irian Jaya. We know the rebellion has failed. It is only a matter of time before the military turns its focus on our little island. The Republic of Eastern Indonesia will die, the responsible provinces punished. The United States will continue to court the Indonesian government, and another generation of young men will grow up blaming the West for their affliction.

"A dismal outlook, no? But it does not have to be that way, Captain. With your help, and only with your help, we can force the hand of the United Nations. The other provinces will fall, yes, but if we act quickly we can bring Bunda's conflict to the attention of the Security Council and appeal for the same kind of U.N. intervention East Timor received. I am certain this can be accomplished. It *must* be accomplished, or the people of Bunda are doomed." Imam moved closer to Edwards and cast a pleading look into his eyes. "You are the critical factor, Captain. The linchpin on which our entire plan will either hold or collapse. How, you may ask? As you know, your men are fleeing from an enemy they cannot escape. If they are killed, we will all lose. You will lose your men, and—as you said before—our movement will lose any sympathy it might have gained in the U.N.

"On the other hand, if your men are captured, Al Islamiyyah will announce to the world that they hold American hostages. Then the U.N. will be forced to turn its focus onto our little islands. While the world is watching, our own troops will rescue your men and apprehend the Al Islamiyyah fighters. The global community will applaud our noble deed. Journalists pursuing Pulitzers will arrive from every part of the Western world to run stories on Bunda's small stroke in the war on terror," Imam grew more intense with each passing word, his eyes blazing with excitement, as if he could see the events unfolding before his very eyes. "Then, Captain, the world will lend an ear to our own grievances. Peacekeepers will arrive from the United States, New Zealand, and Australia. They will put a stop to Jakarta's offensive, and we will have our independence at last."

The rebel mayor stared earnestly at the space above Edwards' left shoulder as if on a vision quest, picturing the realization of all his dreams in his mind's eye. But he quickly came back to the present, fixing his eyes on Edwards.

"Your men must be taken alive, Captain. This plan depends on it. Despite what you say, I believe you know the position they are in. I am asking that you contact them and give them the order to surrender. If you do this, I promise that no harm will come to them. I have dispatched a company of my own troops to join Al Islamiyyah, under the auspices of assisting in the search. Their true orders are to ensure that your men are not injured in any way when they are captured. When the time is right, they will turn on the Al Islamiyyah fighters and rescue your men. It is the best chance they have of survival, and it all depends on you, Captain. You must trust me."

"Trust you?" Edwards said incredulously. "You line your own mayor up against a wall and fill him full of bullets, and then expect me to trust you?"

"Do not patronize me, Captain!" Imam said hotly. "You yourself have not been honest about your true mission here."

"You're talking gibberish to me, sir. We came here to evacuate Dr. Whitehead. That's all! I don't know anything about this agent you keep talking about."

Imam's eyes blazed and he gritted his teeth to the point that his scalp moved. He appeared to be on the brink of flying off the handle at Edwards, but managed to contain himself.

"I do not know what your motivation is, Captain," he finally said with visibly harnessed rage. "You can deny it, but I know you are lying, and your lies upset me. I wish to hear no more of them, so I will be brief and to the point. Either you order your men to surrender, or their fate is sealed along with the fate of my people. If you refuse, I will do my best to protect your men, but only as long as it suits my purpose. If you or your government make any attempt to rescue them, I will see to it that your men never leave this island alive. I loathe threatening you, Captain, but I am devoted to this movement as much as you are devoted to your ship, and I will do everything in my power to preserve it."

"I think we have nothing more to discuss, sir," Edwards said shortly. He had no choice. As much as he sympathized with the people of Bunda, he could not make deals with the leader of an insurgency.

As Edwards turned on his heel and headed for the door, Peto rushed after him.

"Captain, wait!" Peto said, pleadingly. "Imam is passionate about our cause. He does not mean to offend you. You must trust us, please."

"Trust, Peto? Two days ago, I watched you blow your own admiral out of the water. And now you ask for my trust?"

"Yes! As a fellow captain, as a friend, I *do*. You should not mourn Admiral Syarif. He was guilty of a thousand crimes I could not begin to describe. He met his death with the blood of many innocent people on his head."

"And what about the young sailors you killed with him? What had they done?"

"In war, men die, Captain. Sometimes you must kill a few in order to save many. I did what I had to do in the hopes of making a better life for my family, for my children. I swore an oath to that end, and I will never turn my back on it. Just as I know you will not turn your back on us now. I know that the man who risked his life and career to help the distressed *Mendar* crew will not let us down. Not now. Not in our hour of need."

"I'm sorry, Peto, but I just can't do that," Edwards said sadly.

"Can I ask you to at least consider it, Captain?" Peto implored, grasping Edwards' hand firmly. "Return to your ship, think on it, then contact me with your decision. I will be watching the same email account that I used to contact you. Send your response there. I will be waiting."

Edwards cast a pitiful look across the room at Imam, and then back to Peto. Without another word, he shook his head and opened the door to leave.

"You do realize, Captain," Peto said before Edwards could leave, now in a much more forceful tone, "I cannot permit you to rescue your men. The fate of my people depends on it. Rest assured, I will be monitoring *Providence*'s movements. Your sonar equipment will not be able to find the *Hatta,* but you can be certain that wherever you go, she will be close by, *watching you.*"

Edwards paused momentarily in the doorway with his back to Peto. It had sounded like a challenge, Peto's tone now devoid of its former warmth. Edwards got the impression that he had just become another obstacle in Peto's path to freedom. Perhaps another obstacle that would need to be eliminated, like Admiral Syarif.

As Edwards continued out the door, Peto called after him.

"*Selamat jalan*, Captain. If we do not meet again, I wish you good luck. May you die a deep death."

AS the jeep drove down the wet streets, Edwards had a thousand things on his mind. He'd made a grave error in coming back here. He'd placed his ship in danger by bringing her so close to Bunda, and now the shore party possibly faced more hazards, too. This jaunt ashore had accomplished very little, and he cursed himself for letting his emotions get the better of him. The sum of his booty included one dead officer, waiting at the pier, and one live crewman rocking back and forth in the seat next to him. Perhaps it was the isolation from ComSub-Pac that had made him do it. Without guidance, he'd felt obligated to act, but now all he wanted to do was get back to the *Providence.*

As the jeep drove to the waterfront, passing between groups of celebrating citizens, their young driver waved enthusiastically at each one. The youth wore the green fatigues of a rebel fighter but his boyish demeanor carried no remnant of the former warrior. He grinned from ear to ear, periodically letting loose with a cheer that reminded Edwards of his own college football days. There was no doubt this state of bliss encompassed the entire town. It was genuine, and Edwards even caught himself smiling at a few of the young happy faces greeting them. But his personal moment of levity did not last long, and he suddenly felt very sorry for these happy people. With each passing face he saw the portents of the tribulations to come. In every aged eye he saw complete comprehension of what the future held in store. They were not fools. Perhaps they were wise to celebrate one last time before the heavy hand of the Indonesian government descended on their idyllic island. They could expect harsh treatment now, especially after executing their *Walikota* and his staff. As soon as the larger rebel provinces were secure, the Indonesian air force would commence a bombing campaign, the likes of which these islands had not seen since the Second World War, when the Americans dropped their bombs on the Japanese occupiers. There would be little differentiation between civilian and military targets, and another smile would not appear in these islands for many generations to come.

Above the wind thrashing the brim of his navy blue ball cap, Edwards heard the faint sound of a jet engine. It came from high above the gray clouds. No doubt, an Indonesian reconnaissance aircraft.

Seconds later, an incredibly loud noise jolted Edwards upright in his seat. The sound, as deafening as a space shuttle launch, erupted from the jungle on the southern edge of town, and Edwards looked up too late to see the anti-aircraft missile climbing skyward. Only a white smoky trail remained, leading up from the jungle floor until it disappeared into the low clouds. Cheering at this, the townspeople raised their fists in the air as if they could will the missile on toward its target far above the clouds. Minutes passed and soon the missile's smoky trail dissolved into the stiff breeze. No one seemed to know if the little anti-aircraft battery had successfully shot down the high-altitude intruder, and they didn't seem to care. The intruder had gone away and that was all that mattered. Now they could celebrate their freedom a little longer.

After a few more speedy turns, the jeep finally emerged at the waterfront. Carefully manipulating the vehicle along the crowded pier, the driver soon brought the jeep to a stop next to the harbor craft chugging idly in the water. At the head of the gangway, a long black bag lay on a stretcher at the feet of two rebel soldiers. It obviously contained Yi's body, and Edwards had to make a conscious effort not to stare at it. Then he noticed another group huddled on the pier. The ten or twelve men and women were mostly European, and they had a large pile of luggage stacked beside them. Edwards recognized the U.N. envoy Descartes just as the tug's single stack coughed out a dirty brown wisp of diesel exhaust, enveloping Descartes and forcing him to cover his mouth to prevent himself from breathing in the noxious fumes. As the Frenchman emerged from this black smoke, he noticed Edwards' presence. Though Descartes' eyes still watered from the diesel exhaust, his face instantly broke into a relieved smile, and he approached Edwards without pause. Far from the well-groomed diplomat Edwards had seen two nights before, Descartes now appeared disheveled in a hastily-thrown-together assortment of mismatched business apparel. But, notwithstanding his attire, his face still carried that same supercilious mien it had held at the mayor's dinner.

"Edwards!" he said as he reached for Edwards' hand and shook it vigorously. "We heard you had come back. Thank God!"

"Monsieur Descartes," Edwards said, acknowledging the French diplomat, but immediately placing himself on guard by his restrained response.

"Anarchy, Edwards! It's complete anarchy. I tell you, these people have lost their senses. They're barbarians! My staff and I have spent the last two days fortified in our offices, fearing for our lives. With all this madness, we haven't dared set foot outside. That is, until we heard that you had come. These people are unreasonable to a fault. It will be their doom, I think. But, of course, that's all out of our hands now. Now that you are here."

"Excuse me?" Edwards said apprehensively, not certain what Descartes was implying.

"Well, as you can see, my staff and I are ready to depart. That's why you're here, isn't it? We heard the news of your return and came here as fast as we could. I didn't know you had business with that despicable traitor, Imam. If I had, maybe we wouldn't have come so quickly, but regardless we've been waiting almost a half-hour for you. Oh, I see that look on your face, Edwards, but don't worry, that pile over there is the sole encompassment of our luggage. We've managed to dwindle it down to a manageable cargo, I'm sure you will agree?"

"Sir . . ."

"And I'm sure your men will have no trouble loading it when we meet your vessel beyond the reefs. It shouldn't take long, I think. Not for big American boys, no?"

"Sir . . ."

"I assure you, Edwards, my staff and I will stay out of your way for the entire trip. You won't even know we're aboard. We will, of course, expect to dine in the wardroom with the officers, but beyond a cordoned off berthing area for my females and a washroom where they can enjoy some privacy, we'll require nothing from you."

"Sir . . ."

"And please, Edwards, don't even think of giving up your own cabin for me. I'll be perfectly satisfied with one of your officer's staterooms."

"*Sir!*" Edwards finally shouted at the top of his lungs, thwarting any further interruption, and causing Descartes to draw back several steps.

"Whatever is the matter, Edwards?" Descartes said, presenting a bewildered expression.

Edwards could not believe what he was hearing. This same man who had belittled him at the mayor's dinner, who had come so close to questioning his honesty, was now giving him orders. Edwards didn't know what infuriated him more, Descartes' high-handed demands or the haughty manner in which he issued them. Regardless, Edwards had to muster every last bit of self-control to keep from shouting the man down. He tried his best to put on a politician's face.

"Has the Secretary General ordered you to withdraw, monsieur?" Edwards asked firmly.

"What?"

"You know, the Secretary General, your boss, the guy that sits back in New York. Has he ordered you to withdraw?"

"Well, no, but . . ."

"Are any of your people injured then?"

"No!" Descartes said, looking irritated. "Edwards, what is the meaning of this line of questioning?"

"I'm afraid you're not going anywhere with me, sir. I don't run a cruise ship, and I certainly don't have enough space for you or your staff. You'll just have to find other passage."

"Other passage?" Descartes suddenly appeared flustered. "Edwards, what the devil are you talking about? No ships have come. None would dare approach this island with the *Hatta* about. Yours is the last. You must take me off!"

"You and your people don't have a security clearance," Edwards said calmly.

"Security clearance? What the devil are you saying?"

"I can't let an agent of a foreign government on board my ship, sir. Remember what you said at dinner? The U.S. is involved in all sorts of secret stuff, and you might see something we don't want you to see. So I can't let you aboard."

"That's absurd!" Descartes shouted hoarsely. "I've never heard of such a thing! Damn you, Edwards, I've never been treated in such a despicable manner! I'll have your commission over this, I swear it! Do you realize who you are talking to—"

"I don't care if you're Jacques fucking Chirac! You're not going with me! Now get your people away from the fucking gangway."

"You would do this? You would leave me here to die? What kind of a man are you, Edwards?"

"The kind that knows his duty, sir. My duty is to my ship, my crew, and my country. Do you know what your duty is? If I were you, I'd be asking myself that question right about now." Edwards paused, gesturing toward the town. "Look around you. Look at these people. You know what they're facing. You know what's coming for them."

"They're barbarians, Edwards."

"They're desperate, Mr. Descartes. They just want the same freedom you and I have enjoyed all our lives. The same freedom our fathers fought side by side for when they defeated Hitler together. Sure, these people have done a few desperate things. Wouldn't you, if your freedom hung in the balance? They've made some mistakes and now they need help. Just look at what you're doing! You're turning your back on them, running away as soon as your safety's in question. If these people ever needed the U.N., they need it now. Or else, what's the U.N. good for? They need *you*, Monsieur Descartes. You can help them, if you stay. If you leave, you'll just join the ranks of a hundred different failed U.N. missions in a hundred different parts of the world. You'll hand the Indonesian government a permission slip to massacre these people. You know as well as I do none of the Western media outlets will ever cover the story, and it'll be ten or fifteen years before someone ventures to guess how many thousands were murdered. And just like all the other times, the U.N. will issue a formal apology to the survivors, then merrily go their own way. But that doesn't have to happen *this time*! *You* can make a difference! Here, at this moment, it all depends on *you*."

All the rage seemed to leave Descartes' face as he sighed and stared distantly at the town with the colorful banners, his gray hair whipping in the ocean breeze. Sounds of celebrating drums and laughing children still rang out across the water and Edwards thought he saw the middle-aged Frenchman's eyes start to water. Perhaps Descartes had a heart, after all.

"What do you say, sir?" Edwards said. "Will those children over there be free people when you and I are old men, or just another apology?"

Descartes nodded, his eyes cast low. He found a handkerchief and wiped his nose with it several times. Without another word, or another glance at Edwards, the French envoy casually walked over to his staff. The staff looked at each other in confusion as he mumbled a few words to them.

Then, hesitantly but dutifully, they all gathered their bags and followed as he led them back down the pier toward the town.

Chapter 15

THROUGH the small opening in the droplet-coated jungle canopy Lake saw the white smoky trail lead up to the sky until it disappeared into the low gray clouds. The anti-aircraft missile had come from somewhere near Ujungpang, several miles to the south, but the menacing noise was still loud enough to silence the annoying tropical birds inhabiting the jungle all around him. The thousand-bird song had seemed to increase in volume as the morning wore on, the conglomeration of the various species creating a sound so saturating, so tortuous in nature, that Lake had found it hard to hear himself think, and he was grateful for the respite. Only the missile's loud booster had managed to silence the jungle creatures. Though the silence lasted only a moment, it was a moment Lake cherished.

He used the precious silence to ponder their current situation, which depended entirely on the *Providence*'s whereabouts. The ship couldn't possibly have waited all this time. As daring as Edwards tended to be, Lake couldn't see him putting the ship in jeopardy with missiles flying about and rebels and terrorists in possession of the island. Not for the sake of three crewmen. It was unthinkable and would be unforgivable with the admirals back in Pearl. Most certainly, *Providence* had left port by now, and Lake suddenly realized that the shore party had been traveling in the wrong direction all along. Ujungpang held nothing for them but certain capture or worse. There was no safe haven there, only rebels and Al Islammiyyah. Heading to the north side of the island seemed the best option, but exactly how they would get there, he did not know.

"What time is it?" Teresa asked, leaning against a damp

log and flicking an insect off her arm. "Shouldn't they be back by now?"

Lake looked at his watch but did not answer. With mid-morning fast approaching, there was still no sign of Reynoso and Ahmad. The two had been gone for over eight hours.

"I'll go down and see if I can find them," Michaelson said impatiently. With his face contorting from the pain, he tried to get on his feet, but his swollen leg gave way at every attempt.

Teresa moved to help him, but Lake waved her away.

"Don't help him," Lake said. "He's talking nonsense. We can't go down there."

Teresa nodded but still watched the struggling chief with concern.

"Damn it, Lieutenant," Michaelson grumbled after he finally wore himself out. "That gunfire we heard can't mean anything good's happened! Those two have run into trouble and we've got to try to help 'em!"

Lake did his best to ignore the irate chief, but inwardly he shared the same concerns. Almost an hour ago, the jungle rang out with small-arms fire, all originating down by the road. It had been sporadic at first, and Lake thought he recognized the blunt report of the forty-five pistol he'd lent Ahmad. But soon after, a fusillade of automatic weapons erupted, lots of it, as if someone were firing in desperation. It lasted about two or three minutes, ending in a few sporadic single shots. Since then, they had heard nothing. No voices in the distance, no gunfire, no sign of Ahmad or Reynoso—nothing.

"Listen, Lieutenant," Michaelson said, in a more conciliatory tone. "It's been over an hour since that shooting. We don't know what the fuck happened to them. They could be dead, for all we know. But we've got to go down there and find out for sure. There's no other way."

Again Lake ignored the chief. The suggestions weren't helping his train of thought. He was about to tell Michaelson to keep his opinions to himself when Teresa spoke, a small smile appearing on her face, the first Lake had seen since her father's death.

"One time, Chief," she said thoughtfully staring into a

thick patch of brush, "when I was just a kid, and we were living in Raleigh—my dad took me camping up in the Blue Ridge Mountains. It was one of those controlled campsites, you know the kind? The ones with the little pre-made fire-pits and the strategically placed logs to sit on with all the knots and bark conveniently sanded off. I think I remember there being a bathhouse there, too, somewhere nearby. I sure don't remember peeing in the woods at that age. Anyway, I was just a little girl, I guess about nine or ten, and I didn't know anything about camping. It was all new to me. I remember watching my dad as he set up our little tent and thinking about what a smart and strong man he was and how I wanted to marry a man just like him someday. Little did I know I'd end up just like him—or at least just like the man I thought he was. My dad wanted me to have the same appreciation for the environment that he did. I guess that's why he took me camping with him. And I guess it worked too 'cause I've been living in the wilderness ever since I graduated from high school."

Lake glanced at Michaelson and knew that he must be growing impatient, but the dutiful navy chief listened respectfully as this civilian told her story. Perhaps she had reached a point in the grieving process that she needed to talk about her dad to deal with his loss.

"After living in the wilderness all these years, Chief," she chuckled, "I think it's funny that the one story I remember— the one incident that stays with me everywhere I go— happened during that first camping trip with my dad. One morning we went hiking on a trail that led along the edge of a small river valley. The whole area was heavily wooded, thick like this stuff, but not as tropical, of course. The trail was one of those obscure trails used by mountain men in early colonial days. It was totally isolated and that day we were the only ones on it. I'll never forget how scary the woods looked to me at that age, all quiet, dark and twisted. You could almost hear the spirits of the forest, or at least my young ears could. And, of course, Dad didn't help. He told me that a Confederate soldier who had disappeared during the Civil War still haunted the valley, still looking for Yankees. He said that I'd be okay because

I was born in the South, but since he was born in Philly, the Confederate ghost surely wouldn't spare him. He liked to scare me like that. Anyway, the forest was so thick you couldn't see the trail. From ten feet away, you couldn't see it. Of course, the golden rule in places like that is simple: *Don't get off the damn trail.* If you get off, you might never find it again.

"Well, anyway, late in the afternoon as we were heading back on the trail, I was tired and I guess I wasn't paying attention, because I walked right into a low branch. The branch and tree were both dead and thus the wood was very jagged, so I got a nice cut right across the top of my left eyebrow." Her forefinger pointed to a scar above her left eye that Lake had not noticed before. It was barely visible and almost blended in with her eyebrow. "Gosh, it hurt like hell! I bled a whole lot, and of course I cried my little eyes out. My dad had a first aid kit in his pack and he put a wet bandage over it, but it kept on bleeding. Dad began to worry about an infection, since my face was so dirty. He tried to clean the wound as best he could, but he'd used up the last of our water and we were still miles away from camp. The closest water to us was the small river at the base of the valley, not more than a mile from where we were, so dad set out into the woods with both our canteens. I was in no condition to claw my way through the brush, so he left me sitting on the trail. I don't know what it was, but as soon as he disappeared, I felt so incredibly alone. The trees seemed to close in on me, and I got the overwhelming feeling that I was being watched.

"The minutes passed, it seemed like hours, but it just got quieter and darker. The sun had already set beyond one of the distant ridges, and it left our valley covered in shadow. It scared the beejeebies out of me, and all I could think about was that Confederate spirit lurking somewhere. I kept turning around thinking there was someone behind me, but of course there wasn't. I got scared and, like an idiot, I ran into the woods after my dad. I cried and cried as I stumbled over rocks and bushes, and my legs and arms got at least a dozen cuts and scrapes each. In a roundabout way I eventually made it to the river, but of course my dad wasn't there. He'd already been there and was headed back to the trail to find me. The brush was so thick that we'd passed each other without knowing it.

"Somehow my little ten-year-old brain figured that out, and I decided that I'd better stay put or else the same thing would just happen again, and we'd be forever trying to find each other. And as I sat there by the dark waters, shivering and praying, and calling for my daddy until I was hoarse, I began to wonder if he'd ever come for me. Maybe he thought I had gone down the trail in either direction and was looking for me there. Maybe he'd gotten lost himself. Or maybe the ghost had gotten him. I know it sounds silly now, but that's what I thought. But if I'd just stayed put, if I'd just done what he told me to, we'd have already been back at our campsite cooking dinner. Of course, he eventually found me. I think I fell asleep, because the only thing else I remember is resting my head on his shoulder the whole way back. It's silly to remember such a stupid thing about your dad, isn't it?"

"No, ma'am," Michaelson said solemnly. "Not silly at all."

Teresa paused for a moment before adding, "He carried me the whole way back, that bastard. He carried me and we must've had four or five miles to go. Four or five miles with a kid on your back over that kind of terrain is no small chore. That was real, wasn't it, that moment with my dad? He was a good dad, wasn't he, no matter what he became later in his life? You're a father aren't you, Chief? You know. Tell me my dad loved me. Tell me he loved me even though he lied to me all these years."

"I didn't know him, ma'am, but I'm sure he did. Any dad would. Any dad would be proud." It seemed to be all Michaelson could say, and his face lost its previous scowl as he settled down against the log, now obviously resigned to wait.

Lake appreciated Teresa's help and was touched by her grief, obviously still fresh in her mind. Under her rough exterior, she was really a very tender person, and he felt that he needed to console her in some way.

"I think he lived his other life *because* he loved you, Teresa," Lake said, as gently as he could. "I didn't know him either, but I suspect he wasn't too different from the father you remembered. You want to make the world a better place and your dad did too, only he went about it in a different way. You two only differed in methods, not in purpose."

Teresa looked intently at him and he soon regretted ever opening his mouth on the subject. What business was it of his anyway? Where the hell did he get off telling her about her father?

"Somebody's coming," Michaelson said lowly.

Instantly they groped for cover, and soon Ahmad emerged from the thick trees carrying a man on his back. The man's clothes were muddy and stained with blood, a lot of blood, and it took a few moments before Lake realized that the wounded and bleeding man was Reynoso. Ahmad fell to his knees in the center of the little clearing, his chest heaving as he allowed Reynoso's limp form to slide to the ground. Teresa's waiting hands cradled the young radioman's head and guided it gently to the soft earth.

At first glance, Lake thought Reynoso was dead. He wasn't moving and from the amount of blood on the shirt he couldn't possibly be alive. The sight of all the blood, of Reynoso's limp form, of a sailor he had treated so poorly, all overtook him and he suddenly found it difficult to move. The blood covering Reynoso's shirt made it impossible to tell where his wounds were. But then he heard the thin sailor cough and saw his face come to life on Teresa's lap. Spitting up blood and saliva, Reynoso tried to sit up, but he could not. Seconds later Lake found himself on both knees beside him clutching his hand and telling him everything would be all right. He didn't know what had come over him, but the sight of the devoted Reynoso felt like a knife thrust into his soul.

"We . . . we got the box, sir," Reynoso struggled to say in a whisper.

"Don't talk, Reynoso," he said, then tried to sound encouraging. "Just rest for a minute. You did good."

Lake glanced over to see Ahmad staring back at him. The mysterious operative looked exhausted as he knelt in the same spot taking frequent sips from a water bottle Michaelson had given him. Lake noticed the communications suitcase lying on the ground next to Ahmad's right knee. And he had brought back another item too, an AK-47 assault rifle, slung muzzle-down over his left shoulder. Amazingly, after only a few drinks he seemed revived again, almost to the same level of stamina he had exhibited earlier. As his breathing returned to normal, his eyes resumed their intense gaze.

"What happened to him?" Lake prompted.

"He's been shot," Ahmad replied, stating the obvious.

In no mood to play twenty questions, Lake threw him a fuming glance. Ahmad seemed to pick up on it and relented with a sigh.

"An Al Islamiyyah militant shot him. We spent most of the night trying to find the place where he dropped the suitcase. The enemy had listening posts everywhere. I took them out one by one, silently."

Ahmad's hand settled on the fold-out knife holstered at his belt, and Lake suddenly conjured the image of Ahmad's trim form slithering through the jungle, stalking his prey like a ghost, appearing abruptly behind the unsuspecting terrorists, then slitting their throats with a flash of steel in the night.

"One that I did not see shot Reynoso," Ahmad continued. "I found three wounds on his back but there could be more. He's lost much blood and cannot move his legs. I killed the one who shot him, but there were more. I heard them running back to the road. No doubt they've called for reinforcements by now."

With tender care Teresa rolled Reynoso onto his side and slid her hand under his shirt to probe for the wounds. Reynoso groaned at the movement, his blood-smeared face contorting in every possible way.

"*Please* . . . don't, ma'am," he said, struggling with the pain. "There's nothing you can do. I feel dizzy . . . like I'm going to pass out at any moment. Let me lie on my back."

Lake looked with hesitant optimism into Teresa's face, hoping that she would refute the young sailor's morbidity, that she would tell him his wounds were not that serious and that she could save him. Instead her eyes met Lake's with a sad countenance as she shook her head slowly, confirming his worst fears.

The young sailor had lost too much blood. With what little they had to treat him, the wounds were mortal. Gingerly, they rolled the dying man onto his back and he let out a gurgling sigh as the pressure came off his spine. Lake produced a bottle of water which Reynoso strained to sip with trembling lips.

"My lips," he muttered, "I can barely feel them, sir."

"Don't try to talk, Reynoso."

Mucous and blood spattered Lake's face as Reynoso rigorously coughed up the fluid he had managed to swallow.

"Damn it, Reynoso," Lake said despondently as he watched the poor young sailor struggle to catch his breath. "You'll do anything to get promoted, won't you? Why'd you have to go get shot, you son of a bitch? Why d'you always put your ass on the line?"

Reynoso's coughing finally subsided and he regained some semblance of composure. As he allowed his head to rest on the damp jungle floor, he smiled feebly up at Lake, his eyes wrinkling at the corners. Lake smiled too, but only briefly. He was too ashamed to look his leading petty officer in the face and instead stared at the ground.

"You'd have been promoted by now," Lake said almost inaudibly, "if your division officer wasn't such a self-centered piece of shit. You'd have been promoted by now, but I never got off my sorry ass to put your damn promotion package together. I'm a sorry excuse for a div-o, that's for sure."

As he looked again at Reynoso's face, he was surprised to see the radioman still smiling back at him.

"That's . . . good to know, sir," he muttered, wheezing short breaths in between words. "I just figured . . . I wasn't ready yet. That . . . I might not be . . . *chief* material."

"Oh, no, Reynoso, of course not. I don't think that at all. You're more than ready. If anyone's ready, you are. Don't ever think otherwise, okay? The only reason you're not wearing a chief's anchor right now is because of my lazy ass."

"I'll second that, young man," Michaelson chimed in. He had hauled himself to a spot near Reynoso's feet. "You're *chief* material in my book, Reynoso. And that's coming from a *chief*!"

Reynoso cast an acknowledging glance in Michaelson's direction but his gaze soon drifted back to Lake. Looking into the dying radioman's eyes, Lake felt lower at that moment than at any other in his life. Here was the loyal sailor who had busted his ass to please him, who had done everything asked of him and more, who desired little more than a career in the navy, and now he lay dying on a rotting jungle floor some ten thousand miles from his home. At that moment, Lake hated himself. He hated himself for the way he had treated Reynoso all these years, for not finishing Reynoso's promotion package. And he hated himself for the cynical self-serving officer he had become. If only he'd taken the time to get Reynoso promoted, at least he'd be dying with the knowledge that he'd reached his career milestones. Now he would die a mere first-class petty officer, just one of the hundreds of thousands manning the fleet. Lake knew that he alone was responsible.

But if dying a mere first-class petty officer was a tragedy, Reynoso scarcely showed it in his paling face. He appeared serene, content with his life, content with what he had lived for, and content with what he would die for. In fact, he appeared so peaceful that Lake found himself rather envious—notwithstanding the gunshot wounds. Reynoso had lived his life knowing exactly what he wanted, a claim that Lake could never make.

Clutching Lake's wrist with a bloody and bony hand, Reynoso suddenly took a deep breath and lifted his head slightly to say, "Pasternak's a good guy, sir . . . he's just a second class . . . but I've trained him . . . I trust him . . . to take over the division . . . in my place."

"Damn it, Reynoso! Can't you think of anything else at a time like this? Fuck the division!"

Apparently he could not hear Lake, and he began muttering over and over, "Pasternak . . . can take over . . . I trust him . . ."

In all his agony, Reynoso's dutiful mind could only think about the line of succession, about who would take over in his absence. Even in this final moment, his thoughts dwelled on his beloved radio division and the men back on the ship he had done his best to mentor. They would be his last thoughts as his lungs wheezed out one final breath, then never inhaled again. As Lake stared into the lifeless eyes of the trusty radioman, his own began to water. A solitary tear slid down his grime-encrusted face and fell to the earth, colliding with the blood-stained mulch beside Reynoso's still body. Only now, after Reynoso was gone, did Lake realize how much he had cared for the oftentimes bothersome radioman.

The four survivors sat watching in solemn silence as Teresa's dirty but motherly hand closed his eyes.

The silence did not last long. Soon the air filled with sounds that did not belong to the jungle. Trucks and vehicles, lots of them, moving swiftly on the road below, their engines revving high as they took the steep grade in low gears. Within minutes the squealing brakes rang out in succession as each vehicle came to a stop. Then muffled voices in the wind. Voices speaking in Indonesian and Arabic.

"Reinforcements I presume," Lake said to no one in particular but caught an affirming nod from Ahmad.

"Probably dozens down there," Ahmad said. "Rebel troops *and* Al Islamiyyah fighters. We must leave now. They'll spread out in a line abreast and move straight up the hill to flush us out. We can escape if we leave *right now.* If we move laterally, parallel to the road, and if we move quickly enough, we can get beyond their line's flank before it reaches us."

"I want to try calling the *Providence* first. Just in case," Lake said.

"In case of what?"

"There's still a chance those people down there aren't terrorists at all. That they might actually be coming to help us. For all we know those could be Indonesian troops down there, and not rebels at all."

Ahmad's lips formed a diminutive smirk. "If you think that, you are a fool."

"Give me that suitcase, Ahmad!" Lake snapped. "Reynoso didn't die for nothing. I'm calling the *Providence* before we move one more fucking step!"

"I'm afraid you'll get no answer." Ahmad motioned to Reynoso's still body, then shook his head as he offered up the silvery box. "I didn't want to say anything while he lived, but see for yourself. It's beyond repair."

Lake noticed a large misshapen hole in the side of the suitcase. The metallic casing had bent inward, obviously the result of a stray round from a large-caliber rifle. Lake snatched the case from Ahmad's hand and placed it flat on the leafy ground. As he popped the locks, he said a silent prayer that the projectile had missed the contents inside. But when he raised the lid, the extent of the damage was plain. The projectile had wreaked havoc inside the box, smashing the radio transceiver to pieces, leaving nothing more than a hodgepodge of broken circuit boards and exposed wiring. The radio was useless, as Ahmad had said.

"I know this island well," Ahmad said, apparently assured that Lake had now come to the same conclusion. "North is the quickest way off this slope. We must make it to the valleys near the coast if we ever expect to get off this island now. There we can steal a *prahu* from one of the villages and make for one of the islands to the south. Any place is safer than remaining here. If we get lucky your ship will find us. If not . . ."

"And Uru Pass?" Teresa said, searching the Arab's face. "What about that? They're sure to have it blocked. I've lived here long enough to know there're only two ways to get off this slope to the north. One is through Uru Pass, the other is over the mountain summit. Surely your terrorist friends know that too."

Ahmad ignored her, but a small vein visibly pulsed above his left eye, giving Lake the impression that he wasn't used to having his authority challenged. Lake remembered the narrow gorge called Uru Pass. They had passed through it that day in the jeep going to and from the doctor's camp. Uru Pass was an awe-inspiring sight where the road approached a wall of solid rock at least a hundred feet high, the last significant barrier before descending into the hilly coastal valleys on the island's north side. To surpass this barrier, a deep path had been blasted out of the rock, probably decades ago by Bunda's now-defunct mining industry. The jagged gorge sliced right into the mountain ridge and conveniently emerged at the same elevation on the far side. The road narrowed significantly to pass through the chasm but it still allowed enough room for vehicles of most any size to run the short quarter-mile distance untouched. Steep walls of solid rock flanked the road on both sides inside the chasm. Walls that stretched to the sky, it seemed. Walls so steep and so high the sun scarcely touched the road during the course of a day. It was an easy place to set up a roadblock, or an ambush. A fact the terrorists could not have overlooked.

"We must try Uru Pass first," Ahmad said matter-of-factly. "The mountain is too high, and too steep for this man's leg. He surely cannot make it."

"Bullshit! I can make it, damn it!" Michaelson grumbled.

"Ahmad's right, Lieutenant," Teresa said. "I've been to the summit before. The last mile you're walking on nothing but loose volcanic rubble. It's like walking on golf balls. You take one step up and slide back ten. The chief would never make it."

Another expletive came from Michaelson.

Lake had already ruled out going over the mountain ridge, but he felt it was best not to stir the chief's angst any further. He would slow them down for sure. But despite the chief's climbing ability, Lake was much more concerned about the lack of cover on the bare summit. Any lucky bastard with a set of binoculars could see them from miles away.

A few feet away from him, Michaelson groped to stand up, his teeth gritting from the pain.

"I see that look on your face, Lieutenant. Don't worry your little university-nursed ass about me. I can take care of myself."

"Bullshit, Chief. Ahmad and I are taking you on our shoulders and I don't want any arguments! We're heading to Uru Pass like Ahmad said." Lake looked back at Ahmad for assistance in lifting the big chief, but was surprised to see him dragging Reynoso's limp body toward a fallen log. There he dispassionately propped up the dead sailor in a disturbing, yet lifelike sitting pose. From his deep pockets, he produced two hand grenades, and a chilling horror crept over Lake as Ahmad pulled the pins on both and gingerly hid them beneath

Reynoso's legs, carefully positioning the striker levers so that the weight of Reynoso's legs would hold them shut. Whatever unfortunate fool found Reynoso's body would get a face full of shrapnel.

"Now we can go," said Ahmad finally. "Quickly now!"

Teresa grabbed up what little supplies they had. Ahmad took position under Michaelson's left armpit, and Lake moved to take up a position under the right one. But then a thought suddenly crossed Lake's mind and he quickly fell to his knees to rummage through the discarded communications suitcase.

"What the hell are you doing?" Ahmad said anxiously. The Indonesian voices were already growing louder as the troops below began climbing the slope. "Leave the suitcase, Lieutenant! Let it go! Your radio's out of commission!"

"One thing about us submariners, Mister Secret Agent," Lake said as he produced a foot-long object and also a smaller item taken from a pocket concealed along the inner edge of the suitcase, "we don't believe in single points of failure. We always have a back up."

Lake held up the undamaged satellite telephone with its accompanying cryptographic sleeve for all to see before stuffing them both into his front pants pocket. Finally nestling himself beneath Michaelson's right arm to take his portion of the weight, Lake thought he caught a smile from the burly torpedoman. As much as Michaelson disliked Lake, perhaps the chief had enjoyed seeing the smug agent left speechless, bested by the navy. But any gratification was short-lived as they swiftly pressed into the thick brush, heading north, the chief attempting not to wince from the excruciating pain at each jostling step.

Before going a hundred yards Lake was out of breath. The chief was heavy, but he dug deep for the strength to maintain Ahmad's brisk pace. He tried not to think about how drained he was, but instead focused on the satellite phone bulging from his pocket, its antenna jabbing him in the ribs with each step. It was the one thing that could save them. With it, they still had a chance.

* * *

NUCLEAR Machinists' Mate Third-Class Myron Dean placed his toothbrush in the locker beneath his bunk, struggling not to make any noise that would disturb the dozen other sailors sleeping all around him. Like synchronized metronomes, the rack curtains swayed back and forth in the dimly-lit, twenty-one-man bunkroom as *Providence* rocked gently on the surface, and a chorus of snoring sailors kept time with the slow rhythm. Happy to be back aboard once again, Dean smiled at the familiar scene. It was good to be back.

The ride out of Bunda Harbor had been a long one, especially since the captain chose not to converse with him the entire trip. Staring at Bunda's distant hills, clearly visible with the lifting of the storm, the captain spent the ride deep in thought, troubled by matters far greater than any he ever could conceive. But what else did he expect? Did he really think the captain would shoot the shit with him all the way back to the ship? And besides, informal conversation with a junior enlisted man, especially one who was under a suspended mast sentence, simply did not happen on a U.S. warship. Disciplines had to be followed, ranks observed and feared.

Dean could have used some conversation on that long trip back to the ship. It might have helped him sort things out in his head. But no matter. With the wind in his face and the sunlight breaking through the clouds, he had time enough to come to grips with his feelings. After a few full breaths of the thick salt air, he came to terms with the overwhelming feeling of relief that had descended on him. Not because he had been rescued, but because he'd just learned that the engineer had gone missing ashore. It seemed sick to feel reprieve at another man's peril, but he could not help it. The dark cloud hovering over him for most of the last year had lifted and he suddenly felt alive again. It seemed to finally sink in when Lieutenant Coleman, the acting-engineer, dropped by to see him, offering a welcome back to the ship and showing a genuine concern for his well-being. Polite and professional as always, Coleman told him to make sure he got plenty of rest and to make sure he had recovered before reporting aft for duty again. But despite this "free rack ticket," Dean didn't want to wait. He felt restless and eager to get back to his division. The last thing he wanted to do was sit in his rack thinking about the whole ordeal ashore.

As he stepped out of the bunkroom and into the bright light of the lower-level passage, he couldn't stop thinking about the freakish way in which Ensign Yi had been killed. Lack of space on the harbor craft had forced him to sit practically side by side with Yi's tightly wrapped body. Fumes from the noxious fabric, whatever it was, still lingered in his nose, and they served as a constant reminder of his close brush with death. Had he been in the room when those murderous thieves showed up, it would have been his body wrapped with the smelly fabric, instead of Yi's. He felt sorrow for the unlucky young ensign. Yi had never been a good division officer, always fumbling over himself, seldom standing up for his men, but Dean believed that under other circumstances—perhaps in some other setting away from the regimented hierarchy of shipboard life—he would have liked Philip Yi.

Allowing a couple sailors to go before him, Dean headed up the ladder to the middle level, taking each step at his own pace, his ribs still tender to every move. Passing aft to the crew's mess, he smelled the aroma of the galley as lunch was being prepared. Several sailors sat at the mess tables and talked while they watched the monitor at the far end of the room, which seemed to be the focus of attention at the moment. Some looked in his direction and welcomed him back, then turned again to the monitor. It was selected to the periscope view, displaying whatever the officer of the deck or the captain was currently looking at through the periscope.

"Check this out, Dean," a mustached yeoman with over-sized glasses said as he pointed to the screen. "Them Indonesians sent their navy out to help us."

A few men near him burst out laughing as Dean looked up to see what the yeoman was talking about. The screen was focused on a small prahu floating in and out of the waves some distance ahead of the ship. The periscope must have been on maximum magnification because the small canoe-like vessel took up most of the field of view. It appeared to be in bad shape, low in the water and leaning heavily on its outrigged stabilizer. Three heads bobbed actively above the gunwale as the small craft's crew frantically bailed water to keep her afloat.

"Ain't they lucky we happened along?" a sailor said.

"Aw, we ought to let 'em drown," sneered another. "Those fishin' folk wouldn't lift a finger to help us if it were the other way around."

The 1MC keyed and every man went silent to listen to the forthcoming announcement.

"Muster the small boat handling party topside to receive personnel!" the speaker squawked.

"Sounds like the old man's going to help 'em, God bless the bastard," said one of the sailors as he filed out of the dining booth, responding to the call for the small-boat-handling detail.

Dean took a seat and gazed at the screen. Soon the boat detail was crowding the mess, noisily staging their safety harnesses, life vests, fenders, and boat hooks just beneath the aft hatch. He envied them, partly because they had jobs to do, but mostly because they would get to see the world above again. He'd give anything to be topside one last time before *Providence* submerged.

"One, two, three, four, six, eight. . . . there're supposed to be nine of you!" Master Chief Ketterling's voice boomed from down the passage. "Where the hell's Jorgenson? Jorgenson! Jorgenson! Where the hell is he?"

"Jorgenson's on watch, Master Chief," a sailor's voice answered. "His back-up's Reynoso. But Reynoso ain't on board."

"Shit!"

Dean heard Ketterling trudge up the passage toward the crew's mess, the metal hooks on his harness dragging the tiled deck the whole way.

"I need one volunteer!" he said, eying the mass of sailors

lounging in the mess. None looked him in the eye for fear of being chosen for the duty. None except Dean, that is.

"I'll volunteer, Master Chief."

"Not you, Dean. I need someone who's got ribs that ain't broke."

"It's not that bad, Master Chief," Dean said, popping up from his seat far quicker than he should have. His ribs suddenly felt like a horse had kicked them, and it took everything he could muster not to show any outward signs of pain. "Really, it feels a lot better now."

"All right." Ketterling eyed him skeptically. "But you let the other fellas do the heavy heaving, you hear? Let's go."

Dean followed Ketterling down the passage where he gingerly donned a harness and life vest and followed the eight other men up the long ladder through the lower and upper hatches until he emerged on deck into the bright sunlight. Bunda's tall mountains were now little more than tiny peaks on the western horizon, rising far behind *Providence*'s short bubbly wake. The drifting storm front had receded farther still, now only a distant mass of dark cumulus far to the north.

In preparation for bringing the beleaguered prahu alongside, *Providence* had slowed to one-third speed and continued to decelerate until Dean could scarcely tell she was moving. The little craft he had seen on the monitor was much closer than he had expected it to be, and now it lay a mere hundred yards off the port beam, her crew waving hysterically at the officers on *Providence*'s high bridge, as if the submarine might pass them by.

"I guess those bastards aren't taking any chances," Ketterling muttered.

The boat detail's gear came up the aft hatch, and Dean shouldered a coil of hemp to do his part. Ketterling led them forward along the curved deck and stopped when they reached the shade of *Providence*'s tall sail and broad fairwater planes. With the sun behind her, the long shadow of *Providence*'s sail stretched out to touch her rounded bow.

"Prepare to bring the boat along the port side, Master

Chief." Dean recognized the captain's voice and looked up to see him peering down at them from the bridge.

"Aye, aye, Captain," Ketterling called back smartly, touching the brim of his blue ball cap before immediately issuing orders to that effect. Lifelines were made fast and fenders rigged out. The squashy deflectors splashed into the water and bobbed on their tethers half-submerged.

But it was looking more and more like the fenders would not be needed, since the prahu appeared to be sinking. Dean saw the three men in the small craft, now fifty yards away, give up their fight to keep her afloat as all three leaped over the gunwale and into the sea. Watching them closely, Dean tried not to blink as he kept track of their exact location. The three bobbing heads quickly drifted away from their sinking vessel, making it even harder to keep sight of them. It was easy to lose a small bobbing head on anything but a placid sea and Dean had certainly witnessed his share of man overboard drills to prove it. Losing sight once usually meant losing it forever.

A splash and a flailing arm appeared above the surface periodically and helped him to keep track of the three heads. But minutes later, the small boat capsized behind them and soon their flailing and splashing lost its original vitality. Dean guessed that the three men were near the point of exhaustion. They'd been bailing water for who knows how long, and most likely they were having trouble staying afloat. They would not have to tread water for very much longer however, as *Providence* was steadily approaching their position. *Providence* would be alongside them in a matter of minutes, if only they could hang on.

The tricky current was moving swiftly to the northeast, but *Providence*'s conning officer seemed to know what he was doing. *Providence* skillfully maneuvered to a position upstream of the floating men, then with a sharp rudder angle the submarine's bow came over until it pointed exactly perpendicular to the stiff current. This exposed the whole length of her three-hundred-sixty-foot hull to the full force of the current, and since she had more surface area than the floating men, she felt a much greater effect. A short backing bell brought her forward motion to a halt, then nothing more remained to do except drift down to the treading men, now just thirty yards away.

Dean could see that the men were having trouble staying afloat. Their fatigue was getting the better of them as they tilted their heads back, their mouths gasping for air, their arms moving slothfully as if they swam in quicksand and not water. Just then a small wave broke over their heads and submerged all three. After several seconds, only two faces reappeared. The third never made it back to the surface.

Standing next to Dean with fins at the ready, the ship's diver took the nod from Ketterling. He jumped into the water with a splash and immediately broke into a brisk swim toward the two men. It was always a risk sending another man overboard. Oftentimes he became another man to rescue. But the alternative, simply watching the two flailing men drown, was obviously unacceptable. The men on deck cheered as the diver reached the first man and began hauling him back toward the ship.

"Let's get these guys aboard," Ketterling said in preparation to receive the men in the water. "Check them out, and get them below ASAP, boys. These guys have got to be tired, so I want everyone but Dalton and Dean on the rope ladder to help pass 'em up. Once we get them up on deck, Dalton, you'll help the first guy below, and Dean, you'll help the second guy. Understand?"

Dean nodded in unison with Dalton, suddenly not quite sure how he was going to hide the pain when he took the exhausted man's weight on his sore shoulder. Glancing aft, he noticed that two security petty officers were now on deck. They stood by the sail with stern faces and M-16 rifles at the ready, apparently showing up on deck shortly after the boat detail. The captain was taking no chances with these unexpected guests.

As the first man approached the side, the men on the dangling rope ladder reached for his arms and plucked him out of the water like a bath toy. Within seconds they had passed him

up the curved sloping deck to the waiting Dalton, who immediately assisted the weary man—obviously a local, judging
from his Malay features and his drab villager attire. Dalton
slung the man's left arm over his shoulder and directed him
aft to the security detail, who spent a few minutes searching
his wet, raggedy clothing before allowing Dalton to take him
on to the open hatch. The Malay man was so weary that his
feet dragged the deck, forcing Dalton to literally carry him the
whole way.

Silently, Dean panicked. If the next man needed as much
help, Dean wasn't sure he'd be able to do it. His ribs weren't
ready for that kind of pressure yet. He had to tell Ketterling
the truth, that he had no business being up here at all, before it
was too late.

"Master Chief?" he said feebly.

"Get ready for this next guy, Dean," Ketterling said, his
eyes locked on the remaining man in the water. "He's almost
on board."

"Master Chief, I . . ."

"Damn it, Dean, shut up and get fucking ready!" Ketterling
snapped. "Okay, boys, here he comes. Okay Thomas. Okay
Gutierrez. Damn, this guy looks like he's in bad shape! Get
ready to pull him up! Get a good hold! Together now! Heave!"

Dean knew he had no choice. He was going to have to suck
it up the best he could. Who knows, he thought, maybe he
could do it after all. Like an Olympic wrestler, he assumed a
low stance at the end of the line of men as they reached and
struggled to pull the man up on deck.

"Shit, Master Chief!" shouted one sailor near the waterline. "This guy's dead weight! He's a white guy! Must be Australian! His face is all swollen and bruised and shit."

Ketterling reached his arm into the mass of tangled flesh
and helped pull the man up by his tattered wet shirt. The
man's head hung low as Ketterling dragged him onto the level
deck and dropped him onto his stomach. Dean assisted as best
he could, but he knew there was little he could do to help. The
pitiable man showed few signs of movement as he lay with his
face flat against the black, rubber-coated deck.

"That's no Australian, shipmates," Ketterling said flatly. "He's one of ours, though he don't look much like himself. Shit, he must've lost twenty pounds! Here, Dean, you better help him below."

The near-drowned man instantly went into convulsions as he coughed up a torrent of seawater and mucous that streamed down the curved black hull.

"Dean?" the half-dead man's dry voice cracked as he struggled to regain his breath and lift his wet head.

Even the warm equatorial air could not keep Dean's skin from turning to ice as he found himself looking directly into the bloodshot eyes of Aubrey Van Peenan.

Chapter 16

"**LET** me be perfectly frank with you, Captain Edwards." Admiral Chappell's image appeared fuzzy on the laptop computer screen in Edwards' cabin, but the static wasn't enough to hide the admiral's angry scowl. "In order for a modern navy to function, it must rely on a central command and control, a single point of command from which all strategic and tactical decisions emanate. On any high-tempo battlefield, it's the only way for a modern force to properly optimize its combined assets in order to attain the mission objectives. Wouldn't you agree, Captain?"

"Yes, Admiral." Edwards knew where Chappell was going with this, and he wished he'd just skip the mentoring session and get on with the business at hand. Of course, any business could have been handled with voice comms alone, but Chappell must have wanted the satisfaction of watching his errant captain's face while he told him off. There were few enough high bandwidth satellites covering the far-western Pacific as it was, and most were allocated to the pair of carrier strike groups operating in the Sea of Japan. Chappell must have called in a few favors to get the assigned bandwidth for this video conference.

"Then explain to me, please, Captain, why you have trouble following orders. Please explain to me how you can so lose sight of the grand scheme of things that you would take matters into your own hands. Do you think you knew more than your superiors? Do you think you have better intelligence? Please help me to understand how you've managed to be so utterly and unbelievably *stupid*!"

"I assume you're referring to my trip into Ujungpang this morning to retrieve my men, sir."

"You know damn well that's what I mean, you son of a bitch! Shit, you've caused a stir! I got a call from Washington this morning. A very unpleasant phone call, you might say. It seems that the *Providence* showed up on radar imagery during the national security advisor's briefing this morning. Right in front of the President's fucking advisor a picture of one of *my* submarines, sitting on the *surface* no less, hardly a stone's throw away from Bunda. One of *my* submarines! Damn you, Edwards, I've never been so fucking embarrassed in my entire life!"

"I regret very much any humiliation I've caused you, Admiral," Edwards said carefully, not wishing to show his impatience with this exercise. "I doubt if it's any consolation, sir, but the trip inshore wasn't a complete loss. Three of my missing men are now back aboard. One of them dead, I'm sad to say."

"Don't you think I know that?" Chappell fumed. "CinCPac is furious! I've spent my whole damn day going from one meeting to the next answering for that stunt you pulled. The CinC knows all about your little parley with the rebel leaders, Captain, and he's none too pleased about it. He's in contact with the Indonesian government, or didn't you realize that? They've still got loyal citizens in Ujungpang, believe it or not. They know exactly what's going on there, and up until now they've been providing us with regular updates. That is, until today. We're not getting updates anymore because the Indonesian government now doesn't trust us. Damn it, Dave, try to imagine the position you put us in trying to come up with excuses for your little foray! An American submarine captain arrives in Ujungpang in the middle of a major revolt and meets behind closed doors with the rebel leadership? It looks bad, Dave, very bad. Of course, tomorrow the press won't mention anything about the three men you got back. They'll portray things in the worst light possible. And they're going to have a field day! I can't believe you were so stupid. If I didn't need your ship there right now, I'd recall you at once. I'm afraid this could be a career-ender for you, Dave."

"Admiral," Edwards said, then hesitated for a moment,

considering carefully what he was about to say. "I was surprised at something one of the rebel leaders told me, sir. He said that the *Providence* was sent here to extract a covert agent who'd been living with a local terrorist group. Apparently the rebels think this agent is with my shore party right now, wherever they are, and that's why they're after them. Unfortunately, I haven't heard from my shore party in two days. I just thought it was strange, Admiral. My orders didn't mention anything about extracting an agent. Do you have any idea what he's talking about, sir?"

Edwards knew the answer before he even asked the question, but he wanted to see Chappell squirm for a change. It went against his nature to play the game, but even good officers couldn't climb the ladder without an ace in the hole. There were too many flag officers, too many civilian officials who wouldn't think twice about feeding a lowly ship captain to the sharks. He'd just played his ace, and from the look now on Chappell's face he knew there would be no further mention of "career-enders."

"That rebel was correct, Captain," Chappell said in a different tone, much more subdued. He appeared uncomfortable sharing the information with Edwards. "And, yes, the agent he spoke of is with your men ashore. Radio comms intercepted in the last twenty-four hours confirmed this. As for the location of your men, I don't know where they are, just that they're still alive somewhere on Bunda. We're in the process of coordinating a rescue operation with the Indonesian military, but who knows how long that will take. The Indonesians are far more concerned about quashing the rebellion right now."

"Something has to be done, sir. What about our own spec ops? What about the SEALs? CinCPac may be writing off my men, but I'm not going to, sir!"

"We're working on it, Dave. Trust me. You've done your part, now let others do theirs. It's going to take time to get the right team in place, but let me assure you, forces are moving as we speak. I project no more than seventy-two hours before we can launch a successful rescue operation."

"Three days!" Edwards said incredulously. "By that time

the Indonesian air force could be bombing the hell out of the place!"

"It can't be helped, Dave. Besides I don't think there's much chance of that. The Indonesian military's never dealt with anything on the scale of this revolt before. Right now Bunda is last on their target list. Take them another week to mop up things in Aceh and Irian Jaya, maybe two weeks before they can shift their attention elsewhere." Chappell cleared his throat. "Which brings me to the primary reason I've contacted you. I'm tasking *Providence* with a strike mission, tonight. The target package and threat assessment are all in your next TS download, so make sure you copy it before leaving comms depth."

A sudden sensation came over Edwards, as Chappell changed the subject. The admiral had finished talking about *Providence*'s shore party and had now moved on to "more urgent" matters. A simple change of subject was all it took to effectively writeoff *Providence*'s lost sailors. There wasn't much else to it. It was where the "centralized command and control" system Chappell had just lectured him about broke down, where men and ships became mere numbers on a spreadsheet.

"As you've apparently learned," Chappell continued, "a terrorist cell's been operating in the Bunda Islands for many years now, using Wijaya as a training camp and weapons depot. Intel estimates that this particular camp is home to no fewer than two hundred fighters at any given moment, but, more importantly, it serves as a hub for weapons shipments to different Islamic terrorist networks around the world. The place is loaded with weapons and equipment, both light and heavy. Satellite even caught them unloading a light tank a few months ago. It's all hidden in underground bunkers, of course. Who knows how many thousand RPG rounds are stacked under that island, but rest assured if they aren't destroyed they'll end up in the hands of the same guys fighting against our troops in the Middle East. We've notified the Indonesian authorities about the presence of the camp and the threat it poses and they've promised to add it to their target list, but as I said before, their air force has their hands full. They won't hit

Bunda for at least a week. That's a week the terrorists will have to get away, and a week we're not willing to wait."

"We shot off most of our Tomahawks in the Red Sea, Admiral. I've got only six missiles left, and one of those I'm not sure about. My Weps tells me it won't spin up properly during the weekly maintenance checks."

"I know, I know," Chappell said, raising a hand. "I saw it all in your last sitrep. It can't be helped."

"Well, that's hardly an arsenal for you, Admiral. Surely a carrier group somewhere or a long range bomber would be better suited for—"

"What the hell kind of talk is that, coming from a submariner?" Chappell interrupted, poignantly. "I'm surprised at you, Edwards. Never send a plane when a submarine can do the job. Our Tommies don't have pilots, so no one gets shot down and no one gets taken prisoner. And that makes the politicians happy. Besides, the Indonesians haven't given us permission to do this strike, so it's in everyone's best interest if we minimize the evidence. Carrier strike groups consist of thousands of men, most of which don't have TS clearances. In other words, that's a few thousand tongues that can spill the beans to the press. Long range bombers, no matter how stealthy they are, still need airspace and a flight plan. They still have to land and refuel at airbases where the guys in the tower and the guys pumping the gas aren't cleared. Whereas submariners, on the other hand, are a pretty reliable bunch. Small crews who are used to keeping their mouths shut. Small ships that pull into port weeks after the strike takes place. We don't need bases, we don't need flight plans, we don't need to recover our aircraft. We just fire and forget, and the bad guys go away."

Chappell was practically rubbing his hands together in a state of devilish bliss as he touted the obvious, and Edwards thought it best not to further question the wisdom of the operation.

"But you're quite right, Captain," Chappell continued, as he regained control of himself. "Your half-dozen Tommies aren't enough to deliver the big punch in this strike. By my records you've got only Block III missiles on board anyhow. And I'm afraid your standard warheads won't do the trick against those bunkers. We need something with some penetrating power to get to those buried weapons. We need Block IVs. Two days ago, I ordered the *Ohio* to leave her station near Formosa Strait. She's been heading your way ever since. She'll be in strike range of Wijaya by 2300 hours tonight."

Edwards hid his almost audible gasp. Sending the *Ohio* indicated the importance and size of this strike mission. The big nuclear-powered USS *Ohio*, a former ballistic missile submarine of the Cold War, now carried conventional cruise missiles in the same tubes that once cradled her lethal three-story high continent killers. Her design had been conformed to fight the new war, the war on terror, and with her new design came a new designation—*SSGN*—or, more colloquially, a guided missile submarine. Though she no longer carried her nuclear payload, the *Ohio* still gave nightmares to America's enemies. Sluggish as a pig, barely surpassing half *Providence*'s max speed, and limited in her underwater sensor capability, the *Ohio* had never been intended by her designers to hold her own in an undersea engagement. But what she could unleash on a land target more than made up for her shortcomings below the sea. She held one hundred fifty-four tactical cruise missiles of every variety, including the deadly Block IV Tomahawk guided-cruise missile—or TLAM-E—which could hit targets over a thousand miles away and had an accuracy beyond compare. If *Providence*'s Block III missiles could hit a terrorist's front door, the Block IV could hit the peephole. They could target weak points in any structure and penetrate it, or bring it down altogether.

It gave Edwards a sense of comfort to know such a powerful friend was heading this way, and he tried to picture the *Ohio*'s captain in his mind. He couldn't remember ever meeting him, and they certainly wouldn't get the chance to meet on this operation either. More than likely, *Ohio* would launch her missiles from extreme range, never coming closer than a thousand miles to *Providence*'s position.

"At precisely 2330 hours local time tonight," Chappell

continued enthusiastically, "*Ohio* will begin firing a forty-three unit strike package to turn Wijaya into a hell on earth. Those missiles each have a target and a specific mission, and if all of them get through there won't be any man-made structures left anywhere on that island, or beneath it for that matter. We know they've got large munition stockpiles and we're counting on some major secondary detonations to finish the job for us. Any terrorist there at the moment our missiles strike better like his surroundings, because he'll become an integral part of them about two milliseconds later."

"So where does the *Providence* fit in, sir?"

"The terrorist camp is a high value asset to Al Islamiyyah, and as such they've invested in a high-dollar air defense system to protect it. A strategically placed network of Lieying-60 anti-aircraft missile batteries and thirty-millimeter Goalkeeper Gatlin guns, all guided by two state-of-the-art air defense radars, protect the island from air assault. Now, of course, these batteries could never stop *all* of *Ohio*'s missiles, but they might stop a few heading to the more crucial targets. *Ohio*'s Tommies will be skimming the waves as they approach, but we still estimate her birds will get detected thirty miles from the target. That'll leave them plenty of time to line up their missile batteries and guns. So obviously, those radars have to be taken out. Without them, the network will go dark. And that task will fall to the *Providence*, Captain. Your orders are to destroy those radar emplacements before *Ohio*'s strike arrives."

Chappell paused. "But here's the catch, Dave. If you fire from too far out, those radars will detect your missiles and bring 'em down without even sneezing. So you've got to get close in. You've got to override the minimum range interlocks on your missiles and shoot inside twenty miles."

Edwards did the quick math in his head. Shooting from twenty miles away, *Providence*'s missiles would have a two-minute flight time to target. It was still plenty of time for the terrorist radars to lock on.

"I know what you're thinking, Dave, but here comes the

second catch. *Ohio*'s missiles will be coming in from the north, yours from the south. *Ohio*'s birds will reach the detection point at precisely 0113:15 local. We want to let the enemy radars get a good paint on them and get all their defenses pointed in that direction. Then you'll launch your birds from the other end of the azimuth, taking their radars by surprise. You'll be launching a salvo, four missiles total, two at each radar. That should do the job. They'll have to be airborne by 0113:45 local, and there's *no margin for error* here, Dave. The coordination has to be right on this one, or we'll blow the whole show. Get *Providence* in position early and tell your weps to use his best birds."

"Aye, aye, Admiral." Edwards nodded, immediately thinking of Peto's threat as he had left the governor's mansion. The *Hatta* would be waiting for them, and launching a missile wasn't exactly a quiet undertaking. "Sir, if we happen to encounter the *Hatta*—"

"You are authorized to take any means necessary to carry out your launch at the designated time, Captain," Chappell said sternly. "You have authorization to destroy her. And that means without prior provocation, too. If you find her, put her on the bottom. Understood?"

Easier said than done, thought Edwards.

"I wish I had better intel for you," Chappell added, "but the *Hatta*'s unaccounted for. She showed up on satellite imagery twenty-four hours ago, but she's not been seen in any of the data since. Most likely, she's pulled the plug. *Use extreme caution, Dave*. No one's been up against a Type-214 before. We're sending you everything we have on her, but take it with a grain of salt. No one's ever accused navy intel of being accurate."

"I will, Admiral." Edwards decided there was no need to mention that he'd actually toured the *Hatta*.

"Good luck, Dave. Remember, your birds must launch on time at all costs. The success of this operation depends on it. Keep me up to date with regular sitreps."

"Aye, aye, Admiral. Don't worry, sir, we'll shoot on time."

Chappell nodded into the camera with a slight smirk on his face before saying, "SubPac, out."

The screen went blue and Edwards clicked the mouse button to close the window, returning the screen to his email. The admiral had made no further mention of *Providence*'s shore party. Obviously the strike was at the center of his thoughts. If Chappell could add the destruction of a major terrorist camp to his coffers, he might just pin on a second star. Under the spell of the "star fever" it was easy for a flag officer to forget about the heads he was stepping on, the people who were making the actual sacrifices.

Edwards was determined the *he* should not forget. He would find a way to get Lake and his men off that island if it meant losing his command. But first things first. *Providence* had a strike mission to accomplish, and he needed to focus his short-term efforts toward that end. Like a CPU spinning up, his mind began to think of every contingency, every factor, every unforeseen circumstance, every obstacle that might constrain the mission. The *Hatta* was, of course, the deadliest obstacle. She would certainly be there, waiting for them. If they were to have any chance of defeating her, they would need an edge. Another ace in the hole.

Clicking down the list of emails on his laptop, he found the one from Peto. Where was the rebel submarine captain now? Somewhere under the sea, more than likely only a few miles away, intently watching the *Hatta*'s sonar panel as he searched for a flagrant tonal he could use to track the American submarine. Perhaps he'd found the same tonal *Providence*'s sonarmen had detected on the voyage out. The engineering department had turned the engine room upside down trying to find the source with no success.

Peto would certainly find it. He'd find the tonal and track *Providence* right up to the launch point. He'd have the advantage from the beginning, and once *Providence* began shooting missiles he'd know her location to within half a degree.

In the lower corner of the screen, Edwards saw an icon change color indicating it was no longer connected to the Internet. On cue, the sounds of porting hydraulic fluid ran through the jumble of piping in the overhead as the communications mast was lowered. Over the speaker in his stateroom, Edwards heard the officer of the deck making preparations to leave periscope depth. All message traffic must now be aboard, including the mission data for the upcoming strike.

As he searched the far recesses of his mind for a way to defeat the *Hatta*, he found himself mindlessly thumbing the mouse over Peto's email a dozen or more times. How things had changed since he was an ensign, when captains had to draft paper copies of messages which the radiomen would laboriously type into the communications buffer for broadcast at the next comms window. Now submarine captains could communicate directly with a simple click of the mouse. Email eliminated all of the middlemen and broke down all barriers.

Then an idea crossed his mind, a crazy, far-fetched idea. An idea so simple it could not possibly work. Yet so simple that it just might.

He reached over and took the phone from its cradle.

"Officer of the Deck, this is the captain. I assume you've downloaded all the strike mission data?"

"The Weps is in the control room reviewing it now, sir," the young officer's voice replied.

"Good. Pass the word for all officers to muster in the wardroom at 1900 hours." He paused a moment before adding, "And do not, repeat *do not,* go deep yet. I want to stay at comms depth for a little while longer. Have Seaman Shoemaker report to my cabin immediately."

The officer of the deck had barely acknowledged the order when Edwards shoved the phone back into its cradle. His idea was a long shot, but it was the only ace he had.

Chapter 17

PROVIDENCE cruised at five hundred feet as she made her way cautiously but swiftly toward the Bunda atoll, this time heading for the northern island of Wijaya, now some fifty miles away. It had been a long and miserable day for the officers and crew of the *Providence*, having spent most of it on the surface or at periscope depth. After bobbing about all day, the smooth ride at this lower depth was a welcome reprieve. Spirits rose further when news of the upcoming missile strike finally made its way around to all compartments. Understandably, the sailors felt invigorated at the prospect of breaking up the monotony, and, not surprisingly, every off-watch officer showed up for the wardroom meeting a few minutes earlier than required.

The blue-uniformed officers conversed excitedly as they crowded around the long dining table. Bloomfield, for his part, sat quietly in the executive officer's chair, pretending not to hear any of the conversations around him as he sipped at a coffee cup and flipped through some files on the table before him.

"Did you hear about the Eng?" one of *Providence*'s young lieutenants whispered to another as they waited for the captain to arrive.

"I heard he's laid up in the rack," said the second lieutenant. "I heard he got beat up pretty bad."

"Yeah, but they didn't beat the asshole out of him, that's for damn sure," the first lieutenant said between draws on a can of soda. "You know my locker's right next to his rack, right? Well, I keep my soda on the top shelf, right, and I'm reaching for this soda trying to be extra quiet so I don't disturb him, right. I even leave the light off so he won't wake up, and all of a sudden this fist comes shooting out of his rack right through the curtains and punches me in the stomach."

"Ha!" exclaimed the second lieutenant, with bewildered amusement. "I'm glad I don't live with that crazy bastard. I'll take the nine-man berthing any day to your stateroom with the Eng."

"But then get this," the first lieutenant continued. "I pull his curtain back to ask him what the fuck he's doing but he's sound asleep, or at least he looks like it. So I shine my flashlight in his face and nudge him a couple times until he finally opens his eyes. And when I ask him why he hit me he just mumbles something about how he must have been dreaming and for me to make sure I don't tell Captain Christopher about it. Captain *Christopher*! Can you believe that shit? What the hell time-warp is he living in?"

Unknown to the young lieutenant, Bloomfield silently choked on his last mouthful of coffee a few seats away.

"I already knew Commander Van Peenan was crazy," the second lieutenant whispered. "This just confirms it."

At that moment, the wardroom door opened and all came to their feet as Edwards made his way to the head of the table, followed closely by Miller, who immediately flipped down the laptop computer panel on the starboard side bulkhead and started manipulating the imbedded track ball to load up a presentation.

As his officers stared back at him Edwards realized how very green they all looked, even the more seasoned ones like Fremont and Miller. Only Bloomfield, now wiping his chubby face with a paper napkin, looked old enough to be at sea on a warship. Perhaps his extra seventy-five pounds facilitated that impression. The rest were mere boys he would be leading into battle. Boy officers who would have to lead even younger boys and rely heavily on their hardened and often much wiser chiefs for the upcoming trials that awaited them.

"Please, take your seats." He motioned.

As they regained their chairs, he could tell they were anticipating his every word. He had their complete and undivided attention, a difficult task with a bunch of vibrant young men. Obviously, the rumor mill had been churning.

"While the Weps is loading the presentation," he continued, "I'll fill you in on what's been happening. As most of you no doubt know by now, we've been tasked with a strike mission for this evening. The strike is against a terrorist camp located in these islands, an important target and one we can't afford to miss. This will be yet another stroke in the grander war on terror, so you all can be proud of yourselves when we get back home. You won't be able to tell anyone about it, but you can be proud all the livelong day."

A scant few chuckled at his attempt to lighten the mood.

"This will be a coordinated attack in conjunction with another boat taking up position far to the north. We've got to get in close and we've got to shoot on time. You guys have all done this type of thing before. We've done it together, so I'm not too worried about the launch. I know you guys will do your jobs, and I know you'll do them well. What I *am* worried about is our opponent. Weps, please continue."

Miller finished booting up the presentation and touched the button to activate the large flat panel display on the forward bulkhead. The screen took a few seconds to warm up before an artist's concept of the *Hatta*'s stubby, torpedo-like hull filled the field of view.

"This, gentlemen," Miller said dramatically, "is the submarine you saw in Ujungpang, the KRI *Hatta*. She's a new ship, built in Germany—completed only last year—with a sonar suite comparable to our own, and an air independent propulsion system that makes our reactor sound like a three ring circus. She's got a crew of twenty-five officers and sailors and can fire missiles or swimout torpedoes from eight tubes in her bow. She's to be considered hostile from here on out!"

Miller paused for a moment to let the last point sink in with the attentive officers.

"We've good reason to believe she's tracking us right now as we sit here. And with ambient noise as low as it is today, she can probably hear you tapping your pen on the table there, Mr. Frederick!" Miller snapped.

A young lieutenant junior grade sitting down the table stared apprehensively at the pen in his left hand. It hovered over the spot on the table where he'd been nervously drumming it. A few of the other junior lieutenants sniggered as the red-faced Frederick quickly placed the pen back in his left breast pocket.

"Remember this, gentlemen," Miller said to the group in general, "—and be sure to pass this on to your divisions— we're in a hostile area now, and wartime quiet needs to be maintained at all times. We don't know what the *Hatta*'s up to, but if she's close enough she may try to interfere with our missile launch tonight. And by 'interfere,' I mean she may send a torpedo our way. The captain has a plan to deal with her, and he'll brief you on that in a minute. Right now, let's talk about the launch. Launch time is 0113:15 local, and that's *not* flexible. Fire Control Division is already loading missions into the missiles, and they'll be done by the time we finish this meeting. We'll be using the missiles in tubes seven, eight, eleven, and twelve, all Block IIIs. We'll set battle-stations missile at 1150 local, spin-up missiles at 0015, reach launch depth at 0100, and open tube doors at 0112:45. We're opening the tube doors as close to the launch time as possible since the *Hatta* might be close by. She's likely to hear it and we don't want to give her time to react. That way, she won't be able to stop us from launching. She might sink us afterward, but she won't stop our missile launch. I want all weapons and tracking stations fully manned with all interior communications circuits tested before we set battle stations. Understood?"

Several nods and a few audible affirmations came from the room, and Miller relinquished the floor to Edwards.

"Thank you, Weps. As Commander Miller pointed out, gentlemen, our opponent has electric-driven swimout weapons. What does that mean to you, Mr. Frederick?"

Frederick appeared caught off-guard, but after a few searching moments he came up with the answer. "It means his weapons propel themselves out of the tube on their own, sir, at a low speed. They're electric-driven so they make very little noise, unlike ours which are combustion-driven and need the ship's torpedo ejection system to launch."

"Very good. Now can you tell me the standard operating procedure once we detect an incoming torpedo?"

"Yes, sir. We shoot one of our own torpedoes down the same bearing and hope we get a hit on the guy that fired it."

"Right again, Mr. Frederick. So would you say that our standard operating procedure is a sound tactic to use in this case—that is, once we've detected an incoming torpedo?"

"No, sir."

"And why not?"

"Well, Captain, that procedure assumes you've detected the other guy's launch transient, and we won't be able to do that. Not if he's using swimout weapons. We probably won't even detect his torpedo until it's right on top of us. By that time, the torpedo could be well off the line of bearing between our two ships. Conceivably, we could pick up a torpedo closing from the west while the *Hatta*'s off to the south. In that case, shooting a weapon back in the direction of the incoming torpedo would be a wasted effort."

"Excellent, Mr. Frederick!" Edwards said enthusiastically in an effort to keep up his men's confidence. "You keep it up and you just might earn those gold dolphins one day."

Frederick buried a grin after one sly glance at his department head, Miller.

"So this is our quandary, gentlemen," Edwards said, leaning back in his chair and crossing his arms. "We'll be a sitting duck while we're launching missiles. The *Hatta* will have a perfect opportunity to guide a quiet low-speed electric torpedo right into our hull. Now I'm confident we can outrun one of *Hatta*'s torpedoes, if we detect it early enough. Those electric torpedoes don't have the horsepower *Providence*'s main engines do, but the problem is detecting it. As long as their torpedo stays at a low speed, I don't think we have a chance in hell of picking it up in time. But if we can get it to shift somehow to high speed, or maybe even to active pinging mode, we'd pick it up right away. Don't you agree, Weps?"

Miller nodded, adding, "By default, most torpedoes shift into high speed mode once the guiding wire breaks, Captain."

"Exactly! So we've got to force the *Hatta* to cut their guiding wire. In other words, gentlemen, we've got to force her to evade. We've got to send a well-aimed weapon in their direction and leave them two choices: keep the wire and risk destruction, or cut the wire and try to get away."

"But, Captain," Bloomfield spoke suddenly. "We can't detect the *Hatta*. Like Miller said, the Type-214 has an AIP drive. They'd have to be inside a couple thousand yards for our sonar to even pick them up. Surely, their captain's not stupid enough to allow that! Your plan won't work, sir!"

"If you'd be kind enough to let me finish, XO," Edwards said, seething but trying to keep a lid on it for morale purposes. Why did Bloomfield have to be there, he wondered. Why now, when he was trying to instill confidence in his officers, when he was trying to provide them with the optimism they would need to see them through the coming hours with a clear head. He was half-tempted to order Bloomfield out of the room, but he recognized the temptation came more from his personal aversion for the man than fearing the damage his careless mouth could inflict.

"The XO's right," Edwards said in a controlled tone. "We can't detect the *Hatta*'s propulsion system, not unless we're close to her. So we're going to have to rely on something else. I can't go into detail right now, there just isn't time. You all have divisions to look after and I have a thousand things to do before we reach the launch point. Suffice it to say, I expect to detect the *Hatta* before we shoot our first missile. I'm betting the *Hatta* will fire the moment we open missile doors, so expect a torpedo in the water at that moment coming straight for us. At the same instant that we launch our first missile, we'll fire a torpedo in the *Hatta*'s direction. That should give her something to worry about and, God willing, she'll cut her guiding wire to evade. When her torpedo kicks into high-speed mode, we'll detect it, track it, and hopefully outrun it."

He nodded at Coleman sitting on the other side of the table. "Our acting engineer, Mr. Coleman, assures me that *Providence*'s main engines are up to the task, and I believe him. So let's put our faith in the big twins back in the engine room, gentlemen, and in that excellent reactor built by those smart gentlemen and ladies at Bettis Labs. Now, let's take this ship into battle!"

He looked around the room at their blank faces to try to gauge their response to his little pep talk. If they had questions, they didn't voice them. Some looked nervous, others unsure, others naïvely eager. As a captain, it was his job to take all their strengths and weaknesses and mold them into a functioning unit. He'd been working to that end since he took command six months ago, and the next few hours would be the test. If he failed, they all would die, and perhaps some terrorists would live to terrorize another day.

"Good," he said finally, then glanced at the clock on the bulkhead. "Pass the word to your sailors. We man battle stations missile in less than four hours."

They all stood in unison as Edwards strode out of the wardroom and shut the door behind him. He would leave them to their tasks, trusting each man to do his duty.

Entering the middle-level passageway, Edwards headed for the forward ladder and made his way to his stateroom. There, he found a fidgety Seaman Shoemaker pacing up and down outside the door, apparently waiting for him.

"Are you wanting to see me, Seaman?"

"Uh, yes, Captain, sir. You see, it's about this email you had me send, Captain. I'm not sure if it's going to work, sir."

"Fine time to tell me, Seaman, when we're on the verge of going into battle. Why didn't you say something before? I stayed at comms depth for two hours just so you could put that damn thing together."

"Yes, sir, I know, Captain, but you see, sir, it's not like it's ever been done before. I've never sent a trojan to another ship before. I mean, I've hacked into other sub's computers before when they were sitting pier-side, but I've never sent a trojan in an email before, sir. I mean, what if they don't open it? What if you didn't tell me the right operating system? There're just too many ways it could go wrong, sir."

"Shoemaker, relax. They'll open the email. If I know their captain he won't be able to help himself. He's a very clever guy and he might even suspect something, but he's far too idealistic not to open it. And I may not be a computer whiz like you, but I know my operating systems when I see them. Don't worry, I got it right. Are *you* sure that virus will work?"

Shoemaker appeared slightly insulted. "It's a *trojan*, Captain, not a virus, and of course it will work, sir. I took it from my library, sir." Shoemaker patted the CD case he clutched in one hand. "I've got nearly a thousand viruses in this here case, sir, most the world hasn't ever seen before. No anti-virus software in the world will detect what I sent them. It'll work, Captain, as long as they open that attachment."

"Then everything should work out fine."

"Yes, sir."

"Was that all, Seaman?"

"Actually, no, Captain." Shoemaker paused for a moment, twitching nervously. "I hope you don't mind me asking this, Captain, but I was wondering . . . Seeing as how I lost my rank for hacking into that French sub's computer, do you think it might be fitting, sir, assuming this whole thing with the trojan works out . . . Do you think it might be fitting to give me my rank back again, sir?"

Edwards fought back a grin. *Providence*'s survival was a complete uncertainty, yet getting back his petty officer stripes was all that mattered to Shoemaker. The navy needed more like him.

"You're threatened with court-martial, Seaman. That's pretty serious. I took away your rank in hopes that it would spare us a visit from the NIS. But if your program does what you claim it will, I'll see what I can do."

Shoemaker grinned, before being shuffled out of the way as officers and chief petty officers needing their captain's attention formed a line in the passage. Much work remained before the missile launch. The certain confrontation with the *Hatta* was mere hours away.

LYING in his rack going in and out of consciousness, Van Peenan listened through the small crack in the stateroom's partition wall, beyond which lay the wardroom. He'd used the hidden sound hole many times in the past, especially whenever the ORSE team was on board. The ORSE team always used the wardroom to plan surprise drills, but little did they know that Van Peenan was in the habit of eavesdropping on every meeting he wasn't invited to. Consequently, he never experienced a surprise drill that he wasn't expecting. It was cheating, of course, a serious breach of the honor code, but Van Peenan cared little for honor when his career was on the line. That was how he justified it—and a lot of other things.

The meeting in the wardroom next door, another meeting he wasn't invited to, had just ended. Some of the officers lingered and he could hear conversation in low tones about an upcoming strike mission. In another conversation, he recognized the voices of two of his division officers. The two young officers were talking about him, one even calling him a "crazy bastard."

Crazy bastard? he thought in his half-conscious state. *I'll show those impudent lieutenants who they call "sir" once I'm up and around. Tough shit for their sorry asses once I'm on my feet again. I'll make their lives a living hell, those little insubordinate maggots! Captain Christopher better not have heard them. God help me if he heard those snot-nosed lieutenants blabbing at the mouth. He'll think I've gone soft. He'll think I can't run my department and I've let them get the best of me. Captain Christopher mustn't know . . . Captain Christopher . . . or . . . who was it?*

He wasn't sure at the moment. His memory seemed to come and go.

He didn't know how long he'd lain unconscious on the floor of that crumbling warehouse with the mangled bodies of his tormenters lying all around him, but someone eventually discovered him there. A small platoon of Indonesian marines found him and whisked him off into the jungle. There they hid in a makeshift cave while awaiting the outcome of the battle for Ujungpang. With defeat finally certain, the marines cut across the rainy jungle, sometimes carrying him, sometimes helping him along through the twisted trees, muddy slopes, and overgrown brush. He hadn't any notion as to why they would bother to save him, except that maybe they believed their chances for rescue were better with an American in their midst. He remembered stumbling onto a small fishing village of twenty or thirty people near the southern coast. The Indonesian marines were defeated and out of control, and the defenseless village suddenly afforded them a means to take their revenge.

The slaughter was efficient and brutal. No person was left alive, save for the young females who were forced into a small shack not fit for animals where they suffered repeated rapes and torture until the marines were all satisfied. But shortly after the massacre, the marines began to get apprehensive. They panicked. For some reason they felt certain someone from the village had escaped and that rebel troops would arrive at any moment. That's when they decided to shed their marine uniforms and don villager attire. The next morning they took to the village's half dozen prahus and, under cover of the vertical sheets of rain, made for the open ocean. After only a few hours beyond the surf, it became apparent to Van Peenan that his companions were most-decidedly marines and not sailors. They handled their craft with ineptitude and the horrid weather only made matters worse.

One by one, the swift currents running in and out of the small island chain drove them apart. Some capsized within sight of Van Peenan's craft, stove by a shallow reef or flooded with rainwater. Some simply floated away. By late afternoon, all had vanished from sight, leaving Van Peenan's craft alone on the stormy sea. For the next two days Van Peenan and his two companions in their tiny weather-cracked prahu fought the elements. Between the rain from above and the seeps from below, it was all they could do to keep the pitiable vessel afloat. He was already worn out from the terrorist beating he'd withstood the day before.

The biting wind on his swollen, chapped lips, the crashing saltwater stinging across his blistered back, the back-breaking labor to keep the craft from capsizing, all triggered his mind into a state of abstract removal. Only the thought of the here-after kept him going. Only the promise of accolades and as-

sured promotion gave him the determination to bail one useless handful of water after another. If only he could survive
this, his career was set. Nothing would stand between him and
command if he managed to make it through this. It was his
destiny. He could almost feel it. It was the only way the cards
could fall. He felt all the more certain of this when the dark
clouds parted overhead and *Providence*'s sun-bathed black
shape appeared on the horizon.

When the feeble prahu finally capsized and *Providence*'s
diver fished him out of the water, that must have been the moment when his system had collapsed. His mind must have
fallen into a state of shock at that moment, because he began
to have wild visions after that. He began to see things that
made no sense at all, things that could not be. He saw Dean
alive and well, though he knew most assuredly that Dean was
dead. Furthermore, he imagined Dean helping him onto the
deck! It was almost laughable, the tricks the mind played
when it reached the point of exhaustion.

As the conversation continued in the wardroom he struggled to listen, but his eyelids grew heavier by the minute. His
mind was getting groggy again, and he had to lie back on the
pillow to rest his aching head.

He needed to sleep. He needed to get better. He'd figure
everything out once he'd recovered. Then he'd kick that asshole Coleman out of his engine room and set things back the
way they were before.

Chapter 18

THE *Providence* glided gently up toward the shimmering surface like a great sea beast coming up for air, her black hull all
but invisible in the dark waters south of Wijaya Island. A half
moon shone bright blue above the indistinguishable horizon,
but it lent little assistance to the unaided human eye, which
was practically blind in the present blackness. Midnight had
already passed in this part of the world and a new day had begun. Silence dominated the ocean around *Providence*. Distant
shipping, a few light fishing craft hugging the Bunda coast,
and a couple of trembling volcanoes made up the balance of
her sonar contacts.

"At periscope depth, Captain," the diving officer called
from his station.

"Steady on course two eight five, Captain." the helmsman
reported. "Answering all ahead one third."

"Very well, Dive. Very well, Helm." Edwards rested his
arms on the extended periscope handles and used the hydraulic assist to swing around the azimuth. The control room
was rigged for black, but he could feel the mass of perspiring
bodies around him, crammed near every station, console, and
plot. Battle stations missile had been manned for nearly an
hour. The bustling and commotion of manning up had settled
to a quiet murmur as the different stations got into the habit of
communicating via their one-eared wiry headsets. Across the
starboard bulkhead the weapons consoles beamed a ghostly
bluish light onto the faces of their operators. From time to
time a large shadow passed in front of the bright screens,
blocking Edwards' view. The large shadow was completely indistinguishable, but he knew it was Miller, moving swiftly

from station to station, ensuring the launch preparations were progressing as planned.

As Edwards glanced from the periscope lens to the sonar waterfall display in the overhead, he prayed that the launch would pass without incident, but he knew better. Somewhere in the dark sea out there, the *Hatta* was watching his every move. Somewhere, not too far away, Peto had the *Providence*'s solution loaded into his attack computer and had a torpedo ready for launch. He would not fire until he was sure of *Providence*'s intentions, of that Edwards was certain. Peto would wait and give *Providence* the benefit of the doubt, but the moment *Providence*'s missile doors came open, Peto would know that his proposal to Edwards had been rejected.

"We're at launch depth early, Captain," Miller reported from the darkness. "The missiles in tubes seven, eight, eleven, and twelve are spun up and the missions are loaded, sir. All pre-launch parameters are within specifications to support our launch in eighteen minutes."

"Very good, Weps."

"Captain." Miller had stepped up to the periscope stand and was now whispering in Edwards's ear. "Sir, I hate to ask, but we're getting close to launch time, and you said we'd detect the *Hatta* before then. I didn't question you then, sir, because I figured you had something in mind. But since we haven't heard a bleep out of the *Hatta,* and she's probably under our very noses right this minute, don't you think you ought to let me in on it, sir? How're we going to detect her?"

Edwards leaned back from the periscope lens and glanced at the dimly lit digital clock next to the periscope stand. It read 0051. Launch time was 0113.

"In about nineteen minutes, Weps, I'll let you know. Right now I want you to concentrate on the launch. Now, let's see if we have any mission updates." Edwards looked toward the dark corner of the control room's forward port side. "Chief of the Watch, raise number one BRA-34."

"Raise number one BRA-34, aye, sir," came the reply from the darkness.

Edwards peered through the periscope and saw the com-

munications mast pop its head above the surface a few feet
ahead of the periscope, its wide bulk blocking out the moon in
the western sky. With the glare absent, Edwards could see better in the night. Almost instantly he picked out the dark jagged
shapes of Bunda's mountains lying off the port bow, and,
sweeping the periscope to starboard, he saw Wijaya's low hills
against the starry sky beyond. Even from this close distance,
just eighteen miles from Wijaya's southeastern shore, the islands appeared dark and lifeless. After staring a few minutes
more he picked out the fleet of fishing craft *Providence*'s
sonar suite had been monitoring all night. Their dim running
lights held close to Bunda's northeastern coast in reef-filled
waters that *Providence* didn't dare traverse. Deep enough for
fishermen, but not for submarines.

"Radio, Conn," Edwards said into the periscope microphone. "Number one BRA-34 is up. Query the satellite and
download all message traffic."

A few minutes later the speaker behind his head squawked,
"Conn, Radio. All message traffic received. No mission updates, sir. Radio no longer requires number one BRA-34."

So, he thought, Chappell had nothing new for him. The
mission was a go, as planned. Somewhere, far to the north,
Ohio's cruise missile armada was already in flight, a mass of
missiles streaking low over a dark sea at 600 knots, speeding
toward their unsuspecting terrorist targets.

"Chief of the Watch, lower number one BRA-34."

"Conn, Radio, wait!" The radioman's voice suddenly came
over the speaker sounding hysterical. "Don't lower the mast!"

Edwards wasn't used to having his orders countermanded
by the radioman of the watch, but he sensed the real urgency
in the young man's voice.

"Belay my last order, Chief of the Watch!" he said sharply.
"Keep the mast up!"

Removing his hand from the mast panel, the chief of the
watch uttered an acknowledgment. Silence emanated
through the room as all listened intently, expecting the radioman's voice to come back any moment with an explanation
for his exigency.

"Radio, this is the captain," Edwards finally said, impatiently. "Do you have something? Radio, this is the captain, what do you have?"

"Conn, Radio!" An excited voice several octaves higher came back over the speaker. "I think we've got 'em, sir! I think we've got 'em!"

"Radio, Captain. What the hell are you talking about?"

"The shore party, sir! It's the shore party! They're on the satellite phone, sir!"

Groping into the darkness, Edwards found the nearest lieutenant and yanked him to the periscope stand to take over. He wasn't usually as rough, but the instant euphoria at the thought that the shore party was still alive sent an adrenaline surge through his body.

"Radio, Captain," he finally managed to say, as he slid in between the chart tables. "Patch the satellite phone through to the conn."

Seconds later, a weary but solidly familiar voice came over the speaker, unquestionably Lieutenant Lake's. "X-ray Tango Urban, this is Romeo Alpha Foxtrot, over. X-ray Tango Urban, this is Romeo Alpha Foxtrot, over."

Apparently Lake didn't realize he had made it through to the ship. In all the excitement, *Providence*'s electrified radioman had forgotten to answer the phone.

Edwards tried to curb his own enthusiasm as he yanked the microphone from its cradle in the overhead.

"Romeo Alfa Foxtrot," he said slowly and deliberately. "This is X-ray Tango Urban, hold you loud and clear, over."

A silence fell over the line, and Edwards could picture in his mind the physically drained Lake hunkering somewhere in Bunda's dark jungle, staring at his phone set, disbelieving what he'd just heard. The long pause lasted several seconds more before Lake's voice came on again.

"X-ray Tango Urban, this is Romeo Alpha Foxtrot." Lake's voice suddenly carried a new vibrancy, before he abruptly added, "Go secure!"

The smart lieutenant knew that the phone conversation was

most likely being monitored. Switching to a secure mode of communication was a wise precaution.

Agreeing with the suggestion, Edwards leaned over to speak into the control room's open microphone. "Radio, Captain. Go secure, now!"

Edwards waited for the ship's encryption units to align, hoping his radiomen were on their toes tonight. The satellite signal would always be susceptible to interception as it bounded from Lake's position somewhere on Bunda and bounced halfway around the world on a commercial satellite network, then down to a ground station two continents away, then back up to the satellite network, where it bounced around again until it found *Providence*'s communications mast popping out of the waves. With encryption active, any interloper would hear nothing more than meaningless pops and static. Only the crypto gear in *Providence*'s radio room and the similar device attached to Lake's hand-held phone could decipher the code and turn it back into something intelligible.

"Conn, Radio," the radioman's voice finally announced. "You're secure, sir."

With the signal now encrypted, Edwards spoke into the microphone again, "Mr. Lake, I hold you top secret."

"Roger, Captain. I hold you the same." Lake's signal had lost some of its former quality and now sounded distant and metallic, the price of secure comms.

"Nice to hear your voice, Mr. Lake."

"Same to you, Captain."

"What's your situation?"

"Tenuous, sir. We were ambushed on the road a few days ago on our way back to Ujungpang. It's a long story, sir, but I think they were terrorists from Al Islamiyyah. They've been after us ever since, but we've managed to stay one step ahead of them. I don't know how much longer that will last, though." Lake paused. "We've suffered some casualties, too, sir. Reynoso, Dr. Whitehead, and our police escort, all dead."

The news came like spears through his heart. He'd already lost one officer, another badly injured, and now Reynoso dead, too. In his mind each loss was his own personal failure. A failure to protect his men. A failure to get them home to their loved ones safely. And now if the shore party were captured, all those deaths would be for naught.

"And Chief Michaelson's wounded, sir, but he's determined to go on," Lake added. "The rest of us are okay."

"Who else is with you, Lieutenant?" Edwards was almost afraid to ask.

"Dr. Whitehead's daughter, sir, Teresa Whitehead. Then there's this . . . gentleman, who calls himself Ahmad. I don't know his last name, he won't give it, but according to him he's the reason we came here. Do you know what he's talking about, Captain, 'cause I've—"

"Save it, Mr. Lake," Edwards interrupted, hoping to minimize the dissemination of confidential information to the number of listening ears in the control room. "SubPac just briefed me on him. Suffice it to say, we were both in the dark going into this one. He is who he says he is, if that's any consolation to you."

"It helps, sir."

"Captain," Miller whispered. He had suddenly appeared near the chart table looking agitated. "Sorry to interrupt, sir, but we're ten minutes from the launch point."

"Very well, Weps. Listen, Mr. Lake, you've caught us in the middle of something. There's not much time. Are you in a safe place? Can you hold on for a few hours until we contact you again?" Edwards did his best to sound confident for the benefit of both Lake and the men around him.

"I don't think so, Captain," Lake's voice grew tinny over the fragile circuit and it began to fade in and out sporadically. Every man in the control room visibly bent an ear toward the speaker as if it would improve the reception. ". . . sort of locked into a corner right now. We're on the eastern side of . . . island, on a plateau of sorts, with no easy way down to the water . . . trying to head north along the coast to get to the beaches up there . . . bad guys have a roadblock in front of us. It's hard to explain, but . . . no way around it. If you're copying my GPS data . . . see what I'm talking about . . . We keep ducking foot patrols and trucks as they go by . . . larger force coming through the jungle about an hour behind . . . Don't suppose SubPac said anything about sending SEALs any time soon, did they, sir?"

"No, Lieutenant, I'm afraid that rescue is a couple days away," Edwards answered. Though Lake's words were broken, he comprehended the meaning. The shore party was in a precarious position, and risked imminent capture, or worse. "Listen to me, Lieutenant, your signal is weak, and . . ."

"Here they are, sir!" An excited Fremont spoke up from the electronic plot, his finger tapping a spot on the digital map display. "We're getting position information from the GPS receiver in Lake's phone, sir. They're right here!"

Edwards shifted over to the plot table to see what Fremont had.

"I've called up the land map of Bunda, sir," Fremont continued, "and here it is, yes. This is his precise location. See, right here at—I can barely read it—Uru Pass. My gosh, you can see what he's talking about, sir. They're sitting here, about a hundred yards off the coast road, and just to the north of their position, the road enters this steep gorge in the mountain. This must be where he's talking about, sir, where the roadblock is."

The digital map display showed the situation clearly. With the topographical map on maximum zoom, Edwards could see the road leading straight through the steep mountain pass, roughly a quarter mile long. It appeared no wider than a couple dozen yards along its entire length, and a perfect place for a roadblock. A half mile to the east of Lake's position a plateau dropped off four or five hundred feet into the sea. To the west, a sharp slope rose to the summit of Bunda's mountain spine a thousand feet above. Edwards could only imagine the difficultly of such a climb. The elevation marks on the map were packed so tightly together they were hardly distinguishable. Add Michaelson's injury to the picture, and mobility was not a viable option. With a large force closing from behind, a roadblock to his front, and insurmountable barriers on both his flanks, Lake's choices seemed fatal indeed.

"We're getting your GPS data now, Lieutenant," Edwards finally said into the speaker to keep Lake on the line while he tried to think.

After three days of waiting he was finally in touch with the shore party, but now it seemed there was nothing he could do to save them. It seemed cruelly ironic. If only Chappell had put an iron boot in someone's ass, maybe the SEALs would have arrived by now.

As he stared at the map display, and the small yellow dot Fremont had digitally inserted to represent Lake's position, Edwards sighed. The line representing the road wound its way through the narrow pass on the map, and he could just picture the terrorists blocking Lake's path, their vehicles drawn across the road, several guards posted all around the perimeter. There was no way to circumvent it. No escape. Once *Providence* started shooting missiles and the *Hatta* retaliated, it might be hours before the *Providence* made it back up to comm depth—that is, assuming she survived. By that time, Lake and his group would be either captured or killed.

"Captain," Miller said in an urgent tone. "We need to prepare for missile launch, sir. We're seven minutes away!"

Edwards nodded an acknowledgment, but said nothing. At the mention of "missiles," an insane thought had entered into his head. As his eyes fixated on the yellow dot on the map display, his insane thought took the shape of a wild and crazy idea, which two seconds later metamorphosed into a harebrained plan. He seemed to be full of them in the last twenty-four hours, but it was the only solution he could think of to save Lake and his people. The mountain pass was only a quarter mile long, and there were only so many places the terrorist roadblock could be.

"Mr. Lake," he spoke into the microphone assertively, now decided in his course of action. "Is the roadblock concentrated near the southern entrance of the pass?"

"As far as we could tell, sir . . . saw four vehicles blocking the road. They . . . men on foot in close proximity."

"Excellent! Mr. Lake, this is what I want you to do. I want you and your people to find shelter as fast as you can. I want you to get as far as possible away from that roadblock without giving away your position. Is that understood?"

After a long pause, Lake's voice replied, "Aye, aye, sir. What's the plan?"

Edwards did not answer but instead had moved closer to the chart table.

"Those fishermen we've been hearing all night," he prompted of the quartermaster. "Did you get a good position on them?"

"They're right here, Captain. About a mile out from the beach," the perplexed quartermaster said, pointing a stubby finger to a place on the chart near Bunda's northeastern shore. "The reefs must be almost scrapin' their keels there, sir. Must be good fishin' to take that kind of a chance."

Without a word Edwards snatched up a pair of dividers and began taking measurements. While the men around him watched in wonder, he scribbled coordinates, distances, and times in the quartermaster's logbook and then tore off the used sheets. The seasoned calculator in his mind, much more honed than that possessed by any of his subordinates, took only a few seconds to come up with the answers he was looking for.

"All right!" he said with excitement, holding up the final sheet with all the answers, and snatching the microphone. "Mr. Lake, how's the battery looking on your phone?"

"I've . . . about an hour left . . . sir."

"Good! When we sign off here, don't try to call us anymore. The crypto unit on your phone eats up battery juice in no time. Conserve power and use it for GPS information only. In a few minutes you're going to hear one hell of an explosion. After that happens, I want you and your party to move as fast as you can through the pass and make your way to these coordinates: 02-07 North, 126-16 East. You got that? Be there by 1500 tomorrow. We're going to extract you!"

"Aye, aye, sir," Lake's voice replied uncertainly. "But I'd like to ask—"

"Did you get the coordinates, Lieutenant?" Edwards interrupted firmly.

"Yes, sir. But—"

"Then you have your orders. Now carry them out! Good luck, Lieutenant. *Providence* out!"

If Lake had any more questions, Edwards had no time to answer them. Either way, *Providence*'s radiomen took the cue and terminated the connection.

"Chief of the Watch," Edwards called across the room as he scrambled over to the weapons consoles to stand next to the neglected Miller. "Lower number one BRA-34!"

He looked at the clock. It read 0108.

"We're ready to launch, Captain. Request permission to equalize tubes in four minutes," Miller said in a normal tone before leaning over and whispering, "What was that all about, Captain? And where the hell's the *Hatta*?"

"Sonar, Conn," Edwards ignored the question and raised his voice to the open microphone. "In less than one minute, you're going to detect a transient in close proximity, I'm guessing to the south of us. I want you to assign a tracker to it immediately, and pass the bearing to the fire control system. Understood?"

"Conn, Sonar, aye," came the sonar chief's steady response over the speaker.

"Captain, what the—" Miller started but was cut off by Edwards' raised palm.

"Weps, warm up torpedoes in tubes one and two and make them ready for firing in all respects with the exception of flooding tubes. And spin up our two remaining missiles in tubes six and thirteen. I've got another strike mission for them."

As the orders relayed several times from the operators sitting at the weapons consoles down to the torpedo room two decks below, Miller's round face leaned in close to Edwards'.

"Captain, it takes time to spin up missiles," he said in a low tone. "We don't have time, sir. Besides, missile six has been deemed unreliable."

"This is a simple geo position strike, Weps." Edwards shoved the piece of paper into Miller's hand. "Program missiles six and thirteen to strike these coordinates with an air burst at two hundred feet. Give them one waypoint, then send them straight to the target. We'll launch these two after we've launched the rest. Understood? You'd better hurry."

Submitting to faith in his captain's judgment, not to mention his desire for fair markings on his next fitness report, Miller scurried over to the missile console and quickly began barking orders to the missile console operator.

With the machine now in motion, Edwards took in a few deep breaths and moved back over to the periscope stand. He'd have a lot of explaining to do after this one. Shooting missiles at his own discretion would probably cost him his command, but he had to do it. He couldn't just stand by and let his men die at the hands of the terrorists. Not when it was physically within his power to save them.

He relieved the lieutenant at the periscope stand and glanced at the clock.

It read 0110.

"Conn, Sonar," the speaker squawked. "Transient, bearing one six four!"

A small smile appeared on Edwards' lips. The *Hatta* was detected!

Several of the less experienced men in the room cheered at the report but were quickly silenced by the veteran submariners around them. Out of the corner of his eye Edwards saw Miller's shadowy form shoot him a wide grin.

"Mark that bearing, Weps!" Edwards snapped. "Designate that transient as the *Hatta* and enter a zero speed, short range solution into the fire control system. Firing point procedures, tube one." He let the fire control party absorb his last order before issuing another. "And stand by to equalize missile tubes six through eight and eleven through thirteen."

Things were moving quickly in the control room, preparing missiles and torpedoes simultaneously. Still, as his orders relayed around the room, Edwards allowed himself a brief moment of relief. Shoemaker's trojan had worked. It was a simple program really, hidden in Edwards' last email to the captain of the *Hatta* under the simple subject line "YOU WIN." Edwards had thought long and hard about the content and how he should word it. He wrote phrases of capitulation, apology, complete acquiescence, and whatever else he thought it would take to entice Peto to open the attachment, a file entitled "*The Tempest*" which Edwards had cut and pasted from the web. Once opened the file appeared to be nothing more than the complete play by William Shakespeare, line by line. But embedded in the file was a small program from Shoemaker's "library" that found its way onto the user's hard drive. Once there, it waited for a particular moment on a particular day to activate, in this case 0110 local time. At that moment the program took control of the computer's volume settings, raising them to the maximum level to play a small sound byte that sounded much like a hammer hitting the side of a tin shed. This was the noise that *Providence*'s sonarmen had detected to the south.

It wouldn't take long for Peto to figure out what had happened, and Edwards could just imagine his counterpart bolting for his stateroom to unplug and remove the batteries from his clamoring laptop. The simple trojan was the best idea Edwards and Shoemaker could come up with in the short amount of time. They gave no thought to attacking the *Hatta*'s more secure weapons or sonar computers. More than likely, the design of those systems prevented any connection with the *Hatta*'s admin computers for the very purpose of avoiding cyber attack. Edwards had deliberated on the best moment for the program's activation, too. Too soon, and Peto would figure out what happened and send a torpedo their way, perhaps while *Providence* was making preparations to shoot her missiles. Too late, and there would be no allowance for error between the two ships' clocks. In the end Edwards needed only a line of bearing on the *Hatta*, and now he had it.

As the fire control technicians scrambled to prepare *Providence*'s missile tubes and to enter the torpedo solution, Edwards put his face back up to the periscope's eyepiece. Sweeping the field of view across the black night to the south he half-expected to see the *Hatta*'s scope sticking above the water's surface. But, of course, neither periscope could see the other in this dark night, with or without night vision amplifiers.

"Missiles in tubes six and thirteen are still spinning up, Captain," Miller finally reported. "All other missiles are ready for launch. Torpedo tubes one and two are ready for firing in all respects, with the exception of flooding tubes. The single point firing solution has been entered into the system. Forty-five seconds to missile launch . . . Forty seconds . . ."

Edwards grimaced. The missiles in tubes six and thirteen, the ones he'd just added to the mission, were not ready to fire yet and would have to be fired separately from the rest. The first strike mission couldn't wait. *Ohio*'s Tomahawks would be approaching the northern horizon in less than a minute.

"Thirty-five seconds . . ." Miller announced, ". . . thirty seconds . . ."

"Equalize tubes six through eight and eleven through thirteen," Edwards ordered. "Flood tubes one and two. Sonar, watch for inbound torpedoes!"

Small vibrations originated up forward in *Providence*'s bows and reverberated throughout the deck as valves opened and shut automatically, filling the torpedo tubes with a rush of seawater, equalizing the pressure in both missile and torpedo tubes with the sea outside. Seconds later, Miller acknowledged that all had equalized satisfactorily.

"Open missile tube hatches six through eight and eleven through thirteen," Edwards continued, never taking his eyes from the scope. "Open outer doors on torpedo tubes one and two."

Piping bundles in the overhead strained as the ship's hydraulic plant ported the high-pressure fluid to the operating mechanisms on the large doors. Edwards imagined how ominous his ship must look, her bow crowned with open missile hatches, her numbers one and two torpedo tube doors pivoted inward and opened to the sea, the menacing green heads of the Mark 48 ADCAP torpedoes just visible within the dark cavities like two sharks threatening to spring from their lairs.

"Doors open!" Miller announced. "Missile launch in ten . . . nine . . . eight . . ."

By opening missile hatches and tube doors he had announced his intentions—and his exact location—to the *Hatta*. Consequently, a quiet "swimout" torpedo was probably heading toward the *Providence* at this very moment. Each passing second meant less time to escape, and Edwards squeezed the scope handle with sweaty palms as Miller seemed to take an eternity to count down to the launch point.

". . . three . . . two . . . one. Salvo launch!"

"Fire missiles seven, eight, eleven, and twelve!" Edwards ordered with forced coolness. "Shoot torpedo tube one on generated bearings!"

The hull shook on its frame as a loud *whack!* followed immediately by a *whoosh!* filled the room. Two decks below, the torpedo firing ram vented high pressure air inboard, causing a rapid pressure change inside the ship that compressed Edwards' eardrums. The torpedo had left the tube.

Less than a millisecond later the first missile, encased inside its buoyant capsule, shot from its tube. The hydrophone speaker in the control rooms crackled as the differential pressure beneath the tube's protective membrane drove the missile to the surface with lightning speed.

Edwards trained the periscope forward just in time to see the twenty-foot-long all-up round bubble to the surface within its capsule, then disappear in a bright flash of light as the booster section ignited and promptly lifted it skyward. The booster illuminated the rippling waves beneath in a bath of white light that rapidly diminished as the missile climbed higher and higher. Increasing the elevation on the periscope lens, Edwards followed the missile's path as it gained altitude and accelerated into the starry sky. The lapping tongue of flame streaked across the night sky as it reached the peak of its parabolic arc. Then the bright tongue of flame flashed vividly for a split second before extinguishing altogether.

"Booster separation," Edwards announced for the attack party's benefit. "Normal launch."

No sooner had the words left his mouth than the second missile took to the night sky, followed by the third, then the fourth, each showing the same normal booster separation as they settled onto their pre-loaded flight plans. The ship sagged noticeably forward from the fourteen thousand pounds of water weight now filling the empty tubes, but then slowly regained her trim as the diving officer pumped water from one trim tank to another.

The missiles quickly disappeared into the night, free from their cramped capsules and *Providence*'s encumbrance. On their own now, they were programmed with all they needed to know to execute the mission. Fins and stabilizers would deploy automatically. Turbofan engines would take over. The onboard computers would use GPS, DSMAC, and TERCOM data to guide them on their short flight until they hit the terrorist radar sites on Wijaya.

"Normal launch on torpedo tube one, sir. Run to enable, three thousand yards," an operator from one of the starboard-side consoles reported as the *Providence* began receiving telemetry data from the wire guided Mark 48 AD-CAP, now speeding down the same bearing *Hatta*'s transient had appeared.

"Sonar, Conn, any indication of a hostile torpedo out there?"

"Conn, Sonar, negative. Still searching."

He had to give it time, Edwards told himself. Give Peto time to detect *Providence*'s torpedo and evade. Assuming the *Hatta* fired a torpedo of her own the moment *Providence*'s missile hatches cranked open, it would be out there somewhere closing on *Providence*'s position. But from which direction? He couldn't evade properly unless he knew where the threat was coming from. Fleeing down some random evasion course might inadvertently drive *Providence* straight toward *Hatta*'s torpedo. Besides, he couldn't take her deep yet. *Providence* still had two missiles left to shoot.

"Weps!" Edwards called, now unable to hide the tinge of desperation in his voice. The longer the *Providence* lingered at launch depth, the easier she would be to hit. "Where the hell are those last two missiles?"

"Number six is almost there, sir. We're almost done loading the mission. Number thirteen is giving us errors when we try to spin it up. I can't verify that it'll hit the target, sir. As a matter of fact, Captain, I'll guarantee that she won't."

Edwards cursed under his breath. Launching the erroneous missile in tube thirteen was now out of the question. Rules of engagement dictated it. Without a functioning navigation system the missile might go astray and hit some hapless coastal village. *Providence*'s one remaining missile, the one in tube six, would have to do the job.

"Conn, Sonar, torpedo in the water!" blared the speaker near his head. "Torpedo bears one nine five!"

The torpedo was thirty degrees off from the bearing to the *Hatta*. As expected, Peto had tried to quietly steer the weapon in from an unanticipated sector, but *Providence*'s own torpedo had forced him to cut the guiding wire and evade. With the link now severed from its mother ship, the *Hatta*'s torpedo had assumed its default settings and began driving for its enable point at maximum speed.

Ostensibly unmindful of the incoming torpedo, Miller hovered over one of the console operators as he finalized the missile pre-launch checklist. The procedure took time, but it was necessary. One parameter forgotten could mean a fouled launch or a complete miss altogether. But time they scarcely had. Each passing second the *Hatta*'s torpedo closed another twenty-five yards.

"Sonar, Conn, give me a range to that torpedo!" Edwards called.

"Conn, Sonar, triangulation range with the towed array places torpedo at four thousand yards, closing rapidly. Detecting active search mode."

Edwards shot another hasty glance at Miller, but the weapons officer appeared to ignore him. Miller's balding head gleamed in the dim overhead lights as he deliberately directed one operator after another to push this button or that, as if the procedure were written in marble within his nuclear-trained head. Edwards fidgeted, feeling the perspiration beneath his palms as he gripped the periscope handles. The men around him did the same, every eye sneaking pessimistic peeks at the fire control party, knowing their chances for survival depended on getting the next missile airborne quickly. They could do nothing but wait.

"Nav, get these men plotting a solution on the *Hatta*!" Edwards ordered, mostly to give them something else to think about besides the closing torpedo. "Once our torpedo sends back telemetry on that son of a bitch, I want the whole tactical picture updated on the nav plot."

With his expression displaying precise understanding of his captain's motives, Fremont began issuing orders to the men standing around the two plot tables. The men obeyed enthusiastically. How quickly the panic left their faces once given true guidance and leadership, Edwards reflected, once given an assurance, however false, that everything would be okay.

"Conn, Sonar, incoming torpedo bears one nine zero at three thousand yards!"

The incoming torpedo was closing on *Providence*'s port bow. The four-hundred-foot submarine would have to turn sharply once she began her evasion. That turn would certainly take time and the thought led Edwards to reach for the hydraulic actuator above his head and lower the periscope. It was one less thing he'd have to do before ordering *Providence* to top speed. The last missile launch would have to go unobserved. As soon as the last missile cleared the tube, *Providence* would need to run hard and fast.

"Conn, Sonar. Torpedo bears one nine zero, range two thousand five hundred yards!"

"Assuming the *Hatta* fired that torpedo from a range of six thousand yards," Fremont said evenly, calculator in hand, "we'll have to start our evasion in fifty-five seconds, Captain. Otherwise, we won't outrun it. The torp'll be only a thousand yards away at that point."

"Very well, Nav." Edwards grabbed the engineering microphone in the overhead and keyed it, "Maneuvering, Conn, stand by for a flank bell! Answer it smartly and give us everything you have!"

"Conn, Maneuvering, aye," came Coleman's steady voice over the speaker.

"Conn, Sonar. Torpedo bears one nine zero, range two thousand yards!"

"Chief of the Watch, stand by countermeasures," Edwards ordered, deliberately fighting the urge to wring his hands together. "Set one noisemaker deep, one decoy shallow."

As the chief mumbled the order into his headphones, relaying it to the three-inch launcher space one deck below, Edwards turned again to ask Miller for status. This time, the unfaltering weapons officer preempted him.

"Missile tube six is ready for launch in all respects, Captain!"

"Fire six!" Edwards shouted without hesitation.

The weapons console operator pulled the firing handle and, a half-second later, *Providence*'s bow dipped slightly followed by a loud *whoosh!*

"Missile six is away!" the operator announced.

"Conn, Sonar. Torpedo bears one nine zero, range fifteen hundred yards! Torpedo has enabled and is active homing!"

As if to confirm the report, annoyingly shrill beeps came from the WLR-9 active sonar interceptor on the starboard bulkhead, its palm-sized circular display showing the relative bearing to the incoming weapon's active sonar pulses. The *Hatta*'s torpedo had already locked onto *Providence*'s hull. The only chance now was to run.

"Close all missile hatches!" Edwards shouted. "Close all outer doors! Helm, right full rudder! Dive, make your depth six hundred feet!"

Providence immediately angled down toward the deep as the two planesmen pushed their control yokes to the floor. As her bow began to swing to the right, the broadband speaker resonated with the sound of missile hatches clunking shut. With her hull now reverted to its sleek hydrodynamic shape, *Providence* was ready to run, and every man in the control room grabbed a firm handhold in anticipation of their captain's next command.

"Chief of the Watch, launch countermeasures! Helm, all ahead flank, cavitate!"

Hardly before the words had left Edwards' mouth, the chief of the watch hit the fire buttons on the three-inch launcher panel, blasting the set of countermeasures out the port side muzzles in a tumultuous clamor that sounded like cannon fire. At the same time, the helmsman twisted the engine order telegraph knob to the flank position and pushed the cavitate buzzer three times, prompting an almost instantaneous response as the maneuvering room acknowledged with three repeat buzzes of their own, indicating that they would answer the flank bell without regard to cavitation.

Then the sleeping beast came to life.

Several sharp beating vibrations rang throughout the hull and shook Edwards' feet. Every light in the room dimmed, then flickered, as the two-story reactor coolant pumps back in the reactor compartment shifted into fast speed. Moments later, *Providence*'s angled deck lurched forward as her two main engines awoke with a fury, straining the massive shaft to its limits. The hull creaked and groaned from the sudden strain and several loose items in the control room fell from tables and shelves, skidding across the deck. The broadband sonar speaker in the overhead emanated a mass of white noise as *Providence*'s giant screw began to cavitate outside. As the ship picked up speed, millions of tiny bubbles formed at the low-pressure zone created by the screw's eye, then collapsed again as they reentered the high-pressure zone beyond. Cavitation was normally regarded as a bad thing, since the ensuing noise stood out on the passive sonar display like a sore thumb. But at this moment, torpedo evasion took precedence over stealth.

The deck leaned to starboard as *Providence*'s bow continued swinging to the right, spinning the compass in front of the helmsman at an alarming rate. On the same panel, a few gauges over, the digital depth indicator was in a state of perpetual update as the ship drove deeper and deeper, picking up more speed along the way.

"Passing course north to the right, Captain," the helmsman announced, his rudder still angled full to the right.

"Steady on course zero two zero, Helm," Edwards said, glancing at *Providence*'s speed log. It already showed twenty-eight knots.

As the helmsman reversed the rudder to steady on the ordered course, *Providence* passed five hundred fifty feet. The diving officer muttered a few words and the planesmen skillfully leveled her off at six hundred feet with only a few minor corrective plane movements. Now on depth and gradually approaching flank speed, her hull pulsated like a racehorse controlling its breathing.

She *was* a racehorse, Edwards thought. Even with the torpedo closing he could find time to thank God for the miracle of nuclear power. What else could propel something a big as *Providence*, longer than a football field and weighing more than 6000 tons, to maximum speed in a matter of seconds?

Having scooted over to the periscope platform, Miller spoke lowly, "Captain, our evasion's caused us to lose the wire on our own torpedo, as expected. But, just before we lost telemetry, we saw it shift into active homing mode. I think it may have acquired that son of a bitch, Skipper."

Edwards nodded, not taking his eyes from the sonar waterfall display, too absorbed in evading the *Hatta*'s torpedo to worry about his own. *Providence*'s high-speed flow noise showed up as bright green streaks, all but obliterating the other sound traces. Only a well-trained sonarman could make sense of the jumble of lines.

"Sonar, Conn. Torpedo is on the edge of the port baffle, eleven hundred yards astern, closing at a three-knot relative speed. Constant bearing."

"Damn!" Miller exclaimed.

Providence's countermeasures had failed to dupe the hostile torpedo, almost dead astern now and still homing. The WLR-9 on the starboard bulkhead beeped at three-second intervals, needlessly warning of the impending danger.

"It's a race now." Fremont stated the obvious, as he manipulated his calculator. "And it's got three knots on us, Captain."

Edwards waved him off as he did the math in his head. A three-knot closure rate meant the torpedo was gaining a hundred yards every minute. That meant ten minutes to impact. A menacing deduction—that is, unless you carried the math further. Edwards came to the alleviating conclusion a split second before Fremont pressed the "equals" button on his calculator.

"We're going to beat it, Captain!" Fremont cried elatedly. "Damn, sir, we're going to beat it! That electric fish only has a range of about twelve or fourteen thousand yards, and she's already gone at least six or seven thousand by now. At this speed, with this separation, she can't catch us, sir! We're in the clear!"

Edwards couldn't help but smile back at his beaming navigator. Fremont was right. The *Hatta*'s torpedo could not possibly catch up with the *Providence* before the torpedo's electric batteries depleted and went dead. Veterans and greenhorns alike forgot they were submariners and let out a cheer as the news passed around the room and then throughout the ship. A muffled applause wafted up the aft ladder as the news reached the damage-control parties assembled in the crew's mess. As he allowed the men in the room to celebrate around him, Edwards finally breathed a sigh of relief. His plan had worked like clockwork. *Providence* had fired her missiles and had lived to fight another day. He thought to compliment Lieutenant Coleman on the engine room's excellent performance when, all of a sudden, he felt his body lurch forward. The cheering ceased in all compartments as every hand felt the same thing, and the realization sank in.

Something was wrong. Something was terribly wrong. The ship was decelerating!

Every smiling face turned grim in the blink of an eye and all fell starkly silent. Glancing at the speed log, Edwards could plainly see that *Providence* no longer maintained the ordered flank bell. She was slowing rapidly, now at twenty-five knots . . . twenty knots . . . fifteen knots and still decelerating.

At the helm, the engine order telegraph buzzed wildly and the engine room repeater rotated over to the "All Stop" setting.

"Maneuvering answers all stop, Captain!" the helmsman blurted out, rotating his dial from "Flank" to "All Stop" and then back to "Flank" again, to no avail. "Maneuvering's not answering bells, sir!"

Then the uncharacteristically agitated voice of Lieutenant Coleman came over the speaker, "Conn, Maneuvering. We've got a high bearing temperature alarm on number two main engine! Both main engines have tripped off line! Unable to answer engine bells! We're investigating!"

Edwards' hair receded on his forehead as he and Fremont exchanged horrified glances. *Providence* had no propulsion. She was coasting to a dead stop with a torpedo speeding up her wake less than a thousand yards away.

"Fuck those NavSea assholes for their main engine trip!" Miller exclaimed uselessly. "I wish those bastards were here right now! What the hell good does it do to save the fucking main engines if you lose the fucking ship?"

Though he didn't exhibit it in quite the same fashion, Edwards felt the same way. Some NavSea engineer back in Washington, D.C., had decided to build that automatic trip feature into the 688 main engines to make sure some ignorant sailor didn't damage them. Right now, that guy was probably sipping his morning coffee at a Starbuck's in Crystal City, half a world away, completely oblivious to the fact that his design just might have killed every man on the *Providence*.

"Conn, Sonar. Incoming torpedo just passed the towed array, closing fast!"

The thought of the torpedo streaking past the towed sonar array, following the three-thousand-foot tether all the way to the *Providence*'s stern gave Edwards a brief chill. He could hear the torpedo's propellers now over the control room sonar speaker. The shrill sound reminded him of a dentist's drill, only this drill would be a lot more painful.

He shook himself. He had to think clearly in the mere seconds they had left.

"Chief of the Watch, stand by countermeasures! Noisemaker deep, decoy shallow!"

"Standing by, sir."

The WLR-9 unit continued alarming, increasing in tempo and intensity as it detected each sonar pulse from the approaching torpedo.

"Conn, Sonar. Torpedo has gone into terminal homing. Range six hundred yards, dead astern!"

"Launch countermeasures, Chief!"

"Countermeasures away, sir!" the chief said, the cannon-like sound erupting again from the deck below as another broadband noisemaker and acoustic deception emitter shot from the three-inch launcher muzzles.

"Conn, Sonar, torpedo range four hundred yards!"

"Flood all tanks, Dive!" Edwards said wildly. "Flood everything you've got! Get this boat down! Get it down, now!"

Groping for the buoyancy control handle, the chief obeyed, flooding water into *Providence*'s massive tanks. The small graphic indicators on his panel representing the ship's many variable ballast tanks immediately began to light up as thousands upon thousands of pounds of seawater rushed in. The added weight had almost an immediate effect on the *Providence* as she began to descend faster, her digital depth gauge showing her already passing eight hundred feet.

"Conn, Sonar. Torpedo at one hundred yards!"

"Open all main ballast tank vents!" Edwards shouted at the chief of the watch. "Open them, now!"

The chief swiftly raised the fiberglass covers on the main ballast tank vent switches and flipped all five to the open position. It may have been a useless endeavor, but any air pockets that might have accumulated over time in the already flooded tanks, might reduce *Providence*'s descent rate, and Edwards needed every ounce of weight he could get. Normally, submarine captains didn't like air pockets in their main ballast tanks since they could wreak havoc on a submarine's trim. But at this moment, Edwards prayed for a cubic megaton of air. The more, the better. Anything to make the ship heavier.

There must have been some air in the tanks, because the depth gauge began to count down at an increased rate. Not much of an increase, but an increase nonetheless. Edwards wondered if it would be enough.

The torpedo propellers whirred over the control room sonar speaker now and grew louder by the second, complimented by the almost incessant beeping of the WLR-9, as the torpedo's active sonar painted *Providence*'s steel hull with unremitting pulses of acoustic energy.

Edwards looked up at the overhead and imagined he could see through the two inches of steel and several hundred feet of water. Somewhere far above them, *Providence*'s tiny decoy emitted a stepped sound wave very similar to an active sonar return. The first decoy didn't fool the *Hatta*'s torpedo, so there was no reason to believe this one would—but maybe, just maybe.

This time was different from the last. This time *Providence* was essentially dead in the water. Depth alone—not horizontal distance—separated her from her decoy. The incoming torpedo would see two active returns coming from the same bearing. Its onboard computer would have to decide which was the real target and which was the fake. It would have to choose either the one above or the one below. Either way, with the decoy hovering no more than seven or eight hundred feet above them, it was going to be close.

"Conn, Sonar. Torpedo range—"

The report never finished. At that moment, the ocean erupted. A sound louder than any Edwards had ever heard in his life shook *Providence* to her very core. The deck fell out from under his feet, sending most of the unrestrained men catapulting into the overhead. Holding on to a nearby bracket, Edwards didn't fair much better. Attached to the hull, the bracket moved lightning fast in the downward direction, like he was riding a wild bronco desperate to shake him off. The bracket yanked his hands downward until his body was physically parallel to the deck and still several feet above it. Then the downward movement suddenly stopped, and his legs and lower body caught up, violently crashing against the floor.

The deck heeled sharply, the hull groaned, men and equipment flew from one side of the room to the other. While dodging falling equipment, Edwards looked up to read the digital depth gauge, but it was useless, showing erroneous indications ranging from zero to two thousand feet in the space of a few seconds. Then the room suddenly grew warmer, and Edwards realized that the constant whir of the ship's ventilation fans was absent. Air no longer flowed through the ship's ventilation ducts, and the resultant heat from the control room's mass of computer consoles had raised the temperature in no time flat.

Edwards' knees hurt like hell after colliding with the hard deck, but he forced himself to stand anyway. Stepping over bodies, he limped his way over to the periscope platform and reached for the microphone to call the engine room. But before he could, the lights suddenly went out. Everything went pitch black around him and all fell gravely silent, except for the moans of the injured sailors and *Providence*'s groaning hull.

HUNKERING on his knees in the cold mud, Lake hid behind a jagged boulder that had once been molten lava, Ahmad and Michaelson on his left, Teresa on his right. The rock was the only decent shelter they could find without leaving the dense cover of the jungle, and as they waited there, none of them said a word to each other.

It had been a taxing day. A day filled with ups and downs, trudging miles through the forest with the constant fear of an Al Islamiyyah fighter appearing around the next tree or bush. A day spent breaking his back with the weighty Michaelson lodged securely between him and Ahmad. A day spent traveling on blistered feet over loose terrain only to finally reach their objective and discover that it was impassable.

How long the Al Islamiyyah fighters had been blocking the road through Uru Pass was uncertain. Obviously, the terrorist leader, Musa—the one Ahmad kept referring to—had anticipated their escape route.

Before sunset, Lake and Ahmad had ventured within sight of the roadblock for one good look at what they were up against. Bunda's topography prevented them from approaching the terrorist position too closely. The forest receded a couple hundred yards away from the pass entrance, the large clearing in between strewn with lava rock and low grass. It provided little or no cover to get close, but they managed to get a good enough look from their distant jungle cover. From their position, they saw a well-established barricade of four vehicles staggered across the road at the southern entrance to the pass. The vehicles were arranged in such fashion as to form a windy obstacle course for any vehicle wishing to go through. A platoon of heavily armed and well-equipped fighters, numbering perhaps twenty, clustered in small groups behind the vehicles and in strategic positions around the entrance. While Lake and Ahmad watched, a beat-up pickup truck, most likely belonging to one of Bunda's locals, had driven up to the blockade and was allowed to pass only after its bed received a few probes with the bayonet.

Shortly thereafter, Lake and Ahmad returned, found Teresa and Michaelson, and broke the news that all of their hard efforts of the last two days had been in vain. They now faced an insurmountable barrier. It was at that dejected moment that Lake began trying to reach the *Providence* on the satellite phone. Ahmad had advised against it since the enemy obviously still had signal detection gear and could possibly locate their position, but Lake knew it was their only chance. He spent many painful hours dialing *Providence*'s number only to get busy signals. *Providence* was either deep or else all her comms channels were being used. He spent many maddening hours watching the phone's battery indicator dwindle to almost nothing.

Out of frustration he even placed a call to the SubPac watch officer's desk back in Pearl, but the inexperienced fool of an ensign who answered the phone couldn't understand what he was saying. They always put the idiots on the midwatch, and this one was no exception. This fool thought it was a crank call from one of his off-watch buddies. Before hanging up, Lake found himself shouting vulgarities at the young officer, calling him every name in the book. But later, he found a few moments to be sorry for it. After all, the silly ensign had probably never spent a day at sea in his life. Who could blame the young lout for thinking it was a crank call? Who in his right mind would believe some whacko calling in the middle of the night claiming to be a navy officer stuck in some Indonesian jungle with a bunch of terrorists after him?

In a moment of rage, Lake had thrown the phone into the mud, determined never to try again. But Teresa plucked the phone from the mud and handed it back to him. As tired as she was, she placed a gentle arm around his waist and pulled him close to hug him. Given the rough and tumble treatment she'd dished out before, Lake had thought it a strange gesture. It had been soothing, almost loving, in nature, and as much as he wanted to think otherwise, he eventually dismissed it as nothing but an emotional side-effect brought on by the death of her father.

Now, as the group squeezed their exhausted forms behind the boulder and waited for *Providence*'s promised salvation, Lake was ever mindful of the small pressure he felt against his right side. He didn't have to look down to know it was her hip touching his. Perhaps unconscious on her part, perhaps not, but the subtle contact of her rounded hip, rounded and perfect in every way, rounded even more so by her kneeling position, rounded in that way only a woman's hip could be—that way that compelled the beast within him to reach out and grab it— energized the man inside him. He forced himself not to look, though he did not need to look. In the past two days he'd found himself memorizing every curve of her muddy but flawless figure as she moved through the jungle in front of him, bounded over mountain streams and climbed over and around fallen trees. He couldn't help but look. He'd not been with a woman for longer than he could remember. That was it, of course, nothing else—or so he kept telling himself. Something inside him felt an emotional pull to her as well as a physical one, though he scarcely knew why. Two people were never more different. Perhaps it was that difference that attracted him. She was his antimatter, the type of granola treehugger he'd spent his whole life despising.

Maybe now that he'd been to the top of the proverbial mountain and seen the other side, those barriers were finally falling away. Now that he understood that people not too unlike him—good people, people with the same ideals, if not the same means—lived on the other side, maybe he could put aside his old revulsions. This was neither the time nor the place, of course, but if they ever made it off this island, he'd make sure he didn't lose touch with Teresa. He'd make sure she knew how he felt.

Ahmad glanced at Michaelson's watch.

"Where is this explosion your captain spoke of?" he whispered.

"Don't worry," Michaelson said confidently. "If Captain Edwards said it, it'll happen. You can be sure of that. He isn't one to tell a lie. He's a good officer. Takes care of *his* men."

The jibe was intended for Lake's benefit, but once again he chose to ignore it. When would Michaelson give it a rest? Apparently lugging the resentful chief through the jungle all day had had little of an ingratiating effect. How long would that little incident with Jepson remain firmly lodged in the big chief's craw? Michaelson's constant ridicule was starting to grate on Lake's nerves, and he was finding it harder and harder to simply brush it off, a fact that annoyed him more than the ridicule itself.

"What is that?" Teresa pointed to a small opening in the canopy around them through which they could see the dark ocean void in the distance.

Lake looked just in time to see a bright flash appear on the water's surface many miles out to sea. It lit up the ocean around it, painting the water in a shimmering light. Instantly, the bright fire rose to the sky, shooting straight up some three or four thousand feet before it disappeared into the night. It was immediately followed by another, then another.

Lake knew exactly what they were.

"The *Providence*'s shooting Tomahawks! Holy shit, we better get down! Those lights we saw were just the boosters. Once they separate from the missiles there won't be any more tail-fire. In other words, we won't see them coming before they hit."

They all began to dig in the mud where they knelt, trying to get deeper, and now wondering if the rock they had chosen was far enough away to provide adequate shelter. As he crouched lower, Lake felt the cold mud enter his trousers at the bottom and seep up his leg. Several minutes passed, and nothing happened. Looking above him, Lake saw the starry night sky through the break in the canopy. It seemed peaceful enough, matching the stillness engulfing the entire jungle. A few nocturnal creatures growled in the distance. As quiet as it was, they could be miles away for all he knew. The night was so quiet that Lake could even hear the Al Islamiyyah men talking in Arabic and laughing with each other at the roadblock far down the slope. Sound traveled clearly in the jungle at night.

Then, something disturbed the jungle's serenity. A droning sound, faint at first, grew louder by the second until it became a deafening roar. It sounded like a jet fighter on maximum thrusters hovering over their position. Of course, it was not a fighter. It was a Tomahawk cruise missile climbing for the "pop-up point"—a countermeasure, avoiding maneuver—before it descended straight down on top of its target.

Suddenly, the night sky flashed daylight bright and the tall trees formed long shadows. A split second later, the concussion wave hit them, and Lake's ears blanked out as the tremendous blast tore open the night. The massive one-thousand-pound fragmentation warhead had exploded so close that the earth shook beneath his feet, and he noticed Teresa trembling as she tried to get lower. Instinctively, he placed his arms around her, shielding her from the solid blast of hot air that followed, climbing the hillside in a fireball inferno which singed tree, bush, and vine alike. By the time it reached their position the fireball had dissipated substantially, but it still managed to curl the hairs on Lake's forearms and leave his exposed skin with a bad sunburn.

After the heat wave subsided, Teresa looked up into his face.

"Holy shit!" Teresa said, beneath him. "Are we okay? Are you okay?"

Lake rolled off her, inspecting his legs and clothing. A few charred bits here and there, but, otherwise, he was okay. Ahmad and Michaelson faired the same, but as they stood up to peer over their rock shelter they were not prepared for what they saw.

The jungle, what was left of it, lay flat on the slope below. Far down the hillside, nearer the clearing that led to the pass entrance, the slope still burned with a dazzling orange-red flame, lapping at the night sky. Bits and pieces of burning trees and grass lay all around, thrown up the slope by the tremendous blast. The jungle air now smelled like a gas station, the unburned remnants of the Tomahawk's nearly full fuel tanks.

"War," Michaelson uttered with a deep breath. "Glorious war!"

"We cannot wait," Ahmad said, hefting Michaelson's arm around him. "We must go while they're still stunned."

"Stunned?" Lake said as he positioned himself beneath the chief's other arm. "I very much doubt anything survived that!"

"If you care to look down the hill you'll see the jungle is burning more fiercely over there," he pointed down the hill to a patch near the jungle's edge. "It looks like your missile exploded about a hundred yards away from the roadblock. If it was an airburst, I'm sure the blast wave killed most of them, but I seriously doubt they are all dead. Come, we must hurry!"

Lake kept stride with Ahmad as they all headed down the charred slope, skirting fiery patches of timber until they reached the jungle's edge. There, they could see the entrance to Uru Pass across the rocky clearing, still bathed in the light of the burning fires. Where the roadblock had once been, two cars now burned brightly, the intense heat having ignited their gas tanks, while the other two looked mangled and damaged beyond repair. Lake could see a few small mounds burning here and there on the road leading up to the pass, and it took him a few seconds to realize that they were bodies. The poor bastards never knew what hit them. As many times as he'd launched them, he never realized the full destructive power of a Tomahawk weapon until that moment. But as destructive as the blast was, not all of the terrorists were dead. Several figures ran this way and that, in and out of the firelight, their shapes passing in front of the burning vehicles. None appeared to carry weapons, and a few appeared to be naked and smoking, their clothes and hair burned off by the massive blast.

"Take the chief," Ahmad said, gesturing for Teresa to take Michaelson's arm as he unslung the AK-47 rifle from his shoulder. Then to Lake, "Count ten seconds, then all of you follow me."

At that, Ahmad leaped from the cover and started double-timing across the clearing in a crouched stance, the AK-47 pointed toward the enemy with the butt firmly planted in his shoulder. Teresa moved in to take Ahmad's spot beneath Michaelson's arm, then the three hobbled as best they could after him. By the time they got going, the trotting Ahmad had already made it halfway across the clearing. The bright flames of the burning cars had wrecked the night vision of the Al Islamiyyah fighters beyond. They could not see the dark figure rushing toward them with the rifle. Even if they could, they seemed too confused to have taken notice. Frantically, the less injured ones carried their wounded comrades away from the burning cars and laid them in a neat row beside the road. Within seconds, Ahmad was in their midst. A shot rang out in the night, then another, then a short burst, and Lake watched as figure after figure fell to Ahmad's deadly aim. A few of the terrorists, not realizing their attacker was already among them, grabbed up their weapons and fired fruitlessly toward the jungle, but one by one, they fell victim, too.

After Ahmad's thin arm casually waved for them to come on, Lake saw the destruction up close for the first time. The area was littered with body parts and corpses, both victims of *Providence*'s missile attack and Ahmad's rifle. Ahmad had killed nearly a dozen terrorists in less than half a minute, but *Providence*'s missile had done far worse. Horribly disfigured shapes and charred remains twisted in every imaginable fashion redefined Lake's definition of the term "strike warfare." The burning bodies filled the air with the putrid stench of smoldering flesh, and along the roadside the line of eight wounded terrorists wailed from the pain of their burns. Some recognized Ahmad immediately and cried out to him in Arabic. Others cursed at him and spat in his direction.

Ahmad glanced at them for a few moments, seeming to enjoy their suffering. There was a devilish look in his eyes as he casually waved to them and then briskly walked over to Lake who still held the injured Michaelson.

"Your forty-five, please," he said simply, removing the pistol from Lake's holster without waiting for an answer.

With complete calm and no trace of remorse, Ahmad approached the line of wounded men and one by one placed a bullet between their eyes. Some protested, some cried out one last time, some met their fate with silence, but one minute later it was all over and the eight terrorists lay dead beside the road.

Ahmad returned and replaced the forty-five in Lake's holster.

"You sick bastard!" Teresa spat through the tears streaming down her face. "To think that my father associated with the likes of you!"

After one long, emotionless look into her face, Ahmad shrugged and began ransacking the bodies. Lake wished he could say something to her, but he knew he didn't have the right words. How could he? After all, he partly agreed with what Ahmad had just done. Those men would have blabbed to their comrades who were almost certainly driving this way by now, attracted by the huge ball of fire in the sky. Yet he had to admit, it seemed a bit demented to kill an unarmed man, let alone these pathetic, badly burned creatures Ahmad had just dispatched.

"A weapon for you," Ahmad said, slinging a Kalashnikov AK-47 rifle over Lake's free shoulder, "and a weapon for you."

He held out a Kalashnikov for Teresa but instead of taking it she spat in his face.

"Eat shit, asshole! I hope they get you, you bastard!"

Slowly wiping the spit from his eyes, Ahmad drew close to within inches of Teresa's face. He said nothing, but Lake wondered what twisted calculations were going on behind those fiery eyes. He remembered what Ahmad had told him before, and now he could bet that the Arab agent was figuring out how they could manage to carry the chief, the rifles, the water, and the gear with Teresa eliminated.

"We've got to get moving," Lake said quickly to distract Ahmad's thoughts. "We've got an appointment to keep with the *Providence* and I intend to keep it."

Casting one more chilling look at Teresa, Ahmad nodded in agreement.

"I know those coordinates they gave you," he said. "It's an area filled with isolated coves, far from any villages, but your captain would be a fool to bring his submarine in there."

"Why's that?" Lake asked.

"The reefs are far too shallow. He won't be able to approach the coast, not even on the surface. If my memory serves, a Los Angeles Class submarine draws thirty-two feet of water on the surface. Those reefs get shallower than fifteen feet. Obviously your captain wasn't aware of this." He paused before adding, "Now that we can pass through this place, I believe we should continue with our original plan. We'll steal a boat in one of the coastal villages and meet your ship out at sea."

Michaelson shot a glance at Lake, apparently to see how he would respond to this blatant deviation from Captain Edwards' instructions. Lake had to admit, after watching Ahmad kill a whole platoon single-handedly, he wasn't overly eager to challenge him. But, of course, as officer in charge, he had to.

"Sorry, Ahmad," Lake said with forced firmness. "You know this area, and you know this line of work, but I know my captain. And if he says he'll be at these coordinates tomorrow, then, damn it, he'll be there! Besides, I'm fucking in charge here, and we're going wherever the hell I say we go! Understand?"

Ahmad turned to face him. Half-expecting to die a quick and clean death, Lake was surprised when the Arab operative broke into a small smile.

"Okay, Lieutenant." He shrugged again. "Your captain got us past this roadblock, so I guess I'll trust him to get us off this island, too."

Catching an affectionate glance from Teresa, Lake

breathed a small sigh of relief, then hefted Michaelson's weight back onto his shoulder. As the group emerged on the other side of the dark pass, they found a small clearing where they could see the low hills far below, now black and indistinguishable in the moonlight. It felt good to finally see their destination, but it paled in comparison to the dazzling spectacle adorning the northern horizon.

The night sky above the distant island of Wijaya exhibited a pulsating yellow hue that rendered the stars above invisible. Three or four dozen unceasing dark columns of smoke rose far above the island where they congregated into one great ominous cloud stretching out with the westerly trade winds across the dim ocean. Beyond Wijaya's low mountains, the whole island appeared to be on fire. The night air carried the muffled sounds of far-off explosions, like a distant fireworks show. Sometimes the detonations were short and distinct, other times they sounded staccato, like a thousand bombs going off in succession. Every few moments a fireball from one of the larger explosions would appear above Wijaya's hills, but from this distance it was only a small sliver of flame.

Lake believed he had finally put two and two together. *Providence*'s missile strike against the roadblock was merely a small part of a grander strike mission. The terrorist camp on Wijaya was the main target, and from what he could see the strike was indisputably successful. No living thing could have escaped such an inferno, not to mention the multiple secondary explosions that seemed to have no end. As the four dived back into the jungle and headed down the mountain, this time on the northern side of Uru Pass, Lake began to wonder about the orangutans on Wijaya. He remembered the harbor pilot telling him about the apes as he drove the *Providence* into Ujungpang on that beautiful day, seemingly ages ago. Hopefully, the poor apes had escaped the carnage. They probably wished they were back on Borneo right about now.

At first he thought it strange to be concerned with the plight of a few apes as he trudged through the forest, his back sore to the breaking point, his feet numb with blisters. But then he thought how utterly appropriate it was. They themselves were like four apes being hunted by men. They lived in the jungle and had no human friends on this island. And like the Wijaya orangutans, they needed some nice people to come and take them home.

Chapter 19

LIEUTENANT Commander Warren Bloomfield did his best to keep his bulky form out of the way as men all around him groped to don their damage-control gear in the dim light afforded by the emergency lanterns. As the deck finally returned to level and the men tended to their wounds, the dining tables quickly transformed into equipment staging surfaces. Each damage control team gathered around their own table, preparing for action.

Over the sound-powered phones, a fire had been reported in the engine room, and now the faintest hints of acrid smoke wafted through the idle ventilation ducts, reaching Bloomfield's flaring nostrils. Beyond the sporadic damage reports, which continued to come in, *Providence*'s status remained a mystery. The mess contained no depth gauge, so for all he knew the ship was hurtling toward crush depth. All around him, men donned firefighting gear and emergency breathing apparatus, each man's air hose plugging noisily into the air manifolds with a brief wisp of escaping high-pressure air. It sounded much like forty men using a tire gauge to check the air in their tires all at once.

In each corner of the mess, a different hose team assembled and geared up to man *Providence*'s four fire hoses, the front lines in any fire fight. The hose teams were special, and used a different type of breathing apparatus from the rest of the crew. To maximize freedom of movement they wore the same Scott air packs worn by the everyday local community firemen, in addition to the same flash hoods, the same flame-retardant breeches, the same coats and gloves. Each team consisted of a nozzle man, two holders, and a leader. Usually, a phone-talker accompanied the team to keep the control room informed of the fire's status. Also accompanying the lead hose team was a man in charge, whose job it was to take control at the scene of the fire. This task usually fell upon the shoulders of the senior officer present, and today that officer was Bloomfield.

"Here, XO, you better put this on." A stocky chief shoved an air pack into Bloomfield's thick hands. In the dim light he could scarcely see which side was up, but he finally wrestled the tank onto his back and the mask over his head. In his days as a junior officer, the submarine force didn't have Scott air packs. Everyone made do with the cumbersome EABs, or emergency air breathing apparatus, like most men in the mess wore now. Sucking rubber, it was called, a euphemism for the airtight seal formed between the man's face and the rubber mask.

Bloomfield cursed into his mask, his hot breath instantly fogging up the Plexiglas shield, but no one heard him. He'd spent enough time as a junior officer sucking rubber, and he was far too short in his career for this kind of work.

"Team One, ready!" a voice called out.

"Team Two, ready!" another called. Then another, until all teams announced their readiness to take on any flooding or fire anywhere in the ship.

Bloomfield stood at the head of the room with the chief petty officers while the rest of the men sat at the booth tables staring at each other and waiting for orders. With the loss of power, and the fans shut down, the room was deathly quiet except for the respirator-like sounds of the two dozen breathing devices, including Bloomfield's, which audibly sucked air at a much greater rate than the others.

The XO hated being there. He could barely breathe in the mask, and the air pack's straps pulled uncomfortably tight under his flabby armpits. He shouldn't have to endure such treatment this late in his career. Edwards could go to hell as far as he was concerned!

"Should we send a team into the engine room, XO?" Senior Chief McKennitt asked, his voice muffled by his mask. "There's a report over the line they've got a fire back there."

"Ah . . . no, Senior Chief. We'll stay right where we are and do what we're told. I have no desire to be a cowboy, unlike our self-indulgent captain."

At that moment, the emergency lights flickered to life, and someone reported over the phone circuit that battery power had just been restored. Not surprisingly, with power now available for the announcing circuits, the mess's 1MC speaker intoned: "Attention all hands!"

It was Edwards' voice over the speaker, calm and unruffled. "There is a fire in engine room upper level, in the number two R-114 power panel. The fire has spread to the local area and needs to be contained. Damage Control Central, send a hose team to fight the fire. There is also flooding in engine room lower level, but the flooding has been isolated. Damage Control Central, send a team with band-it kits to engine room lower level to restore the main seawater system."

Edwards' voice remained steady as he added, after a slight pause, "We've survived the torpedo explosion, gentlemen. Thanks to God and our countermeasure, it exploded well above us. Now let's make it through the aftermath! All stations make regular reports to the control room. That is all."

Bloomfield felt his heart leave his throat. They were indeed lucky to be alive. The men around him may not have understood the gravity of Edwards' report, but he sure did. When a torpedo explodes underwater, the majority of its explosive force travels upward in the water, not downward. If the *Hatta*'s torpedo had detonated beneath *Providence* instead of above her, the ship would have cracked in two—and he never would have made it to retirement. And he still might not, but the steady tone in Edwards' voice gave him confidence, oddly enough. He hated Edwards, of course, but at least the bastard had the knack to imbue a desperate situation with a sense of calm.

"You coming, XO?" McKennitt asked as he and his hose team headed through the aft passage toward the engine room.

"I . . . uh," Bloomfield stuttered as every man in the room stopped what he was doing and directed his attention squarely at him, waiting for his answer. He was the only officer in the room. There was no excuse now. "Well . . . of course, Senior Chief. Lead the way."

At that, the men returned to their tasks, apparently now satisfied that their XO at least was not a coward, and Bloomfield found himself bounding down the passage after McKennitt's hose team cursing the men in the mess who had shamed him into it. The passage narrowed and turned sharply as the team approached the watertight door leading into the engine room, and Bloomfield's air tank swung uncontrollably from side to side across his oblong back, banging into the passage walls with every step.

"Differential pressure's good," McKennitt announced, reading the pressure gauge next to the door wheel. "That's a relief, XO. I was sure we'd have to bleed off air, with all the flooding back there."

"Whatever you say, McKennitt." Bloomfield had an itch in his nose and he couldn't get his finger to it with the mask over his face. Without a second thought, he lifted the mask, breaking the airtight seal, and reached in to scratch the offending nerve.

McKennitt opened the hatch and directed his hose team to proceed through. All four men ducked under the senior chief's arm and scrunched through the hatch, trailing the saggy fire hose behind them. After the team had gone through, it was Bloomfield's turn, but McKennitt stopped him abruptly, barring his passage with one firm arm.

"XO, sir, it's bad enough I've got to train these boys day in and day out not to take their masks off, but when I see an officer do it, I just want to shoot myself. The boys look to you for example, XO. *Be* an example to them!"

Bloomfield reacted instinctively to the senior chief's boldness. "Get your ass through the hatch, McKennitt, and stop lecturing me! You're out of line, damn you!"

McKennitt nodded and ducked through the passage, carrying his gripe no further as he hurried to catch up with the hose team. Still smarting from the senior chief's reprimand, Bloomfield cursed as he tried three different ways to get his rotund body through the small tunnel door with the bulky air

tank on his back. He finally resorted to taking the tank off in
order to squeeze through the small opening. Once through he
shut the hatch behind him, again slung the tank onto his back
and huffed briskly down the smoky passage to find the hose
team. He followed the trailing hose up one ladder and then
down the next. The fire had created a lot of smoke, and visi-
bility in the engine room was poor, especially in the far aft
corners of the upper level where Bloomfield soon found visi-
bility reduced to only a few feet. The fact that his mask had
fogged up again didn't help matters either. The temperature
was much hotter back here. Hotter due to the fire and hotter
due to the large-diameter steam piping from which most of
the heat emanated, heat normally removed by the now idle refrigeration plant. Bloomfield had trouble seeing the deck beneath his feet, but kept walking aft, kicking the hose
periodically to make sure he was still going in the right direction. Soon he came upon a sailor wearing an EAB and manning a set of headphones.

"Where's the hose team?" Bloomfield shouted through
the mask.

"They're further aft, sir. I'm phone talkin' for 'em, but my
cord don't reach that far. One of 'em's coming back again to
give me status."

"Right," Bloomfield said, moving past the sailor into the
denser smoke beyond. The fire hose was rock solid at his feet,
so at least he knew the hose was pressurized. Somewhere
ahead of him, the hose team was discharging the hose onto
the fire.

As he came upon the small space above the shaft where
the ship's R-114 refrigeration plant resided, the back of
McKennitt's shirt appeared out of the smoke. Just ahead of
him, the three other men held on tight to the fire hose as they
trained it onto a section of burning lagging in the overhead.
The high-velocity jet stream ate away at the burning lagging,
eroding it until it fell in large, spongy chunks onto the steel
deckplates. With the lagging extinguished, McKennitt
scarcely acknowledged Bloomfield's presence, and immedi-

ately directed the team to shift their focus to the burning refrigeration plant.

Bloomfield found himself standing there, watching and out of breath. His heart pounded fast from his poor physical condition, but he suddenly felt the need to be a useful part of the team. Call it a spark of personal honor, he felt the sudden pressing need to be accepted by these men who followed McKennitt—and Edwards for that matter—without question.

"What's the classification of this fire, Senior Chief?" he shouted above the water stream. "Has that panel been deenergized? When's the last time you gave a report to control? That nozzleman's not holding that nozzle correctly . . . Senior Chief? Senior Chief?"

"Yes, XO! Yes! Yes! And fucking *yes*!" McKennitt swung around, his face snarling behind the mask, his previous demeanor all but vanished. "With all due respect, sir, you haven't fought a fucking fire in two fucking years! You're a worthless piece of shit, so why don't you just shut your fat ass and let me put this fucking fire out!"

Bloomfield's blood began to boil at McKennitt's insolence. The comment hurt his ego, but most of all it hurt his pride, something he thought no longer possible this close to retirement. Perhaps it hurt most of all because deep in his heart he knew it was all true, and he found himself wondering where were the snappy salutes and inherent respect enlisted men used to give him all those years ago when he was a young ensign fresh out of the academy. It seemed he got more respect as a lowly ensign than he did as an executive officer, and the thought made him want to punch McKennitt in the mouth. He wanted to take over the hose team and show them all he could still lead. Instead, his anger made him breathe even heavier and caused his mask to fog up until he could not see a thing. He groped around, a sudden blind panic overtaking him. Then he did the unthinkable. He reached up and lifted his mask's rubber seal in order to wipe off some of the condensation. It was a rookie mistake, and one he wouldn't have made if he'd participated in any of the ship's fire drills over the past year.

As soon as he lifted the seal, the smoke-filled air rushed in to mingle with the fresh. Bloomfield breathed the smoky mixture once and instantly fell to the deck in convulsions. He began coughing so hard he could feel the veins popping out on his temples and the blood rushing to his head as his face turned bright red.

Within seconds, McKennitt restrained him and forced the mask back onto his face, verifying that the seal was secure. Bloomfield felt fresh air flowing again, but he still coughed uncontrollably. Moments later, McKennitt and a member of the hose team hefted his arms around their shoulders and began carrying him forward. He could scarcely put one foot in front of the other as he fought for breaths between coughing fits. Sweat poured down his face, drenching his flash hood, T-shirt, and blue jumpsuit at the neck. The two men grunted as they conveyed his two hundred fifty pounds along the port side all the way forward, then down the ladder to the middle level, then into the passage leading back the way they had come.

Before he knew it, he was sitting on the deck in the breathable air of the forward compartment just on the other side of the watertight door. He leaned against the bulkhead as he took deep breaths, his hair a disheveled mess, his torn-off mask and dangling flash hood resting on his large belly. It took several minutes before his rapid heartbeat began to subside and the coughing fits to grow further apart.

"Go back and help the team finish off that fire!" he heard McKennitt order the sailor that had helped carry him aft. Obeying the senior chief, the sailor ducked back into the smoke-filled compartment, and McKennitt closed the door behind him

Bloomfield was surprised when McKennitt then took his own mask off and looked down at him pitiably. They were the only two in the narrow passage.

"Come on, XO," he said, offering a hand. "Let's get you to the wardroom. The doc can check you out there."

"No, McKennitt . . . No!" Bloomfield struggled to say between coughs. "Don't let . . . anyone . . . know about this . . . Just . . . let me stay here . . . for a while."

He looked up to see the weathered senior chief return a slight nod, his face twisted in a disgusted scowl as if he utterly detested what his eyes beheld. The scowl remained as McKennitt donned his flash hood and mask once again, then opened the tunnel door and headed back into the engine room to rejoin the hose team.

He must have been a pathetic sight, Bloomfield thought, especially to a hardened undersea warrior like McKennitt who had spent his whole life in the trenches aspiring to his senior enlisted position. Obviously, the senior chief had little or no respect for him.

As he sat in the passageway all alone, his heaving chest slowly returning to normal, his sweat-streaked face glistening in the emergency lighting, Lieutenant Commander Warren Bloomfield thought about how different he was from the young Ensign Bloomfield of twenty years ago. Honor, courage, commitment, they were words to live by at the academy. How strange that he would only come to understand their true meaning twenty years later when he was on the verge of retirement. How strange that he would discover after all these years, that he had little respect for himself.

"**DAMAGE** is extensive, Captain, but the fire is out, and we should have the main seawater system up and running within the hour."

Edwards stood with crossed arms on the periscope platform as a very smoky and grimy Lieutenant Coleman made his report in person. Battle stations were still manned in the control room, though a few sailors with some very nasty contusions had to be carried off to the wardroom for medical attention. Most of the loose equipment dislodged by the torpedo detonation still lay strewn about on the deck.

"I can give you five knots on the EPM right now, Captain," Coleman continued. "It'll drain the battery, but we should be okay. There's nothing wrong with the reactor, and we can start it up once main seawater's restored."

"Good. We need that five knots, Mr. Coleman. As you can

see, we're six hundred feet below test depth, and I've used up just about all our high-pressure air to keep us from going any deeper. I'm this close from an emergency blow."

As if on cue, a loud groan of overstressed steel filled the room and passed fore and aft before subsiding. The hull was under an enormous strain. At this depth *Providence* could be likened to an aluminum soda can with a heavy weight on top. One slight twist in the wrong direction, and the can would undergo a catastrophic collapse. Most of the leaks caused by the explosion had been stopped by automatic isolation valves, and that was a good thing. But fighting leaks under this kind of pressure was not a simple task. Two decks below, the auxiliary machinery room had reported a tiny leak the size of a pinhead. Nothing to be overly concerned about, except that one of the unlikely mechanics had stupidly passed his index finger through the water stream and was horrified to see it neatly sliced off.

"Helm, ahead one third. Dive, make your depth one hundred fifty feet," Edwards ordered before turning back to Coleman. He wanted to get *Providence* out of the danger zone before going any farther, and there was still much to do. The smoke-filled engine room would have to be ventilated with the outside atmosphere, the air banks needed recharging, and the refrigeration plant needed restarting. With all the electrical power these tasks would require. he half-considered snorkeling to preserve the battery, but he hesitated. Starting up *Providence*'s noisy diesel generator was a risky proposition with the threat of the *Hatta* still out there.

"What about the main engines?"

Coleman shook his head. "The main engines may take awhile, sir. I've got both off-line right now. From what we've been able to discern, we definitely had an oil flow problem on the forward bearing of number two. I'm not sure what caused it. The only way to tell is to crack open the main engine housing and conduct a full inspection."

"That will take time," Edwards said gravely, briefly imagining the ordeal of conducting such an inspection. The area would have to be cordoned off, every tool tracked, every dis-assembled item properly tagged and marked for reassembly. The whole process could take ten or twelve hours, and they needed a whole lot more than five knots to keep their appointment with the shore party.

"What about number one main engine?" Edwards asked suddenly. "Why is it racked out?"

"Well, Captain, I'm not sure what caused the loss of flow on number two. I can't be certain we don't have the same problem on number one. I thought taking it off-line was the wiser approach."

Edwards shook his head. "I need that engine, Mr. Cole-man, or should I say *Eng*, because you *are* my acting engineer. One day when you become a full-time engineer you'll learn that a captain never likes to be robbed of his mains." Coleman started to speak but Edwards cut him off. "Always remember, your job is to maximize propulsion in any way possible to the extent of breaking your equipment. Once you get the reactor back, I want you to restore number one main engine and place it back on-line, please. Thanks for your report, Eng. Keep me informed up here."

"Aye, aye, sir," Coleman said halfheartedly, then headed for the aft ladder. He obviously didn't agree with his captain's order, but Edwards knew that someday he would learn. They all did, just like he had years ago.

As the deck angled upward and the ship crept up to her creeping five-knot speed, Edwards considered how fortunate they were to still be alive. *Providence*'s decoy had done its job, drawing the torpedo shallow just before the smart weapon detonated upon detecting *Providence*'s magnetic influence field. The explosion had been too high to rupture the pressure hull, but it had been close enough to do some serious damage, and he couldn't help but wonder what might have happened if he hadn't ordered the main ballast tanks vented at the last minute. Did that act alone take *Providence* deep enough and give her the extra cushion of seawater she needed to absorb the blow? Perhaps they would never know. Or at least not until some pencil-necked geek back at NavSea spent five million dollars doing a study on it to come up with the conclusion that he had acted stupidly.

"Passing eight hundred feet, sir," the diving officer called out. Everyone in the room seemed to breathe a collective sigh of relief now that *Providence* was well within her design depth specifications. The hull felt the relief too as the HY-80 creaked and popped, expanding to its former shape.

He noticed Miller in the starboard corner conversing in a low voice with Chief Ramirez, who had just emerged from the sonar room.

"Any contact on our assailant, gentlemen?" Edwards called over to them.

Miller and Ramirez exchanged glances, then approached the platform together.

"The chief was just telling me, Captain," Miller said. "Sonar picked up a loud explosion to the south of us before that enemy torpedo exploded."

"We were too busy tracking the enemy torpedo, Captain," Ramirez uttered, abashedly. "That's why we didn't report it before, but I can bring it up for you on the historical display."

Ramirez reached up to the conn's sonar display and rapidly pressed a series of buttons on the touchscreen, passing the display through several screens before stopping on the one that had the passive sonar waterfall showing the last four hours' worth of data. He pointed to a small bright green blip just above a saturated portion of the display that represented the close-aboard torpedo explosion.

"You can see here, sir, this distant explosion on bearing one eight five just before the *Hatta*'s torpedo went off. That lines up well with our last known position for the *Hatta*."

"So, you think we got her?"

Ramirez looked to Miller for support. "I think so, Captain."

"It sure looks that way, sir," Miller affirmed.

Edwards nodded. It could be. The *Hatta* would have had a tough time escaping if *Providence*'s torpedo had acquired her. The Mark 48 ADCAP could travel three times her speed and had a range of close to twenty-eight miles. It could have run

Peto's impressive new submarine into the ground, if it found her. There was a reason for the popular saying among submariners, "Once an ADCAP had you, it *had* you."

"Well, until we know otherwise, we'll proceed with caution."

"Approaching one hundred fifty feet, Captain," the diving officer announced.

"Very well, Dive." Edwards suddenly reconsidered. He had much to do, and he had an appointment to keep. "Proceed on to periscope depth, Dive, and prepare to ventilate!"

The diving officer acknowledged the order as Edwards moved over to the nav plot and squeezed in next to Fremont. He glanced at the chart for a few moments, then ordered, "Helm, right fifteen degrees rudder. Steady on course zero eight five."

"Right fifteen degrees rudder, aye, sir," the helmsman responded sharply. "Coming to course zero eight five."

"Zero eight five, sir?" Fremont looked puzzled. "That'll take us away from Bunda, Captain. If we're picking up Lake and his men in twelve hours, shouldn't we be heading west, sir?"

Edwards did not answer. His plan was far-fetched enough without advertising it to the rest of the crew. Right now they needed to concentrate on damage control efforts, and he wanted their entire focus on that endeavor.

He glanced at the clock. It read 0302.

He needed his main engines back, or at least one of them. Right now the rendezvous point was only about twenty miles to the west of their present position, and it seemed insane to be heading away from it, but if they were ever to have any chance of rescuing Lake and the others from that reef-bounded island, *Providence* would have to head east first. If Coleman could get the number one main engine back on-line within the hour, *Providence* could make a good twenty-one knots. At that speed she could make it just in time for the rendezvous with Lake's party.

But it wasn't the *Providence* he was worried about.

"Who's the best diesel mechanic we have on board?" he asked Fremont impulsively.

"That would be Chief Louis, sir," Fremont quizzically answered. "The A Division chief. He's probably up to his armpits right now putting things back together in the machinery room. It was one of his guys who got his finger cut off."

"Chief of the Watch, have Chief Louis come to the conn . . . No wait . . ." Edwards suddenly conjured up the image of the grizzled chief two decks below, shouting orders, directing his wide-eyed young mechanics as they made speedy repairs to the ship's big diesel engine and the jumble of atmosphere-control equipment. "On second thought, call Chief Louis in the machinery room. Tell him I'm coming down to see *him*."

"I guess they're bringing main seawater back up again," a grimy and very tired-looking lieutenant junior grade said as he poured himself a cup of coffee and collapsed into one of the wardroom chairs. "My division's back together again. At least as much as it can be after taking a close hit like that."

"Shit! We were lucky!" another junior grade lieutenant said as he too fell into a chair. "Reactor should be back up soon."

The wardroom door opened and a gaunt and ghoulish figure in a T-shirt and boxers ambled in.

"Holy shit, Eng, I didn't know you was up and about!" one lieutenant said, looking up. "Shit, you look like death warmed over! Want some coffee?"

The lieutenant didn't wait for an answer but poured a cup and placed it on the table as Van Peenan slowly sat down in the chair nearest the door. The ship's engineer said nothing but instead stared silently at the simmering cup.

The lieutenant glanced at his buddy with a snide smirk.

"So, Eng, what the hell happened to you over there? They must have beat the living crap out of you."

Van Peenan did not respond. He did not touch the cup, but continued staring at it vacantly with his hands on his lap.

The lieutenant shrugged, then continued chatting with the other lieutenant.

"Did you hear what Coleman said?"

"No."

"He said they don't know why the main engine seized up like that. He thinks it might be a maintenance issue or something like that. If those lower level looies haven't been cleaning the strainers out every night there's going to be hell to pay, that's for sure."

Van Peenan raised his eyebrows, but still remained silent.

"Captain wants him to get the other engine up so we can get out of here," the lieutenant continued. "That's what I heard. I guess they're gonna open up the other one. Damn, it's hot in here! Wish they'd get that fucking reactor back up. We need some AC up here."

"You been back there to see it?"

"See what?"

"The main seawater system leak."

"No."

"Pipe ruptured on a corner piece. Put a thousand gallons in the engine room bilge before they could shut the isolation valves. I could stick three fingers in the hole it made. Some crazy shit back there!"

"What'd they do about it?"

"Took a couple laps around the pipe with a band-it patch. The rest of the system needed some tightening up too. Had the whole M division back there workin' on it at one point. It was a sight to see, I tell you. I've never seen so many M div-ers in one spot. The diving officer must've had one hell of a time keeping trim. I even saw Dean back there, bandages and all, with his ass in the bilge. They worked hard, those sons of bitches."

Van Peenan looked up now, his eyes blazing at the lieutenant. "Who did you say?" he asked urgently. "Who was back there?"

"Dean."

"Dean?" Van Peenan muttered incredulously.

"I couldn't believe it either, Eng. Here that son of a bitch fell three stories down a ladder not five days ago, and now he's already itching to get back to work. Shit, if I was him I'd spend the rest of the trip in my rack. Hell, no one would say anything if he did. Shit, I don't see why you're up either, Eng. Has the doc said it's okay for you to get up yet?"

Van Peenan stood slowly, leaving the coffee cup undisturbed on the table. The two officers said some things to him, but he did not hear them. He left the wardroom and closed the door behind him.

Dean was *alive*! First, Coleman had taken over his department, and now Dean was alive! The thought made him nauseous and he quickly peered around the corner to make sure no one saw him clutching his stomach. He had to make sure Captain Christopher didn't see him . . . or was it Edwards? His head suddenly hurt, and he swiftly ducked into his stateroom, took two steps, then collapsed into his rack. He wrapped himself in his blanket but cold shivers overcame him at the thought of what this would mean to his career.

It was over now, just over. Coleman, that conniving bastard, would probably find some reason to blame him for the main engine seizing. It sounded like he was already setting the stage, citing maintenance problems as the probable cause.

And what if Dean remembered who pushed him down that ladder well? On top of dealing with a bad fitness report, he'd have to deal with a court-martial as well. He couldn't let that happen. He couldn't let Dean have the chance to destroy him. It was, after all, a long trip back to Pearl, and an opportunity was bound to arise.

This time, he'd leave nothing to chance. He'd do the job himself, and he'd make sure Dean never spoke to anyone ever again.

Chapter 20

LAKE wiped the sweat from his eyes as he sat on the shaded rock not twenty yards from the water's edge and gazed out on the turquoise ocean. He strained his eyes to find *Providence*'s black sail rising up from the flat blue waters stretching as far as his eyes could see, but there was no sign of her. The rendezvous time had come and gone, and the only vessels in sight were a few coastal fishing craft. Most of the fishermen bobbed on the waves in the deep channel between Bunda and Wijaya, but one or two oddballs attempted to make their trade on the less restrictive seas near the northeastern reefs. The channel between the two islands was probably a good spot for fishing, Lake pondered. The island currents forced ocean fish through the narrow passage and straight into the nets of the waiting fishermen. Rebellion or no, the island economy had to function. Still, he found it odd that the Indonesian air force, which had periodically appeared high above the islands, chose to spare the defenseless craft. They were, of course, legitimate targets, since they probably fed the insurgent forces ashore with a good portion of their catch. But perhaps Jakarta had chosen to use restraint with the Bunda rebellion, instead embarking on a "hearts and minds" strategy.

Off to the north, a pall of smoke still hung over Wijaya, reminding Lake of the dazzling destruction he had witnessed the night before. The *Providence*'s missiles had laid waste to the far side of the island, very evident from the large number of fires that continued to burn there. Even now, twelve hours later, secondary detonations rumbled across the six-mile channel between the two islands. An endless sheet of rising black smoke filled the northern sky and continuously fed the enormous dark cloud above.

"Anything?" Ahmad said, climbing up the rock behind him.

"Nothing but fishermen," Lake answered wearily. "They're over an hour late. I'm beginning to think your plan was a better one."

Ahmad shook his head. "I've reconsidered. This is a good place. Your captain was wise to send us here."

Lake didn't know why Ahmad seemed so agreeable all of a sudden. Perhaps it was the rough morning they'd had getting here, carrying Michaelson between them down the jungle-covered slope. The first two miles had been the toughest. The descent to the hilly coast was steep going, and they found themselves tripping and tumbling many times over fallen logs and dense brush. At each stumble Michaelson's face turned beet red from the pain in his knee, but he never let out a single peep. Lake had not made out much better. He bore cuts and bruises all over his body, and on more than one occasion he came very close to impaling himself on a protruding frond. Descending the slope while carrying a wounded man was difficult enough, but it became an almost impossible task when Musa's helo showed up again. Above the jungle canopy, the thundering Huey swept north to south across the hilly coast, then back again, forcing them to dash for cover on at least a dozen occasions. Many times they thought they were done for, when the helo's door-mounted machine gun blasted away at the jungle close to where they lay. But on each occasion the helo cut short its hunt, departing abruptly and retreating inland until the sound of its thumping rotors faded away. At first they had wondered why Musa had beat such a hasty retreat, but moments later the reason became apparent, when the roar of jet engines filled the forest. Apparently, the Indonesian air force had begun low-altitude sweeps over the rebel island, probably searching for targets of opportunity.

"Musa knows we're on the north side of the island," Ahmad had said after one such incident. "He knows we're here somewhere, but those jets keep forcing him to take cover. He'll send men on foot to scour these hills soon enough."

Despite the delays brought on by the harassing helo, the party of four had made good time reaching the somewhat secluded cove where they expected to be extracted. Their exhausted, blistered and sore bodies collapsed beneath the palms on a small outcropping a few feet above the shoreline, overlooking the white sandy beach. And there they waited, searching the vast horizon, gazing straight into the strong ocean wind until their eyes teared from the salty air. They watched and waited the entire hour before the scheduled rendezvous. They watched and waited again the entire hour after the scheduled rendezvous, but no submarine appeared to take them away.

From time to time, they heard the helo still beating the skies above the jungle, but it was further inland, searching the low hills yet again. The terrorist leader probably wasn't bothering to search the coastal area, since he'd easily see well in advance if any American or Indonesian warship approached the coast to take them off.

"So you think this was wise, do you?" Lake said bitterly to Ahmad, as the two stared out to sea. "For the life of me, I can't figure out why Captain Edwards chose this place. This whole coastline is ringed with reefs. That white fishing boat out there's coming in pretty close, but even *he's* taking it slow. And *Providence* draws a hell of a lot more water than he does. There's no way they'll get the sub in here without running her aground. Shit! Where the hell are they?"

"My plan would not have worked," Ahmad said evenly. "Musa is bound to have men in every village along the coast. Stealing a boat would have been impractical, if not impossible. Especially with your chief in his condition."

Lake nodded. "Well, I hope *Providence*'s not just sitting out there beyond the reefs, at periscope depth, waiting for us to swim out to them. I'm tempted to call them on the phone again."

"Don't do it!" Ahmad said firmly. "Any transmission would give our position away. Remember, I know how these people operate. They've got direction-finding gear that would make the U.S. Army envious."

"Well, I didn't—"

Just then Ahmad raised a hand, motioning for him to be

silent. Lake turned one ear out of the wind and heard the sound of vehicles driving on the coastal road a half mile up from the beach. The road was well out of sight from their position, hidden by the dense jungle between them, but close enough that he could clearly hear the squealing brakes as the vehicles came to a stop.

"Have they found us?" Lake asked.

"I doubt it. Probably foot patrols searching along the road. I don't think they will come down this far. I will go check, just in case. You'd better notify the others to find cover."

Ahmad darted in the direction of the road and disappeared into the brush while Lake hurried over to the clump of bushes where the other two rested. Teresa lay flat on the cool shady sand, but the lively chief sat propped against the trunk of a nearby palm doing his best to elevate his now purple and grotesquely swollen knee. As Lake approached him, he noticed that Michaelson was gazing out to sea as if he were in a trance.

"Vehicles on the road, Chief," Lake said, nudging him with one foot. "We need to move to better cover. What the devil are you staring at?"

"That fishing boat out there, the white one. It's coming awfully close to the shore. Something about it looks familiar."

Lake turned to see the same white fishing vessel he'd been examining before, only now it had closed the distance from the beach by several miles, much closer than when he last glanced at it. The flying bridge above its single-story structure swayed to and fro in the choppy shallows as it came on at a moderate speed of about ten knots, its high bow plowing up a frothing foam at the waterline. From this distance Lake could see no one on deck except for one figure, barely distinguishable, standing in the window of the high-flying bridge. As the boat kept coming toward the shore, Lake and Michaelson stared in bewilderment. Not until the craft had approached to within a thousand yards did Lake suddenly recognize the craft.

"It's the *Mendar*!" Lake said excitedly. "Call me a liar, but I think it is! Holy shit, that's them!"

Lake snatched up the pair of binoculars Ahmad had taken from one of the dead terrorists the night before. His arms were so tired that they trembled, and he had to lean against the tree to hold the field of view steady as he examined the vessel. As he zoomed in on the flying bridge he instantly recognized the black arms and face of Chief Louis at the wheel. Who better to conn the decrepit diesel-driven vessel than *Providence*'s best diesel mechanic. Lake's heart filled with hope once again. He may have been an hour late, but Captain Edwards had held true to his word. He had found a means to pass the reefs and get the shore party off Bunda. *Providence* must have spent all morning locating the drifting and abandoned vessel, and Louis must have nurtured the *Mendar*'s aging engines like a baby to get her here so quickly.

The boat continued driving toward the shore, heading generally toward their location, no doubt guided by the same GPS satellites Lake and the shore party had used to lead them there. Lake and Michaelson exchanged glances, and the big chief actually smiled. Lake wanted to run down to the beach and wave his arms so that the men on the *Mendar* could see him, but he didn't dare leave cover for fear of the watching Al Islamiyyah eyes on the road above.

"Those rocks will stop him from coming any closer," Michaelson said pointing to the breaking surf a couple hundred yards out from the beach where a pattern of jutting rocks poked above the surface. Even from this distance Lake could see the sudsy seawater rivulets from the last series of waves streaming back into the sea through the rocks' myriad of time-eroded fissures. The rocks' narrow spacing afforded no safe place for the *Mendar* to pass through, and this became apparent when the fishing boat spun her shaft astern and came to a complete stop on the rocks' seaward side.

"Looks like we've got a good swim ahead of us," Lake said. "I don't know if we can swim a hundred yards in that surf. Especially you, Chief."

Still looking through the binoculars, Lake saw activity now on the *Mendar*'s deck. Several U.S. sailors in blue jumpsuits and blue ball caps were rigging something off the fishing boat's fantail. It was *Providence*'s dinghy. The same one used to sneak up on the *Mendar* several nights before. Edwards had thought of everything. Within minutes the rubber craft had set out for the shore, two muscular sailors briskly paddling as they skillfully maneuvered it through the rocks.

"They'll be here any minute!" Lake said, then shook the sleeping Teresa. "Teresa, our ride's here! We've got to get moving!"

Just then Ahmad broke through the trees, his face as concerned as Lake had ever seen it.

"I got close enough to the men by the road to hear them talking," Ahmad caught his breath. He must have sprinted the whole way back to be so winded. "I counted sixteen of them, definitely Al Islamiyyah. They've seen the fishing boat and the dinghy and they're coming to investigate. We have only minutes before they get here."

Teresa gazed at the beach where the two men in the dinghy had just touched the shore and were dragging the craft onto dry land. "How are we all going to fit in that?" she asked.

They all stared at each other as the cold realization sank in. The rubber boat could hold only four people at most, and two of those spots would be occupied by the sailors who had paddled it ashore. Not all of them could go. At least, not all in one trip.

"I will swim," Ahmad said matter-of-factly as he pulled off his shirt and kicked his shoes into the sand. "You all must decide as you will."

Without further hesitation, Ahmad darted from their concealed spot and sprinted toward the water. Lake watched with envy as the iron-man agent ran past the confused sailors, standing with paddles in hand by the beached dinghy, and dived head-first into the sea. Surfacing a few seconds later, his lean arms and legs broke into a brisk stroke that propelled him seemingly without effort through the waves toward the waiting *Mendar*. Even after the intense physical exertions of the last few days, Ahmad still had enough stamina left in him to qualify for the Olympics. His abrupt departure and willingness to abandon his comrades of the past few days so quickly did not surprise Lake. After all, Ahmad had made it no secret that his mission came first. Lake, Michaelson, and Teresa were merely means for him to escape and thus accomplish his mission. Now that the means of escape had appeared, he no longer needed them and cared little if they lived or died.

Now Lake was solely in charge and knew he had to make a quick decision. There were three passengers, and two seats. The choice was clear.

He moved out of the brush cover and waved to one of the sailors on the beach.

"O'Shea!" Lake shouted.

O'Shea was mindlessly staring after the strange Arab man who had just sprinted past him and jumped into the water when he heard Lake's voice.

"O'Shea!" Lake said hurriedly, "Get your ass up here and help me get Chief Michaelson down to the dinghy!"

O'Shea tossed his paddles into the raft and headed up the sandy slope toward Lake, leaving his comrade alone on the beach.

"All right, here he comes," Lake said, turning first to Teresa and then to Michaelson.

"You get your ass on that raft, Lieutenant!" the chief seethed.

Lake turned to see that Michaelson now held Ahmad's discarded AK-47, and it was leveled squarely at Lake's torso. Leaning against the tree while biting back the pain in his knee, the big chief's eyes met Lake's with a fierce, determined look.

"What the hell?" Lake gasped.

"Take Miss Whitehead with you and get the hell out!"

"Are you nuts?" Lake said, advancing toward him. "Give me that thing!"

Michaelson snapped off the weapon's safety, startling both Lake and Teresa.

"I'm not joking, Lieutenant! I'm staying behind! Somebody's got to cover the raft, and you're sure as hell not suited for it!"

As Lake wiped the sand from his eyes he heard faint voices

coming from the jungle. Michaelson was right about one thing. There was no way the raft could make it out of rifle range before the Al Islamiyyah fighters showed up. Once the terrorists reached the beach, the raft would be an easy target. Someone would have to divert their attention until the raft made it to a safe distance.

"Good to see you, sir! Chief!" O'Shea said excitedly as he finally reached their position, totally oblivious to what had just transpired. "By the way, who the hell was that guy who jumped in the water back there? Are we taking him with us, too?"

Lake locked his eyes on Michaelson's. The indomitable chief's face was fixed in a feral stare that clearly communicated his intention to remain. Lake knew that any argument on his part would be futile.

"Come on, O'Shea," Lake ordered, not taking his eyes off Michaelson. "Let's get Miss Whitehead on the raft." Lake then looked to Teresa. She was obviously moved by Michaelson's decision to stay.

"Go with O'Shea, Teresa," he said in a gentler tone.

O'Shea appeared confused but didn't argue with his superior officer. "Ma'am," he said as he motioned for Teresa to follow him.

A solitary tear streamed down Teresa's dirty face as she glanced from Michaelson to Lake and then back to Michaelson again. She awkwardly approached the brutish chief, leaning up to kiss him on his sweaty cheek, before running down the sandy slope to follow O'Shea.

A small smile appeared on Michaelson's lips as he stared after her, then his eyes met Lake's again. The two had been at odds for the past three years, and shaking hands would have seemed terribly out of place. Lake gave the chief a simple nod, then followed the others down the slope, leaving him alone on the shady hill with the shore party's small cache of weapons.

Lake had trouble keeping up with O'Shea and Teresa. His legs were sore from the two days of cross-country travel, and it made running in sand extremely difficult. The two reached the raft well ahead of him. When he finally caught up with

them, the two sailors had already started hefting the raft down
to the water. Teresa had the paddles in her arms as she encour-
aged him to hurry. Lake nodded to her after catching a
glimpse at Ahmad's swimming form, far out in the surf, already half the distance to the *Mendar*.

As the raft splashed down into the water, the two sailors
immediately helped Teresa get aboard.

"Get in!" Lake directed them, as he grabbed hold of the
raft to hold it steady.

O'Shea and the other sailor dutifully obeyed, throwing
their legs over the spongy floatations until they were straddling them with their paddles held at the ready. The weight of
the two men quickly bottomed the raft, which was sitting in
only a few inches of water. With the dinghy firmly planted in
the sand, O'Shea tossed his paddle down and prepared to get
out and push, but Lake stopped him.

"Stay in there, damn it!" Lake shouted. "I'll push you off!"

Lake buried his shoulder into the rubbery stern and pushed
with all his might, his feet sliding in the wet sand until he was
on his knees. Then a small wave slapped against the shore,
raising the water level just enough to make his efforts successful. The raft slid off the sandy bottom and into the deeper water just a few feet beyond.

As Lake picked himself up out of the knee-deep water and
stood facing the raft, the two sailors brought the raft under
control with their paddles. Teresa and O'Shea frantically motioned for him to jump in, but instead Lake reached out and
gave the raft a good push away from the shore.

"Row for the *Mendar*!" Lake ordered from the shore. "And
hurry!"

O'Shea looked confused as he began to paddle, but the
gloomy smile on Teresa's face indicated that she knew all
along what Lake was going to do. She knew that he would
never leave Michaelson alone on this island, and Lake suddenly thought it funny how after only a few days she knew
him better than he knew himself.

Catching one last warm look from Teresa, Lake turned and
rushed back up the sandy beach.

* * *

"YOU'RE a damn fool!" Michaelson muttered as he stacked their few extra magazines on a fallen palm tree frond to keep them out of the sand. "Young and stupid, that's what you are!"

"I guess that makes you old and stupid, doesn't it?" Lake said with a grin as he slid to a better position to observe the beach, trying hard to keep the AK-47's breech away from the fine powdery sand.

In the few moments they had to spare, Lake and Michaelson had taken up position in a thick patch of brush on a small hill overlooking the beach. The voices in the jungle had grown louder, then fainter, and were now growing louder again, and Lake could only assume the terrorists were having problems finding the beach through dense forest. From experience, he knew it afforded few opportunities to collect bearings. He had had the luxury of the GPS unit on the satellite phone. The terrorists probably weren't as lucky. Regardless of whether they had a GPS or not, they seemed to have finally found the beach. The voices were getting much closer now and were almost upon them.

Lake looked out at the water. A hundred yards away or so, the raft crept along at a snail's pace, the sailor's paddles kicking up white splashes as they rowed smartly. They were moving as fast as they could but they were still well within small-arms range. He could see Teresa's face between the two sailors as she stared back at the island, and he wondered what she was thinking. He had already written off his own chances, but if she made it, that would be enough.

"Keep quiet and follow my lead. Understand?" Michaelson whispered. "I've got a little more experience at this kind of thing than you do. So, don't shoot until I tell you to."

Lake had no argument since the only time he'd ever fired a gun was during his bi-annual qualification at the weapons range on Oahu. Like most officers, he'd never taken the qualification seriously. As a full-fledged certified navy marksman, Michaelson was by far the better gun expert. With that in mind, Lake nudged the spare Kalashnikov rifle lying between them a little closer to Michaelson, figuring it would be better to have the spare weapon near his hands.

"There!" Michaelson whispered, pointing toward the jungle's edge.

Down the hill and not thirty yards from where they lay, a dozen heavily armed men emerged from the trees. They wore camouflaged uniforms of various types. Some even wore the traditional red and white Islamic turbans like Lake had seen so many times during Persian Gulf port calls. Many had beards and they all appeared to be of Middle Eastern descent. They crept out of the forest at a crouch, holding their weapons close to their chests as if they expected an ambush at any moment. Most likely, they knew what Ahmad was capable of and were proceeding with due caution. But once they sighted *Providence*'s dinghy bobbing on the waves, any semblance of precaution gave way and a blood-craving frenzy took over. They began yelling in Arabic, raising their weapons above their heads, and running forward to gain better vantage points from which to shoot. They made no attempt to take cover but instead spread out at several-yard intervals along the open beach, some crouching, some standing, each taking aim with whatever weapon he had.

One terrorist stood about ten paces behind the rest. He carried an RPG, which he was in the process of loading when Michaelson pointed him out as their first target. As the other terrorists started shooting to get the range on the defenseless rubber raft, Lake saw the RPG man's head jerk to the side. The man fell into the sand and rolled limply down the steep slope until his body came to rest in an inch-deep puddle of water. It took Lake a few seconds to realize that Michaelson had shot him. Though the death shot had been fired right beside him, the loud clamor from the various small arms on the beach had masked the AK-47's report.

Before the other terrorists even noticed their fallen comrade, Michaelson had killed three more. Lake found himself staring in wonder at the chief's deadly aim, but quickly snapped out of it when Michaelson rapped him in the shoulder with the butt of his rifle.

"Shoot, you asshole!" Michaelson shouted.

Pulling himself together, Lake noticed the two terrorists closest to him leveling their weapons in his direction. He squeezed the AK-47's trigger and sent several bursts in their direction. His muzzle was so close to the ground that it kicked up sand, which the wind blew right back into his eyes, blinding him momentarily. When he could finally see again, one of his targets lay motionless, apparently dead. The other was crouching and appeared to be wrestling with a jammed weapon. Lake squeezed off another burst. The man took the rounds across the neck in a spatter of blood and then dropped to the ground, vainly reaching for his jugular vein as it emptied the contents of his arteries onto the white sand. He was dead within a minute.

With half their number down, the Al Islamiyyah men abandoned the fight and darted for the cover of the jungle. Many must have been uncertain of Lake and Michaelson's location, because they ran straight across their field of fire. Michaelson never stopped firing, expending one magazine after the other into the backs of the fleeing terrorists. When all his magazines were finally shot, he grabbed up the spare Kalashnikov and continued firing, cheering as he knocked one enemy down, then two, then three. Lake noticed a wild expression on the chief's face as he sat up, then eventually stood to get a better angle on his prey, completely ignoring the pain in his purplish, swollen leg.

Then Lake heard the chief's bolt slide back.

"I'm out!" he shouted, picking up his AK-47 again. "I can still see two of those bastards through the trees! Here, Lieutenant, toss me your spare magazine!"

Lake obeyed, hurling his extra clip in Michaelson's direction. The chief caught the clip in mid air and with one motion slammed the fresh cartridge in place. Then he moved away from the cover of the brush and limped to a new spot beside a grove of palm trees where he could get a better shot. Lake watched as Michaelson drew a bead on the fleeing men. Lake could not see them from his position, but apparently Michaelson could. Michaelson then squeezed off a couple of rounds and gave a whooping yell that made Lake wonder if the chief's swollen knee had gone to his head.

"War! Glorious war!" Michaelson shouted, almost laughing, then glanced back at Lake. "I got one, Lieutenant! But, damn it all, that other bastard got away!"

Not knowing quite what to say, Lake gave a smiling thumbs-up then, looked out to sea to check on the dinghy's status. It had reached the rocks. Good. A few more minutes of rowing would put it alongside the *Mendar*. It was well out of range now and only a very lucky shot from the shore could hit it. At least Teresa was safe.

"Let's restock our ammo," Michaelson said as he limped over to one prostrate terrorist stretched out on the sand. Making certain the man was dead before he searched through his ammo pouch, Michaelson sprayed the terrorist with a short burst from his rifle and sent the limp body into convulsions.

"We better stay under cover, Chief," Lake yelled from the concealed position. "There might be more of them out there."

Michaelson ignored him and continued rifling through the dead body.

Then Lake heard it. A thumping, thunderous noise. It shook the ground and seemed to come from all directions at once, growing louder at an alarming rate. He knew it could mean only one thing.

The charging Huey helicopter suddenly appeared above the tall trees, its whirring rotors almost low enough to touch the jungle canopy. The sole surviving terrorist more than likely had access to a radio and more than likely had vectored Musa's chopper directly on top of them. Before Lake could think straight, the helo had moved above the beach. The two men in the cockpit were clearly visible from his concealed position, both wearing headsets and one eagerly pointing to the exposed Michaelson down on the open beach. Which one was Musa? Lake wondered. If only he hadn't given his last magazine to Michaelson, if only Ahmad hadn't used the last of his forty-five caliber rounds to execute those terrorists last night, he could end this terrorist's reign right here and now. Even *he* could make the shot at this range.

As the menacing helo rotated around, Lake saw the door gunner swing his mounted machine gun toward Michaelson's position. The chief was caught in the open, in the sand, with a bum leg, and a look of horror fell over his face as he realized that he could not get away. But, true to form, fierce aggression soon replaced the horror and the muscle-bound chief brought his rifle up to challenge the hovering helo. But the challenge was short-lived. Before Michaelson could get off two rounds, the door machine gun opened up with a long burst, the heavy caliber weapon ringing out over the thundering rotors. The ensuing fusillade of large-diameter shells tore into Michaelson's body at the waist, splitting him into two distinct pieces in the blink of an eye. Lake had to turn away as Michaelson's torso fell on one side of the dead terrorist he'd been rifling only a few moments before, his legs on the other, a large patch of blood-spattered sand all around.

Expecting the helo to fire at him next, Lake was surprised when it turned and headed out to sea. The men inside must not have seen him hiding in the tall bushes. The helo was now headed for its primary target, the *Mendar*, helplessly riding the waves just beyond the rocks. Of course, the terrorist Musa would have concluded by now that this fishing boat was Ahmad's means of escape, and that simple fact marked the *Mendar* and everyone aboard her for certain death, including Teresa.

The Huey pointed toward the vulnerable fishing boat, then dipped its nose and accelerated. Lake knew that he had to do something. The fishing boat didn't stand a chance against the Huey, no matter how good Ahmad was with a gun. *Providence* had nothing in her small-arms arsenal that could easily bring down a helicopter. Most likely, the men on board the *Mendar* were armed with nothing more than a few M-16s.

He had to do something, or Teresa was dead!

Then Lake saw it. The unfired RPG launcher still lay in the sand only a few yards from the bloody spot where Michaelson's bullet had brained its owner. It was his only chance. Every passing second the helo drew farther and farther away. He had to hurry!

Lake dashed from his hiding place and bounded across the sloping beach, covering the distance in seconds, leaping the final yards to the weapon, where he unintentionally fell face-first into the bloody sand. Assuming a kneeling position, he plucked up the weapon and hefted it onto his shoulder. He'd never fired an RPG before, never even held one. It seemed very cumbersome, a lot heavier than he'd imagined, and this one reeked of grease and grimy hands.

How hard could it be to shoot? he thought.

The range to the helo was rapidly increasing as it picked up speed. A few moments more and the RPG would be useless. Lake knew it was now or never. Leveling the weapon on the helo's tail rotor, he aimed a little higher at the last second, then squeezed the trigger. The launch tube shook violently on his shoulder as the rocket roared away, its white smoky trail completely obliterating his view.

As the smoke cleared, he saw the rocket-propelled grenade speeding toward the Huey in a corkscrew-like fashion. For the first forty or fifty yards it flew relatively straight, but shortly thereafter it seemed to lose all control. It veered right, then left, then dove at a steep angle straight for the water's surface, exploding harmlessly with a large geyser to clearly mark the spot.

"Shit!" Lake shouted, hurling the launcher into the sea.

The *Mendar* had no hope now. Teresa had no hope. The Huey would certainly destroy her. Lake's frustration brought him to the point of throwing sand in the helo's direction. But after he tossed two handfuls, the helo made a large banking turn to the left and headed back toward the beach. Though the Huey was still a couple hundred yards away, he could clearly see that the nose had steadied on his position. Someone on the helo must have seen the RPG hit the water, and now the helo was coming back to take care of him as it had Michaelson.

Lake stood alone and in the open. He knew there was nowhere to run. He was near the water's edge and would have to clamber up the steep sloping beach to find adequate cover. The helo would be on him by the time he reached it. Lake suddenly had visions of Chief Michaelson as he faced the charging helo, and hoped he could meet his death with the same display of courage. The rotors pounded the air and made the sand vibrate under his shoes, and now he could see the muzzle of the heavy machine gun protruding out of the helo's side door.

The pain would be brief, and then it would all be over. Only one tiny moment of agony, he kept telling himself. Funny how two weeks ago he'd expected to leave the navy, and now he was about to die on a forgotten island at the hands of some terrorist. He was going to die in the service of the same navy he'd detested all these years. Lake almost chuckled at the irony of it all. As the helo drew within fifty yards of the beach, it started to turn to the side to expose its lethal machine gun, and Lake closed his eyes to wait for the inevitable.

But then, an earth shattering roar much louder than the Huey's rotors suddenly filled the air. It resembled the sound of a low jet engine buzzing the ground, but this noise was even louder. Lake felt it coming from the jungle behind him, increasing with such volume and intensity that Lake instinctively dropped to the ground, anticipating his eardrums were about to break.

Then a streak of white smoke and flame appeared over the jungle. It shot low across the sky, skimming over the treetops before heading out to sea. It was obviously a missile, and Lake watched with quivering awe as it headed straight for the Huey. Musa and his men had about two point four milliseconds to pray to Allah before the missile slammed into their helo's left windshield at one thousand knots, almost certainly impaling the co-pilot before exploding in a tremendous fireball that blew out the helo's backside along with the aircraft's internals and a few incinerated body parts. A thousand pieces of burning metal, fabric, and flesh rained down on the sea below, followed closely by the big blackened shell, its rotors still spinning as they impacted the glistening surface and snapped like fragile twigs, ricocheting in all directions.

Lake clutched the cold sand in his hands to make sure he was still alive, and breathed a deep sigh of relief. Just as he began to wonder where the timely missile had come from, a distant jet engine roared above the island behind him. Holding his hand up to block the sun, he caught a glimpse of an F-16 fighter dropping flares at regular intervals as it maneuvered sharply in and out of Bunda's high mountain peaks. The jet was the wrong color to be U.S. Air Force, and Lake quickly deduced that it was most likely the same Indonesian warplane that had been hunting Musa's helo all day. The fighter loitered for only a few seconds more before it hit its afterburner and disappeared into the sun, its pilot apparently satisfied with his kill.

As the helo's swirling remains sank into the shallows, Lake suddenly felt numb. The terrorist leader, Musa Muhammad, was dead, but at what cost? Michaelson, Whitehead, and Reynoso. Was it worth losing those good men to kill that terrorist madman? How does one come out on top in such an exchange?

Ahmad would accomplish his mission now, though Lake cared little. Teresa was safe, and that was all that really mattered. Somehow he had managed to convince himself over the last few days that it was his personal duty to get her through this thing alive. Perhaps that duty had given him the strength to go on.

As the dinghy shoved off again from the distant *Mendar* to retrieve him, Lake walked up the sloping beach and came upon Michaelson's mutilated body. He forced himself to go though the chief's bloody pockets and pick out anything his family might want to cherish, for they would not be getting his body back. There were more Al Islamiyyah fighters on this island, and once they realized their leader had been reduced to atoms, they would all converge on this spot.

The *Mendar* needed to leave, and leave quickly, before any new threats popped up. Strangely, Lake actually smiled at the thought of returning to the waiting *Providence* lying submerged somewhere beyond the reefs. For the last three years he'd been counting the days until he got off her, and now he couldn't wait to be aboard her again.

Chapter 21

"DIVING Officer, submerge the ship to two hundred fifty feet."

"Submerge the ship to two hundred fifty feet, aye, sir."

The klaxon sounded throughout the ship, and Edwards watched through the periscope as the main ballast tanks vented their air volume and filled with water, the resulting geysers shooting fifty feet into the air. Through the misty spouts in the fading light, Edwards took one last look at the fishing boat, now cast adrift. He breathed a sigh of relief that *Providence*'s surviving shore party members were now safely back aboard.

Providence had rendezvoused with the *Mendar* just as it emerged from Bunda's reef barrier over three hours ago. Not wishing to attract the attention of any onlookers ashore, Edwards had kept the *Providence* submerged until the two vessels were well beyond visual range of the island's coast, all the while keeping a sharp eye and ear out for any pursuers. It wasn't until the sun had set behind the just visible peaks of the distant Bunda Islands that *Providence* finally surfaced to transfer personnel from the fishing boat. Edwards remembered seeing the worn-out and beaten faces as they came down the forward hatch one at a time. Whitehead's daughter, the operative called Ahmad, and a barely recognizable Lieutenant Lake. Lake's face spoke volumes without ever having to utter a word, and Edwards knew that the young officer who had stepped off his ship four days before was gone forever, replaced by this hardened, wiser, and much more mature man. As much as Edwards ached to know what had happened, he had refrained from asking him any questions. The whole lot of them were beaten and exhausted, and rest was the only remedy to restore their spirits. On the long trip back to Pearl there would be plenty of opportunities to discuss the events that had transpired ashore.

His plan had worked thanks to the trusty *Mendar* and her shallow draft. Finding the drifting vessel that morning had not been difficult. Thankfully, the Indonesian Coast Guard hadn't yet gotten around to retrieving the abandoned vessel. Chief Louis had one hell of a time getting the *Mendar*'s aging diesel engine to cooperate, but he worked one of his miracles with the ancient engine and forced it to put out the needed horse-power, eventually making a good sixteen knots. But despite his efforts, the *Mendar* still arrived over an hour late. An hour that proved to be fatal for Chief Michaelson. Edwards couldn't help but think what might have happened if *Providence* had been able to use both her main engines, instead of the one she limped on now. It was a simple math problem. The extra fif-teen or so knots put out by the second main engine might have made the difference. *Providence* would have found the drifting *Mendar* earlier, and Louis would have had more time to get her back to Bunda to pick up the shore party. Perhaps he would have arrived on time, perhaps even early. The thought haunted Edwards, but there was nothing he could do about it now. It was all over. The rest of the shore party was safe. The *Mendar*, for all her shortcomings, had served them well. Of course, Louis deserved most of the credit, and Edwards made a mental note to decorate the chief the next time he had the opportunity.

"Forty-five feet," the diving officer called as *Providence*'s deck tilted down. "Five-five feet . . . five-six feet . . ."

The periscope soon went under, and Edwards turned the hydraulic ring in the overhead to lower it.

"Helm, ahead standard. Steady on course zero seven five."

The helmsman acknowledged the order and *Providence*'s bow swung around to steady on the first leg of her voyage home.

"Captain?" Coleman had appeared on the periscope stand behind him. He held an oil-soaked and badly torn industrial Kimwipe in one hand and a long metallic extraction tool in the other. Odd implements to bring from the engine room to the conn, but Edwards understood the meaning before Coleman said a word.

"Is *that* what caused the main engine to fail?" Edwards said incredulously.

Coleman nodded, staring at the twisted Kimwipe as he turned it over several times in his hand. "We had to tear apart the whole engine to get to it, Captain. We found it in the lube oil suction line for the forward turbine bearing. It was blocking oil flow completely."

"Damage to the turbine?"

"Minimal, sir. Amazing, since we were answering a flank bell when it happened. I've looked it over and I think everything's okay. I think the automatic trip saved it." Coleman paused when he saw Edwards looking distant, then added, "If you'd like to come back and take a look at it, Captain . . ."

"No, no. You're my acting engineer. I trust your judgment." Edwards waved dismissively. His mind had already moved on from the main engine failure and was now concentrating on its cause. Something troubled him deeply, and he wondered if the same thought had already crossed Coleman's mind too. Kimwipes didn't just magically appear inside main engine housings.

As if on cue, Coleman said, "I'm a little concerned as to how this Kimwipe got in there, Captain." He lowered his voice so that only Edwards could hear him. "The lube oil strainers should've caught it. The only way it could've made it past them is if someone intentionally removed the strainers and placed this Kimwipe downstream."

Edwards nodded. His thoughts exactly. The look in Coleman's eyes told him they had both come to the same conclusion. Someone had intentionally sabotaged the main engine.

Someone on board was a saboteur!

The chilling thought made the hairs on the back of Edwards' neck stand up, as he searched his mind for who the culprit might be.

Coleman made to speak, but then hesitated.

"What is it?" Edwards prompted.

"Well, sir." Coleman hesitated and looked over his shoulder before continuing. A few men near the chart tables chuckled and joked, completely oblivious to the situation Coleman and Edwards now discussed. "I'm no detective, Captain, but that guy we pulled out of the water with the Eng has bothered me ever since he came aboard. I know he claims to be an Indonesian marine and all, and I know he had an I.D., but he asks a lot of questions. Too many questions, if you ask me."

For the most part, Edwards had given the Indonesian marine free access throughout the ship. The man seemed harmless enough at first glance, and appeared to be enjoying his stay. Most times when Edwards saw him, he was socializing with the crew on the mess deck. That seemed to be where he spent most of his time. Edwards had considered denying him access to the engine room but once he found out that the man was a chain smoker, he abolished that thought. The engine room's shaft alley was the only designated smoking area on the ship, and he didn't see the need to deprive the man of a good smoke to pass the time.

Coleman's theory was certainly plausible, but Edwards wasn't sure. Either way, he couldn't take any chances now.

"Chief of the Watch," Edwards called across the conn to the ballast control panel.

"Yes, sir," the chief said, swiveling in his chair.

"Have the security petty officer apprehend our Indonesian guest and confine him to the doc's office."

"Aye, aye, Captain." The chief looked puzzled, but removed the phone off the panel to contact the security petty officer down in the torpedo room.

Coleman appeared satisfied. "With your permission, Captain, I'll start putting the main engine back together. It shouldn't take too long. Of course, we'll have to do a bowed rotor warm-up before we place it back on the line."

"Good. Let me know if you run into any troubles."

Coleman nodded and made to walk away, but Edwards stopped him.

"Just in case we're wrong about our guest," Edwards said in an uneasy tone. "I think it'd be a good idea if we exhausted every possible option. Make sure you check the propulsion lube oil system on both port and starboard sides for total integrity. And don't forget to check the engineering logs. There might be some clue for us in there as well."

"Aye, aye, sir," Coleman said before disappearing down the aft ladder.

Resting his hands on the cold railing surrounding the periscope stand, Edwards glanced at the men manning the various stations around him. They seemed unfazed by the curious order to arrest the Indonesian marine, and Edwards chalked it up to numb indifference. Most of them probably could not care less at this point. They'd had their brush with death, and now they had homes and families to think of. *Providence* was once again on her way home, and this time she would make it *all* the way home. With her missiles expended, her food supplies running low, and her crew's fatigue at its zenith, ComSubPac would have no choice but to bring her in. The crew certainly sensed this and Edwards could tell by the warm smiles on their faces that they would need little of his leadership on the voyage back to Pearl. They were on autopilot now, with only one goal in mind.

"At two hundred fifty feet, Captain," the diving officer announced.

"Steady on course zero seven five, Captain" reported the helmsman immediately after.

"Very well, Dive. Very well, Helm."

The control room quickly settled in to the same quiet cruising routine of all lengthy voyages. The extra quartermasters left the room, leaving the lone quartermaster of the watch to man the chart table by himself. The messenger of the watch moved silently around the room collecting coffee orders. Near the OOD's podium, Fremont reviewed the deck log in preparation of relieving the conn. The gentle rumble of a distant volcano, almost tranquilizing in nature, emanated from the overhead sonar speaker. It and the whirring fans were the only noises in the room.

Edwards struggled to keep his eyes open as he focused on the sonar display above him and the bright green swath marking the volcano's location. He politely refused the messenger's offer to bring him coffee. Fremont would be relieving him soon, and he was in dire need of a few hours' sleep. He been living on coffee for the last twenty-four hours, and the last thing he needed now was more caffeine in his bloodstream. Even with all that had transpired in the last twenty-four hours, his weary mind could focus only on the bunk in his stateroom.

Suddenly, Fremont stood before him. "I'm ready to relieve you, sir," he said cheerfully. The navigator still reeked of garlic from the wardroom's evening meal.

Edwards was too tired to be annoyed at the odor. "I'm ready to be relieved."

Just then, the overhead speaker cracked, "Conn, Sonar. Picking up funny noises astern, bearing two three four. Sounds like intermittent cavitation."

Edwards glanced up at the display to see tiny bright green dots appear at irregular intervals along the southwesterly bearing. He shook his groggy head to make sense of what he was looking at. Edwards then glanced at the *Providence*'s depth and speed. It took only a few moments before the realization set in, and he and Fremont exchanged panicked expressions.

"Helm, ahead full, cavitate!" Edwards shouted across the room. "Chief of the Watch, sound general quarters!"

Everyone in the room appeared puzzled at first, some apparently convinced it was a drill. But as the *Providence* picked up speed, they gradually realized that this was anything but a drill, and that the ship was certainly in danger. The fourteen-bell gong rang throughout the ship and soon the room filled to capacity as each man once again occupied his battle station.

Miller appeared in the room, zipping up his blue jumpsuit, his khaki belt completely forgotten.

"What is it, Captain?" he asked as one of the fire-control technicians tossed him a wireless headset.

"Helm, left fifteen degrees. Steady on three four zero," Edwards ordered before turning to Miller and pointing at the green blips on the display. "Torpedo in the water. The *Hatta*'s out there. That's one of her torpedoes trying to sneak up on us. She probably fired it while we were still on the surface and was trying to guide it in at silent speed. They'd have to keep it slow at this shallow depth, otherwise we'd hear it cavitate and detect it. I'm guessing we dove at just the right moment, and when we picked up speed a few moments ago they were forced to adjust the torpedo's speed accordingly. Fortunately for us, their torpedo cavitates a lot easier than the *Providence*'s does."

"Holy shit, sir, they must've been trailing us all along." Miller stared disbelievingly at the display. "I guess we didn't hit her after all, sir."

"Not necessarily, Weps. There has to be a reason they didn't attack us earlier. It wouldn't have been that difficult. We certainly didn't break any speed records while we were in company with the *Mendar*. I bet your torpedo exploded close enough to damage her propulsion systems at least, and the *Hatta*'s spent the better part of the afternoon catching up with us."

Miller raised his eyebrows and shrugged, then focused his attention on the fire-control consoles.

Glancing at the speed log, Edwards saw that the *Providence* was making only twenty-one knots, just as he expected. Coleman had not had enough time to put the port main engine back together. The starboard engine was having to turn the big shaft by itself.

"Chief of the Watch," Edwards called. "Tell Maneuvering to push number one main engine as far as its limits will take it. I need every last knot."

The chief of the watch nodded as he relayed the order into his phone set.

Once again, the WLR-9 active intercept unit squawked from the starboard bulkhead.

"Conn, Sonar. Torpedo has increased speed. It's gone into active searching mode. Range, two thousand yards off the port quarter."

Good, Edwards thought. As long as that torpedo was in active pinging mode, they might have a chance. *Providence* couldn't outrun it on one main engine, but she could certainly lead it on a chase. He watched and waited as the torpedo line on the sonar display passed into *Providence*'s port baffle. Now he had the torpedo following him on a northwesterly heading.

"No countermeasures, Captain?" Miller asked hesitantly.

"Countermeasures will only fool that torpedo for so long, Weps. Besides, I *want* this torpedo to follow us." As Miller returned to the starboard-side consoles with a quizzical expression on his face, Edwards called after him. "Warm up the weapons in tubes two and three and prepare the tubes for firing in all respects. Open outer doors as soon as you're ready, and stand by!"

"Aye, aye, Captain," Miller answered, then quickly began issuing orders to his people.

"Nav, give me the range and bearing to the *Mendar*'s last position. Helm, left full rudder!"

As *Providence*'s deck heeled over to port Edwards grabbed the railing to stay on balance, eagerly awaiting the response from Fremont, who now fumbled with the chart table's compass ruler. After what seemed like an eternity, he reported, "The *Mendar*'s position bears two six one, range twenty-two hundred yards, Captain."

"Helm, steady on course two six one!"

Fremont's calculation had taken so long that the *Providence*'s nose was already close to the ordered heading, forcing the helmsman to jerk his control to the "right full" position in order to check the submarine's swing in time to steady on the new course.

As *Providence* righted herself and the deck leveled, Edwards examined the sonar display. The thin green line had passed out of the port baffle momentarily due to *Providence*'s sharp turn, but it soon edged back into it as it mirrored *Providence*'s course. Edwards could picture the torpedo speeding through the dark water a thousand yards astern, following the maneuvering submarine as if the two were connected by an invisible string.

"Conn, Sonar. Torpedo bears zero eight one, directly astern. Range eight hundred yards!"

Edwards' sweaty palms squeezed the metal railing. The torpedo was closing *Providence*'s stern at five hundred yards per minute. It would all be over in less than two minutes. He glanced at the clock on the bulkhead. The digital display read 2033. He suddenly wondered if it would ever read 2035. Or would it end up a thousand fathoms below scattered on the lonely ocean floor with the rest of *Providence*'s wreckage?

"Recommend course correction to intercept the *Mendar*, Captain," Fremont said, now apparently understanding Edwards intentions. "Two five eight's a good course. Range four hundred yards"

"Helm, come left to two five eight," Edwards ordered, nodding an acknowledgment in Fremont's general direction.

As the helmsman skillfully nudged *Providence*'s bow over to the new course, Miller reported from the starboard side, "Outer doors are open on tubes two and three, Captain. Torpedoes two and three are ready for firing in all respects. Standing by."

"Conn, Sonar. Torpedo has shifted to terminal homing. Range, five hundred yards!"

This is it, Edwards thought. *It's now or never.*

"Dive, make your depth seventy feet! Helm, watch your heading!"

"Full rise on the fairwater planes!" the diving officer shouted. "Full rise on the stern planes! Establish a thirty degree up bubble!" The diving officer normally muttered commands to his planesman, but the adrenaline rush of the moment must have compelled him to shout the orders unconsciously.

Providence's deck tilted at an alarming rate as she drove toward the surface. Within seconds her deck was too steep to stand and everyone without a chair groped for something to hang on to before careening into the aft bulkhead. Any sailor walking down the fifty-foot straight section of the middle level passage would soon find himself riding an "E" ticket to the crew's mess.

With a firm grip on the platform railing, Edwards heard *Providence*'s hull creak from the rapid change in depth and felt the vibrations in his hands. The digital depth gauge continued to count down rapidly. Two hundred feet . . . one hundred fifty feet . . . one hundred feet . . .

Just as Edwards was beginning to think the ship wouldn't be able to pull down in time, the diving officer shouted, "Zero bubble! Make your depth seven zero feet!"

Instantly responding to the order they'd anticipated, the two planesmen pushed their control sticks to the floor until they reached the hard stops. The plane angle indicators on the ship's control panel flipped to the opposite direction as *Providence*'s giant control surfaces responded to the three-thousand-pound hydraulic fluid. The change in angle had an immediate effect and, remarkably, the ship never went a foot above seventy feet, instead leveling off just one foot below. Edwards watched as the two expert planesmen exchanged a silent nod. Their training and teamwork had paid off.

"Mark on top!" Fremont reported. "We're passing beneath the *Mendar* right now, sir."

Edwards wiped his brow. The *Mendar*'s keel hung down some twelve to fifteen feet. If *Providence* hadn't pulled out in time, her sail would've plowed into the fisherman's keel right about now. Even at this depth, the two were separated by only five or six feet of water, too close for comfort, but necessary to adequately fool the pursuing torpedo.

Edwards glanced at the WLR-9 active intercept display. Now only a couple hundred yards astern, the incoming torpedo still transmitted the terminal homing frequency. But now its transducer would be aimed up at the surface as it followed *Providence* to her new shallower depth. It would be painting both hulls with acoustic energy, receiving active returns from both the *Providence* and the *Mendar*. It would now have to choose between the two targets. One might expect the choice to be obvious, that a three-hundred-sixty foot submarine would present a much larger return than a fishing boat one tenth its size. One would be right too, if it weren't for the thin rubbery layer of anechoic foam covering *Providence*'s hull from stem to stern. Many of *Providence*'s own sailors probably thought the spongy substance was there to provide them better traction on deck, but in fact its *only* purpose was to absorb acoustic energy, and Edwards was counting on it to come through for them now. He was counting on the torpedo to shift its focus to the *Mendar*'s larger acoustic echo.

"Our stern's past the *Mendar*, Captain," Fremont reported, hovering over the tactical display.

"Dive, make your depth five hundred feet! Fast!" Edwards ordered.

He had to open the distance now and get some depth separation from the *Mendar*. And as *Providence* tilted to head back into the deep, it became a simple waiting game. With the *Hatta*'s torpedo traveling at thirty-six knots, he would not have to wait for very long. He squeezed the railing, praying that he had managed to trick the pursuing weapon.

Moments later, he had his answer. A loud *whack!* followed by a booming explosion shook the hull and seemed to thrust the deck forward several feet. *Providence* creaked and moaned as the shockwave rippled along her length from her spinning screw all the way up to her bulbous bow. Several men fell to the deck, but this time Edwards held on firmly to the railing. He knew the answer before sonar reported it.

"Conn, Sonar," the sonar chief's voice reported with audible relief. "Torpedo has detonated well astern!"

A cheer sounded throughout the room as every sailor at every station seemed to realize in unison that the ruse had worked. The torpedo had blown the abandoned *Mendar* to bits. But Edwards' face quickly suppressed any jubilation as he motioned for the men to attend to their stations. They were not in the clear yet. The *Hatta* was still out there.

The waterfall display in the overhead now showed a swath of bright green covering every point on the azimuth. The ship's hydrophone sensors were momentarily useless, saturated from the multiple pressure waves generated by the exploding torpedo. But all passive sonar systems used the same sound-pressure-level measurement as the means to detect contacts, including the *Hatta*'s. All were susceptible to this downside of the technology, and at this moment, Edwards was counting on it. If the *Hatta* were anywhere nearby, her sonar sensors would be experiencing the same exact anomaly. The sensors would take about a minute to recover, like a brief time-out for both teams, but Edwards intended to use it to *Providence*'s advantage.

"Helm, all stop. Dive, continue to five hundred feet," he said as he moved over to the weapons consoles to stand beside Miller. "Firing point procedures, Weps, on tubes two and three. We'll wait a few more seconds before firing. I want some of this speed off her to make sure we don't lose the guiding wires."

"Aye, aye, Captain," Miller acknowledged, then added quizzically, "Where shall we shoot them, sir? We've got no solution on the *Hatta*. Shit, we haven't even detected her yet."

"Don't worry about that. Just select a zero degree gyro angle and make sure you don't lose the wires."

As the puzzled Miller scrambled down the line of consoles to make sure all were ready, Edwards checked the speed log. *Providence* had slowed to less than ten knots. Any flow noise the *Hatta* could use to track her would be gone. The suspicious tonal that had pinpointed *Providence* like a beacon for the past week had disappeared in the last twenty-four hours, the offending equipment probably dislodged by the close torpedo explosion the night before, and at this moment Edwards was thankful for it. Now *Providence* could transform herself into a silent void in the ocean.

"Chief of the Watch," he called across the room, "Pass the word to all stations to rig the ship for ultra quiet. No repairs are authorized without my specific permission!"

Stopping all repairs would ensure no butterfingered sailor dropped a piece of equipment on the metal deck, or slammed a panel shut, or created some other transient that would give away their position. From this point on, silence took precedence over anything else.

"We're ready, Captain," Miller said, after his men finished entering the torpedoes' settings.

Edwards checked his watch and looked at the waterfall display, still saturated from the explosion. He hoped Peto's display on the *Hatta* was taking just as long to recover.

"Fire two!" Edwards said, and waited for the loud *whack!* The deck vibrated as the water ram launched the weapon from its tube three decks below, followed shortly thereafter by the customary pressure change throughout the ship. The torpedo was away.

"Fire three!"

The same sequence followed and Edwards immediately glanced up at the sonar display to make sure both torpedoes had launched while the system remained saturated. It was only another half minute later that the passive sonar system recovered and the bright green saturation disappeared. With her weapons now away, *Providence* would sit quiet and wait.

As a captain, Edwards always tried to place himself in his opponent's shoes. With any luck, Peto's display would have taken just as long to clear, perhaps longer, and Edwards began to wonder how Peto would react when the *Hatta*'s sonar display suddenly revealed two Mark 48 ADCAP torpedoes on the hunt and no trace of the *Providence*.

THE torpedo detonation had rocked the ship along its length, every compartment feeling the forceful jolt and shaking violently. The middle level officers' quarters was no exception. At the moment the torpedo detonated, Van Peenan had been resting his aching head on his pillow. The next moment, his rack spit him out like a piece of stale chewing gum, sending him careening across the room to impact with the wash closet on the opposite wall.

"Son of a bitch!" he cursed, as he rubbed the fresh bump on his head. "What the hell was that?"

It took Van Peenan only a few moments to realize *Providence* had just been rocked by a torpedo explosion, though this one seemed much farther away than the one that shook him out of his rack the night before. This one sounded farther astern.

What the hell is going on? he wondered. The ship must be under attack again. The speed was falling off. Shit, she must be damaged! Damn that asshole, Coleman! He couldn't run an engine room to save his fucking life! Captain Christopher will have his ass for that!

He heard footfalls in the passageway outside his stateroom and saw shadows intermittently blocking the small sliver of light at the foot of the door. Men ran to and fro, probably damage-control teams on their way to fight fires or make repairs. The mirrored wash closet cabinet above his head had popped open from the impact, and he picked himself up off the deck to close it. He flicked the light switch on the bulkhead and a single fluorescent bulb over the sink sputtered to life. In the dim lighting he could see the cuts and bruises on his face, the sunburned skin now peeling from his brow, the disheveled sun-bleached red hair.

He looked like shit, like some pathetic loser. Somewhere back in the engine room right now Dean was probably laughing his ass off at the thought.

Just then, the deck trembled beneath his feet. A loud *whack!* came from the torpedo room one deck below, soon followed by another. *Providence* was firing torpedoes. The battle must not be over yet.

As Van Peenan splashed his blistered face with cool water, an evil thought suddenly entered his aching head. He wondered why he hadn't thought of it before and could kick himself for keeping to his rack for so long when such a golden opportunity awaited. The thought revived him, and he suddenly felt a burst of adrenaline as he wiped his face with the towel. As the towel came down and he stared at his face in the mirror, he could not hold back the sinister grin rapidly forming there. Moments later he was pulling on his blue uniform jumpsuit, hardly able to keep from salivating at his perfect luck.

The battle was not over yet, and sometimes men die in battle.

"**ALL** stations report rigged for ultra quiet, Captain," the chief of the watch reported.

"Very well," Edwards responded over his shoulder before returning his attention to the weapon consoles. *Providence* was now invisible to any hydrophone more than two miles from the ship, and even inside that range a sonar operator would have to be pretty keen to detect the spinning pumps in the engine room, presently the only source of noise. This gave him a little peace of mind as he and Miller leaned over the operators' shoulders to see the telemetry data coming back from *Providence*'s two torpedoes. Both units were running normally with their guiding wires still intact.

"You ever heard of UUVs, Weps?" he asked.

"Unmanned Underwater Vehicles?" Miller replied. "Sure, Captain. UUVs for littoral ops. I've heard of them, but I've never seen one. Apparently the things are loaded with a ton of hydrophones and transducers with a thirty-mile spool of cable to stay in touch with the mother ship. You can launch 'em from miles away and let the UUV's robot brain go sniff out the bad guy. Then it transmits the data back to you via the cable. But what does that have to do with—"

"Think of it this way, Weps," Edwards interrupted him. "Our torpedoes are UUVs right now. They may be crude substitutes, but they've got transducers and we can steer them. That's all we need. I want you to send both weapons on a snake pattern search covering the southwestern quadrant."

"But, sir, the *Hatta* could be anywhere . . ."

"She's in the southwestern quadrant, Weps! I'm sure of it. Bunda is far to the southwest of us. If the *Hatta* spent all afternoon following us, she would have had to come from that quadrant. And if we damaged her propulsion system last night, as I suspect we did, she wouldn't have wasted the time to get around us before firing. I'm sure she fired the moment we came in range. *Think about it.* If *you* were her captain and *you* had just caught us on the surface, wouldn't you go ahead and shoot while you had the shot?"

Miller nodded. "I see your point, sir."

"And I'm sure she's no more than five thousand yards from us right now. She probably fired somewhere in the vicinity of the *Mendar*, so we must have closed the distance to her with our evasion maneuver."

As the console operators, each controlling one torpedo,

pulled up the tactical map view on their displays, Edwards and Miller watched intently. The maps were centered on the *Providence*'s position and had two green symbols, each representing one of *Providence*'s torpedoes, both now a few hundred yards away from the ship. As the operators typed in commands, the two torpedoes changed course toward the area southwest of the ship.

"Commence active search," Miller ordered.

The two operators responded and the dots on both weapons began tracking off in snaking arcs that wound far to the right and then returned far to the left, sweeping out every portion of the southwest quadrant. A rotating "V" shape, with its apex affixed to each symbol, swept from side to side across the torpedoes' bows, representing the aimed direction of the built-in sonar transducers.

Edwards could only imagine the horror Peto and his crew must be feeling at the moment to see two shipkillers searching for them at forty-five knots with active transducers pinging away. Despite his brief friendship with the rebel captain, their submarines were on different teams now, and only one could sail away from this contest. For the first time, he had the upper hand on Peto, and he could not let personal emotion keep him from exploiting it. The life of every man on the *Providence* depended on it.

Within moments, the operator in front of Miller reported, "Number two torpedo has acquired the target!"

Edwards was not surprised, and he felt almost guilty for his own mounting excitement when he saw a bright green "V" with a dot in the middle of it appear on the display ahead of *Providence*'s number two torpedo. It represented the *Hatta*'s position, a mere four thousand yards to the south-southwest. His deduction had proved to be correct.

"Conn, Sonar. Torpedo in the water!"

"Sonar, Conn, aye. Keep an eye on it," Edwards said calmly, knowing full well that Peto had fired the torpedo blindly, a last ditch effort, hoping *Providence* would take evasive action and reveal her position. Edwards knew Peto was grasping at straws, and he would not take the bait. The rebel captain had to know that his ship was doomed. With *Providence*'s number two torpedo now bathing his hull in acoustic energy and accelerating to sixty-five knots, Peto had few options left. The *Hatta* could not escape unless the *Providence* did something foolish and noisy, like running from an ill-aimed torpedo.

"Conn, Sonar, torpedo is tracking off to the east. It does not appear to be a threat."

Edwards smiled, a little relieved, but not surprised. Peto was indeed shooting in the blind, and had not detected *Providence*'s position.

"Target is picking up speed now, Captain," the console operator reported, as he read the data coming back from *Providence*'s torpedo. "Target is now heading two two zero, range five thousand yards, speed twelve knots. Torpedo number two has shifted to terminal homing!"

Edwards could picture the screaming twenty-one foot killer driving straight for the *Hatta*'s spinning screw. With a damaged propulsion train, Peto had to be pushing his battery to the limit to get the twelve knots out of his sub, but he had no hope of outrunning a Mark 48 ADCAP.

"Conn, Sonar. Picking up a countermeasures launch to the southwest."

The *Hatta*'s last chance, Edwards thought, but it was far too late to save her now.

"Warhead armed!" the operator for number two torpedo reported. "Torpedo detonation!"

One second later, a distant blast rumbled across the deep expanse, pulsating the billion water molecules between the one-thousand-pound HBX warhead detonation and the *Providence*'s steel hull. Though three miles away from the blast, the deck still shuddered beneath Edwards' feet from the massive explosion.

A loud cheer erupted throughout the room, and this time Edwards made no effort to stop it. The *Hatta* certainly could not recover from such a blast. Even if her countermeasures had managed to draw the weapon off at the last second, her engine room and shaft were most likely a mangled mess.

Miller could not contain himself either and began slapping Edwards on the back with undue familiarity.

Edwards let it go. He didn't care, but he didn't join in either. He simply stared at the small blip on the console, the blip that represented the sinking *Hatta*.

The loud whoops and cheers drowned out all other sounds, and Miller probably did not hear him when Edwards sadly mumbled, "Goodbye, Peto."

BACK in the engine room, Lieutenant Coleman heard the *Providence*'s torpedo explode as did the half dozen nuclear mechanics staring blankly at him as they lounged beside the half-assembled port main engine. Coleman had made it his priority to get the main engine back together once he heard that the *Hatta* was nearby, but the recent order to set ultra quiet conditions had ground that effort to a halt. Despite the ultra quiet order, they had made good progress and the only thing remaining was one final access plate, now lying on the deck with its associated metal bolts and fasteners. Of course, once that was done they'd also have to conduct a long warm-up cycle on the potentially bowed turbine, a long laborious process that required spinning the engine with steam in both the ahead and astern directions a couple times a minute for an entire hour.

Coleman felt fairly satisfied with the men's performance, especially since they had managed to assemble the engine without the experienced eye of the M division chief, Chief Hans, who was at this moment laid up in sick bay with a terrible contusion on his head from the previous night's action.

"Why we sittin' at all-stop?" one mechanic asked another, who was wearing a sound-powered phone set. "Did we get that bastard or what?"

"That's what it sounds like," the sailor replied. "Electrical operator came up on the line a few minutes ago. Said we got a hit. Said that's what the chief of the watch told him on the JA circuit."

Coleman could just picture the electrical operator in Maneuvering acting in his role as the central point of information dissemination—or gossip—to the forgotten watch-standers in the engine room. Why the men so direly needed to know always puzzled Coleman's duty-filled mind, and he tried to get the thought out of his head as he continued to review the engineering log bundle lying across his arms. He was certain that the now handcuffed and confined Indonesian marine was the saboteur, but Edwards had ordered the logs reviewed, so Coleman figured he'd knock it out while they waited.

He'd already made it through the last month's main engine logs, looking for anything out of the ordinary, but everything looked fine. Now, as he went through them a second time, it wasn't long before his scanning eye focused in on the forward-bearing temperature for the number two main engine. The readings all fell within limits, but the warming trend over the past few weeks was alarming, to say the least. Temperatures had risen several degrees higher when compared with their normal values only a month before.

"Shit!" Coleman let out an audible sigh as he came to the realization that the Indonesian marine could have nothing to do with it. The main engine condition had existed well before *Providence* had plucked him from the sea. He had accused the man falsely, and he felt ashamed for it. He felt like going forward and telling the captain immediately, and had resolved to do just that when another chilling thought entered his head.

If the marine didn't sabotage the main engine, then *who did*? The thermal trends had started weeks ago, well before this mission had even started, indeed well before *Providence* had even reached Pearl Harbor. The first indications of rising temperature dated back to a time when *Providence* was still crossing the Indian Ocean, just after she had left Diego Garcia and only a few days after the failed ORSE examination.

Tiny beads of sweat suddenly formed on Coleman's forehead and he began to pale.

"Hey, Mr. Coleman," one of the mechanics said. "What's wrong? You don't look so good, sir."

Coleman ignored the sailor as he desperately tried to recall those days after the ship left Diego Garcia. He searched his brain but could not remember *Providence* having any more visitors after the ORSE team had left. In fact, no visitor set foot on board the ship for the entire trip back to Pearl Harbor. That left only one option. *The saboteur had to be one of* Providence*'s crew!*

The thermal trends had started during the mid-watch on the fourteenth of May, exactly one month ago. Coleman now flipped violently through the logs, turning page after page almost to the point of ripping them as he searched for the one containing the watchstanders' signatures. It was the page each watchstander signed when he assumed the watch, and then signed again when he was relieved at the end of his watch. Finally finding the signature page for the engine room lower level watch, Coleman yanked it from the bundle. Only the engine room lower level watch had access to the propulsion lube oil strainers. Only the engine room lower level watch could easily remove the strainers and introduce a Kimwipe into the system. Sweat dropped from Coleman's brow as his finger sped down the list of signatures, stopping only when it reached the midnight entry on the fourteenth.

There was a printed name, and a signature that he recognized. And suddenly everything became very clear to him.

"Hey, Acting Eng!" a mechanic called after him. "Where you going? Ain't we gonna put this thing back together? Mr. Coleman?"

Coleman did not hear him but continued marching aft in stunned silence. He had to report his discovery to the captain, but before he did, he wanted to make sure. He didn't want to accuse another man falsely. The gaggle of nuclear mechanics gazed on as their lieutenant reached the portside ladder, tucked the log page under one arm, and descended out of sight.

"CONN, Sonar. Still picking up transient noises coming from the *Hatta*. Sounds like a lot of pipe patching going on over there. But I think they're losing the damage control battle, sir. We've already heard one compartment implode."

The sonar display showed exactly what the chief had described as Edwards and Miller looked on. Sporadic green dots appeared on the same bearing as the *Hatta*.

"Damn, sir," Miller commented. "Those Germans build their boats well, don't they? One of her countermeasures must've stopped our torpedo just short of hitting her. But she's damaged bad enough to sink her. I'm guessing she'll be on the bottom before the hour's up."

Miller was right. The *Hatta* was definitely in trouble and sinking into the abyss, but *Providence*'s sonar could clearly hear the survivors as they desperately tried to save her. Edwards guessed that the *Hatta*'s engineering compartment was the one sonar heard implode moments before. She had no flow noise, so her propulsion was gone, and after coasting another thousand yards she had come to a dead stop. Just the thought of what the *Hatta*'s survivors must be going through right now gave Edwards chills. Wet bodies, some dead, some not, struggling to move around in partially flooded compartments with freezing high-pressure water shooting at them in all directions from a hundred different leaks, blinding them as they cut sheet metal for patches and hammered shoring into place. The effort was hopeless, and Edwards seriously considered ending their misery with *Providence*'s still-running number three torpedo before it ran out of fuel, but he could not bring himself to do it. The *Hatta* was finished as a fighting submarine. His mission was accomplished. He did not harbor any hate toward Peto, and if through some miracle the rebel captain could make it to the surface again to get his men off, Edwards would not interfere.

"No telling what shape their forward compartment's in," Miller commented. "For all we know she can still shoot. Hell, she might even have sonar, too. That is, if her forward batteries held up."

Strangely, the thought had never occurred to Edwards, and he cursed himself for letting his emotions cloud his judgment. The lion was wounded but she was still dangerous.

"Chief of the Watch," he called, "Pass the word again throughout the ship. Remind all stations to maintain the rig for ultra quiet. I don't want to hear a peep out of anyone."

"Aye, aye, sir," the chief said as he keyed his phone to pass the word.

MACHINISTS Mate Third Class Myron Dean strolled through the lower level of the engine room with his log clipboard in hand, dutifully make his rounds from one bay to the next, despite the ominous explosions he'd heard outside the ship. This was his first time standing watch after his fall, and though he could still feel the tenderness in his bandaged ribs, he was glad to be contributing once again. His rescue from the island, coupled with the courteous treatment he'd received from Lieutenant Coleman, had changed his outlook on everything despite all the tragedy he'd witnessed over the past few days. He felt as thought he'd been granted a new lease on life.

Standing watch in the lower level of the engine room was generally a lonely one, and tonight was no exception. The explosions, as unsettling as they were, offered only brief moments of distraction from the secluded feeling of the watch. All of the bays, tanks and column-like pump housings made the vast and dank lower level seem like a virtual maze and could easily make a sailor feel that he had been completely forgotten. Dean sometimes wondered what would happen if the decision were ever made to abandon ship. Would anyone remember to tell him?

As he walked through the flood doors into the auxiliary seawater bay pondering his loneliness, one of the 2JV phones mounted on the bulkhead whooped. Thankful to talk to anybody, he lurched to pluck the phone off its rack.

"Engine Room Lower Level," he said into the phone.

"Engine Room Lower Level, this is the engineering officer of the watch." Dean recognized Lieutenant junior grade Kemper's voice on the other end. "Petty Officer Dean, make sure you maintain the rig for ultra quiet down there, understood? Control says we've still got a hostile out there, so make sure you don't go and drop something on the deck or do anything stupid to make a transient. Understand?"

"Aye, aye, sir. Understood," Dean answered, the line going

dead on the other end as Kemper probably dialed to inform another watchstander in one of the engine room's various spaces.

Dean wasn't sure if he liked knowing about the potential danger somewhere out in the water on the other side of *Providence*'s metal skin. There was little he could do about it, so why should he have to know. But, looking on the bright side, at least now he wouldn't have to do any maintenance. He could relax, take his logs every fifteen minutes, and daydream in between.

Then he heard footfalls on the metal ladder rungs. Someone was coming down the ladder from engine room upper level. A pair of shoes descended through the portside ladder well and eventually Dean saw that it was Lieutenant Coleman. Coleman's face looked visibly shaken, his expression indicating that he had come down to the lower level specifically to see him. As Coleman reached the base of the ladder and began crossing the bay, walking between the various pump housings, Dean noticed the single paper log clutched in one of his hands.

A moment of panic suddenly came over Dean when he realized what it was. But his panic quickly turned into brute shock when he saw a long dark object flash out from behind one of the pump housings and strike Coleman squarely on the back of the head. Dean heard the thud from the impact and watched the lieutenant's limp form fall facedown on the deck, a trickle of blood flowing from beneath his hair to mix with his blue uniform and white T-shirt.

Coleman was not moving and Dean instinctively knelt down to try to help the unconscious officer, but his blood ran cold as a shadow suddenly blocked the light above him. Looking up, he saw Van Peenan step out from behind the pump housing, his blistered face wearing a scowl that could cut through the pressure hull, his right hand clutching a crescent wrench red with Coleman's blood. He must have been hiding behind the pump housing while Dean was taking his rounds in the other bays, and Dean shuddered to think what might have happened if Kemper hadn't called him on the 2JV at the moment he did, or if he had walked past the pump first instead of Coleman. It might have been him lying on the deck in a pool of blood.

"Well go ahead and fuck me," Van Peenan snarled with a sickening smile as he glanced down at Coleman's still form, giving it a swift kicked in the ribs. "It looks like I've got my department back, ay, Dean?"

"What's going on, Eng?" Dean said, trying hard not to show any fear. "Why'd you hit him?"

"Funny thing about close explosions outside a submarine!" Van Peenan said almost in a different voice as he stepped closer to Dean, "You never know what they're going to do to the people inside."

Dean began to scoot backward, moving away, but Van Peenan kept moving closer, slapping the bloody wrench into his left hand, seemingly oblivious to the bits of blood, hair, and flesh that came off in it.

"You've fucked with my career once too often, young Dean! Now I'm going to make sure you never fuck with it again!"

Dean ducked just in time to avoid the fast moving wrench as it whipped past his head and collided with the bay's metallic bulkhead, the resulting crash reverberating throughout the entire lower level of the engine room. Before he could think, Van Peenan lunged again, this time kicking him in his bandaged ribs. The pain put Dean on the deck, but he was still able to roll in time to avoid the next swing of Van Peenan's wrench. It hit the metal deck where Dean's head had been a millisecond before, sparking and sending vibrations along the linked deckplates.

Van Peenan was off balance for only a moment, and Dean took the opportunity to get away from his reach, stumbling aft. But the immense pain must have affected his judgment, because going aft brought him to a dead end. The auxiliary seawater bay ended with the sharp curvature of *Providence*'s pressure hull, and there was no way out. As Dean realized his error, he turned to see that Van Peenan had realized it too.

The crazed engineer slowly walked toward him, his face wearing an evil grin as he once again rapped the bloody wrench into his open palm.

*   *   *

EDWARDS and Miller had just been discussing what to do with *Providence*'s still-running torpedo when the sonar chief's agitated voice squawked from the overhead speaker.

"Conn, Sonar! Transient, own ship! Transient, own ship!"

"Damn it!" Edwards shouted. He normally didn't lose his temper, but this really was *Submarining 101*. "Chief of the Watch, didn't I tell you to remind all stations?"

The chief nodded hesitantly, "Yes, Captain. All stations, fore and aft, acknowledged, sir. I don't understand what could've happened."

Edwards spoke into the open microphone, clear aggravation in his voice, "Where did the transient come from, Sonar?"

"Conn, Sonar. Transient originated aft, in the engine room."

Edwards needed only to glance at the chief of the watch.

"I'm on it, Captain," the chief said as he keyed his phone set to call Maneuvering.

Edwards and Miller gazed at the waterfall display with hidden trepidation. Damage control was still in full force on the *Hatta* as was evident by the small blips popping up around her location. A rough estimate from the fire control system put her at six thousand yards off the port bow, due southwest of *Providence*'s position.

"Only time will tell if she heard us," Miller stated the obvious. "If her sonar's still functional."

All watched in stark silence as the waterfall display scrolled on.

Then came another transient. This one even louder than the first. It sounded like metal striking against metal, and it was so loud, that everyone in the control room clearly heard it over the open sonar speaker.

Frustrated and feeling powerless, Edwards reached up to grab the engineering microphone. If the men in the engine room would not listen to the chief of the watch, maybe they'd listen to him over the loudspeaker. But before he could key the handset, Miller touched his arm and pointed at the waterfall display.

"Captain, look!"

On the display, a large swath of green blips obscured the *Hatta*'s position, then the swath receded into a thin green line. The line moved ever so slightly to the right, then steadied on a constant bearing.

"Conn, Sonar. Picking up bulkheads imploding to the southwest. The *Hatta* has imploded! Torpedo in the water, bearing two two eight!"

Edwards could only imagine what had happened. After detecting the *Providence*'s transients, Peto must have decided to give her one final parting shot. But something had happened as the *Hatta* fired the torpedo, something that caused a catastrophic bulkhead failure. Quite possibly, her torpedo tube breech mechanism had been damaged by *Providence*'s earlier weapon, and then fractured entirely when she fired her last weapon. At near test depth, with a torpedo tube open to sea, the column of high pressure seawater twenty-one inches in diameter would have gutted her forward compartment like it was made of jelly, bending solid steel and ripping bodies apart.

This time the *Hatta* would not be coming back, but she had left the *Providence* with a very deadly parting gift.

"Torpedo bearing constant! Range five thousand five hundred yards and closing!"

On cue, the WLR-9 active intercept panel blurted out an alarm. The torpedo was in an active pinging mode and had already acquired the *Providence*'s hull.

"Helm, ahead full! Cavitate! Right full rudder, steady on course north!"

The helm rang up the engine order and *Providence* answered, accelerating from her stopped position, but Edwards suddenly wondered if it would be enough. The pickup was already painfully slow. Twenty seconds passed and *Providence* had only just surpassed ten knots. The hardworking starboard engine was doing its best to turn the big shaft alone, but it would need its twin's help if Edwards expected any kind of strong acceleration.

"Conn, Sonar. Torpedo bears two two zero. Range four thousand five hundred yards."

Providence's speed log took another full minute to steady out on her maximum single engine speed of twenty-one knots. Once again, the *Providence* had a torpedo driving toward her stern at thirty-six knots, closing the distance by five hundred yards every minute, only this time the *Mendar* wasn't around to trick the enemy weapon. The only hope was to run, as fast as her single main engine could take her. A dismal look from Fremont gave a clear indication of their chances. He had already done the math on his calculator.

"At this speed that torpedo will overtake us in seven minutes, Captain," Fremont said gloomily. "We can't outrun it on one main engine."

Edwards knew that, of course. He had no clue what the status of the port main engine was, but regardless of its condition, Coleman would have to get it back on line, and fast.

"Maneuvering, this is the captain." He spoke calmly into the engineering microphone. "Report status of number two main engine."

After a long pause, Kemper's voice came back, "Number two main engine status unknown, sir. I can't find Lieutenant Coleman! Sir, we . . ."

Edwards cut off the nervous young officer and switched the microphone circuit over to the 1MC. Wherever Coleman might be, he would certainly hear him now.

"Lieutenant Coleman, this is the captain." He heard his own voice reverberating throughout the passages beyond the control room. "Restore number two main engine immediately! Conduct an emergency start-up! Repeat. Restore number two main engine immediately! Conduct an emergency start-up and place number two main engine back on line!"

Edwards waited for several minutes, but no response came.

"What the hell's going on back there?" he said through his

teeth, exchanging desperate glances with Miller. "And where the hell's Coleman?"

WARREN Bloomfield lingered by the port-side electrical panels in the upper level of the engine room, trying to stay out of Chief McKennitt's way. A circuit breaker fire had been reported to the crew's mess and McKennitt's damage-control team had been the first to respond. Bloomfield tagged along as the damage-control officer, but every sailor in the team knew who their real leader was. They kept their wide eyes glued on McKennitt for both guidance and orders. Bloomfield suffered no small blow to his ego, when he arrived on the scene and, recalling his days of DC training as a junior officer, announced, "This is Lieutenant Commander Bloomfield! I am the man in charge!" His announcement was met by a burst of laughter from every sailor in the area, each man having to be silenced by a swift whack on the side of the head from McKennitt's open palm.

McKennitt quickly took charge of the situation, which turned out to be nothing more than a little arcing and sparking. One sailor de-energized the panel while McKennitt emptied the contents of a CO_2 fire extinguisher on it for good measure. Slowly and quietly, Bloomfield made his way to the back of the group, utterly humiliated. He felt like the odd man out. The men made all of their reports to McKennitt, and McKennitt in turn reported his status to the control room, bypassing Bloomfield altogether. He had no useful purpose, and he knew that the men felt the same way about him. In fact, he was certain they considered him to be some sort of ship's fool. They'd laughed for months at their blundering XO behind his back, and now apparently, they had no compunctions about laughing to his face as well.

Bloomfield was tired of it. He was tired of a lot of things.

As he shuffled aft, he overheard one of the headset-laden sailors say that one of *Providence*'s torpedoes had hit the *Hatta*. That being the case, he couldn't understand why the ship had suddenly gone to full speed, and he suddenly wondered if there could be another enemy torpedo out there. Then he heard Edwards' announcement over the 1MC, ordering Coleman to restore the number two main engine, and at that moment he knew there was an enemy torpedo out there, and *Providence* was running from it. It could be the only explanation.

With McKennitt's damage control team focusing on the de-energized panel, Bloomfield slipped away unnoticed and nosed his way aft along the port side of the big turbine generator. The port main engine was only a few frames aft, and he was suddenly curious as to whether Coleman had gotten the word to restore it. As he came in sight of the number two main engine, he was shocked by what he saw.

The big engine was completely assembled and appeared ready to go, but a gathering of petty officers who should have been starting it up looked anything but ready. Hovering over an open technical manual laying flat on the engine casing, the sailors were actually studying the emergency start-up procedure while a torpedo was traveling up *Providence*'s stern. All were nuclear mechanics, but none had more than a single stripe on his sleeve. They were third-class petty officers with no leadership in sight.

"What are you men waiting for?" Bloomfield approached them. "Didn't you hear the captain's order? Restore this engine to service immediately!"

They stared back at him blankly, and it soon became obvious to Bloomfield that they had no idea where to begin. They had obviously heard the order over the 1MC and were trying to comply as best they could. Like all good nukes, they had consulted the technical manual. There was just one problem. No written procedure existed for an emergency start-up of a main engine with a potentially bowed rotor. NavSea would never publish such a procedure because of the liability involved in damaging a multimillion dollar engine. Any experienced nuke would have known that. Bloomfield knew it from his junior officer days, long ago, when he spent several years qualifying as a ship's engineer. The procedure was not written anywhere. It only existed in the minds of those who had done it before. And Bloomfield had done it before, twelve years and eighty pounds ago, when he had served as the main propulsion assistant on the USS *Phoenix*.

"XO," one of the sailors pleaded. "You've got to help us, sir! We can't find Mr. Coleman and we can't find the procedure either! I don't think it exists, sir!"

Strangely, Bloomfield felt calm and composed in front of the distressed sailor. It felt good to be needed again. He hadn't felt needed for a very long time, and it almost made him smile in spite of the imminent danger that threatened them all.

"XO?" the sailor said, obviously wondering if he had heard him.

"You men put that manual away," Bloomfield said in a steady but authoritative tone. "And do everything that I tell you to . . ."

"YOU'RE not getting away from me a second time, asshole!" Van Peenan snarled as he rushed Dean and kicked him again in the ribs.

Dean winced and had trouble breathing from the pain. His ribs had almost certainly fractured again. By now Dean realized that Van Peenan meant to kill him. Putting two and two together, he surmised that he had not actually fallen down the ladder as previously thought. Van Peenan had pushed him, and now the mad engineer was trying to shatter his skull with the same lethal implement used to fell Coleman.

Dean waited for the next lunge, then sidestepped it, managing to get to one side of the starboard seawater pump. As Van Peenan tried to get around it, Dean moved to keep the pump between them. As Van Peenan doggedly attempted to get around, Dean managed to counter every one of his moves. When Van Peenan went right, he went left. When Van Peenan went left, he went right. The crazed engineer's curses were swallowed up by the din of the engine room's spinning equipment as the ship answered full speed, and Dean began to think he could play the game indefinitely, or at least until help showed up. He probably could have, too, if he'd looked up in time to see the metal wrench hurtling through the air before it hit him squarely in the temple. The blow from the thrown object knocked him senseless and sent him stumbling into an equipment locker where he noisily fell to the deck.

Dean felt woozy as he feebly staggered to his feet, subconsciously aware that Van Peenan had recovered his weapon and now stood within striking distance.

He had to get away. As much as his head hurt, and as dizzy as he was, he had to try. In a fervent effort to escape, he drove himself to run forward along the deck as fast as he could, his boots clomping on the metal deckplates as he ran.

He could hear Van Peenan running after him.

"No sense in running, you little shit!" Van Peenan called from only a few steps behind. "I'm going to bash your fucking head in!"

Dean felt the breeze on his neck from a swipe of the heavy wrench. The wrench had missed, but it was only a matter of time before Van Peenan caught him. Dean kept running, heading for the next bay forward. He ran between the auxiliary seawater pump housings as Van Peenan wound up for another stroke. Anticipating a smashing blow to his skull, Dean was surprised when he suddenly heard his pursuer stumble and fall noisily onto the deck behind him, the wrench ricocheting off the bulkhead and falling into the deep bilge below the catwalk.

Dean turned to see Van Peenan lying motionless on the deck. A few feet aft, Coleman's body quivered, his arm lay extended across the path. The injured officer had obviously tripped up Van Peenan as he had run by, causing the engineer to fall and hit his head on a solid steel eye used for looping block and tackle. Dean couldn't tell whether Van Peenan was alive or dead, but either way, he wouldn't be getting up for a while. The protruding metal object had knocked him out cold.

Coleman, still dazed from his own injury, tried to speak, but he could not. Hobbling over to him, Dean helped him roll onto his side.

"Are you okay, sir?" Dean said, wincing at his own aching head and ribs.

Coleman mumbled something but it was unintelligible. The concussion to the back of his head had shocked his senses. His jerky eyes indicated that he was having trouble seeing, and he was probably suffering from memory loss too.

In his shaky condition Coleman didn't see or feel Dean remove the crumpled log page from his clenched fist. He also didn't see when Dean tossed the wadded page into the dark and grimy bilge water below.

"TORPEDO'S two thousand yards away now, Captain!" Miller reported after emerging from the sonar shack's sliding door. The fidgety weapons officer had nothing to do now that *Providence*'s target had been eliminated, so he occupied his time by nervously pacing in and out of the sonar shack, more of a distraction than anything else to the row of sonarmen beyond the door.

Edwards wanted dearly to jump down the aft ladder and make for the engine room. Something had to be very wrong back there, and with no response from Coleman, he couldn't be certain of anything. But he held back. His place was in the control room, and he needed to trust his officers to carry out their orders. With that in mind he had dispatched two of the junior officers manning the tracking consoles and sent them aft in an effort to locate Coleman.

"We need flank speed in two minutes, Captain, or we're not going to make it," Fremont commented.

The information only added to Edwards' sense of helplessness. There was nothing he could do at this point but wait and pray. If the men in the engine room had not yet begun to start up the main engine no interference on his part could get it started in time.

Coleman was a good officer, he kept telling himself. He had to trust his acting-engineer to come through for him.

Just as Edwards was convincing himself to reach for the engineering microphone to ask Maneuvering for another update, he felt the deck suddenly decelerate. The log showed *Providence*'s speed falling below twenty knots.

"Maneuvering answers all-stop, Captain!" the helmsman cried as he twisted the engine order telegraph back and forth. "They're not responding! What the hell are they doing?"

The outburst was very inappropriate behavior for a low-ranking helmsman, but his frustration was understandable given that he was not an engineering rate but a yeoman by trade. Edwards knew exactly what was happening, and he couldn't help but smile as all around them the ship took on a new murmur. The lights dimmed throughout the space and the deck shook as *Providence*'s big reactor coolant pumps shifted into fast speed. Then, like a big Mack truck shifting into gear, *Providence*'s massive thrust bearing felt the full force of her spinning shaft. The deck lurched forward with an abruptness that sent books flying out of lockers, and jostled coffee cups in their holders all around the control room. Every man groped to find a handhold, and the surprised helmsman took a firm grip on his control yoke like he had suddenly been placed in the saddle of a wild bronco. The puzzled yeoman smiled widely when he saw the engine order telegraph jump over smartly to the *All Ahead Flank* position followed by three distinct buzzes. *The engine room was answering the bell! All ahead flank, at last!* For further confirmation the yeoman needed only to glance up at his panel where the speed log showed *Providence* accelerating at the rate of two knots per second.

Within half a minute *Providence* had come close to doubling her single main engine speed, and her deck shook and shuddered from the strain. The big twins were pulling together once again. *Providence* was once again a *fast* attack submarine.

A smiling nod from Fremont told Edwards that they were in the clear now, and after another eight minutes of running at flank speed, sonar made the expected report.

"Conn, Sonar. No longer receiving active pulses from the hostile torpedo. Weapon has shut down."

Edwards walked over and patted the helmsman on the shoulder as the fast-moving ship continued to vibrate under his feet.

"The engine room had to disengage the starboard main engine momentarily in order to bring the other one on line," Edwards explained, smiling down at him. "That's why they rang up *All-Stop*. I'm sure you'll remember that for the rest of your life, helmsman."

The sailor nodded, visibly relieved as he wiped the sweat from his brow. "Aye, aye, Captain."

The men in the room chuckled as they all breathed a sigh of relief.

Edwards did not want to be remiss in his duties. He wanted to place credit where credit was due. The *Providence* had survived only because Coleman had been so quick to restore the number two main engine, and even though Edwards would have preferred that Coleman keep him better informed, the young acting engineer had done a fantastic job.

Edwards grabbed up the engineering microphone and keyed it. "Mr. Coleman, this is the captain. Excellent work! You and your men can drink up when we get back to Pearl. I think every man on this ship owes you a beer!"

Everyone in the control room smiled at the thought of drinking alcohol again. Edwards waited by the speaker for a response from the engine room, but none came.

After several minutes, the headset-wearing chief of the watch finally spoke up.

"Captain, I've got a message for you on the JA phone circuit. The XO would like you to come to engine room lower level right away, sir."

Bloomfield? Edwards thought. What the hell was he doing in the engine room?

"Nav," Edwards said, dispensing with the normal watch relief formalities, "Take the conn, please. I'm going below."

EDWARDS ducked through the flood bay doors into the auxiliary seawater bay and came upon a sight he most certainly didn't expect to see. On one side of the bay, Van Peenan lay propped against the bulkhead, mumbling something as the corpsman shined a flashlight into his groggy eyes, an ugly gash very visible on his forehead. Two steps away, an armed security petty officer rested one hand on his holstered forty-five, watching Van Peenan's every move.

On the other side of the bay, Petty Officer Dean sat on top of an equipment locker with his head in his hands, while at his feet a prostrate Lieutenant Coleman received medical attention from the corpsman's assistant. Standing in the middle of the bay Bloomfield conversed with the two lieutenants Edwards had sent to find Coleman.

"Captain," Bloomfield said, with uncharacteristic enthusiasm. "I thought you'd want to see this, sir."

"What happened?"

"Apparently, Mr. Van Peenan there attacked Lieutenant Coleman with a crescent wrench, then went after Petty Officer Dean. Don't know the reason yet, sir, but I've ordered him taken into custody after the corpsman checks him out."

Van Peenan continued mumbling, and Edwards thought he heard him say to the probing corpsman, "Don't tell Captain Christopher, okay? Don't tell Christopher . . ."

"What's Coleman's condition?" Edwards asked.

"I think he'll be okay, sir. Or, at least, the corpsman thinks so. Got a pretty tough nut, that lieutenant."

Edwards watched as the corpsman turned Van Peenan over to the security petty officer, then moved over to help his assistant with Coleman. Van Peenan now wore handcuffs, as the petty officer led him forward into the next bay. He never once looked in Edwards' direction. He just kept mumbling, staring straight ahead as if in a daze.

Next in the procession, the two corpsmen carried Coleman between them. He was in no condition to walk. As they passed Edwards, Coleman grabbed hold of his uniform.

"Stop!" Coleman shouted to his bearers, his eyes still jerky, his face covered with sweat. "I've got something to tell the captain."

Edwards knelt down and looked him in the face. "What is it, Lieutenant?"

"If only I can remember, Captain. I was coming to see you when someone hit me."

"Commander Van Peenan hit you, Lieutenant," Edwards said gently.

"Yes, sir. That's right. Commander Van Peenan hit me. And then he tried to hit Dean, but I stopped him."

Coleman looked distant for a few seconds as Edwards waited.

"Maybe you'd better get some rest," Edwards said finally. "We'll talk about it later."

"No!" Coleman said firmly, grasping his arm. "I remember now, sir. I remember what I was coming to tell you."

"Tell me what?"

"It's Dean, Captain!" Coleman struggled to get the words out. "Dean's the saboteur! He tried to destroy the main engine!"

Edwards glanced back at Dean, who gave no apparent reaction, still sitting on the locker with his head between his hands, staring blankly at the bulkhead.

"Get some rest, Lieutenant," Edwards said kindly, as he removed Coleman's hand from his arm and nodded for the two corpsmen to proceed. The two lieutenants followed as the corpsmen carried Coleman forward, leaving Edwards and Bloomfield alone in the room with Dean. Dean still did not move.

"Are you all right, Petty Officer Dean?" Edwards called to him.

Dean didn't respond initially. He kept staring at the bulkhead as if Edwards and Bloomfield were not there. His voice was barely audible when he finally began to speak.

"It's true, sir," he mumbled through his hands.

"What's true? Speak up, Dean."

"I mean Mr. Coleman, sir. What he said is true."

Edwards and Bloomfield looked on skeptically.

"What are you saying, Dean?" Edwards prodded.

"That I'm the reason the engine seized up, sir. That I'm the one who put the Kimwipe in the lube oil system. I did it, Captain."

"Damn it, Dean!" After all he'd been through in the last few days, Edwards wanted to lay into the young mechanic. He wanted to take his frustrations out on this sailor who had placed all their lives in jeopardy, but he refrained, instead asking simply, "Why on God's green earth would you do such a thing?"

Dean kept staring at the bulkhead.

"The Eng was riding me hard, Captain, after that last ORSE. He rode me real hard. Everything I did was wrong to him. Everything I said was wrong. To him, *I* was wrong. He blamed me for everything. He was riding me, sir, and I guess I just couldn't take it anymore. I wanted to get back at him somehow, to try to defend myself, but what could I do? I'm a lowly petty officer and he's a lieutenant commander. Crapping out the main engine was the only thing I could think of, sir. I knew Naval Reactors would blame him for it, and it'd wreck his career. I didn't want to hurt the ship, sir. You gotta believe that. I didn't know it was going to be so important. I'm just glad nobody died because of it."

Edwards bit back his temper. He thought about reminding Dean about Chief Michaelson's death because the *Mendar* didn't make the rendezvous on time, but he quickly decided this was neither the time nor the place.

"How can he do that, Captain?" Dean continued, this time facing him. "Commander Van Peenan's a crazy son of a bitch! How the hell can he get away with treating people like he did me?"

Edwards made to speak, but was surprised when Bloomfield answered first.

"I guess that's just the nature of the beast, Dean," Bloomfield said distantly. "The men above us sometimes make us do crazy things—things we wouldn't normally do. They turn us into the kind of people that we really aren't, deep down inside. Each of us reacts to such situations in different ways. Some of us go insane, some of us do stupid things, and some of us . . . just stop caring." Out of the corner of his eye, Edwards saw Bloomfield wipe his nose, or was it his eyes, before continuing in a more authoritative tone, "I'm sorry to have to tell you this, Petty Officer Dean, but you're under arrest."

Chapter 22

THE warm Pearl Harbor sunlight shone through the open weapons shipping hatch and cast long shadows on the deck outside the stateroom, as Edwards took the report from a spry-looking Lieutenant Lake, who was wearing an insignia-ornamented, summer-dress khaki uniform. The ship was quiet outside in the passage and throughout all her compartments as she rode the gentle swell beside the pier at the submarine base across from Ford Island. She had pulled in earlier that day, and what was once a vibrant living vessel teeming with life now seemed completely deserted. With the exception of a small skeleton crew, most of *Providence*'s sailors had departed hours ago, their families or girlfriends whisking them away the moment the ship touched the pier, as if *Providence* might put to sea again if they lingered one moment longer.

Edwards realized just how empty the ship was when he dropped down to the wardroom and ended up having to make his own pot of coffee. But who could blame them for leaving? They'd been at sea for seven months. They deserved some leave and liberty. And so did he.

"That pretty much says it all, Captain," Lake said, handing Edwards his written report on the shore party's activities. The report would go into the much thicker mission report that Edwards was preparing.

"I trust you saw Miss Whitehead off okay?" Edwards said, trying not to appear overly curious as he filed the report in a drawer beside his desk.

"Yes, sir. I just got back from driving her to the airport. She's probably already in the air by now, on her way to take care of her father's funeral arrangements in Raleigh. I guess the Indonesian government's going to send his body back there. Apparently they recovered the doctor's body as a part of the U.N.-negotiated cease-fire."

Edwards nodded grimly, but also with a small amount of personal satisfaction. The doctor's body had been recovered as part of a cease-fire that was now in effect all across Indonesia. A cease-fire attributed in no small part to the efforts of the U.N. envoy Descartes, who was quickly becoming a celebrity in the world-wide media for his selfless devotion to achieving peace in the troubled islands. Neither the *Providence* nor any of her lost crewmen would ever be mentioned in the media, and Dr. Gregory Whitehead would be remembered at home and abroad as a peace-loving humanitarian who cared for the Indonesian people more than he did his own life.

Teresa Whitehead seemed to be handling her father's death as well as could be expected. Of course, she had a devoted confidant in Lake, and that had certainly helped. Obviously, the two had grown close during their ordeal ashore, and Edwards scarcely saw them apart during the week-long transit back to Pearl. She seemed nice enough from the few chances he had to speak with her. The secretive Ahmad was another matter. Ahmad had uttered no more than two words the whole trip back.

And, true to form, the moment *Providence* touched the pier, two men in dark brown suits whisked the unfriendly agent away in an unmarked sedan before the ship could even shift its colors. Somehow, Edwards knew that he'd never hear another word about the man named Ahmad ever again.

"Now I suspect you'll be leaving us too, Mr. Lake?" Edwards asked hesitantly.

"Actually, Captain." Lake paused and seemed to blush. "I was wondering, sir, if you might authorize an extension for me, sir."

"An extension?"

"Yes, sir. I'd like to pull my resignation letter. I've looked into it, sir, and if you authorize it, they might even let me into department-head school. I know I'm already behind my class, but I know I can catch up."

"Yes, Mr. Lake," Edwards said, smiling. "I think you can

do anything you set your mind to. I'll gladly endorse your request, as I'm sure ComSubPac will, too."

"Thank you, sir," Lake said, now grinning from ear to ear. He made to leave but stopped short at the door. "Oh, sir, I almost forgot."

Lake removed a folder from the stack of files under his arm and placed it on Edwards' desk.

"What's this?" Edwards asked.

"Promotion package, Captain, for Petty Officer Pasternak, my leading petty officer in radio division. He's a good guy, sir, and he ought to be wearing first-class stripes." Lake paused before adding solemnly, "He comes with a good recommendation, Captain."

Edwards nodded, knowing all too well the meaning.

"I'm sure it'll be approved, no problem, Lieutenant."

"Thank you, sir," Lake said, donning his khaki garrison cap and heading for the hatch. As he scaled the ladder Edwards heard him call back, "Have a good leave, Captain!"

"You too, Mr. Lake!"

Edwards smiled. His predecessor had been all wrong about Lake. Edwards was glad that Lake would be staying in the navy. He even hoped the young officer would consider coming back to the *Providence* after he completed department-head school. Officers like Lake were hard to find.

As Edwards tried to get back into the right mindset to finish his report, he heard the door to the CO/XO washroom slide open behind him. He turned to see Bloomfield's big form enter his stateroom wearing civilian attire, his packed bags hanging from shoulder straps and loosely tucked under his chubby arms.

"I was waiting until you were finished with Mr. Lake, Captain," he said, his face beet red and perspiring from the Hawaiian humidity.

"Come on in, XO. You're shoving off, I presume?"

"Yes, Captain," Bloomfield said, dropping one bag on the deck. "I wanted to say goodbye, sir. ComSubPac should approve my early retirement request before my leave runs out, so I probably won't be coming back."

Edwards stood up and shook his hand. He'd had his problems with Bloomfield, but the man had certainly changed in the past couple weeks. Perhaps he'd been too impatient with him in the beginning. In the seven months they had spent together, Edwards had uttered some harsh words to the bumbling executive officer, and he felt that he owed him some kind of apology. At least now, anyway, since Bloomfield was leaving the navy.

"Before you leave, XO, I wanted to tell you that I'm sorry," he said stiffly, "I'm sorry I assigned you to the damage-control unit. I know that was embarrassing to you. It may have been an inappropriate move on my part."

"Don't apologize, Captain. I'm glad you did it. It helped me to sort some things out. It helped me to come to grips with some decisions I've needed to make for a long time—like the one to retire."

Edwards shook his hand again, and an awkward silence descended on the room as Bloomfield made no move to leave.

"It's a shame about poor Dean," Bloomfield said finally.

"Yes, quite," Edwards said simply, but then continued when Bloomfield's expression indicated he wanted to know more, "They've got him over at the brig on Ford Island now. He'll have to wait there for his court martial. And Van Peenan's been admitted to the Psych ward up at Tripler. The JAG's still trying to figure out what to do with him. They're trying to figure out if Van Peenan wigged out and harassed Dean because he knew Dean was a saboteur, or if Dean only became a saboteur *after* Van Peenan started harassing him. That whole situation's one big mess. Kind of a 'chicken before the egg' syndrome, you know?"

"But who was the original chicken?" Bloomfield said distantly. "I wonder if they're asking that. Believe it or not, Captain, I can remember a time, three years ago, when a young Aubrey Van Peenan first reported aboard this ship. Believe it or not, he wasn't too different from young Mr. Lake, there. Wide-eyed and very impressionable."

Bloomfield leaned over and removed a well-worn notebook from the side pocket of his dropped bag. He turned the notebook over several times in his hands, rubbing the covers and sighing heavily. He held it in both hands, staring at for a while, and then suddenly tossed it onto Edwards' desk as if it brought him physical pain to part with it.

"What's that?"

"That, Captain, is a personal log. I've kept it since the day I reported aboard this ship, four years ago. I've kept it, I'm ashamed to say, to cover my own ass in case the JAG ever came snooping around this place." Bloomfield chuckled awkwardly, and added, "You know, Captain, we can spend our whole damn careers learning how to find enemy subs that go deeper than ours, but sometimes we find—in the end—the deepest enemy is the one within ourselves."

"I don't want this," Edwards said, picking up the notebook. "Why don't you keep it as a—"

"Read it!" Bloomfield said, suddenly very serious. "Promise me you'll read it, and then we'll shake hands and say goodbye. It may help you to understand why Van Peenan's the way he is. Hell, who knows, maybe Dean's lawyer'll be able to use it in his trial. I'm sure you'll know what to do with it."

EDWARDS climbed the weapons-shipping hatch ladder and emerged into the late afternoon sun. The warmth felt good on his face as he took a full deep breath of the fresh Hawaiian air and relished the picturesque surroundings. It was after working hours for most people, and already some sailboats rode the gentle breeze around the tranquil harbor, the white houses of Aiea and Pearl City dotting the green hills just beyond. Wearing his best summer khaki uniform, Edwards felt strangely out of place as he crossed *Providence*'s brow and stepped onto the sub base pier for the first time in seven months. He headed straight for the parking lot at the end of the pier, adjusting his stride to accommodate his sea-accustomed legs. One of *Providence*'s lieutenants had been good enough to retrieve his car from the deployment lot and it now sat in the closest space to the pier, reserved only for commanding officers. As he climbed in to the new-smelling sedan, he tossed the notebook he'd been reading for most of the afternoon onto the empty seat beside him. The feel of being behind the wheel after so long at sea was always a rare treat, a treat that landsmen never got to experience. After every deployment, he always felt like a sixteen-year-old kid with a brand new driver's license.

As he drove along the harbor road, past the long row of black submarine sails jutting above the quay, past the softball field, past the officers' quarters and the enlisted barracks, he tried to let the strains of command fade from his clouded mind. But when he came to the first intersection, he found himself facing one final command decision. Turning left would take him off the base and place him on the road to Honolulu. Going straight would take him onto the main surface base with all of its supporting command buildings.

He glanced at his watch. His daughter's flight would be arriving at the airport in an hour. Her mother, his ex-wife, had been kind enough to send her to spend a week in Hawaii with her dad, a week Edwards had looked forward to since he got the email telling him about it, only three days ago. Apparently, his ex-wife had originally planned to send his daughter to see him as a surprise for his birthday, but the *Providence* had been diverted to Bunda only days before. Now, though his birthday had come and gone, he still couldn't wait to see her, and he half-wished his ex-wife had come along too. How he could use some time with the opposite sex. Who knows, maybe her pony-tailed boyfriend would kick her out someday, and she'd come back to him. He smiled at the thought.

What was he doing? he asked himself as he sat at the intersection. He knew he was only stalling, now. He had left the ship with plenty of time to spare. The airport was only ten minutes away, fifteen tops. There was plenty of time now to do what he had to do. Besides, he'd never enjoy the week with his daughter unless he first cleared his conscience.

Driving straight through the intersection, Edwards maneuvered the sedan toward the cluster of white buildings on the left side of the road. As he pulled into the parking lot of the JAG building, he hoped his friend had not already left for the day. It was already 1700.

He returned the salutes of several passing sailors in the parking lot, then darted up the stairs to the second floor, relieved to find the door to his friend's office still open.

"Can I come in?" he said, knocking on the frame.

"Well, holy shit!" A smiling commander roughly his same age stood up from a desk and shook his hand briskly. "Dave Edwards, home from the deep, eh?"

"How's it going, Thomas?" Edwards chided. "Isn't it tee time yet for you JAG types? I thought you'd be on the golf course by now."

"Hell no!" Thomas said, gesturing for him to sit down. "How can I make it to the golf course with people like you barging into my office at the end of the day?"

"Well at least I'm not the first."

Thomas sighed heavily and plopped his arms down on his desk. "Oh shit! Don't tell me you didn't just drop by to say hello."

Edwards shook his head.

"Oh well." Thomas threw his arms up in the air. "I work late for half the assholes down on the waterfront. I might as well work late for my old OCS roommate. What's on your mind?"

"I want to know how to go about bringing up charges against another officer," Edwards said gravely. "Can you help me?"

"That all depends on who the officer is," Thomas said, chuckling. "Or at least how many gold stripes he's got on his sleeves! Ha, ha, ha!"

Edwards did not smile and Thomas quickly sensed that he was no longer in the joking mood.

"Oh, all right, Dave. Whatcha got?"

"What kind of charges would be appropriate for an officer who's created an oppressive environment among his subordinates such that they suffer mental breakdown, an oppressive environment that disrupts the free flow of communication among unit members, and, worst of all, an environment that jeopardizes the very survival of the unit during the execution of its mission?"

"Well, let's see now. That's pretty heavy, Dave." Thomas

tapped his pen on the desk while he looked at the ceiling. "*Conduct Unbecoming* comes to mind. I'm sure I could find a few more—that is, if you have proof. If you have hard evidence, you see. These days, it's so hard to prosecute an officer unless you have real hard evidence."

"I've got that," Edwards thumbed the notebook in his hands.

"Well, all right. Then why don't you tell me who this asshole is and we'll prosecute the hell out of him!" Thomas said, half-joking.

Edwards did not smile as he said calmly, "He's the Chief of Staff for the Commander of Submarines Atlantic Fleet."

Thomas' jaw immediately hit the floor and his whole career flashed before his eyes at the thought of what he'd just gotten himself into. A chief of staff had lots of friends in high places. This wouldn't be easy.

Before Thomas could think of a reason to back out, Edwards added, "His name is Captain Carl J. Christopher."

R. CAMERON COOKE
PRIDE RUNS DEEP

Shattered by the surprise attack at Pearl Harbor, the U.S. is
rebuilding its fleet while the badly damaged Submarine Division
Seven holds the line against the Japanese Navy. The loss of ven one
more submarine could be devastating—and every enemy ship
that slips through means more lives lost.
But Lieutenant Commander Jack Tremain is determined to whip
into shape a boat that's returned from a hellish patrol and make
the Japanese pay—even if this is his last mission ever.

**"One of the most original new voices in suspense
fiction...on a par with *The Hunt for Red October*."**
—NELSON DE MILLE

**"Powerfully captures the heroic highs and hellish lows
of our WWII submariners."**
—W.E.B. GRIFFIN

"Terrific...the best I've read in years."
—STEPHEN COONTS

0-515-13833-9

**Available wherever books are sold or at
penguin.com**